"Her powerfully moving love stories
will touch your heart and soul."
Jill Barnett

~~~~~

BEST LAID PLANS GONE
SCANDALOUSLY AWRY

Clutching her well-worn copy of *Blunders in
Behavior Corrected* Miss Lydia Westland comes
to London with dreams of marrying a British
lord. But the first titled man she meets in society is Rhys Rhodes, the Marquess of Blackhurst, who is anything but the "gentleman"
Lydia is seeking. It was whispered that he was
a man so thoroughly ruined that no proper
lady would be seen with him.

Just when Rhys believes all hope of love is
lost, Lydia walks into his life—the exquisite
picture of pure innocence, yet with a fiery
temperament that delights him. But although
he longs to make her his, he knows that no
respectable woman could marry him. Lydia,
it's clear, seems to know the rules of proper
decorum by heart, but Rhys has learned that
rules can be broken, and perhaps this time
his willful ways will allow him to win . . .

LORRAINE HEATH

Love With A Scandalous Lord

An Avon Romantic Treasure

AVON BOOKS
An Imprint of HarperCollinsPublishers

This is a work of fiction. Names, characters, places, and incidents are products of the author's imagination or are used fictitiously and are not to be construed as real. Any resemblance to actual events, locales, organizations, or persons, living or dead, is entirely coincidental.

AVON BOOKS
An Imprint of HarperCollins*Publishers*
10 East 53rd Street
New York, New York 10022-5299

Copyright © 2003 by Jan Nowasky
ISBN: 0-380-81743-8
www.avonromance.com

First Avon Books paperback printing: June 2003

Avon Trademark Reg. U.S. Pat. Off. and in Other Countries, Marca Registrada, Hecho en U.S.A.
HarperCollins® is a registered trademark of HarperCollins Publishers Inc.

Printed in the U.S.A.

10 9 8 7 6 5 4 3 2

For my Dad.
You dreamed such big dreams for your children.
Wish you were here to share this one coming true.
I miss you.

Prologue

London
1879

The young woman's breathless cries rose to a fevered pitch, as he skillfully urged her toward the pinnacle of pleasure. Against his palms, her hips quivered.

"Geoffrey, ah, Geoffrey!"

Confound it!

He stilled, knowing beyond any doubt what would follow. A tiny whimper and then tears. More quickly than most, she succumbed to both insipid reactions.

Ever so slowly he lifted his head from between her thighs and captured her horrified green gaze for only a heartbeat, before she looked away and her tears began in earnest.

"I'm frightfully sorry," she rasped.

As well she should be. It was exceedingly bad form

to call out for one's husband while in another's bed.

Rhys Rhodes pressed a light kiss to the inside of her thigh, which only served to make her flinch and escalated her weeping into abhorrent sobbing. Tenderly he positioned her shapely leg in order to extricate himself from the intimate place she obviously no longer wished him to be.

Sitting on the edge of the bed, he opened a drawer in the small mahogany bedside table and withdrew a neatly folded monogrammed handkerchief, one of a dozen he kept readily available for just such an occasion. Of late they were occurring with irritatingly increasing frequency.

He truly needed to speak with Camilla regarding the women she was sending his way.

He glanced over his shoulder. This latest one had turned away from him, presenting him with her lovely back. Reaching over her curled shoulders, he dangled the linen in front of her. "Here now, make use of this."

She snatched at his offering and proceeded to wipe away her tears, sniffing inelegantly during the process.

"It's not fair," she muttered. "He's with his dreadful mistress tonight. Why can't I take on a lover without feeling guilty?"

He retrieved his dressing gown from a nearby chair, slipped into the silk, and tightened the sash. Experience had taught him that absolution was best given when flesh was not pressed against flesh. Stretching out on the satin sheets, he folded his hand around her quaking shoulder. "Come here."

She shook her head. "I can't. Not yet."

"Countess, let me hold you. I'll even allow you to beat on my chest if it'll make you feel better," he said quietly.

She peered over her shoulder. Tears dampened her cheeks and pooled at the corners of her mouth. "Don't you want to finish?"

He bestowed upon her a wry grin. "Dear lady, trust me on this matter: we are well and truly *finished*."

More tears surfaced in her limpid eyes as she rolled toward him. Cradling her in his arms, he rocked her gently.

"I want to hate him, truly I do, with all my heart, but I can't seem to find it within me to feel anything beyond disappointment that our marriage is no more than it is," she whispered.

"I know."

"Why can't Geoffrey love me?"

"Perhaps he does," he offered.

Although he knew in all likelihood the Earl of Whithaven did not love his wife. Love wasn't always a consideration for matrimony among the aristocracy. As evidenced by the tragic marriage of his brother Quentin, the Marquess of Blackhurst.

"My coming here was a silly notion. I can't fathom why I even considered it." She looked up at him, her eyes searching his. "Was I unfaithful, do you suppose, if you never actually . . . if we were never truly . . . joined?"

He touched his lips to her forehead. Women sought him out because he was adept at giving them what they desired, even when all they truly wanted were carefully chosen truths, bordering on but not quite crossing over into the realm of lies. "No, you weren't unfaithful."

"Truly?"

"Not to my way of thinking, but I don't believe I would broach the subject with your husband if I were you. He might not be nearly as understanding as I."

She smiled then, a sweet, shy smile that made him want to search out her errant husband and beat the unappreciative man until he came to his senses.

"Thank you," she said softly.

"My pleasure."

Her smile grew slightly, almost impishly. "It really wasn't, was it? Your pleasure, I mean."

It seldom was. But he had no plans to oblige her with the truth and risk having it whispered about London.

"Why don't I pop downstairs and scrounge up some warm cocoa for you to drink, before I fetch the carriage to take you home?" he offered.

She sniffed once more, wiped her eyes, and nodded. "Splendid."

While he rolled off the bed, she scrambled to cover herself with the sheets. Ah, how soon modesty returned when roles were remembered.

He walked out of his bedchamber and down the stairs. At the sight of William sitting on the bottom step, Rhys sighed. His valet was scratching his head as though he possessed lice, but Rhys had dispensed with the vile creatures long ago. He wondered what the lad was fretting over now.

As though hearing his master's descent, William twisted around and lunged to his feet. "A message arrived, sir. I wasn't sure if I should take it to you"—he cast a furtive glance up the stairs—"what with one of her ladyships bein' up there and all. The bloke what delivered it—"

"Who delivered it," he corrected gently.

The lad creased his brow as though deep in thought. "I don't know his name. Never seen him before."

Had he not long ago lost his ability to laugh, Rhys might have done so now. Instead he simply stated,

"You said the bloke *what* delivered, and you should have said *who* delivered. I was instructing you, not asking a question."

"Oh, right. Right."

"I'm also fairly certain he was a gentleman and not a bloke."

"Oh, right again you are, sir. The gentleman said it was of an urgent nature."

"I'm certain it is, coming this time of night." And would no doubt require his visiting the shadowy corners of London as soon as his guest took her leave.

William handed him the letter, and Rhys tilted his head slightly. "Fetch me some warm cocoa that I can serve to my guest before she departs. Then see to having the carriage readied."

"Yes, sir." The lad took off at a lope.

"William?"

William stopped and looked at him with such earnestness that Rhys wondered how it was that the boy's mother had ever found it within herself to sell the lad at six. Two years had passed before he and Rhys had crossed paths. They never spoke of the horrors that might have transpired during those years. "Have Cook make some cocoa for you while you're at it."

The lad's face broke into a delighted grin. "Thanks, Guv'ner."

Rhys opened the missive and stared at his father's precise script. The Duke of Harrington was not prone to elaborate jokes, not prone to joking at all actually, but surely his words were designed to impart some sort of cruel jest.

In a fogged daze, Rhys walked into the drawing room and headed for his favorite cabinet. With a trembling hand, he poured whiskey into a glass. Whiskey his half-brother had sent him from Texas. "Guaranteed to give you a kick in the gut," Grayson had written on the note accompanying his gift.

He'd neglected to mention it also burned like a raging fire on the way down. Coughing, his eyes watering, Rhys welcomed the whiskey's warmth saturating his numb body. Reading his father's words again, he slumped into a chair, while his carefully built world crumbled around him.

"So how did our little countess fare once she experienced the reality of your skills?" a soft, feminine voice asked, slicing through his despair.

Camilla. Once wife to the Earl of Sachse, now widow. His benefactor, and more often than not, his tormentor. Because she generously provided him with a roof over his head, she had the nasty habit of dropping by at all hours, unannounced.

He glanced up at her. With her brown hair, brown eyes, and perfect patrician features, she was truly beautiful. Unless one happened to search below the surface. "As any woman might who is in love with her husband," he answered.

She released a sigh of annoyance. "Why in God's name would she love the Earl of Whithaven?"

He shrugged. "I assure you that I haven't the foggiest notion. I'm hardly well versed in matters of the heart."

He gazed back at the missive crumpled within his white-knuckled grasp. The words were no longer visible, but they would be forever emblazoned on his memory.

"Don't look so devastated, Rhys. It doesn't become you. I can assure you that love is highly overrated and does little more than sticky up the situation—as our countess upstairs has proven."

Ignoring her senseless prattle, he slowly rose to his feet. "My brother's dead."

"I must confess that I'm not terribly surprised he met an early end. From what I hear, Texas is a lawless wilderness. Your father was asking for heartache when he sent his bastard there. How did he die? Indians? Outlaws? Was it terribly gory? Do share the details."

Shaking his head, he was as yet unable to fathom the significance behind the fact that Satan had called his minion home. "Not Grayson. Quentin."

She gasped and pressed a hand against her throat. "The Marquess of Blackhurst? How in God's name—"

"Apparently he drowned in the family pond."

Her shock quickly gave way to her penchant for schemes, as evidenced by the triumphant smile that slowly spread across her strikingly beautiful face.

"Well, well, well. So the *spare* becomes the *heir*." Stepping closer, she placed her palm over the spot where he had once possessed a heart. "I've always wanted to be a duchess."

He wrapped his hand around hers and flung it aside. "Then you can *want* awhile longer, Countess."

"Don't be absurd. We've worked well together these many years. We're well suited, you and I."

"I daresay I've never considered us as such." He turned on his heel. He could be packed and out of her house, permanently out of her presence, in five minutes.

"And what, pray tell, do you think will happen the first time you attend a ball or dinner?" she threw at his retreating back. "When my ladies discover exactly *who* you are?"

He froze, his heart thundering.

"Do you honestly believe, after all you've done, that tongues will not wag, or that any woman would want you?"

"I am well aware that marriage is not an option for me, Countess."

"Then why not settle for me?" she asked. "I am more than willing to accept your carefully guarded sins."

"Because I am unwilling to accept them."

Not only the sins that he'd committed in this house, but the one that had come before he'd taken up residence here. The one he found truly unforgivable.

Striding from the room, he accepted that he would never possess the one thing for which he'd always yearned: the love of a woman.

Chapter 1

A true lady shall comport herself in a dignified manner which will serve to draw little attention to herself.

Miss Westland's Blunders in
Behavior Corrected

As the dark crimson coach sped along the narrow country lane, Lydia Westland gazed out the window and fought to maintain an air of casual indifference, to give the impression that traveling in a coach bearing a ducal crest was an everyday occurrence for her, to be taken in stride. When in fact, it was the most exciting adventure of her life.

With a contented sigh, she settled back against the plush interior padding. Traveling back home had never been this comfortable or elegant. She couldn't help but be impressed by the pomp and ceremony.

The coachman's beautiful crimson coat was adorned with silver braid. His white trousers fit snugly and stopped just below his knee, leaving his white stockings and black shoes clearly visible. Beneath his hat, he wore a white wig. As did the two footmen who stood on the back of the vehicle. She was amazed they didn't fall off.

As the coach passed beneath a massive archway supported by two stone columns, her heart picked up its tempo to beat in rhythm with the pounding hooves of the six gray horses that led the way. The well-built vehicle smoothly turned onto another road where magnificent towering elms lined both sides like a regiment of well-trained soldiers. Dappled sunlight broke through the abundant leaves overhead to create a breathtaking scene.

"I'd forgotten how large Harrington is," her stepfather said quietly.

Lydia darted a glance his way. The lines in his beloved face had deepened since the new Marquess of Blackhurst had sent a cable to inform him of their father's failing health. She ached for her stepfather and all the sorrow he would endure in the following days.

Grayson Rhodes had been a constant in her life for almost as long as she could remember. She was seven when he'd arrived at her family's farm to help them harvest cotton shortly after the War Between the North and South had ended. His hair had been a little blonder then, his face considerably paler. Now it clearly revealed where the sun and wind had staked claim to it. More tan, more weathered.

The distinguished lilt of his voice had intrigued her and been a bit more pronounced then than it was now. His impeccable manners had fascinated her. They alone had remained steadfast through the years, while every other aspect of him had changed. His shoulders had broadened, his hands had roughened, and every time he looked at the woman sitting beside him, Lydia knew his love for her mother had grown stronger.

He was unlike anyone else she'd ever known. In spite of the unfortunate circumstances that had brought him to their door, he was incredibly worldly. She'd hung on his every word, badgered him with questions regarding his homeland, and prayed for the day when he might decide to return, taking his new family with him.

Remorse swamped her because her prayers had at last been answered, but not as she'd hoped. She hadn't wanted her stepfather to suffer simply so she could live in a fantasy world for a brief time. She felt guilty because she harbored any joy at all regarding this trip. But she'd wanted to travel to England ever since he'd first regaled her with stories of brave knights and damsels in need of rescue.

She'd often thought she needed rescuing from dull Fortune, Texas, where each day melted into the next with seasons separated only by planting and harvesting.

Unlike London where the Season had an entirely different connotation. It evoked images of gilded balls and beautiful gowns from Worth's. Etiquette. Elegant manners. Rituals. Traditions. Here courtship was much more intriguing and complicated than anything she'd experienced back home.

Her cousin Lauren, older by three years, had written lengthy letters to Lydia describing her exciting Seasons. She'd gone into great detail regarding the various men of distinction who had called on her. Dukes, marquesses, earls, barons. Men with titles other than mister. Lydia found it all incredibly romantic.

She knew she was being selfish, perhaps even unkind, to hope she might be allowed to experience a short Season while she was here. But she couldn't quite relinquish her hold on a dream that had wrapped itself around her at such a tender age: to move beyond the mundane and ordinary into the realm of the English aristocracy.

"How much longer, Papa?" Sabrina asked, gnawing on the tip of one of her braids.

Lydia's eight-year-old half-sister was the main reason she'd been given the opportunity to come on this trip. Her mother wanted someone available to watch over the younger children, so she could devote her full attention to her husband during this difficult time. And there had been little doubt that the Duke would want to see his true grandchildren.

"We should arrive at any moment now," Grayson said, his mouth curving into a loving smile for his youngest child.

Sitting beside Lydia, Colton shifted on the bench seat. At thirteen, he'd been fascinated with the ship they'd traveled on, but passing scenery held little interest for him. Her other brothers, Johnny and Micah Westland, with whom she shared a deceased father, had stayed in Fortune to oversee the crops and the cattle. Her stepfather had succeeded in making farming and ranching extremely profitable enterprises for his family. Of course, he took no credit for the achievement, and instead always pointed to the diligent efforts of each family member as being responsible.

Lydia was grateful Johnny hadn't accompanied them on this trip. He always teased her unmercifully about her aspiration to be perceived as a refined lady.

When she was twelve, he'd caught her walking with a book balanced on her head. He'd laughed for days.

When she was sixteen, he'd tried to foist some of his friends off on her—as possible beaux—and had taken it personally when she'd shown no interest whatsoever in the young men he thought so highly of. She readily admitted that an ability to dance without stepping on a lady's toes, to shoot straight, to break a wild mustang, and to curtail a stampede were admirable skills.

But she was looking for something very different in a man. The projection of an image that was readily apparent the moment he stepped into a room. A heritage so ingrained nothing could shake it loose.

She'd tried numerous times to explain to Johnny what she wanted, but it was intangible, without concrete form. She simply knew she'd recognize it when she saw it.

Johnny couldn't understand the reason she longed for a world so different from the one in which they lived. She didn't find her life lacking. Rather it seemed incredibly mediocre. And she yearned for much, much more.

"Look! Swans!" Sabrina said excitedly.

Returning her attention to the scenery flittering by the coach window, Lydia caught sight of a large pond. Its surface was as smooth as blue glass except for the ripples created by the white swans gliding gracefully across it. A curved stone bridge spanned its width.

She wondered if that was the pond in which her stepfather's brother had drowned. Although her stepfather had expressed sorrow upon receiving the Duke's letter telling him about the accident, Lydia understood no love had been lost between the two brothers.

Beyond the pond loomed a huge house. No, *house* was too tame a word for this immense structure. It greatly resembled her idea of what a palace would look like. She pressed a hand against her throat. "Goodness gracious."

"Is that your house, Papa?" Sabrina asked. "Is it?"

"My house is in Fortune," he said warmly. "That's the Duke's house."

"But you lived there," Sabrina insisted.

"For a time, yes," he acknowledged.

Lydia could hardly fathom that her stepfather had been raised within the confines of those massive, towering brick walls. She counted three rows of windows. How could he find contentment with the home they had in Fortune? Granted, it was larger than many in the area, and she had her own bedroom, but surely ten of their houses would fit inside this one.

The coach rolled onto a cobblestone drive that circled in front of the palace. A riotous array of colorful flowers lined the drive and bordered the house.

Out of the corner of her eye, Lydia saw her mother wrap her hand around her husband's and squeeze with reassurance. Lydia knew this moment could not be easy for him, could not be easy for either of them.

Grayson Rhodes had been born on the wrong side of the blanket. Although he was not legally acknowledged as the Duke's son, the Duke had taken great care to do his duty by his child. He recognized him and allowed him to use his surname. Still, Lydia couldn't overlook the fact that the Duke had sent Grayson to Texas to earn his own way, while the Duke's legitimate sons had everything handed to them. Her stepfather's insistence that he had no quarrel with English law did little to convince Lydia that he'd been treated with absolute fairness.

Lydia's parents planned to divide all they'd acquired in land and wealth equally among their five children. It didn't matter that three of those children had a different father. They all shared the same mother, and to Grayson Rhodes, each child was his—a child of his heart if not of his blood.

Lydia couldn't love him more if he had been the man

who had sired her. He loved her without reservation. He'd comforted her when she was ill and kissed her scraped knees. She'd danced her first waltz with him.

The coach rocked to a halt, and everyone inside—except for her stepfather—exchanged nervous glances. She could hardly believe they'd arrived at last.

An unsmiling footman immediately opened the coach door and helped everyone clamber out. Other servants began to quickly unload their luggage.

A stern-faced man wearing long pants and a black coat approached. He bowed slightly. "If you'll follow me."

He escorted them up the tall flight of stone steps, opened the intricately carved heavy wooden door, and stepped discreetly back so they could enter.

Lydia's breath almost didn't follow her into the immense front foyer. The gleaming marble floor branched off into three different hallways, two nearly hidden by the wide, curving stairs on either side. A long balcony joined the stairs at the top and looked down on the entrance hall. Huge gilded-framed portraits adorned the walls above and below.

She craned her neck to better study the painting on the domed ceiling: a man dressed in a toga drove a chariot through an abundance of clouds. She thought it entirely inappropriate. He should have been a knight, dressed in armor, sitting astride his great destrier.

She lowered her gaze at the tap of quiet, dignified footsteps. She assumed the staid man was the butler. He was dressed as she imagined a gentleman would be: black trousers, jacket, white shirt, and cravat. He looked as though he was afraid his face would break apart if he cracked a smile.

"Mr. Rhodes, I have been instructed to escort you

and your family directly to His Grace's bedchamber. If you will be so kind as to follow me?"

Lydia bristled at what everyone else probably thought was a warm welcome. Although her stepfather wasn't a legitimate heir, she thought the servants, at least, should address him as "my lord." After all *his* father was a duke, and that connection should have garnered him a great deal of respect.

She'd studied everything she could find on the aristocracy, finally managing to unravel the maze of titles, rank, and hierarchy. In Texas, a man earned his position. Here, he was born into it.

Grabbing Sabrina's hand and directing Colton with a touch on his shoulder, she fell into step behind her parents. They ascended the sweeping staircase. More portraits lined the dark paneled walls. In some of the men's faces, she detected a resemblance to her stepfather, although most of these people had dark hair and dark eyes. She wondered if they represented the generations who had resided here.

"Is this a castle?" Sabrina whispered, obviously as awed by the majesty of the residence as Lydia was.

"Almost," Lydia whispered back.

She wished they'd had a moment to make themselves presentable. Because they'd been in a hurry to be under way this morning, she'd done little more than brush back her hair and tie a ribbon around it to hold it in place. While her navy wool serge traveling dress had served her well during the journey, it was wrinkled and hardly fresh. She'd hoped to make introductions in something a little more flattering.

With all the rooms in this house, surely one could have been made available to them for a few minutes.

They reached the top of the stairway. It opened on to

an impressive corridor, a hallway that more closely resembled a large room with its tables, chairs, lamps, portraits, and potted plants. Only the myriad of doors that converged on it identified it as a hallway. Lydia was beginning to hope the palace came with a map.

The door closest to the stairs opened, and an elegantly dressed woman stepped out of the room. A few dark strands of her hair gave testimony to the fact that the others had faded from black to silver. As her gaze fell on Lydia's stepfather, her eyes took on a murderous gleam. She slammed the door and fisted her hands at her sides.

Everyone stopped walking. Her stepfather bowed slightly, and Lydia thought that in spite of his weariness from traveling and his disheveled clothes, he'd never appeared more regal.

"Your Grace," he said quietly.

"You bastard!" she spat, spittle flying between her thin lips. "You are not welcome here. I will not allow you in my house, let alone inside this bedchamber."

"Is she the witch?" Sabrina whispered.

"I think so," Lydia forced out, horrified by the woman's treatment of her stepfather.

"Your Grace—" the butler began.

"I simply will not allow it. If you value your position here, Osborne, you will escort these people off the premises immediately!"

The opening of a distant door had Lydia turning her attention to the young woman who stepped from the room into the hallway. She wore an apron over her black dress and a cap perched on her head.

"Mary, fetch His Lordship," Osborne instructed the servant.

"Yes, sir, Mr. Osborne." Mary scurried toward the stairs.

"You will not fetch him!" the Duchess screamed.

In spite of the order, Mary rushed down the stairs.

"Little chit. The servants Rhys brought here know nothing of discipline. He does not rule this dominion. I do. As for you, you bastard—"

"You will stop insulting my husband—"

"Abbie," her stepfather interrupted quietly, shaking his head.

"Quite so. He understands his place, and it is not within my house," the Duchess said. "Now out with you, out with you all, before I set the hounds on you!"

Her tirade continued, her voice growing louder with each unkind word she threw out.

Lydia had expected elegant behavior from a noble-woman, not screeching like the fishmongers she'd seen on the wharves when they'd arrived in Liverpool.

"Lyd, you're hurting my hand," Sabrina said softly.

Lydia loosened her hold, while her heart ached at the spectacle taking place before her.

How humiliating for her stepfather. How devastating for his younger, impressionable children. Based on the immense size of the house, Lydia assumed it would take Mary several minutes to locate *His Lordship*, longer for him to make his way there. She wanted to stand her ground, but she couldn't allow her brother and sister to witness the degradation of their father any longer.

She wasn't retreating. She was protecting.

Quickly she glanced around. Darting into another room was out of the question. She had no idea what she'd find inside. Besides, she didn't think a door or four walls would block out the Duchess's ranting.

"Come on," she whispered. Tugging on Sabrina's

hand and prodding Colton's shoulder, she guided them back the way they'd come.

Ushering her charges down the flight of stairs, she simply couldn't believe this woman's anger over her stepfather's arrival. They'd sent for him, for pity's sake.

She stopped when she noticed three men rushing toward them. The man in the lead radiated power and grace, his fluid movements tightening his gray trousers around his thighs. His dark blue coat sat well on his broad shoulders. His white shirt, waistcoat, and cravat indicated he was a man who clearly recognized his own worth—dressing in his finery despite the lack of a special occasion.

She had little doubt he was her stepfather's brother. Rhys. The Marquess of Blackhurst. Although he looked nothing like Grayson Rhodes. He was dark, foreboding. His silvery-gray eyes reflected the fury of the storms that often whipped along the Texas coast. She was caught in the tempest of his gaze, unable, unwilling to move beyond him.

As though suddenly and equally stunned by her presence, he came to an abrupt halt. The servants behind him promptly stopped as well.

Lydia's heart hammered rapidly against her ribs with the intensity of his stare. Ensnared by his commanding presence, she was acutely aware of his nearness, his harsh breathing. His hair, the black of midnight, had fallen across his brow. She desperately wanted to reach up and brush it back into place.

A high-pitched shriek shattered the moment. Rage, fast and furious, flashed in his eyes. At that moment, Lydia thought she should have feared him, and yet she felt completely and absolutely safe. Surely he was here to rescue her stepfather from the abusive woman at the top of the stairs. A woman protected by the privilege of her rank.

Although the staircase was wide enough for anyone to have passed by them, Lydia grabbed her siblings. She pressed them and herself against the wall, giving the man ample room to charge past them and put an immediate end to the shrew's shrieking.

"No need to run away," he said with a voice as warm and soothing as the nectar of honey beneath a Texas sky.

"I wasn't running." But her unexpected breathlessness belied her statement.

He arched a dark brow in skepticism. Then he continued up the stairs, his long legs taking the steps two at a time. His servants quickly followed.

As did Lydia, with her brother and sister in tow. She had a feeling the Duchess was about to get her comeuppance, and she wanted to be near enough to witness it.

When she reached the landing, only a step or two behind the others, she pulled Sabrina and Colton off to the side so they'd be out of harm's way, but she'd have a clear view of the Marquess. The Duchess had yet to notice him, and yet to Lydia his presence dominated the hallway.

"Mother." His Lordship's deep voice echoed around them, carrying a hint of warning.

The Duchess swung around. "You! You sent for him!"

"Yes." The single word made no apology for what she obviously viewed as an unforgivable betrayal.

"You're a worthless excuse for a son. As long as

your father breathes, your title is nothing more than a courtesy."

"As long as Father is alive, I am obligated to carry out his wishes. He wants to see the son he loves, and you *will* allow it."

She thrust up a chin supported by layers of fat. "I will not."

"You will." He made a waving motion to the two young men who had accompanied him. "Escort Her Grace to her chambers."

Her Grace shook her fist in the air. "I shan't go!"

"You may either leave with a measure of decorum and respectability, or you will leave flung over my shoulder like a sack of potatoes, but one way or another, Your *Grace*, you will leave so Father may visit with his son in peace. The choice is yours, but make no mistake, you have all of two seconds to render a decision."

Fury contorted her features. "I wish to God it had been you who had drowned."

Sadness touched his gray eyes as he said with a wealth of compassion, "I know."

He angled his head slightly, and the servants stepped toward the Duchess. She cast one last scathing look at Lydia's stepfather and then at her son before lifting her skirts, tromping to the stairs, and going down them. Not soon enough, as far as Lydia was concerned.

The Marquess turned to her stepfather. "My apologies. I hope you'll forgive the Duchess's unpleasant behavior. The past few months have been exceedingly difficult for her, and she is a bit overwrought."

On the stairs, he'd impressed Lydia as a man filled with conviction and passion. She could hardly reconcile that image with the frigid greeting he'd bestowed on her stepfather. Nearly fifteen years had passed since Grayson Rhodes had left his home and traveled to Texas. Fifteen years, and he was not greeted with smiles or hugs of welcome. Instead he was spoken to as though he was an unwelcome stranger, his presence barely tolerated.

However, her stepfather, true to his nature, more than made up for the lack of hospitality. He smiled broadly. "It's good to see you, Rhys."

The Marquess looked as though he'd been slapped. "It's Blackhurst now."

"Of course. My apologies for the slight. I was sorry to hear about Quentin."

The Marquess nodded slightly. "As we all were. I trust your journey was a pleasant one until you arrived at our hallowed halls."

Lydia knew little about the Marquess because her stepfather rarely mentioned the family he'd left in England. After witnessing the encounter with the Duchess and now listening to this uncomfortable exchange, she certainly understood the reason he'd been reluctant to speak of them.

With his blue eyes twinkling, her stepfather seemed unaffected by all the rudeness that had come before. "Actually I have the misfortune of suffering from sea-sickness."

"I regret hearing that. It will, however, make your willingness to travel much more meaningful to Father. He awaits you." He stepped back as though he fully intended to leave without another word.

"How is he?" her stepfather asked quickly.

The Marquess halted, seeming to hesitate, apparently unsure of how he should respond. "Not well at all, I'm afraid. He shan't be with us much longer. I think he's only been holding on because he wished so desperately to see you."

"I'd hoped for a more optimistic outlook."

"Perhaps I'm mistaken, and your arrival will turn the tide for him. By the way, on the off chance that no one explained to you before Mother flew into her tirade, you are welcome to use any of the rooms in this hallway, while you are here. I've assigned my personal servants to this wing and given them specific instructions to tend to all your needs. They will be most honored to do so."

"That's very generous," her stepfather said solemnly, as though he'd suddenly realized they were all in a play and expected to perform certain roles. "May I present my family?"

"Certainly."

While her stepfather introduced her mother and the two children she'd had by him, everyone was formal, stiff, and somber.

Awaiting her introduction, Lydia heard a roaring as though she held seashells to her ears. She was in desperate need of air, but her chest was constricted so tightly, she could scarcely draw in a breath. An eternity seemed to pass before she heard her stepfather finally say, "Allow me to introduce Lydia, our other daughter."

"*Your* daughter?" the Marquess questioned.

Something—she couldn't quite determine if it was admiration or disgust—flashed in his eyes. She sensed that his earlier impression of her taken on the stairs had suddenly shifted and tilted for him. Now he was taking a new measure of her.

"My stepdaughter, Lydia *Westland*, to be precise," her stepfather said.

"There is much to be said for precision," the Marquess murmured.

She'd feared he would find her lacking in some regard, but with his attention riveted on her, she felt confident in her desire to fit into this society. She lifted her hand.

He looked momentarily startled. Then he took her hand with fingers that contained no calluses, abrasions, or scars from years of picking cotton. Fingers that despite a lifetime of leisure managed to reveal strength.

He bowed slightly, and his warm breath wafted over her wrist. Her knees weakened, while he did nothing more than leave the shadow of a kiss against her skin.

"A pleasure, Miss Westland," he said solemnly.

"The pleasure is mine, Your Grace," she rushed to assure him, her voice almost as unsteady as her legs.

He released her hand and straightened. "*My lord.* You should not address me as Your Grace until after my father has drawn his last breath."

"Oh, yes, of course, I knew that. Really I did. I apologize for the blunder."

"No need to apologize. We learn more from our mistakes than we do from our successes, do we not?"

She blinked back the sudden sting of tears threatening to mortify her further. She'd expected so much of her first encounter with an English lord. As much as she'd wanted to impress him, she'd wanted him to see— wanted them all to see—how very well her stepfather had done for himself. That his family was equal to theirs.

The Marquess turned to her stepfather, his dismissal hurting far more than she wanted to admit.

"I'll be in the library," the Marquess said. "When you've finished visiting with Father, you're welcome to join me there. Do you remember how to find it?"

"I have forgotten very little about this place," her stepfather said.

"Hell does have a way of leaving an indelible mark on our souls, doesn't it?"

With a curt bow, the Marquess left them to the purpose of their visit.

"Lydia," her mother said, "will you please see to our things while your father and I visit with the Duke alone?"

Lydia tore her gaze from the stairs down which the Marquess had disappeared. She nodded, trying not to be disappointed that her first encounter with the aristocracy had not gone at all well.

Chapter 2

~⌒◯⌒~

Rhys abhorred weeping women. He stood within his mother's bedchamber, his hands clasped behind his back, waiting patiently while she drenched one handkerchief after another.

"Stabbed me in the back," she muttered. "You might as well have stabbed me in the back."

"You would be wise not to fill my head with tempting notions, Mother," he murmured.

She snapped up her head, her flow of tears abruptly stopped as though she'd quite quickly and efficiently erected a dam. With her lips compressed into a tight line, she rose gracefully—always gracefully—from the sofa before the fireplace and paced. "I can't possibly stay here."

"Grayson and his family will reside in Father's wing of the house while they are here. You should seldom see them."

"I shall go to the seaside—"

26

"I should think that would be entirely inappropriate in light of the fact that your husband of almost forty years lies upon his deathbed."

"My husband," she spat. "My husband, who never let a day pass without reminding me that his true love was some scandalous actress. You cannot imagine the agony of knowing you can never hold a favored spot within the heart of someone you love."

Oh, he could well imagine it, but he was attempting to ease her pain, not his own.

"If you love Father as you claim, then you must know in his final hours he would desperately want to see Grayson. Nearly fifteen years have come and gone since Father sent him away, Mother, sent him away in an effort to appease you."

Tears spilled over onto her cheeks, while she dropped back onto the sofa. "Quentin wouldn't have allowed the bastard to step foot in this house."

He decided his best course of action was to hold his tongue regarding the brother he had despised and stand his ground for the brother he had loved.

"Father pleaded with me to send for Grayson. I could not deny him so compelling a request."

Although even if he had been uncaring enough to ignore his father's appeal, he wouldn't have. He'd wanted to see for himself how Grayson had fared in Texas.

By all appearances, he'd done rather nicely for himself. His wife had looked on the verge of rushing into battle to defend her husband when Rhys had first ascended the stairs.

But it was Grayson's older daughter—his *step*-daughter—who'd initially captured his attention and nearly distracted Rhys from his purpose in flying up the stairs to begin with.

That he'd terrified her had been evident in the widening of her violet eyes, eyes that held far more innocence than he'd seen in any woman's in a good long while. He'd wanted to untie the ribbon holding her hair in place and comb his fingers through her long, blond tresses simply to determine if they felt as silky as they looked.

That she'd sensed a need to pull her brother and sister aside had taken him momentarily aback. He'd not meant to be frightening, but he'd berated himself as he strode through the manor and up the stairs, while his mother's shrieking pierced his ears. He'd scolded himself for not warning her that he'd sent for Grayson, chided himself for not handling the matter in a more satisfactory manner.

He'd put off what he'd known would be an unpleasant confrontation and, in so doing, had merely exacerbated the uncomfortable situation. His father would no doubt be seriously disappointed in his handling of the matter.

As a result, he'd ascended the stairs with his anger threatening to escape the boundaries he'd placed on it. It had ignited his fury further to see Miss Westland's reaction to his appearance and to know she'd accurately read the rage he'd tried unsuccessfully to conceal.

He remembered reading a letter Grayson had written to his father years ago describing his new family. How old would the girl be now? Twenty? Twenty-one?

A child really. Rhys would be wise to remember that and to forget the slight trembling in her fingers as he'd held her hand, the scent of her warm skin at her wrist, and the completely inappropriate flaring of desire in his own body at her nearness.

"Please send them away, Rhys," his mother begged

once more, bringing him back to his current dilemma. "Please."

"The best I can offer is to ensure they are not in the west wing of the manor when you visit with Father. I'll speak with Grayson and make arrangements for him and his family to take an outing each afternoon between the hours of two and five. You may visit with Father during that time, knowing you will not cross their paths."

She sniffed. "I shan't dine with them."

"I hardly expected that you would. I shall have your meals delivered to your chambers as always."

She stared at the empty hearth, suddenly appearing defeated and vulnerable. "Why couldn't he have loved me?"

"Once again, I must apologize for Mother's rather unpleasant behavior earlier this afternoon," Rhys said as he poured port into two glasses.

Only moments before, Grayson had joined him in the library, appearing more haggard and weary than he had upon his arrival. It could not be easy for him to see the deteriorating condition of the father who'd adored him.

"I should have expected her outburst," Grayson murmured. "I had assumed the respect I've earned in Texas would be evident in my bearing."

"It is," Rhys assured him as he handed him a glass.

He walked to the window and gazed out on the garden where Grayson's wife and daughters were taking afternoon tea. If the rapid movement of her mouth was any indication, the younger one was talking excitedly, while the elder one gazed dreamily at something. The petals of a rose, perhaps, or the garden as a whole. Maybe in Texas they didn't have gardens with no purpose other than to bring pleasure.

Miss Westland's delicate profile should be immortalized in marble. Her hair, the soft shade of a full moon on a winter's night, was still held in place with a ribbon fashioned into a bow. Such a simple arrangement. Yet he found it incredibly enticing. The lure of innocence.

He sipped his port before commenting. "You've a lovely family."

Coming to stand beside him, Grayson leaned against the wall and also gazed out. "Indeed, I've been most fortunate. Fate seems to have smiled upon you as well."

"It is a grim smile, if it is there at all."

"You may not believe this, but I was sorry to hear about Quentin's death. Drowning cannot be an easy way to go."

"He was so far into his cups, he obviously didn't notice. Apparently he had a nasty habit of drinking himself into oblivion. Had he fallen but two steps sooner, he would have missed the pond completely. Mother, of course, was devastated. Shortly afterward, Father became ill. As I mentioned earlier, it's been a trying few months."

"I can't imagine it has been easy for you, either. The responsibilities involved in the managing of Harrington and Blackhurst are many. Although I have the utmost confidence in your ability to handle them."

"Speaking of responsibilities, I would ask that you take your family on an outing each afternoon from two until five. I'll have a carriage readied for your convenience. Mother will visit with Father during that time. The less often your paths cross, the better."

"You didn't tell her that you'd sent for me."

It was a statement, not a question. Rhys shrugged. He'd informed various servants that guests would be arriving because rooms needed to readied and the coach sent for them. "I had planned to inform her this evening. I misjudged how soon you would arrive."

"I'm grateful you sent for me."

"It was Father's wish."

"But not yours," Grayson said.

"I'm pleased to see you've done remarkably well for yourself." He stepped away from the window. "Now, if you'll excuse me, I have pressing matters to which I must attend. I will dine with you and your family this evening."

He sat at the desk and began arranging papers as though they were of great importance, hoping Grayson would understand without being told that he was being summarily dismissed.

"He forbade me to take you with me," Grayson said quietly.

Rhys lifted his gaze, allowing his resentment to surface. "Remarkably convenient—how you chose to disobey him in all matters save that one."

"You are his son."

"As are you."

"Your place was here."

"My *place* has been in hell."

Chapter 3

"I should have taken him with me."

With his wife's arm wound around his, Grayson walked through the elaborate gardens that had calmed him as a child. He found little comfort in the bright blossoms or the perfectly pruned hedges now. How was he ever to have known how much he would miss never-ending fields of cotton?

Or how much he would come to rely on the inner strength of the woman strolling beside him. Through the years, they'd become adept at judging each other's moods, reading each other's thoughts, so that even now she did not prod him to continue but waited patiently for him to unravel his misgivings at his own pace.

"He begged me. He was only fifteen, pleading for me to allow him to travel to Texas with me. Knowing Father was opposed to the notion, I refused to even consider taking Rhys."

"You can't feel guilty. You were traveling across an ocean and had no idea what might be waiting for you in Texas. As I recall when you were told that Fortune awaited you, you thought they were referring to money, not a town."

He chuckled low. "Indeed, I quickly learned more than one kind of fortune existed."

His wife represented the best type of fortune that could be bestowed on a man.

"Unfortunately, Abbie, I can feel guilty about not taking him, and by God, I do. Rhys has changed."

"I should hope so. We've all changed. It's been fifteen years," she reminded him.

He glanced over at her, this woman who had seen beyond the accident of his birth, the first and only woman to give him unconditional love.

"I am not referring to the way he looks or the fact he is no longer a callow lad. Rather I fear he may have suffered because of my leaving. I was only a little older than Colton is now when Rhys was born. I should have had little interest in him. Yet as he grew, he seemed as lonely as I. A bond developed between us. Perhaps because we had a common enemy. Quentin. We avoided him at all costs. But there were times when he was not to be avoided. Quentin took his wrath out on me, and with me no longer here, I believe he may have turned his ugly temperament on Rhys."

"That's not your fault."

He shook his head, unable to explain fully the horrors that had surrounded him here. The heir apparent had possessed an evil nature unlike any Grayson had ever encountered since.

"Rhys was within his rights to admonish me. I stood

firm in my disobedience on every matter save this one. I did as Father asked and would not entertain the thought of taking Rhys with me."

"Again, Grayson, he was not your child, not your responsibility."

He gave her a wry grin, and she sighed before saying, "Lydia, Johnny, and Micah are another matter."

The children John Westland, her first husband, had given her. They'd long ago won his heart.

"I would protect them from all the unpleasantness in the world, Abbie. I should have extended the same consideration to Rhys."

"We could argue about this matter all day, but if you're feeling guilty, then I'm not going to be able to convince you to let it go."

He stopped walking and pulled her into his arms. "Is that what we're doing? Arguing?"

Reaching up, she brushed her fingers—scarred from years of plucking bolls of cotton from the stalk—into his hair. "You can't change what happened fifteen years ago, or what might have happened here after you left. Quentin is dead. Let him rest in peace."

"It's not his peace that concerns me, but Rhys's."

"You're here to say good-bye to your father," she reminded him.

But his father had not awakened. Grayson had gazed on his shrunken features, held his withered hand, and spoken to him. To no avail.

"I shouldn't have waited so long to return."

"Considering the welcome you received, I'm surprised you returned at all. I shudder when I contemplate what your life must have been like while you lived here."

He smiled warmly, trailing his fingers lovingly over

her face. "If not for my life here, I might never have had my life with you."

"Maybe the same will hold true for Rhys. In time he'll come to appreciate what he gained by your leaving instead of wondering what he might have lost."

Grayson could only hope, but he thought it highly unlikely.

"Why can't you eat dinner with *us*, Lyd?" Sabrina asked in the singsong voice she used when she was disappointed.

Lydia didn't bother to look up from the books and papers she'd spread across the bed, where she sat with her legs folded beneath her—quite unladylike—and pillows mounded behind her back. She'd had to use a small stepstool to climb onto the canopied bed.

"Because I'm no longer a child," Lydia responded distractedly. "I've been invited to dine with the Marquess. And please, don't call me Lyd while we're here. It makes me sound as though I belong in the kitchen."

"But I've always called you Lyd."

At the hint of sadness in Sabrina's voice, Lydia glanced over at her sister. She was sprawled on the floor, her sketch pad in front of her. She took such delight in drawing that Lydia always encouraged her.

"I know you have," she said kindly, "but we're visiting an enchanted world. Lady Lydia sounds so much better than Lady Lyd. Don't you think?"

Sabrina scrunched up her pixie-like face. "But you're not Lady Lydia."

"Not yet. But if I finish studying my books, then maybe I can be. Dining with the Marquess will be my first test."

She didn't want to consider the debacle during the

introductions as a test since she'd failed miserably. Not only had she addressed the Marquess incorrectly, but she'd offered her hand. They should have merely bowed at each other.

Staring into the Marquess of Blackhurst's stormy gray eyes had somehow muddled her mind. This evening during dinner, she'd look at his nose. Although it was a very handsome nose, she didn't think it would distract her as much as his eyes seemed to.

She considered looking at his mouth, but she grew warm whenever she thought about how close it had come to kissing her hand. Of course, his nose had released the breath that had skimmed along her wrist like the first balmy breeze of summer. Maybe she'd be better off looking at his ears when they spoke. They had yet to turn her knees into jelly.

"Test? Are we going to go to school while we're here?" Sabrina asked, completely misunderstanding where Lydia was headed with her explanation.

"No, silly." She pointed toward the paper. Time was quickly running out, and she still had a number of things she wanted to go over before dinner. Not only for herself, but for her stepfather. Had they received a warmer welcome, she wouldn't be as determined to prove her worth. She didn't want to embarrass him. "Finish your drawing."

Sabrina turned her attention back to her sketching, and Lydia returned her efforts to her studies. As soon as her trunk had been delivered to the room, she'd scrounged through it until she'd located the books she'd packed at the bottom. *Hints on Etiquette and Their Importance to Society*, *The Laws of Etiquette*, and *The Young Ladies' Friend*. She'd brought numerous

issues of *Lady Godey's* and *Harper's Bazar*. Whatever
information they could not provide, she was certain she
would find in *Miss Westland's Blunders in Behavior
Corrected.*

The last book was not a published work, but to Lydia's way of thinking it was more valuable than all the
others combined. It was a collection of the rules Lydia's
cousin had shared in her letters over the years. Lydia
had decided on the title herself. Lauren had made so
many blunders after she'd first arrived in England. Lydia had no desire to travel her cousin's path.

Lauren had been incredibly forthright and honest in
sharing her experiences. Some of her letters were
marred with withered spots that Lydia was certain had
been caused by the dampness of her cousin's tears. Lydia had painstakingly compiled all the important facets
of each letter, learning from Lauren's mistakes, creating her own book on etiquette that she hoped to share
with Lauren when she saw her again.

And she was certain she would see her again. Surely
her mother would not leave England without traveling
to London to visit with her sister at least once. Lydia intended to be completely ready to take full advantage of
the time she was there, and her readiness depended on
practicing at Harrington.

She'd never had a gentleman sit in her front parlor,
join her for tea, or take a stroll with her. Oh, she'd
walked with a fella or two, but "Hey, Lydia, you wanna
go on a walk?" simply didn't have the same romantic
ring to it as "Miss Westland, would you do me the
honor of taking a turn about the garden with me?"

She couldn't believe the Marquess of Blackhurst had
called her Miss Westland. The formality of the intro-

duction had set her heart to fluttering. This evening the formality would continue. She could hardly wait.

"How come Papa didn't know his brother's name?" Sabrina asked.

Lydia glanced over at her sister. She had such an earnest face. "He did know his name. It's just that in the past few months, Papa's brother has become the Marquess of Blackhurst. A title is much more important than a name. So people are supposed to call him Blackhurst."

"Uncle Blackhurst? I don't like that."

Lydia sighed. "Not uncle. Just Blackhurst."

"But we call Mama's brother Uncle James."

"Yes, I know, but things are a little different here."

"What's a bastard?"

Lydia slammed her eyes closed and rubbed her temples. She'd wondered how long it would take Sabrina to ask that question. Opening her eyes, she shoved the books and papers toward the foot of the bed. She patted a spot beside her. "Come here."

Sabrina clambered onto the bed and curled against Lydia's side. Lydia circled her arms around her and held her close.

"Many years ago," she began quietly, "the Duke fell in love with an actress. But his family wanted him to marry someone else, and he did. Still, the actress gave him a son. Our father. But some people frown on women having children when they aren't married." Actually everyone she knew frowned on it.

In her youth, Lydia had witnessed the heartache caused by improper behavior. Perhaps that was the reason that behaving properly mattered so much to her. She never wanted to experience the embarrassment of scandal.

"That woman in the hall made it sound like a bastard was a terrible thing," Sabrina said.

Shaking her head, Lydia smiled softly. "*Bastard* is not a nice word, but Papa is a very good man. It wasn't his fault that his parents didn't get married. The Duchess isn't Papa's mother, so I suspect she's simply jealous."

"Is Blackhurst her son?"

"Yes."

"I thought she was mean to him, too."

"Yes, she was."

"I felt sorry for him."

"He's a marquess. He's very powerful and influential."

"But who loves him, Lyd?"

Who indeed? Lydia placed her hand over Sabrina's chest where her heart rested. "I'm sure his mother does, deep down in here."

The knock on the door made them both jump.

"What if it's the witch?" Sabrina asked.

Lydia laughed lightly. "I don't think she'd knock. She'd simply huff and puff and break the door down." Tickling Sabrina until she was laughing, Lydia called out, "Come in."

Mary—the young servant who'd been sent to fetch the Marquess earlier—entered. She held a light blue gown. Lydia had ordered the gown for the special celebration her parents had hosted in honor of her eighteenth birthday.

It was no longer completely stylish, but the rush with which they'd prepared for this journey hadn't given her time to have new gowns made. She'd barely had time to have a new everyday dress sewn. Fortune was so lacking in sophistication, Lydia seldom had an opportunity to don a proper evening gown.

Lydia squeezed Sabrina. "Finish your drawing now."

Sabrina scrambled down to the floor and stretched out on her stomach. Lydia turned her attention to the maid.

Mary had helped her unpack their trunks earlier and get settled in. Before she'd left home, Lydia had packed her trunk herself. She'd felt a little silly standing in the room and watching while Mary had removed the items, but when she'd tried to help, Mary had insisted she be allowed to see to things. Lydia didn't want the young woman to think she considered her incapable of unpacking a trunk, so she'd finally let the maid take care of everything.

Lydia felt as though she were trapped between two worlds. The world she understood and inhabited and the world she dreamed of becoming a part of.

"I've pressed your gown, miss," Mary said as she carried it to the armoire. "Will you be wanting a bath before dinner?"

"Yes, please," Lydia said.

She absolutely couldn't believe she was dressing up for dinner. Back home, she merely washed her hands after a long day of helping with the chores. She didn't exactly resent that her parents had never bothered with servants, but she knew they could well afford them. Having spent the afternoon with Mary scurrying around her, attending to her needs, Lydia knew she could quickly grow accustomed to being pampered.

"And will you be wanting me to help with your hair, miss?" Mary asked.

"Yes, please."

"Lyd, you know how to fix your hair!" Sabrina cried.

Lydia moaned, fighting to keep the exasperation out of her voice. Her sister was simply too young to fully appreciate the subtleties of this new life. After dismissing Mary, Lydia waited until the servant had closed the door behind her before turning her attention to her sister and her earlier comment. "Tonight is a special occasion, Sabrina."

"Is fixing your hair part of the test?" Sabrina asked.

"Yes, as a matter of fact it is."

"The teacher made Andy Warren stand in the corner of the classroom with a dunce cap perched on his head, because he cheated on his spelling test. Aren't you cheating on the test if you have someone else do your hair for you? If you get caught, no telling what that old witch will do to you."

Lydia would have laughed if Sabrina didn't look so serious. "This test is all about knowing one's position in society. It's impossible to cheat."

"I don't want to take a test," Sabrina grumbled.

"You won't have to, at least not for a while yet." But since she couldn't say the same for herself, she turned her attention back to her books.

With her mother at her side, Lydia descended the stairs, the hem of her gown whispering over the polished wood. Mary had done an exquisite job managing Lydia's thick, often unruly, blond tresses.

"I was always putting some ladyship's hair back to rights after she'd visited with His Lordship—before he was His Lordship," Mary had explained.

Lydia wasn't quite certain what to make of that comment, although she'd pondered its meaning while she'd prepared for the evening. Obviously the Marquess had frequent female visitors, and their hair had often become mussed. Maybe when he took them riding in the park, or they sat in the garden sipping tea while the breeze was strong.

She glanced over at her mother. She hadn't done anything special with her hair, no curls framing her face, no ringlets dangling enticingly along her neck. No bows, ribbons, or tiny silk flowers. She looked to be exactly what she was: a no-nonsense farm woman.

"Are you sure you know where you're going?" Lydia asked.

"Certainly. Your father gave me detailed directions for finding the drawing room. I think he wanted a few minutes alone with Rhys," she said.

"I think maybe the ladies are supposed to *join* the gentlemen," Lydia explained.

They reached the foyer, and her mother raised a brow. "Oh?"

"I simply think that it's part of their etiquette. And I'm not certain we're supposed to address Papa's brother as Rhys. After all, he is a marquess."

"You've been reading your books again," her mother mused.

"Of course I have."

"I'm surprised you don't have the things memorized by now." She slipped her arm through Lydia's as she directed her down another wide hallway. "Simply be yourself, Lydia. It'll take you much farther than all that tripe you've been reading."

"It's not tripe, Mama. A person's manners reveal a great deal. I know you agree; otherwise you wouldn't scold Colton when he belches at the table."

"I suppose that's true enough."

"I do have to confess, though, that I feel a little guilty for looking forward to this dinner—considering the reason we're here: the Duke's failing health."

Her mother smiled softly. "Don't feel guilty. Your father and I are well aware that you've wanted to come to England for some time. It's a pity the trip couldn't have been under different circumstances, but we want you to enjoy your time here as much as possible."

She squeezed Lydia's arm. "Honestly, Lydia, although we'll experience sadness while we're here, I see no reason for us to be morbid the entire time. I'll admit I've enjoyed seeing certain aspects of the country in which Grayson grew up. It helps me to understand him a little better."

"I was under the impression you understood each other very well."

"Where he's concerned I'm always willing to learn more."

"Did the Duke tell you anything special when you were visiting him?" Lydia asked.

"No, he slept the entire time we were in the room. Tomorrow I think we'll all go see him for a short time. It makes it easier on Grayson having all of us here."

"Maybe the Duke will be awake tomorrow," Lydia said.

"I hope so. I would like to thank the man for sending his son to me."

A male servant standing before a door bowed slightly, before he pulled it open. "His Lordship is expecting you."

Lydia felt as though she were living in a fairy tale. Everyone catering to her whims, anticipating her needs. If only her joy at being there wasn't tainted by the sorrow her stepfather would experience.

When she spotted Rhys leaning casually against the elaborate scrollwork that surrounded the massive fireplace, her heart began thundering. He was strikingly handsome, wearing a black jacket over a black waistcoat. Holding a glass, his hand was poised near his lips as though he'd been on the verge of taking a sip and had suddenly decided he'd rather be doing something else.

Like watching her.

She warmed considerably with the attention, acutely aware of his stormy gaze traveling over her, caressing her cheeks, her throat, her bare shoulders—

"My goodness, Lydia, when did you grow up?" her stepfather asked.

She tore her gaze from Rhys. She hadn't noticed her stepfather greet her mother and was surprised to find him standing beside her. "Father, you know I grew up a long time ago."

He arched a brow. "Father? This morning I was still Papa."

The heat of embarrassment crept up her chest, her throat, her face.

"Perhaps it's the formality of the occasion," Rhys said.

He moved away from the fireplace and set his glass on a table near a large, gleaming piano. A harp rested beside the piano. Lydia wondered if both instruments were merely for decoration or if the Marquess knew how to play them.

She smiled tentatively, wishing only he and she were in the room. She didn't relish having an audience who seemed intent on ruining everything—not intentionally, but through ignorance. How could her parents not understand what this moment meant to her and how desperately she wanted to be perceived as a true lady?

"*Papa* just sounds so Texas," she admitted.

"I daresay you do as well, Miss Westland," the Marquess said. "You have a most delightful accent."

"I'm afraid, my lord, *you* are the one who has an accent."

"In England, one does not correct one's betters," he said.

"We'll keep that mind if we run across any," her mother retorted.

Rhys jerked his gaze from Lydia to her mother. Lydia wanted to die of mortification on the spot. Honestly, would it have hurt for her mother to know some of the rules and to abide by them?

"Abbie," her stepfather warned.

"I kept quiet this morning when that old battle-ax was harping on you. I didn't come here to be insulted, and I won't put up with it, Grayson."

"You're quite right, Mrs. Rhodes. I apologize. Grayson, will you allow me the honor of escorting your wife into dinner?" he asked.

Lydia couldn't have been more disappointed if he'd announced she had to eat in the nursery with the children. She wanted his attention, and here he was offering his arm to her mother.

She watched as they led the way out of the room. Rhys bent his head and spoke quietly to her mother, obviously enchanted with her. Yet she'd never opened an etiquette book in her life.

"Lydia?"

Startled, she fought to regain her composure. She glanced up at her stepfather. "I guess you get to escort me to dinner," she said softly, trying to hide her frustration.

"It is truly my honor to do so."

She rested her hand on his arm. "I can't believe you grew up surrounded by all this."

"It was more like *I* surrounded *it*. I was always skirting the edges, attempting to find my way in, but never succeeding."

"It would be sweet revenge if one of your daughters married an English lord, don't you think, Papa?" she asked.

Sadness and loss filled his eyes, as he touched his knuckles to her cheek. "Are you thinking you'll be that daughter?"

"I wouldn't mind."

"Remember, Lydia. Simply because something glitters, it does not mean that it's gold. Fifteen years ago, were I given the opportunity to change places with Lord Blackhurst, I would have gladly done so. Today, I am far too wise to accept such an offer."

She knew his change of heart had come about because he loved her mother.

But Lydia loved no man. Why not find one here?

Chapter 4

Rhys was fairly certain he'd dined on the glazed duck—after all nothing except bones remained on his plate as the footman carried it away. But he could not remember its taste or texture, because ever since he and his guests had sat down to dinner, he'd been unable to distract himself from the enticing Miss Westland.

Had he thought her a child? Dear Lord, but she had alabaster shoulders that begged for a man's lips to play lightly over them. While *her* lips were incredibly quick to smile. He could well imagine their taste, their softness, their warmth. He clearly envisioned them parted in passion, while her violet eyes smoldered and darkened with desire.

Clearing his throat, he signaled for the next course to be brought to him. He had no business thinking of Grayson's stepdaughter in any manner other than as a respected guest.

Despite the fact that this evening she resembled an

alluring woman, he didn't dare overlook the fact she was still an innocent, or that his half-brother had, on more than one occasion during the meal, glowered at Rhys as though he knew the exact path down which his wayward thoughts traveled.

He had little doubt Grayson had adopted some rather savage tendencies while he'd been in Texas. Rhys had no wish to put them to a test.

"Tell me, Miss Westland, do you play the piano?" Rhys asked, suddenly desperate to break through the uncomfortable silence hovering in the dining room.

The woman—no, *the girl*. He had to train his mind to view her as a girl, an innocent, a naïve child. But his mind refused to be trained, refused to see her as anything other than the beguiling young woman she was.

She lifted her napkin and touched it to each corner of her luscious mouth before responding with a hesitant smile. "No, my lord."

"A pity. The harp?"

She shook her head slightly, her cheeks blossoming into the shade of a faded rose. "No."

"I'm afraid working the farm hasn't given the children much time to learn the finer arts," Grayson explained.

"I see," Rhys murmured. Taking a sip of wine, he glanced at his brother. "Then you engage in the actual labor yourself?"

"We pay laborers to work in the cotton fields. We hire cowboys to watch over the cattle and drive them to market. But a good deal of what needs to be done, we either do ourselves or we oversee those who do it."

"The ladies as well?"

"The ladies as well," Grayson answered, almost in a challenge.

Rhys shifted his gaze to Miss Westland. She was staring at her plate as though she hoped to see the Waterford imprint on the bottom. Mortified. She was clearly mortified.

"I find that dedication admirable," he said quietly.

She shyly shifted her gaze to his and bestowed upon him a grateful smile that made him wish he'd never instigated the conversation. So sweet, so charitable, so wrong for him.

"Do you read, Miss Westland?" he asked, fighting to keep the formality in the dining room, when he had an irrational urge to lean toward her and ask what he could bestow upon her that would keep the smile gracing her face.

"Oh, yes, I love to read."

"Perhaps you would be so kind as to honor us with a reading following dinner?"

Her eyes lit up as though he'd just offered her a chest filled with diamonds, emeralds, and rubies.

"I'd like to read aloud very much," she said.

"Splendid. It has been some years since my mother read to us in the library during the evening. I rather miss it."

"I suppose Papa missed it as well once he moved to Texas. He always reads to us after supper."

"Grayson was never included in our little family gathering," he said.

She jerked back slightly as though he'd slapped her. He didn't know why he felt a need to talk bluntly, to reveal the ugly side of his family.

"I hope you'll forgive me if I speak frankly, but I'm having a difficult time seeing your mother as anything except cruel."

Her outburst intrigued him, not only because it

seemed out of place when she was clearly mortified each time her mother spoke her mind, but because it caused him to realize that her mother might not have been the only one willing to go to battle for Grayson this afternoon or now. He found himself wondering what it would take for Lydia to jump to his defense, and just as quickly he dismissed the fanciful thought. If he had learned one thing over the years it was that he was not prone to receiving loyalty from ladies of quality. And for good reason.

"With the exception of your stepfather, my entire family is cruel."

"I don't believe you are," she said.

"Trust me. I can be most unpleasant when the mood strikes."

"I don't recall you having unpleasant moods when you were younger," Grayson said.

"We all change."

Blast it! He didn't know what had prompted him to say that or why he felt he needed to behave irascibly. If he didn't want to dine with these people, he need not have invited them to join him.

"I suppose since your father is ill, you'll have to miss the Season," Lydia said softly, as though testing his mood.

"The season?" He'd rather been enjoying the milder weather of late. May was upon them. What was there to miss?

She nodded quickly. "In London. The balls—"

"Ah, yes, the Season." Even if his father were not ill, he doubted he would be welcomed into any homes. The gentlemen might not know who he was, but many of the ladies would recognize him, and none would risk a careless word or an intimate gaze that might reveal they'd spent time alone in his company. "Yes, I fear I'll miss it this year."

And every year hence.

"Lauren suspects this Season will be her last," she said.

"Lauren?"

"My cousin. Mama's niece. The Earl of Ravenleigh's stepdaughter."

"Ah, yes." The task of unraveling the intricate weaving of these families was certain to give him a headache. He shifted his attention to Grayson. "Ravenleigh's brother was one of your mates, was he not?"

"Kit still is, as a matter of fact. Now he represents the law in Texas."

"Who would have thought such incorrigible young men would do so well? What of Bainbridge?"

"Harry owns a saloon, a pub, so to speak. He provided the whiskey I sent you."

"You're indeed fortunate to have such good friends." He lifted his glass for another sip of wine, suddenly acutely aware that should Grayson ask after his friends, he would have to readily admit he had none.

He couldn't prevent his gaze from wandering back to Miss Westland. She sat with her head bowed as though she'd been duly chastised. It occurred to him that she'd been attempting to engage him in conversation, and he'd shifted the dialogue away from her to Grayson.

If he put her in his bed, he could communicate with her throughout the night. He was less skilled at dinner conversation.

"Miss Westland, you were saying that your cousin expected this Season to be her last," he prompted.

She gave him the loveliest of smiles, obviously pleased he'd paid the slightest bit of attention to her.

"Yes, my lord. She hopes to settle on a gentleman very soon." She leaned toward him and whispered conspiratorially, "She's very near to being considered unmarriageable."

"Lydia!" her mother said sternly.

"Well, she is, Mama. She's twenty-three." She looked to him for affirmation. "Don't you think if she doesn't choose someone soon, she may lose all hope of choosing anyone at all?"

"I should think if she is half as charming as you, her age will matter not at all. Any man will consider himself most fortunate to be the beneficiary of her affections."

He saw the shallow rising and lowering of her chest as she fought not to be flustered by his flattery. Much could be said for the modestly low cut of her gown.

"You're very kind to say so, my lord."

He almost reminded her that *he* wasn't kind, only the *words* had been kind, but the warm pleasure in her eyes was as intoxicating as his wine.

"I suppose I have my moments."

And he needed to ensure he had fewer of them. Miss Westland looking at him as she now was could lure him into forgetting his past mistakes, and in so doing, bring harm to them both.

Lydia sat in the library, mystified. The walls were at least two stories high with a landing along two of them, halfway between the floor and ceiling. A staircase spiraled to the landing. On the second level, a ladder with wheels provided access to the shelves near the ceiling.

And books. She remembered the thrill she'd experienced the first night her stepfather had shared his single book—*Ivanhoe*. And here an incredible number of leather-bound books lined the shelves.

An immense desk stood at one end of the room. A sitting area occupied the area in front of the huge fireplace that dominated the lower portion of one wall.

She imagined all the nights when the residents of the manor curled up in a chair before a cozy fire and selected readings to their heart's content. The abundance of good fortune visited upon these people was overwhelming.

Yet in spite of all the finery and possessions that surrounded them, she had yet to see the Marquess offer even a hint of a smile. He sat in a chair across from her, while her parents shared the sofa beside her chair. The Marquess looked dreadfully bored while he listened to her stepfather explaining various aspects of his cattle venture.

Lydia heard the click of the door opening behind her but refused to turn around, to give any indication her curiosity was piqued. A true lady did not exhibit vulgar curiosity.

The Marquess simply raised his hand and motioned for someone to enter, barely taking his gaze from her stepfather. He hadn't glanced at Lydia since they'd entered the room. Feeling plain and uninteresting, she wished she'd never agreed to spend the evening in his company.

She became aware of several quiet footsteps and a hushed whisper. She glanced over her shoulder to see half a dozen young servants surrounding her brother and sister. In her surprise, she blurted, "What are you doing here?"

"*They* said we were supposed to come," Sabrina answered, pointing her finger toward the servants.

"I must apologize, Miss Westland. When I asked if you would read, I neglected to clarify that my servants would be joining us," the Marquess said. "I hope you don't mind. The younger ones, in particular, enjoy listening."

"No, of course, I don't mind," she said, forcing herself to smile. She'd hoped to dazzle him with her reading, but she hadn't expected a large audience.

"Did you pass the test, Lyd?" Sabrina asked as she skipped forward and wedged herself in the large chair, worming her way between Lydia and the side of the chair.

"What test?" her mother asked.

Heat suffused Lydia's face, and she thought she finally had Rhys's undivided attention. At this moment, she didn't want it. She shook her head. "Nothing."

"Lyd was taking a test tonight," Sabrina announced.

Lydia wanted to die of mortification, when Rhys's gaze intensified as though he wanted to decipher this strange announcement.

"She was studying her books before dinner—"

Lydia interrupted Sabrina. "Speaking of books, I'm ready to begin reading at any time."

The Marquess took a book from the table beside him, stood, crossed over, and handed it to her.

She glanced at it and then up at him. "Mark Twain. I would have thought you'd prefer British authors."

"I find his works revealing. If you'll excuse me, I wish to spend some time with my father now. I truly appreciate your willingness to read to my servants. A chapter or two should suffice for them this evening."

Disappointment rammed into her with the realization that she was obviously being dismissed. "I'm happy to oblige."

He stepped back, and the servants quickly gathered

in front of her, sitting on the thick, lush carpet at her feet.

"I'll join you if you've no objection," her stepfather said.

"None at all," the Marquess murmured. He bowed slightly. "Ladies, it was my pleasure to dine with you this evening. Now, I bid you good night."

She watched him stride from the room. Her stepfather brushed a kiss across her mother's cheek before following his brother out.

"His Lordship got as far as chapter ten last night," a young man said, his voice riffed with impatience.

Lydia glanced down on him. He was probably only a year or two older than Colton, but his brown eyes looked much older. "His Lordship reads to you?"

"Every night," he answered. The other servants bobbed their heads. A couple of the girls looked to be only a few years older than Sabrina.

"William came and got us when it was time to come," Sabrina said, as though the boy sitting beside her, the one who had recently spoken, was the most wondrous of creations. "He told us about the readings."

"That I did," the boy said.

"Well, I'll try to do as fine a job as His Lordship."

Lydia opened the book to the page that had been marked with a bit of silk, and wondered what sort of man could appear to be so distant, and yet take the time to read to his servants?

Rhys sat in the dimly lit room, the flame in the lamp resting on the table beside his father's bed burning low. The draperies were drawn closed, as though someone feared a spot of moonlight might serve to make the room less gloomy. And that simply would not do under the circumstances—to give any indication at all that they were not on the verge of mourning.

He'd hoped for a few minutes alone with his father, but he could not fault Grayson for wanting more time with the old man. After all, for all intents and purposes, he'd been exiled these past fifteen years. He had a great deal of catching up to do, and their father's lucid moments were few.

Grayson sat in a chair on the opposite side of the bed. They had not spoken since leaving the library, and Grayson's gaze seldom shifted from their father's face. Rhys found it difficult to draw comfort from the awkward situation.

But then, comfort was as foreign to him as the land upon which his brother now resided.

"Do you intend to allow Miss Westland to experience a Season here?" Rhys asked quietly, although he doubted any noise would disturb his father's deep sleep.

Grayson sliced his gaze to Rhys, his brows drawing together. "I had not contemplated doing so. Have you a reason to care?"

"It is only that she seemed to express an interest in doing so. I should think she would not require more than a ball or two to snag herself a man of distinction."

"She could be no more my daughter had I sired her."

"That is obvious."

"It is equally obvious you have an interest in her."

"I assure you that I view her as nothing more than my guest. Would you have me ignore her?"

"I would have you recognize she is far from being worldly. Fortune is a very small town. Lydia has no experience with the flirtatious games that are played here. I would not have her harmed or her heart bruised."

"She is exceedingly lovely. But I assure you that I would never exploit her innocence."

With a heavy sigh, Grayson plowed his hands through his hair. "My apologies. It's been a long day. Every man should be blessed and burdened with a daughter. It's difficult to see her as a woman and to know the lurid thoughts that often find purchase in men's minds."

Rhys averted his gaze. Grayson would no doubt be appalled to know his exact thoughts. Although he wouldn't classify them as *lurid*. They leaned more toward the sensual. Erotic. Pleasurable. He was grateful his chambers were in a distant wing far from the one he'd designated for his guests.

"I suppose once you step into Father's shoes, you'll need to give serious thought to marriage," Grayson said speculatively.

Rhys turned his attention back to his brother. "I hadn't planned to."

"You'll need an heir."

"I'm certain a scrounging of the family tree will uncover a distant cousin somewhere who will suffice for that purpose."

Grayson leaned forward, planting his elbows on his thighs. "You can't be serious."

"Deadly so."

"But you have a responsibility—"

"To what?" He lunged out of the chair and began to pace. "To make a woman miserable? My mother has never known a day of happiness. And Annie, dear, sweet Annie . . ."

He turned his back on Grayson and wrapped his hand around the bedpost. He thought his chest might cave in on him as the painful memories swamped him.

"Annie was Quentin's wife, wasn't she?" Grayson asked quietly.

Swallowing hard, Rhys nodded.

"Father wrote me when she died."

He faced Grayson. "Did he share the specifics?"

"No."

Rhys twisted his lips into a cynical smile. "Trust Father to avoid the reality of the situation. Perhaps he was so fascinated with your mother because she lived on the stage in a world so far removed from this one. He no doubt wished to join her in the realm of make-believe."

"How did Annie die?"

He lowered his gaze, the ache in his chest increasing. "She took her own life."

"Marriage to Quentin could not have been pleasant."

No, Rhys was certain it hadn't been. He'd often caught Annie crying in the garden, and while she'd refused to admit Quentin was the cause, Rhys could think of no other explanation. On occasion in their London town home where his room was adjacent to Quentin's, he'd thought he'd heard Annie's muffled cries during the night. But he was also certain that Quentin's cruelties paled when compared with his.

He shook his head slowly, painfully acknowledging the truth that until this moment had only been shared by the immediate family, by those who had read the words she'd inscribed on Harrington parchment during her last moments.

"Quentin didn't compel her into doing the unthinkable. I did."

The confession left a bitter taste in his mouth. He

thought he might be ill, as ill as he'd been the night Annie died.

Hating the heavy silence, he glared at Grayson. "Have you nothing to say? No condemnation?"

"Based upon what I'm seeing, I suspect you received enough of that when it happened. What exactly did you do that caused her to take her life?"

His lips twisted into a wry smile. "I loved her."

Chapter 5

A true lady shall converse gaily on pleasant
matters which offer no opportunity for of-
fense to the listener.

Miss Westland's Blunders in
Behavior Corrected

Unable to sleep, Lydia stared at the shadows haunting the corners of her bedroom. Not quite comfortable with the unfamiliar surroundings, Sabrina had
asked to share Lydia's bed tonight. Lydia hadn't
minded. She found comfort in her sister's soft breathing and her small body curled against Lydia's back. For
Sabrina, dreams no doubt had arrived shortly after she
closed her eyes.

Lydia knew she should find solace in dreams as easily, but the day's excitement had yet to wane, even
though disappointment had threaded its way through
portions of it. Although their journey had begun as a result of sad news, she'd hoped the trip would give her an
opportunity to see a part of the world she'd only heard
about.

Now her enthusiasm for traveling to London had
lessened. Repeatedly she'd made mistakes throughout
the afternoon and evening. Rhys had often dismissed

her. She was certain he was accustomed to wittier, live-
lier conversation. It had been years since she'd felt like
a child trying to peer into the grownups' world. She
would fail miserably in London.

Casting aside the blankets, she eased out of the bed,
reached for her night wrapper, and slipped it on. As
large as this house was, she suddenly felt it closing in
on her.

She padded barefoot to the door. Quietly she opened
it and peered into the hallway. No one stirred. But then
why would they? It was long past midnight.

Creeping along the hallway, she neared the Duke's
bedchamber. She wondered if Rhys was still visiting
with his father. Her stepfather had returned to the library shortly before they'd retired for the evening. He'd
looked more haggard than ever.

She was almost to the stairs when she heard a low
moan come from the Duke's bedchamber. Was someone with the man now? Surely they hadn't left him
alone in his weakened state.

She wondered if she should fetch her stepfather to
check on him. But she couldn't bring herself to disturb
her stepfather if the slightest chance existed that he was
already asleep. She didn't think he'd slept well since
he'd received the news of his father's failing health.

Surely no one would fault her for looking in on the
Duke. If a problem existed, she was sure she could find
a servant somewhere in the house. And if not, she could
wake her stepfather then.

Placing her hand on the cold knob, she turned it
slowly, quietly. Pushing open the door, she was greeted
with the overpowering fragrance of far too many flowers. She would have opened a window to allow in some
fresh air, but the scene beyond the shadows riveted her.

With the low flame in the lamp on the table beside the bed casting a halo around his bowed head, Rhys held his father's hand. A heart-wrenching pose, a son with his father in the final hours.

She felt like an intruder, and yet she couldn't leave.

Several times during her encounters with Rhys, she'd thought he appeared to be a solitary figure, alone within his own family. He seemed even more so now.

She wanted him to know he wasn't alone. They'd come here to offer their support and their strength. As a family, they would endure these troubling times. They would make it through.

She stepped silently into the room, intending to approach and offer him comfort, but the sight of the withered and frail man lying on the bed stopped her. This man was her stepfather's father.

He looked nothing like her stepfather, nothing like the great nobleman he must have been at one time.

"Father?" Rhys prodded in a low voice.

She thought she detected the Duke moving his head almost imperceptibly. Was he awake or simply reacting to the baritone of his son's voice?

"Father, I don't know if you can hear me, but I beg of you, do not leave this world without telling Mother that you love her. Even if the words are false, I implore you to give them to her. She has served you faithfully these many years. And despite her faults—of which I know there are many—she has great feelings for you.

"If you will but do this, I swear to you that I shall ensure Grayson receives whatever property is not entailed. I shall give to him all things the Crown has not expressly forbidden. All you hold dear, I shall bestow upon him. He will always be welcomed here and shall want for nothing."

"He wants for nothing now," Lydia said quietly.

Rhys snapped his head around to glare at her, standing at the foot of the bed, her hand wrapped around the post supporting the heavy canopy. She didn't remember crossing to the bed. She only knew Rhys's pleading voice had drawn her toward him.

He came up out of the chair like a man possessed. Without a word, he grabbed her arm and hauled her from the room. His grip was firm, but not painful. Fury shimmered off him.

She fully expected him to release her as soon as he entered the hallway. To yell at her and wake her stepfather. Instead he proceeded down the stairs, taking her with him. Her toes dancing over the steps, she struggled to keep up with his rapid strides.

Across the foyer. Through the front door. Down the stone steps to the cobbled path.

It finally occurred to her that he had no intention of stopping until he'd escorted her out of the country. She wrenched free.

"What in God's name did you think you were doing?" he demanded, turning on her like a cornered animal. "What right did you have to intrude on my private moment with my father?"

Before she could answer, he'd again wrapped his hand around her arm and was tugging her away from the house, away from prying eyes or ears, away from any witnesses who might see his outburst as undignified. He struck her as an extremely private man, a man who needed distance to rebuild the walls he'd lowered in his father's bedchamber. He certainly seemed intent on achieving distance.

"My lord?"

Her feet skittered over the cobblestones and onto the

cool grass, velvet beneath her soles. So much like home, even if it was considerably chillier. Home, where she understood all the rules. Home, where her strength resided.

"Blackhurst?"

She saw they were nearing the pond. Lamps on either side of the bridge provided a faint glow that reflected off the inky water.

"Rhys?"

She dug in her heels and jerked back. His hold loosened. Flailing her arms, she lost her balance and landed on the ground with a thud.

He spun around. "You had no right."

His voice was calm, calm enough to be frightening in its intensity. As though he'd harnessed all his anger, but at any moment he'd give it freedom. Like the calm before the storm. She'd experienced enough hurricanes to know the most frightening moments came just before the fury was unleashed.

Lying on her back, appearing weak when she wasn't, was hardly where she wanted to be. She scrambled to her feet, acutely aware of her disheveled state and her nightclothes shifting over her body in the breeze.

"I was concerned. I heard a noise—"

He took a step toward her. "You had no right to poke your nose into my affairs."

"Well, pardon me all to hell for giving a damn about your father!"

He looked momentarily startled. As though she'd tossed a bucket of cold water on him. He turned on his heel, took two steps, and then faced her again. "Pardon you all to hell? What the devil does that mean?"

He sounded truly baffled. More importantly, his voice no longer carried the hard edge of rage.

That she had used profanity embarrassed her no end. She hated reverting to her roots, not appearing to be the refined young lady she dearly wanted to be.

"It means I'm sorry. I didn't mean to intrude. I heard a moan and thought maybe your father needed something," she rushed to explain.

"He needs to set matters to right."

"By telling your mother he loves her?" she dared ask.

"That would be a fine place to start." Releasing a deep sigh, he raked his fingers through his hair. "Are you not wearing slippers?"

She suddenly became aware of exactly how cold the air and ground were. She supposed she should have put on her shoes, but she hadn't expected to find herself outside. She'd only wanted to get away for a little while. An odd notion when she was already thousands of miles from home.

"I didn't expect to be run out of the house."

"No, I suppose you didn't. Back to the house with you now. And I trust you to keep what you heard to yourself."

He walked toward the pond, dismissing her as he had for most of the day and evening. "Back to the house with you now," she repeated beneath her breath. Not unless she wished to head back to the house.

She hurried after him. "Is that the pond your brother drowned in?"

"Quite so, but you need not worry. As tempting as the notion is, I have no plans to drown myself."

"Why would you even consider it?" she asked as she caught up to him.

He came to an abrupt halt. "Can you not fathom that I seek solitude?"

"I don't think you have to seek it. You wear it like a shroud."

She walked over to the curved bridge and sat on the sloping surface. She drew her knees up and wrapped her arms around herself to capture as much warmth as possible. She finally had him all to herself. She wasn't about to rush back to the house.

She felt a measure of satisfaction, as she saw him approach from the shadows. The lamp on either side of the bridge cast a pale glow around him as he removed his jacket.

"I can hear your teeth chattering," he said, as he draped his jacket around her shoulders.

She welcomed the warmth and scent of him that permeated the cloth as she drew the jacket close around her. Kneeling before her, he placed his hands over her feet.

"Your feet are like ice," he murmured. "You should go back indoors."

But she had no desire to return to the house, to her bed. It was a moonlit night, and she was finally alone with a man who intrigued her. Her stepfather wasn't here to distract Rhys. Her mother wasn't here to question anything she said.

"Why would you be willing to give up so much just to have your father tell your mother he loves her?" she asked.

"Do you know what curiosity did to the cat?" he asked.

"I'm not a cat," she assured him.

"Indeed you're not."

Twisting, he sat with his back against the wall of the

bridge and placed her feet on his thighs. Firm thighs. Warm enough that their heat penetrated through his trousers to remove the chill from her soles. He ran his palms from her toes to her ankles, enveloping her skin with more delicious heat.

"What are you doing out and about at midnight, my little dreamer?" he asked quietly.

My little dreamer. Not exactly *my sweetheart*, *my darling*, or *dearest*, but for now she had the attention of an English marquess, and she wasn't going to squander it by wishing for more.

"Why do you call me a dreamer?" she asked.

"It's simply an impression I have of you. Now answer my question."

"I couldn't sleep."

"I suppose it's late afternoon back home in Texas. Would you just be coming in from the fields, then?" he asked.

"No, I would have come in earlier. I'd be helping Mama prepare supper," she admitted.

"You resent that chore?"

"It's not exactly how a lady wants to spend her time."

"And how does she like to spend it? Primping and pampering?"

She thought she detected disapproval in his voice. Wasn't the aristocracy known for its idleness? In her letters, Lauren had certainly indicated they preferred fun to work.

"I'm really terribly boring," she admitted. "I'd rather talk about you."

His hands stilled. "Indeed? I've never known a woman who thought beyond herself."

"I suppose, with your father being a duke, you know a lot of women."

"I've known a fair share."

"Mary mentioned she was always tidying their hair after they visited—"

"What?" His fingers dug into her soles. "What exactly did she say?"

"Only that she often put their hair to rights. Or something close to that. I assumed after you take them for a ride in the park or on a walk through a garden. The wind always messes my hair."

"Ah, yes, quite so. I shall have to speak with Mary about keeping her master's indiscretions to herself."

"I didn't mean to get her into trouble."

"I have no intention of punishing her, if that's your fear. She's only been in service for a short time. She has yet to learn the value of silence."

"Your mother doesn't think much of your servants."

"Yes, well, there is much about me of which she has a low opinion." He began rubbing her feet again. "We all have our crosses to bear, and I would ask that you not repeat what you heard in my father's bedchamber."

"It never occurred to me to tell anyone."

"I thought gossip was a lady's favorite pastime."

She remembered how it had hurt to overhear women in town gossiping about her mother and Grayson— even after they were married. "I despise gossip and don't participate in the practicing of it."

"Then you are a rare lady, indeed."

She wasn't certain if he'd truly complimented her or was mocking her. She wasn't quite comfortable flirting with him, and yet she so wanted to master the art of flirtation before she traveled to London. She certainly couldn't practice with Colton.

"I don't think I'm rare at all."

"Then you are unfamiliar with what is common." He

eased up until her knees rested against his thighs. "Do Texas ladies think nothing of being alone with a man at midnight?" he asked in a voice so provocatively low that it fairly purred with unspoken promises.

"I wonder about it all the time," she admitted candidly.

For the first time since her arrival, she saw a true smile cross his face, a smile that washed away the cynicism that seemed such a part of him. She'd thought him handsome when she first set eyes on him. But when wearing a smile, he was devastatingly gorgeous.

"And what do you wonder?" he asked softly.

"I wonder if a man will find me lacking."

"Believe me, Miss Westland, no gentleman would find you lacking."

"I wonder if his kiss will steal my breath away."

"Fascinating." The conversation certainly hadn't gone in the direction that Rhys had expected it to, and he realized too late that having Lydia alone in the moonlight was not a wise course of action. Especially when she'd obviously just risen from bed. He was sorely tempted to carry her to her bed and join her there.

"Are all Texas ladies as candid as you are about revealing their thoughts?" he asked.

"Most are. I suppose I shouldn't be. Especially if I want to play the games over here."

"What do you know of our games?"

"Only what I've gleaned from books and Lauren's letters. It's not quite the same as experiencing it."

He wasn't certain when his hands had begun traveling past her soles to her ankles and a little higher. He remembered Grayson warning him that Lydia was not accustomed to the games played here. The women he'd entertained in recent years had continually dared him to break the rules with them. He had to take into consideration that simply bending the rules with this one could very well cause him to end up shattering her heart.

A risk he was unwilling to take.

"Tell me of your life in Texas," he demanded, wanting the distraction, wishing he'd never begun to rub her feet, but unwilling to separate himself from her.

She shrugged slightly. "Not much to tell. Papa pretty much explained everything during dinner. We work the fields, clean the house, and cook the meals. Boring."

"The gown you wore this evening was hardly boring."

Her eyes widened slightly, and he could sense she was pleased by his comment.

"You must have occasion to wear it," he murmured. "And I should think the occasion would be quite exciting indeed."

She smiled fully. He was grateful to both the lanterns and the moonlight for allowing him to see her so clearly.

"It was a gift for my eighteenth birthday."

"How long ago was that?"

"Two years."

"Is that so?" He knew her age for certain now. Twenty. Much too young for his cynical years.

He gave his gaze the freedom to travel the length of her. How he was tempted to draw her onto his lap and warm every inch of her.

"I find your world fascinating," she said in a sultry voice that carried a hint of twang.

She spoke as though she was in no hurry to get the words out. He found himself savoring every syllable, every inflection. Her wholesome speech contained an honesty that lured him in.

"I find *you* fascinating, Miss Westland."

He heard her breath catch. Her eyes were limpid pools with the ability to take a man under and make him not care that he might never again surface.

"We're practically related. You could call me Lydia."

"We're not related at all," he said, while not revealing the honest truth: that he was absolutely grateful they weren't.

"You play with fire, when you approach a man wearing nothing but your nightclothes," he informed her.

Lydia felt as though she weren't only playing with fire, but completely surrounded by it. When had the night grown so incredibly warm? When had heat begun to pulse through her like sweltering springs?

"It wasn't my intent to approach you in my nightclothes." Holding his gaze, she was aware her voice sounded as though it came from far away.

"Your intent hardly matters when I find you so distracting. Have you any notion how truly lovely you are?"

"You ignored me for most of the evening," she pointed out.

"Not for one moment."

His hands left her ankles to cradle her face. "You tempt me, as I have not been tempted in a good long while."

She found it difficult to draw in air, to think. She was certain she was supposed to respond with some sort of witty repartee, but she couldn't think of anything clever or interesting.

"I'm hardly dressed as a temptress."

"You're hardly dressed at all. That was your second mistake."

"And my first mistake?"

"Was not returning to the house when I ordered you to go."

Before she could protest that she wasn't one to take orders, he settled his mouth against hers, demanding, insistent, giving the one command to which she was more than willing to surrender.

She was no stranger when it came to kissing. Chaperones were practically unheard of in Texas. Ladies went on picnics with gentlemen and took rides in buggies. They went on walks and swam in rivers. They shared each other's company, and on occasion, they shared a kiss.

Lydia had never believed in encouraging men in whom she had no interest. But neither had she discouraged them from giving her kisses. She understood some things in life were better learned by doing, and she'd certainly been unable to learn how to kiss by reading a book.

But the men who had kissed her before had failed to teach her what Rhys was skillfully teaching her now. Their kisses had captured her mouth. His enticed her entire body into participating.

She'd never experienced anything like it. Total and complete surrender.

Lydia didn't remember Rhys easing her down so she was lying on her back. She only knew she was suddenly aware that his large hands pillowed her head, protected her from the hardness of the bridge. His arms, trembling, were braced on either side of her, while his mouth continued to work its magic over hers.

Of an English lord, she'd expected restraint, something a bit more proper, more refined. She certainly hadn't expected him to build a raging fire deep within her belly, to have his tongue swirling and dancing within her mouth with a wildness that bordered on primitive. To have his chest pressed against her breasts, causing her nipples to harden into sensitive pearls.

In the farthest recesses of her mind, it occurred to her that what they were doing was entirely improper. Yet he possessed the power, the skill to make her not care.

If Englishmen kissed with such passion, then it was little wonder that her mother had married one. As the flames of desire licked at her flesh, she set her sights not on scouting out the lords in London, but on conquering one.

And she realized the one she was with now might be an excellent choice. Something had sparked between them the moment they'd met on the stairs. Something that took little more than a kiss to change it into a tempestuous inferno.

She'd never in her life experienced the tumultuous sensations she felt now. She twisted her body against his, caressed her bare foot along his calf. She ran her hands over his back, his shoulders, his strong arms, arms that supported him above her while she wanted to be crushed beneath his weight.

Dragging his mouth from hers, he rolled away from her. She heard his harsh breathing echoing around them.

"Return to your bedchamber, Lydia."

Reaching out, she touched his back. "Rhys."

"Do it now!" He shot to his feet and looked down on her. "Or by God, I swear I'll take you to mine."

Her heart kicked painfully against her ribs, while her stomach knotted with trepidation. "Is that a threat?"

"It's a promise. A promise I swear you'll not want me to keep."

She scrambled to her feet and slowly began to back away from him. "You wouldn't hurt me."

"Not intentionally, no. But that doesn't mean I wouldn't cause you pain. Now run!"

He lunged toward her. She spun on her heel and raced toward the house. She traveled a good distance before she dared to look back. Standing on the bridge with his head bent, he stared into the dark waters below.

The woman inside her screamed for her to return to him. But the lady insisted she continue on. She wasn't afraid of him, but of herself, of what she was feeling. She was incredibly tempted to let him make good on his threat.

Chapter 6

~❦~

Lydia Westland was a temptation any man in his right mind would find difficult to resist. But for a man who had been without a woman in his bed for several long months . . .

Rhys sat at the table, glaring at his cold poached eggs. He'd always prided himself on his mastery of his baser instincts. He could pleasure a woman and, if need be, refrain from experiencing his own satisfaction.

He approached lovemaking as a form of art, a well-choreographed series of movements designed to enhance sensations, stimulate, and titillate. But he kept himself at a distance. The master in command of the production, watching from the wings, but never fully participating in the play.

Why did Lydia Westland make him feel like a lion that had pounced on his prey? A beast that had yet to be tamed? Why did she make him feel as though he was auditioning for a role he had no desire to play?

She was the sweetest of creatures. During their kiss, he'd become lost, completely and absolutely. Adrift in the sea of her innocence. Her sighs and moans had ignited tiny sparks within him that had quickly flared. His own groans had filled the night, echoed around him, the growl of an animal seeking its mate, laying its primal claim. He wanted to declare her as his: possess her heart, her body, her soul.

"The physician looked rather grim when he left Father's bedchamber this morning," Grayson said as he took his place at the table.

Rhys looked up. So wrapped up in his thoughts, he'd been unaware his brother had entered the dining room or that he'd already loaded his plate with the offerings from the sideboard.

"Yes, well, old Fitzhugh always looks grim," Rhys assured him. "I wouldn't worry overmuch. He wouldn't have left had he expected this day to be Father's last."

"I wasn't aware that death kept a schedule."

"You're quite right. I misspoke. I suppose we must all face the inevitable in our own way." Anxious to change the subject, he said, "You look as though you rested well."

"You look as though you didn't."

An understatement. He'd lain in his bed with the scent of Lydia still filling his nostrils, the feel of her soft skin a memory against his fingertips, the taste of her lips remaining on his tongue to be savored awhile longer. He shifted in his chair in a futile effort to ease an ache that refused to be eased. He'd never been obsessed with women.

They used him. He used them. It was the way of things.

"I simply have a great deal on my mind," he murmured.

"Is there anything I can do to help?" Grayson asked.

Take your stepdaughter and get the hell out of here.

"No, but I appreciate your offer."

"I'm not accustomed to a life of leisure, Rhys. While I intend to visit with Father often, I'm also quite sure frequent visitors tire him. So if there is anything I can do to ease your burden, I'm serious about wishing to help."

"I'll keep your offer in mind. I take it Father was awake this morning."

"For a short time, yes. He fell asleep before I was able to usher in the children. But it was good to have a few minutes with him."

"His moments of lucidity are rare. I'm glad he's aware that you're here."

He unfolded the newspaper and stared blankly at the words that seemed to run together, a string of letters that made no sense. He could scarcely concentrate for thinking of Lydia. In the moonlight, in the library, during dinner. He was aware of her every movement, her every sigh, her every smile. She unsettled him, and he was not one who cared to be unsettled.

"I suppose you're kept quite busy fending off the young bucks where Lydia is concerned," he said lightly.

"She has her share of suitors, but she's hardly shown a bit of interest in any of them—to their everlasting disappointment, I might add. She and Abbie should be down any moment."

Rhys set the newspaper aside. His chair scraped across the floor as he stood. "If you'll excuse me, I need to take care of a few matters."

He strode from the room, a man bent on escape.

* * *

Lydia sat in a cheery room the butler had identified as the morning room. He'd also assured her the Duchess rarely made use of the room anymore, so Lydia needn't worry about being disturbed.

Sabrina was napping. She hadn't quite recovered from their long journey. Lydia knew she should probably rest as well, but she was loath to give up a moment in sleep.

Her stepfather had taken everyone into the Duke's bedchamber shortly after they'd finished breakfast. The Duke had failed to wake up while they were there.

Lydia was saddened whenever she realized she might never have a chance to talk with this man. She hoped he'd at least have an opportunity to get to know Colton and Sabrina.

The immense size of the house helped to take them away from the sick room and made it easily forgotten. The fact that none of them was needed—or truly wanted—caused her to often overlook the reason they'd come. Although her parents had explained before they left Texas that they didn't expect the children to spend their time here with puppy dog eyes, Lydia still felt guilty whenever she snuck away to have a few minutes to herself.

Now she tried to concentrate on reading her book, but her efforts were futile. She'd memorized so many little rules. How one left a calling card—which she did not possess. When it was appropriate to wear gloves. When one should don a hat.

Her problem was that for all the rules she knew, she didn't know exactly how to put them into practice. Her studying had prepared her for much of what she would experience over here, but she was quickly discovering many subtleties were still unknown to her. Something she hadn't considered when she was half a world away, but something that was suddenly glaringly obvious to her.

Her mother would have had a conniption fit if she'd seen Lydia last night—wearing her nightclothes and traipsing over the lawn with Rhys. And if she'd happened to spot Lydia lying on the bridge with Rhys hovering over her, his mouth devouring hers . . .

She fanned her heated face and tried to erase a memory she had no wish to forget.

What happened last night could not be repeated. Not at Harrington, not with Rhys. While he'd claimed to be intrigued by her, and she was completely fascinated with him, she was fairly certain she could expect little more than misery by marrying into this family when the Duchess so hated her stepfather.

No, she'd definitely started out on the wrong foot where Rhys was concerned. She needed to prepare herself for a possible sojourn into London. As soon as the butler brought in the tea, she would begin practicing. Meanwhile, she turned her attention to memorizing more rules she would probably never have an opportunity to put to use.

But at least concentrating on them took her mind off Rhys and the inappropriateness of her behavior last night.

The last thing she wanted was to be embroiled in any sort of scandal. Her mother's experience with Grayson Rhodes had taught her that.

As strange as it might seem, English society appealed to her because of all the rules. No behavior was left to chance. Etiquette dictated every action. It seemed such a safe world, a world where men of rank were as anxious to avoid scandal as the ladies were.

Grayson Rhodes's birth had excluded him from that upper tier. Lydia was certain that within London's high society, a lady was protected at all costs. Lydia dearly wanted what the Duchess possessed: respect that came from one's position regardless of one's actions.

She could only achieve that by conquering London.

Rhys spent the early hours of his morning secluded in his study. He reviewed the ledgers and studied the copious notes his father had made some months earlier regarding improvements he wished to make at Harrington.

Then Rhys met with Mr. Willis. The man was nearly as old as his father and as steadfastly set in his ways. He'd overseen Harrington long before Rhys was a disappointment in his father's eyes or a curse upon his mother's lips.

That Mr. Willis failed to comprehend the significance of modern technology was only mildly troubling. That he was nearly deaf, blind in one eye, and suffering from rheumatism that caused him to move in what appeared to be an extremely painful shuffle was more disconcerting.

He would have to be replaced soon, and that action would not sit well with those who held an allegiance to Mr. Willis. He'd always been well liked and treated the workers fairly. It was unfortunate enough that everyone was going to have to grow accustomed to a new duke. Change was seldom welcomed, and Rhys had hoped to keep it at a minimum.

He was strolling through the manor, pondering his

dilemma, when he passed by the morning room. Usually he found the gloom of the room's darkness, with its heavy drapes that were never drawn back, somehow comforting.

This morning, however, the room was awash with sunlight. Rainbows danced over the walls, reflecting off the crystals on the lamps on either side of the sofa. And through the windows of the closed French doors, he could see Lydia pouring tea.

He was so ensnared by her joyous smile, her sparkling eyes, and her tinkling laughter that he was halfway tempted to overlook the fact that she was absolutely, completely alone.

Surely not.

Keeping to the side so he was neither directly in front of the door nor squarely in her view, he eased closer and peered through a window, striving to see into a corner. No one came into his vision. He glanced the other way. The room appeared to be quite empty—except for the intriguing Miss Westland.

He directed his attention back to her. She was no longer entertaining an imaginary friend, but had shifted on the sofa and was running one of her fingers over the page of an open book.

What a strange creature she was.

Was she perhaps practicing her role in a play?

He contemplated the advantages of silently stepping back, out of sight, and pretending he'd never spotted her to begin with. But none of the advantages outweighed his desire to remain as he was and simply watch her.

He could not remember a time when anything had brought him as much pleasure. Yet he knew he was being unaccountably rude, invading her privacy, behaving as a voyeur. Unfortunately, he seemed unable to nobly retreat.

She'd apparently lost interest in whatever she was reading, because she began to turn to the tea service resting on the small table in front of her. At the same moment, her body twitched, her eyes widened, and she pressed her hand just above her left breast as though to still her pounding heart.

The fact that her gaze was locked on his revealed the cause of her surprise. He should have been ashamed to be caught as he was, longingly peering through the glass of the closed doors, but he could not manage to feel anything except grateful that he was now forced to speak to her.

And more gratified that he'd failed so miserably at his attempt to escape her.

Gathering his wits about him, he quietly opened the door and strived to sound as though he were the master of decorum and had not just been caught with his hand deep in someone else's pocket. "Miss Westland."

"My lord," she responded breathlessly, her raspy voice causing his insides to tighten. "How long have you been standing there?"

"As a gentleman, I should say I only happened by at the exact moment you managed to look up—"

"If that were true, I don't think your breath would have fogged the window."

He glanced back at the door. No evidence of her claim remained. Not that it mattered. Unless she'd purposely fibbed to test his words. Was she that clever? He was certain she was, and more. He turned back to her. "It is impolite to interrupt."

"It's impolite to spy!" The teacups rattled with the force of her rising to her feet.

"I believe I spoke similar words last night," he reminded her.

"That was different."

"How so?"

"Concern took me into your father's room."

"And concern brings me into this one. I assure you that I was not spying. I was merely . . ." What could he admit? That if he was wise, he would steer clear of her? That he found himself drawn to her as the waters of an ocean were drawn to the moon?

"I merely wished to apologize for my behavior at the pond. It was entirely inappropriate and shan't happen again."

"You mean your kissing me?"

Kissing you, ravishing you, enjoying you.

"Quite so."

She visibly relaxed. "I'd come to the same conclusion earlier. That my behavior was inappropriate for a lady."

"Then we're of a like mind. I find that rather reassuring."

"You were looking for me then? To apologize?"

"No, I was simply passing by when you caught my attention, and I thought to make the most of the moment. It has been some time since I've seen sunlight allowed in here."

He walked farther into the room bathed in yellow, orange, and green. He'd always thought it looked as if his mother had planted a garden within the fabrics of the furniture and draperies. It had been a place that had once sparkled, where she had always seemed happy.

But as he looked toward a window, he understood now that his mother had turned the morning room into a mourning room, because a small sliver of the window had the misfortune of bringing into view the family pond.

"I didn't think I'd bother anyone here," she said defensively.

He studied the high color in her cheeks, a red almost as vibrant as her lips. "And you are quite right. I was not bothered by your presence. Merely intrigued."

He tilted his head toward the tea service and the two cups filled to near overflowing with tea. "Were you expecting company?"

Her blush, if possible, deepened. She appeared positively mortified and so breathtakingly beautiful he thought he might be content to simply sit and watch her for hours on end. He'd never before felt this way about any woman. Perhaps because he'd always known he'd had no hope of ever winning any woman's favor on a permanent basis. Yet that explanation fell short, because he knew he had no hope of ever having anything permanent with Lydia, either.

"I was . . . uh. . . ." She cleared her throat. "I was very thirsty."

He couldn't prevent a corner of his mouth from quirking up as he raised an eyebrow. "So pouring tea into two cups instead of one twice allows you to drink more quickly?"

"Twice as much tea is able to cool in the same amount of time. Therefore I can drink one right after the other instead of pouring one, letting it cool, drinking it, and then pouring another—"

"And having to wait for it to cool," he finished.

She nodded enthusiastically as though she truly thought he believed her tripe.

"Fascinating," he murmured.

He crossed the room and sat in the high-backed padded chair. She jerked as though he'd slapped her—clearly not wishing him to stay. Yet he was loath to leave.

"What other ingenious time-saving habits do you Americans practice?" he asked dryly.

Suspicion darkened the violet of her eyes. "You're teasing me."

"Only because I sensed that you were teasing me. What are you doing in here, Lydia?"

She seemed as startled by his using her first name as she'd been by seeing him standing in front of the door like some beggar child gazing longingly in a store window at Christmas.

She sat on the sofa and folded her hands in her lap. "I was practicing," she admitted quietly.

"Practicing?"

"Serving tea to a gentleman."

"I see. And where is this gentleman who is the fortunate recipient of your kind regard?"

"You're being deliberately obtuse."

"Perhaps. Why don't you straighten me out?"

Lydia considered tossing the warm tea into his face, but since he had yet to laugh out loud, she hoped maybe he was trying to put her at ease with his teasing. Or perhaps he simply wanted to embarrass her more. Still, she decided to take a risk, to hope with her confession he might see his way clear to help her.

She lifted her book off the sofa and extended it toward him. His eyes widening in surprise, he took her offering and trailed his fingers over the cover.

"*The Laws of Etiquette*," he murmured. He raised his gaze to hers with a question in his eyes.

She thought if she kept blushing under the heat of his perusal, she'd be able to boil a new pot of tea. "I'm trying to educate myself on what is acceptable behavior."

"While I must confess to not knowing you well, I can hardly fathom you engaging in unacceptable behavior."

She gave him a pointed stare.

He cleared his throat. "Last night was a rare exception, I'm quite sure."

She scooted to the edge of the seat. "May I speak candidly?"

"By all means."

She licked her lips and took a trembling breath. "I don't wish for your father to die."

"Extremely charitable of you."

"Please don't make snide remarks."

"A tiger cannot change its stripes. Still, I shall endeavor to be more pleasant." Setting the book aside, he sat up straighter and gave her his complete attention, as though he intended to at last take her seriously.

She hesitated, but she wanted success too much not to take the risk, not to dare to explain. "It is my fervent hope that while we're in England, I'll have a chance to travel to London before the Season is over."

He rested his elbow on the arm of the chair and stroked his finger along the edge of his lower lip. She loved the shape of his lips. Not too thin, like those of so many men she knew. His mouth was full, but not at all in a feminine way. Not pouting, but sumptuous. Wide. Incredibly soft. Not chapped by dry Texas wind or sun. The way it had molded against hers had been sheer heaven.

He cleared his throat, and she jerked her gaze up to his.

"Do continue," he prodded, looking as though he

were fighting not to allow that mouth to curve into the half-moon of a smile.

She licked her lips again, wondering why they tingled. Did they have the ability to remember what she remembered? Had his kiss branded her? Did his lips tingle as well?

She shoved her distracting thoughts aside. "My time in London will be short, and I want to make a favorable impression. I need to learn everything I would have been taught had I lived here for years. I don't want to stumble through my first ball like the country cousin who has come to the city."

"Surely you have attended a dance."

"In a barn!" She lunged to her feet, skirted around the edge of the table, and began to pace, unable to repress her agitation. She spun around and looked at him imploringly. "We hold our dances in the barn. No matter how much you clean it or lay down new straw, it still smells of manure and horsehide.

"I've never had a gilded invitation. Word of mouth or a note tacked outside the general store is the way people are invited. This dress"—she swept her hands from her bosom to her hips—"is fancier than anything I've ever worn to a dance—except on my birthday. Calico, homespun . . . oh!"

Frustrated, she took up her pacing again. How could she explain the unexplainable? As a general rule, she despised whining women. She didn't want him to perceive her as such, but she'd traveled so far—not only in miles, but in her efforts to achieve her dream.

"I don't mean to sound ungrateful, but for years I've read Lauren's letters. Everything she wrote about the glitter and gold of London. All I've had is tin. It's not anyone's fault. It's simply the nature of Fortune. To be dull and boring and wrapped in shades of brown." She pivoted and captured his gaze. "You must think me terribly shallow."

What Rhys thought was that Lydia Westland belonged in a glittering ballroom, with gentlemen thronging around her. Granted, he had to admit that there were undoubtedly more pressing issues in the world than the cut of a ball gown, but for a young woman nothing was more important, nothing else served as effectively to determine the remainder of her life than her Season.

Lydia was quite right that a gentleman's perception of a lady's mastery of etiquette influenced his interest in her as marriage material. During the Season, women were auditioning, flaunting their grace, showing their ability to charm, demonstrating their worthiness to indeed be married to a peer.

He could hardly fault Lydia for wanting to make a good impression—particularly if she did not expect to have much time in London. The month of May and the Season were already under way.

Raised up on her toes, her hands clasped before her, she looked at him as though she expected him to provide her with some profound answer.

"I find most women to be shallow," he replied drolly.

She rolled her eyes and presented her back to him.

"But I also understand," he continued, unable to comprehend the reasons he desperately wished not to disappoint her, "what it is to desire what you've never possessed. Unfortunately in your case, Lydia, I fear you'd discover the reality is far removed from the dream."

She glanced at him over her shoulder, a definite challenge in her eye. "It wouldn't be that far removed if you were to help me."

He ceased to breathe. "I beg your pardon?"

She hurried across the room, knelt before him with her skirt billowing around her, and grabbed his hands. "You could teach me what I don't know."

The warmth of her palms was as compelling as the plea in her eyes. It took all his willpower not to fold his fingers around her hands, squeeze gently, and pull her nearer to him.

"You seem to know a great deal," he finally managed.

"But not everything. And I get flustered. Like when we met. Addressing you as Your Grace. Honestly, I did know better, but I've had so little experience. If you would simply practice with me—"

"Practice with you?"

She nodded enthusiastically. "Have tea with me. Escort *me* into dinner instead of my mother. Murmur in my ear if my touch is not light enough or is too light. If my steps are too slow or too quick. Anything at all."

Shaking his head to clear it, he slid his eyes closed. What he wished to murmur in her ear had little to do with etiquette and everything to do with seduction.

Fighting to control his baser instincts, he opened his eyes. "Impossible."

"Why? We're practically related, and I know often a man takes a female relative under his protection."

Dear God, what he wanted was to take her under his body, to have her thrashing about beneath him and screaming his name. Was she so incredibly innocent she could feel none of this passionate stirring? None of this blasted desire that raged through him?

He felt like a fiery volcano, while she seemed as cool as a wintry night. He wanted to melt her frost and fan the flames of what they'd begun in the sheltering darkness at the bridge.

"As last night proved, our spending any time together would be unwise," he told her. He spoke the truth. His restraint was close to giving out on him.

"You're not ravishing me now."

Not from a lack of wanting.

She released her hold on him, and he mourned the loss of her touch. She sank back on her heels.

"I've read the books, but there are so many little things that they don't tell me. Things *you* would know."

"I did not do the social rounds while I was in London."

She furrowed her delicate brow, and he wanted to press his thumb against the creases and ease them away.

"Not at all?" she asked.

"I had no interest in the balls. And while as a second son I might have been considered a fair catch, Quentin was the favored one, sought after, and invited to every soiree that took place."

"But surely you were taught how to behave in case you were invited."

"I'm not saying I am not without knowledge. Rather I lack the experience you seek."

He shifted in the chair, not entirely comfortable with the way she was scrutinizing him, as though she sought to decipher exactly what knowledge he did possess.

She lowered her gaze to her lap. "What if I get to London and make a fool of myself?"

"You shan't make a fool of yourself."

She slowly lifted her gaze to his, her incredible lavender eyes revealing her vulnerabilities and fears. "How can I not when I've never had the opportunity to put to practice what I've learned? Wishful thinking and imaginary gentlemen have hardly prepared me to walk into a ballroom with confidence, and confidence is what I'll need if I want to be a success."

"Which of course, you do."

She chose that moment to bestow upon him a smile filled with wonder and awe. "I've lived my entire life almost as though I were Cinderella. Do you know that story?"

"A tale written by Perrault. I wasn't aware you had a wicked stepmother. Or in your case, perhaps it's a wicked stepfather."

Her smile blossomed. "Neither. But I'm a farm girl who has spent most of her life dreaming of one night of magic. With your help, maybe it can turn into more."

He narrowed his eyes. "What do you mean by that?"

"I'm not interested in going back to Texas. I want to live among the glitter."

"And when you discover it is not gold, but merely a poor imitation?"

Concern etched itself across her features. "Papa said something similar. I think it's only because you're men, and you can't comprehend what I'm talking about."

"Oh, I understand. Far better than you think. I cannot help but wonder if it is better to have the dream rather than the reality."

"You're too cynical. I don't know why I bothered to ask you, or why I thought you'd be willing to help me."

She started to rise. He reached out and grabbed her wrist, halting her progress and quickening the beat of his heart. He was certain he would analyze this moment until his death and never fully comprehend what had possessed him to say, "I'll offer you my assistance, teach you what you think you don't know."

Unadulterated joy swept over her face. Then her arms were wrapped around his neck, her cheek pressed to his, her backside nestled within his lap. "Oh, Rhys, thank you!"

He dug his fingers into the sides of the chair to keep himself from digging them into her, from burying his hands in her hair, or cupping his palms around her waist.

She eased back until he could look within the depths of her eyes. She slid her hands around until they cradled his neck, her thumbs pressed below his chin. Surely she could feel the rapid thrumming of his pulse.

He felt as though the sun had suddenly moved into the room, heating his flesh. All the joy seemed to flow out of her as awareness crept in. For him, it had been immediate. For her, it was a slow dawning, but he could see its arrival as clearly as he noticed the first signs of spring. The budding of her breasts, the blossoming of her lips.

He recognized that he should have possessed the presence of mind to move her off his lap, but he feared if he touched her at all, it would be to press her closer, to bring her mouth directly in line with his.

Blinking, she gave her head a quick shake before she scooted off his lap. Her cheeks flamed red. "I'm sorry."

"Yes, well, lesson number one is that a simple thank you will suffice in the future, should I do something that pleases you."

"Thank you," she said softly as she stepped back.

"You're welcome." He loosened his grip on the chair, fearing it would forever carry the imprint of his fingers.

He stood and she stepped back again, failing to meet his gaze.

"Lydia."

She lifted her eyes to his.

"We shall need to curb your enthusiasm."

She nodded. "That was a very unladylike display."

"Indeed. I, for one, am in favor of no formal lessons. I shall simply instruct you when our paths cross."

She bobbed her head. "That's fine."

"Very good." He started to stride from the room.

"When do you think our paths will cross?" she asked.

He halted, with his mind racing. *As seldom as possible* hung on the tip of his tongue. He glanced over his shoulder and knew he could not bear the thought of disappointing her. "I shall endeavor to make it often."

"Thank you."

He gave a brisk nod before continuing out of the room. What he needed was a taxing ride over the countryside, although he doubted anything he did would cause him to no longer regret his decision to help her.

Chapter 7

❦

The shrieking began at precisely four o'clock.

Rhys was absolutely certain of the time, because he'd just returned from his afternoon ride and was striding toward his chambers when he passed the large clock in the hallway, and the ear-splitting crescendo reverberated throughout the manor.

The last time his mother had issued such a shrill cry, she'd spotted a mouse hovering in fear beneath her vanity table. Fortunately William had an uncanny talent when it came to catching rodents—a skill he'd mastered during his time in the London streets—and he'd managed to capture the errant creature and remove it from the premises.

Or so he claimed. Rhys suspected William had made a pet of it.

William was already on his way up the stairs when Rhys reached them.

"I'm bettin' it's another mouse, Guv'ner," William

tossed over his shoulder, slowing his steps so Rhys could catch up.

"*My lord*," Rhys corrected him.

"No need to be prayin' about it, Guv. I can catch the fella right quick."

Rhys repressed a groan. "I wasn't praying. I was indicating how you are to address me now that we are in residence here."

"Ah, right, right. I keep forgettin'."

Before Quentin had taken his unfortunate spill into the family pond, Rhys had distanced himself from his family to such a degree that only a few people had known of his noble heritage. Certainly none of his ladies had known.

They much preferred thinking he was some coarse commoner trained in the art of seduction by Lady Sachse. Lady Sachse whom Rhys had never kissed, much less bedded.

He'd never understood why she took such an interest in other ladies' affairs—so to speak—when she was as celibate as a nun.

All thoughts of Lady Sachse flew from his mind when his flight up the stairs came to an abrupt halt at the top. William, obviously quickly deducing a rodent wasn't the cause of the commotion, was gingerly backing down the stairs in an effort not to be noticed.

Rhys scarcely blamed him for his cowardly retreat.

It was not often in this household that two furious women faced off. He would have given the upper hand to his mother, whose voice was causing the walls to reverberate, but for the fire in Lydia's eyes as she stood between his mother and her brother—the fire, the passion, the warning.

Good Lord, she was a tigress defending her cub.

Waiting, waiting for the battle to shift from verbal to physical, at which point, God help his mother.

"Mother?" he dared to utter into the fray.

She spun around, her palm connecting with his cheek, resulting in an echoing crack that caused an unnatural stillness to descend over the hallway. Her eyes flooded with tears. Tears for him that made his own eyes sting. He took a step toward her, fully intending to wrap his arms around her—

"You promised!" she retorted. "Promised to keep them at bay. And now that wretched, horrible boy—"

"Did nothing more than step into the hallway," Lydia protested, her voice seething.

"I was looking for Lyd," the lad said, stepping out from behind his sister, who quickly moved in front of him.

At any other moment, Rhys might have thought their actions amusing. Right now, however, his cheek, mouth, and heart still smarted.

"You promised!" his mother reiterated.

"I know I did," he said quietly. "I shall rectify the situation posthaste."

"I want them out of my house!"

"That wish I cannot grant."

"I want the bastard's boy flogged!"

"Over my dead body," Lydia snarled.

"That can be arranged," his mother said haughtily.

"Mother, is anyone with Father?" he asked in an effort to distract her from the problem at hand. Anything to diffuse the escalating tempers.

She snapped her gaze to his, horror clearly etched across her aging face. "Do you suppose he heard?"

Surely she was joking. His father would have heard

even if he were already lying in his grave. Still, Rhys shook his head. "Hopefully not, but if he did, tell him you saw a mouse."

"Yes, yes," she murmured absently before turning toward the door. "He knows I'm frightfully terrified of the vile creatures."

She entered the Duke's bedchamber, and Rhys shifted his attention to Lydia and Colton. He did not welcome the unpleasant task that awaited him, but order needed to be maintained. "We shall discuss this unfortunate matter in my study."

"Colton did nothing wrong," Lydia insisted.

Rhys narrowed his gaze. "I am in no mood to be corrected or questioned at the moment. And considering the fireworks shooting from your eyes, I would think you would appreciate a few moments to calm yourself, before we discuss why *you and* your brother are in this hallway when I specifically requested that Grayson and his brood vacate the premises each afternoon between the hours of two and five."

His comment only served to ruffle her feathers more if her deepening glare was any indication. She opened her mouth. He held up a finger to silence her. "In my study."

She snapped her mouth closed, squared her shoulders, bunched up her skirt with tightened fists, and marched down the stairs. Her brother started to follow and then halted, glancing up at Rhys.

"You really don't want to get on Lyd's bad side," he warned before traipsing after his sister.

On the contrary. Rhys was definitely looking forward to the encounter. Perhaps afterward she would demand he rescind his offer to help her practice her etiquette. Based on what he'd just witnessed, she did indeed need a tutor when it came to learning about the proper way to handle unpleasant situations.

Removing a monogrammed handkerchief from his pocket, he pressed it to his mouth, disappointed to discover blood. He didn't fancy being a wounded warrior, he mused as he followed them down the stairs. In the entrance hall, Lydia had already turned to the right.

"To my study," he called after them.

She spun around, her brow furrowing, her gaze quickly darting around the foyer. She pointed over her shoulder. "The library—"

"Is not my study," he interrupted. "If you will be so kind as to follow me?"

He knew by the mutinous set of her mouth that she preferred to be the one leading. How different she was when someone she loved was threatened. He'd perceived her to be young, sweet, and innocent. At this precise moment, she looked as though she wished to scratch out his eyes. He couldn't determine why he found that aspect of her character appealing.

He led the way along the wide hallway and entered a room that, like the library, looked out on the garden. But here no books for pleasure were housed on the shelves behind his desk. Here, there was little more than ledgers and books designed to help run massive estates. Here, he could not escape his obligations. Nor, in this smaller room, could they escape him.

He crossed the room, turned, leaned his hips against his desk, and curled his fingers around its polished edge. He did not invite his belligerent guests to sit. What he had to say was better received standing.

"Did your father not inform you that you were to vacate the premises during the afternoon?" he asked.

"He did," Lydia replied succinctly, "but—"

"I didn't want to go for a carriage ride," Colton finished.

Lydia turned to him. "I'll handle this."

"I can take care of myself."

Rhys recognized the battle raging within Lydia. The older sister wanting to protect the younger brother who wished to prove himself a man. Rhys was captivated by the various emotions sweeping across her face, and yet within each one was shadowed the depth of her love for the boy.

She gave the barest of nods, and the boy stepped forward, his mouth set in a grim line.

"It's more boring than a month of Sundays to sit in a carriage, doing nothing. Pa said I could stay here as long as I stayed in my room. I was looking out the window and saw you riding in. I wanted to find Lydia to see if I could borrow a horse and go riding. I stepped into the hallway about the same time the Duchess came up the stairs." He shrugged. "Bad timing."

"I daresay that's an understatement," Rhys mused aloud.

Out of the corner of his eye, he saw Lydia's mouth twitch. He leaned forward slightly, and all the humor fled from her face. She took an almost imperceptible step toward him and closer to the lad. He eased back. She retreated.

Fascinating.

"How is it you don't find riding a horse, looking out over the countryside, as boring as a . . . what was it? A month of Sundays?"

"You're not doing anything while you're sitting in a carriage. Riding a horse"—an excitement came into the boy's eyes—"you're the master."

"Don't you think your father would object to your riding alone about a countryside which is so decidedly foreign to you?"

"Nope. I ride to town by myself or go in search of stray cattle on my lonesome."

"Quite so. But in Texas you are familiar with the area. Here you could quite easily get lost."

"I know how to mark a trail and look for landmarks. I could always find my way back. Even at night, I'm bettin'."

"Could you now?" Rhys asked, unable to keep the skepticism out of his voice.

"Yes, he could," Lydia said.

Her voice carried no reservations, dared Rhys to doubt her or to question her brother's claims any further.

"I see. I'll take the matter up with your father. If he's in agreement, then I'll arrange for a horse to be made available for your use while you're here."

Colton's eyes lit up. "Thanks."

"Are you as skilled at telling time as you are at marking a trail?" Rhys asked.

"Yes, sir."

"Then explain to me how it is that you were out and about in the hallway during the forbidden time."

"I don't have a watch. Felt like I'd been sitting there forever."

Rhys straightened his stance, easing away from his desk slightly, noticing at the same time that Lydia inched closer to her brother. He pitied the man who harmed a hair on the lad's head.

Reaching into a pocket on his vest, he removed his watch and unlatched the chain. He rubbed his thumb over the ducal coat of arms etched in the heavy gold cover.

"This watch belonged to my father," he said quietly. "Given to him by his father."

He extended it toward the lad. It pleased him no end to see the boy take it with the reverence it deserved.

"Wow! It's fancy," he said in awe. "Look at it, Lyd."

Easing closer, she murmured her agreement.

"It's yours," Rhys said.

Colton and Lydia looked at him as though he'd clearly lost his mind. Perhaps he had. He knew tradition dictated that the watch follow the line of legitimate sons.

"You mean you want me to use it while I'm here?" Colton asked.

"I mean it's yours to treasure forever. It was my father's intention to pass it down to his firstborn son . . . which is your father. *He* would in turn pass it down to his firstborn son. That happens to be you. I seem to recall the Duke giving your father a watch when he left for Texas. Therefore your father has no need of a watch, and this one rightfully belongs to you."

The lad beamed up at him. "I'll take real good care of it. Thanks, Uncle Rhys."

Rhys felt his heart lurch at the familiarity that had no place in this house. He cleared his throat. "See that you do. You're dismissed."

Lydia placed a hand on her brother's shoulder. "Go wait for me in the hallway."

She watched the boy until he walked out of the room, then she turned to Rhys. "Thank you," she said softly.

"The gift is of no consequence. I have another watch which I prefer."

Shaking her head, she stepped closer to him. "I wasn't thanking you for the watch. I was thanking you

for not correcting him when he called you uncle. I overheard my father explaining the way of things to my
mother once. I know under English law, as a bastard,
he's considered a nonperson. Certainly not your real relation. That you treat him with dignity is a credit to
you."

"You're making much of nothing."

"I don't think so. Lauren explained to me that even if
I do make it to London for part of the Season, I won't
receive the welcome she did, won't be sought after like
she is. Her stepfather is a peer. Mine is nothing under
the law."

Strange how she'd managed to impart that *nothing*
was something of great importance to her, held dear
and loved.

"I assure you, Lydia, you would be sought after, regardless of Grayson's standing within the law. Now if
you'll leave me—"

"Your lip's bleeding again."

Gingerly he touched his tongue to the corner of his
mouth and tasted the rusty flavor of blood. "It's nothing
to be concerned over."

Still, he reached into his pocket and withdrew his
handkerchief again. As he lifted his hand, hers closed
around his, her pale fingers against his tanned ones,
delicate against strong.

"Let me," she offered with a sultry voice that should
accompany moonlight laced over a bed of satin sheets.

He was fairly certain she had not meant to sound seductive. Although he did not move while she took the
linen from him and gently dabbed at the bruised corner
of his mouth, his mind played all sorts of havoc with his
imagination, imagining her touch not just against his
lips, but over every inch of his flesh.

Her delicate brows knitting together, she angled her head slightly and looked more closely at his mouth. When was the last time anyone had shown concern for him? He could have sworn his lips tingled, swelled from wanting to press against hers. Was she remembering the kiss they'd shared?

She wrapped a corner of his handkerchief around her finger and touched it to her tongue before bringing the damp cloth back to his face. "Some of the blood has dried," she explained.

He swallowed hard, trying not to envy a scrap of linen, because it now held the taste of her, the scent of her, and the warmth of her.

"I can't believe she slapped you," she said with a wealth of sympathy.

"It was not on purpose, I assure you. She's simply overwrought and reacted without thinking."

She ceased giving her tender ministrations to his mouth and lifted her gaze to his. "You spoil her."

"She is a duchess. Being spoiled is a privilege of her rank."

"A good tongue-lashing is what she needs."

Tongue-lashing? An image flashed through his mind of the sort of tongue-lashing he'd like to bestow on Lydia, certainly not in the manner to which she was referring. No, his tongue would deliver lashes that would more closely resemble velvet against silk in the most intimate of places, until she was writhing against him and crying out his name.

He shoved away the thoughts, before he did something he'd regret, like take her in his arms and begin his seduction. She wasn't a bored lady who'd sought what he could offer in the ways of pleasure. She was an innocent, his guest, his bastard brother's stepdaughter. What he had in mind for her would be entirely inappropriate. It was best to turn to the matter at hand if he had any hope of restoring his sanity.

"I trust as our guest, you will refrain from giving the Duchess what you've deduced she needs."

Those damnable, kissable lips of hers shifted into a soft smile. "I've managed so far, haven't I?"

"Just barely. I suspect had she bothered to take a breath, into the silence, you would have stormed like a knight on a crusade."

Her smile withered. "That would have been unladylike."

"Indeed." Reaching out, he cradled her cheek and trailed his thumb across her sumptuous lips. "Although in truth, I cannot envision you being anything except a lady."

And not a very wise one at that. For she did not move, but simply watched him. Waiting. Waiting for what he saw in her eyes she knew he wished to bestow. Waiting for what he knew in his heart he should not.

"Your cousin is absolutely incorrect in her assessment of your situation," he murmured. "You will have besotted men flocking to your side should you make it to London before the Season is over."

"You're much too kind." She sounded breathless, as though she found it as difficult to draw in air as he did.

"I assure you, I'm anything but kind. And I'm going to give you your second lesson. Something your books undoubtedly failed to teach you. Something you failed to learn last night. Never allow yourself to be alone with a man."

He lowered his head. Her eyes widened a fraction before they slid closed and her lips parted. His gut clenched with her acquiescence, and the blood roared through his head, as he touched his lips to hers.

The fire was instantaneous. Not a spark needing to take hold and grow, but a deafening blaze. She melted against him, her breasts flattened against his chest, her arms going around his waist, her hands stroking his back.

He was acutely aware of every inch of her entwining around him like a vine seeking purchase against the mighty oak. Her innocence filled him, swamped him, and took him under. He wanted to possess her, own her.

As his tongue swept through her mouth, he cupped her buttocks and ground her hips against his aching body. His guttural groan sounded like that of a wounded animal, an animal that recognizes the prey has become the hunter.

He'd thought to intimidate, and instead, he'd discovered her arsenal was far superior to his. Innocence unleashed was devastatingly powerful.

"Lyd!" Colton yelled from the outer hall. "Pa's back."

Lydia sprang away at the precise moment that Rhys abruptly straightened. They were both short of breath, trembling with needs unfulfilled.

With her blush creeping over her face and along her throat, she extended his handkerchief toward him with a shaking hand. He saw no help for it but to take it.

As she darted from the room, he closed his fingers around her warmth which still lingered within the cloth. But it wasn't enough, failed to restore his sanity.

Chapter 8

Lydia couldn't explain what drew her into the shadowy hallway long past midnight. She couldn't sleep. Her mind swirled with too many questions and too few answers.

Rhys had been the perfect gentleman that evening. Too perfect. She found herself irritated with him for reasons she couldn't explain and more fascinated with him than she cared to admit.

He'd kept his promise to help her learn what her books couldn't teach her. He'd escorted her into dinner, murmuring near her ear that it was considered ill-bred to wait until everyone was served as she had the night before. Rather she was expected to begin eating as soon as food was placed before her. She'd somehow missed that little caveat.

Her family always waited until everyone was served. Maybe because they put their own food on their plates and passed the pots and bowls around the table.

Although Rhys had conversed openly with her step-father more than he had anyone else, Rhys and she had engaged in a silent conversation during the entire meal. The challenge had been to discreetly convey her messages only to him, in a way that no one else would notice. A dropping of her gaze to her plate, the arching of her brow in question. His nods were indiscernible to everyone except her. She'd never found herself so attuned to someone else's thoughts or moods.

Especially when they kissed. She answered every stroke of his tongue, each movement of his lips. He guided her without words. Yet she never doubted the direction in which he wished to travel, was never bored with the journey.

He represented everything she'd ever dreamed of acquiring.

Handsome. So handsome that she'd be content to look at him for the remainder of her life.

Kind. Hadn't he demonstrated that by inviting her stepfather there against the Duchess's wishes?

Generous. He'd given Colton the Duke's watch, a family heirloom, something he no doubt could have passed on to his own son.

A gentleman. His manners were impeccable. Even when they were alone, she didn't consider his kisses as taking advantage. By the bridge, he'd warned her off. She simply hadn't wanted to heed the warning.

Respectable. Unlike her stepfather, he hadn't been sent away because of scandal.

He was lord of the manor. How easily she thought he could become lord of her heart.

Yet he seemed as quick to retreat as he was to advance. One moment willing to teach her, the next obviously wishing he hadn't agreed to any such thing.

She had little doubt he had a great deal on his mind because of his father's failing health. The responsibilities regarding the management of the estates fell to Rhys. A part of her felt selfish for asking him to devote any time to her at all, but she so enjoyed his company when he wasn't being irascible.

Earlier, just as he had last night, he'd left her in the library to read to the younger servants, while he'd gone to visit with his father. This time, her stepfather hadn't joined him. She didn't know whether Rhys was still there.

She'd been listening for the opening of a door, the tread of dignified footsteps. But she'd heard nothing except the steady pounding of her heart.

He might have left this wing before she'd ever retired upstairs. Or he might still be in this portion of the house.

Taking a deep breath, she knocked softly on the Duke's bedchamber door. She heard the hushed sounds of someone trying to walk without disturbing anyone, and wondered briefly what she'd do if the Duchess were inside.

Rhys opened the door slightly. Behind him, pale light flickered and the shadows danced. He stared at her as though he couldn't quite comprehend what she was doing there.

She wasn't certain she could have answered that question had he asked. She only knew he appeared weary. At some point, he'd untied his cravat, but it still hung around his neck. He'd removed his jacket. Three buttons on his shirt were undone, providing her with the barest glimpse of his chest. She supposed a true English lady would have been shocked. But she'd worked in the fields beside men who often took off their shirts when the sun beat down unmercifully.

She licked her lips, and he immediately dropped his gaze to her mouth. She would have smiled if the occasion weren't so somber.

"Are you alone in there?" she whispered.

His dark eyebrows drew together until they resembled the wings of a raven. "My father is inside."

"Of course, I knew that. I meant anyone else? In particular, the Duchess?"

A corner of his mouth quirked upward. "No. It has been some years since my mother has been in the habit of visiting my father's bedchamber during the evenings."

Embarrassment caused her to blush, as she realized exactly what he was revealing. It seemed intimate, in a way a violation of the privacy one would expect in marriage.

"Is he awake?" she asked.

"No."

"Would you like some company?"

His eyebrows shot upward, almost becoming lost in the heavy, dark strands of hair that had fallen over his forehead. "This is hardly teatime, Lydia."

"I know. But whenever we were sick and Mama would sit beside the bed taking care of us, Papa was always there as well. More to offer support to Mama than anything else. I thought since you don't have a wife to share your sorrow, perhaps you'd settle for my company."

"You fancy yourself an angel of mercy then?"

"I fancy myself a friend."

Regret washed over his face. "I apologize. I am indeed going quite mad listening to nothing but the ticking of the clock and the crackling of the fire. By all means, join me."

Stepping back, he opened the door wider and swept his hand to the side in invitation. She eased inside, acutely aware of the clicking of the door as he closed it. He moved past her, and she watched in fascination, as he hefted a chair and placed it beside another one that was situated near the head of the bed. She took pleasure in the rippling of his shirt as his muscles bunched and relaxed with his efforts.

With a slight tipping of his head, he indicated the chair he'd just placed beside his. As quietly as she could, she glided farther into the room and sat. He dropped down beside her.

A fire burned low within the fireplace, providing the only light in the room. Darkness hovered in the corners, threatened the large canopied bed. Its thick velvet curtains were drawn back, tied in place with golden corded tassels. The posts on the bed were massive, intricately carved, and she wondered briefly if Rhys had been conceived there. If her own stepfather had been.

"Who watches him when you're not here?" she whispered.

"A nurse is sleeping in the adjoining room. She'll move in to sit at his bedside when I'm of a mind to retire. With his frail health, we dare not leave him unattended."

His low voice didn't carry the rasping of a whisper. It didn't hint at the sharing of secrets. Yet it managed to weave a cocoon of intimacy around them, caused her to lean toward him.

"You left him alone last night," she reminded him.

"Yes, well, I think we can both attest to the fact that I was not behaving as I should."

She knew he was referring to his misbehavior going far beyond simply leaving his father with no one to watch over him, but she thought it wise to divert the conversation back on to safer ground.

"Your father was asleep when Papa brought us in to introduce us. Does he ever wake up?"

He held her gaze. "Seldom. He sleeps more deeply now."

"It's very generous of you to allow everyone else to visit during the day and to save your visits for night."

He gave her a wry grin. "You flatter me with false assumptions. I have many responsibilities in regard to Harrington and Blackhurst. They are best handled during the daylight hours."

She felt like a little girl chastised for sticking her hand in the cookie jar before dinner. She didn't know why he tossed all her compliments back into her face. It was as though he had no desire for anyone to recognize the goodness in him. Perhaps he wasn't aware of it himself.

She shifted her gaze to the man lying on the bed. The shallow rising and falling of his chest were the only indications that he remained with them. His hair—fine, snowy-white strands brushed back off his brow— looked as though it had recently been washed. Responsibilities she could not imagine had carved deep lines within his face. She wondered if they would do the same to Rhys.

Yet she sensed peacefulness had come to the Duke. She would have liked to have known him, this man who'd had such a profound influence on her life. He had sired Grayson Rhodes, raised him, and then sent him away. And in the sending, he'd provided her with a father to replace her own.

"What color are his eyes?" she asked quietly.

"The shade of pewter."

She shifted her gaze to Rhys and smiled softly. "Like yours?"

"They hold much more wisdom."

"You admire him."

"Of course. He's accomplished a good deal in his lifetime."

"You're close, then?"

"Hardly."

She was taken aback by the bitterness she heard reflected in his voice. "But you were raised here—"

"You were correct this afternoon when you stated that within English law a bastard has no rights, no claims, and no family except the mother who bore him. But within this household, my father's legitimate sons had little hold on him. He thought Grayson walked on water. My mother believed Quentin did."

"And you?" she prodded gently.

She watched his throat work as he swallowed, his jaw tightening.

"I oftentimes floundered."

Reaching out, she wrapped her hand around his. "I'm sorry."

"I don't want your pity. I long ago accepted my place within their hearts. I have settled for scraps for so long, I fear a feast would no doubt make me ill."

She tried to make sense of his words, to decipher his meaning. Was he referring to love? That he neither wanted nor needed it?

"I can't imagine how difficult it would be to feel like you were less favored than one of your brothers. My parents have always loved us all equally."

"You do not think Grayson loves Colton, a child he sired, a child who carries his blood within his veins, more than he loves you?"

"I know he doesn't."

"You are naïve." He averted his gaze to the bed. She fought her urge to punch him in the shoulder.

"You're cynical," she tossed at him before removing her hand from his.

"I am a student of life. Love is overrated."

"Spoken by one who has obviously never experienced it fully."

He jerked his head around, his gaze as hard as flint. This conversation wasn't going at all as she'd imagined. She'd hoped to console and comfort him. Instead she had a strong inclination to shake some sense into him and self-pity out of him.

He leaned casually back in his chair and studied her insolently. "You know of the love between a parent and a child. What of the love between a man and a woman?"

"What about it?"

"Have you ever experienced it?"

She shrugged, trying to keep her temper in place. "There have been boys I've *liked*, men whose company I've *enjoyed*. But no, there's never been anyone I couldn't live without."

"In my world, it is better to settle for someone you can live *with*."

"Like your mother and father did," she shot back. "Settling for each other when the love of his life was someone else."

"Exactly," he answered smugly.

All her irritation vanished, and sadness swept over her. "It must have been a lonely existence for them both, don't you think?"

"That is the nature of a marriage of convenience."

"And that's what theirs was."

"Most marriages among the aristocracy are such."

She hadn't taken into consideration that unflattering aspect to marrying a peer. As much as she'd thought she wanted to marry a man with a title, she'd always assumed she'd meet a man who had the power to sweep her off her feet and entice her into falling head over heels in love with him—and having him feel the same way about her.

"There are some who marry for love, though, aren't there?" she asked.

"None I know of, although I must confess to my acquaintances being few."

"Lauren's stepfather is an earl. He married her mother, because he loved her," she said, pointing out what she hoped wasn't the only exception to his rule.

"A rare occurrence, I assure you."

"How sad," she murmured.

She'd always thought it unfair that her stepfather hadn't been considered part of the aristocracy, but now she had to wonder if perhaps the Duke had done him a great service by not marrying the actress. The Duke had left his illegitimate son free to marry a woman based on his love for her and hers for him.

"Don't distress yourself over it," Rhys said. "Those of the aristocracy know well their roles in society."

"I'm not distressed. I just . . ." She was incredibly tempted to raise her feet to the chair, tuck her legs beneath her, and settle in to tell him all the things she truly wanted in a husband. Love, of course, but respectability as well.

"Believe marriage should be based on love," he finished for her.

"Yes, well, no. I mean, based on love, yes, but not only on love."

"How like a woman not to be content with the jewel but to insist it be surrounded by gold as well."

She scowled at him. "I don't think respectability in addition to love is too much to ask."

He quirked a brow. "Respectability?"

She hesitated. She'd never shared this secret with anyone, not even Lauren. It resided in her heart, a part of her that she didn't particularly relish revealing. Yet surely a man such as he was, a man who understood honor, who would place the welfare of his dynasty over the comfort of his heart, would understand.

"If I confide something to you, will you promise never to tell a soul?"

"Who would I tell?"

She darted a glance toward the man lying on the bed. His even breathing was still shallow; his eyes were closed. She looked back at Rhys.

"I love my stepfather."

"That is quite apparent."

She took a deep breath. "Do you know the story of his marriage to my mother?"

"He never shared specifics with me, but it doesn't take a wise man to know a child born so soon after his parents have wed seldom survives unless he was conceived long before the vows were exchanged."

She nodded. Her guilt at revealing the situation was eased by the knowledge he'd already suspected the truth. Besides, he was family, in a manner of speaking.

"When my father realized my mother was with child, he became ugly, hideous. I remember he yelled, called my mother a whore—"

"Your father? You mean Grayson?"

She shook her head, her stomach roiling with the

memories she'd fought for so long to suppress. But they refused to be cast aside as worthless. They were like a toothache, worsened by the constant attention paid to it.

"My real father," she rasped. "John Westland."

Although to say he was her *real* father didn't accurately describe him, either. She had no memories of him before the war. His return had brought only sadness and tears.

Confusion filled his eyes. "Perhaps you'd better start at the beginning."

"We thought my father died during the war. Soldiers were returning home. When my Uncle James came back, everyone was happy. It wasn't that way with my father. One day he simply showed up in the fields. I didn't know who he was at first. I simply thought he looked lost. Someone trying to find his home, but he couldn't remember where he left it.

"Grayson had been living in our barn. He moved into town once Mama told us the man in the field was her husband, our father. A few days later Father was yelling at Mama. Calling her a whore. Calling Grayson a bastard. Calling the baby she was carrying a bastard.

"Most of what he said didn't make any sense to me at the time. I was young. Mostly I remember the way his rage contorted his face. It was frightening. And the loud voices when Grayson confronted him. The way people in town looked at Mama. Even after my father died, after Mama married Grayson, some women still stared at her like she was beneath them, something to be scraped off their shoe.

"I've always tried to be above reproach. To be a good daughter. A woman to be admired for her principles. I never want people to look at me the way they did my mother. As though they could carve my sins into my forehead."

Rhys studied her. The determination in the set of her jaw. The plea for understanding in her eyes. She loved all three of those people, and yet they'd managed to betray her with circumstances beyond her control. Perhaps even beyond theirs.

"Then you place respectability above love," he murmured.

Even in the firelight dancing around the room, he could see her blush, could see the discomfiture in her eyes. For all her musings about love and her apparent disregard for strictures that applied to marriage between those of rank, she was hardly any different.

"I suppose I do," she said softly. "I mean I'd never marry an outlaw or a criminal, even if I loved him. Although I can't imagine placing myself in a situation where I'd even have the opportunity to fall in love with someone I couldn't respect."

She angled her chin with resolve. "I'm certain I'd never have to choose between respectability and love."

"In his youth, I imagine my father thought much the same thing," he said quietly.

She snapped her gaze to the bed. "Would it have been so awful for him to have married an actress?"

"Scandalous at the time. Perhaps more acceptable now. Who is to say? I, for one, believe we should not judge the past by the present."

She turned her attention back to him. "But the past is what leads us to the present. How can you separate them? My life would be completely different if your father had married his actress lover. *Your* life would be different."

"I would not exist."

"Exactly," she said, as though she found philosophical discussions in the middle of the night fascinating. She brought her legs up to the chair and tucked them beneath her. "So how can you discount the importance of the past?"

"I did not say I discount it. Rather I do not judge past actions by today's acceptance of what is correct."

"So you don't look harshly upon those who waited to begin eating until everyone was served—when it was in vogue to do so. But you do look down on someone who waits now."

"Exactly."

She leaned toward him, bringing her sweet fragrance with her. He wondered if she'd applied a bit more perfume to her throat before her foray into the hallway.

"Why do you suppose there are so damned many rules?"

God help him. He laughed, a soft chuckle that was as inappropriate at this time and place as the young woman perched in the chair beside him. She smiled softly, somehow shifting the mood in the room, and he found himself incredibly grateful she was here.

"As your tutor, I should instruct you that a lady does not use profanity."

"But it caught your attention, didn't it?"

"Indeed." *She* caught his attention, caught it and held it until he almost forgot that anyone else existed in the world.

Chapter 9

Rhys meticulously calculated the sum of the numbers written on the paper resting on his desk. He cleared his throat. "You've made a mistake on this one."

"What difference does it make?"

He brought his head up sharply and glared at William as he stood in front of the window, staring out at only God knew what. Did the majority of those who resided in this household spend their time gazing out and wishing they were somewhere else?

"The difference, William, is that one way is correct, and all the other ways are distressingly wrong."

William spun around, his black hair falling into his eyes. He brushed it back with obvious impatience. "I only need to understand how one and two work. *One* cravat. *Two* gloves. Or *one* pair of gloves. Which is really *two* gloves. A pair of trousers. Why is it called a pair when there's really only one?"

With a sigh, Rhys leaned back in his chair. Of late,

he'd been trying to engage William in philosophical discussions in order to expand his mind. Deciphering the absurd particulars of garments was not what he had envisioned.

"What's bothering you, lad? Are you not content being within my employ?"

"Aye, I'm content."

He hardly sounded it. William turned back to the window.

"You mustn't take my correcting you as a poor reflection upon you," Rhys said. "We must view our mistakes as an opportunity to learn."

"I'm learning, all right," William mumbled.

"Did someone take you to task?"

"Nope. She walloped me upside the head."

"Who?" Rhys asked, his voice sounding dangerously close to a snarl.

A corner of William's mouth quirked up. "Not literally. Metavically."

"Metaphorically?"

"Aye, Guv. That's it. What you taught me the other day."

"So that lesson wasn't totally wasted. And here I'd thought you hadn't been paying attention."

Numbers gave William a fit, but words were another matter entirely. Unfortunately, the lad refused to infuse his speech with what his mind could comprehend. A sort of rebelliousness. But what was one to expect of a fourteen-year-old?

"Mr. Rhodes's daughter. Is she a commoner?" William asked.

"Quite so."

"So she won't be expected to marry no lord?"

Nor, he suspected, would she be in favor of William.

His sympathies went out to the lad. He'd tried to instill in him that nothing was beyond his grasp. Yet, in truth, many things would be. Especially when it came to women.

"She isn't the one who walloped you upside the head, is she?" Even from where he sat, even though William stood in profile to him, he could see William's cheek turning red.

"I think she's 'bout the loveliest thing I've had pass my way," William admitted.

Ah. Hence the reason for his melancholy, no doubt. Rhys stood and walked to the window. Gazing out on the garden, he realized immediately what had captured William's attention.

Lydia. Lovely Lydia. Her hair, caught up in a chignon, looked thick and heavy, and he expected at any moment the delicate threads holding it captive would break from the weight and send the strands cascading along her back.

She held a croquet mallet and appeared to be listening to her sister, whose mouth was once again moving at incredible speed. A little chatterbox. He shifted his gaze back to Lydia. She wore an indulgent smile.

"She is indeed lovely," Rhys said quietly. "But a good five years older than you."

"Caw! Blimey, Guv! She can't be! She ain't even got breasts yet."

"What are you on about? Of course she does. I'll grant you that they aren't as large as some, but I've no doubt they'd fit quite nicely within a man's palm. And her waist. My hands can span its width. Her hips have yet to expand from childbirth, and yet . . ." His voice trailed away, as he realized where his thoughts were leading, and how quickly his body wished to follow.

He cleared his throat. "That lesson was an example of what a gentleman should not discuss. Even with another gentleman."

He shifted his gaze to William. When the lad put his mind to it, he was sharper than most.

"You've set your eye on the older one, then?" he asked.

"Don't be absurd." Then he realized what William had revealed with what he hadn't said. "Is she not the one you were inquiring about?"

William grinned. "No, Guv. It's the younger one that's caught me fancy."

"Good Lord, lad. You're twice her age."

William wrinkled his brow. "So then when she's fifty, I'll be a hundred?"

He shook his head. "No, as you get older the disparity between your ages will become less."

"Makes no sense."

"It would if you'd work to master your numbers." But conquering mathematics suddenly seemed less important. "William, she's a child."

"I've got no plans to take advantage of her," he responded hotly.

"I didn't think you did, but any sort of *courtship* at this time is entirely out of the question."

"Wasn't even plannin' on any courtship. She just smells so bloody clean, and when she looks at me, she makes me feel like a king instead of what I am."

"Which would be what?"

"A bastard, like her father."

Rhys gave a brusque nod and turned his attention back to the window. He often wondered if bringing the lad here had been poor judgment. His mother made no secret of her intolerance for the illegitimate.

"That boy, her brother, he showed me the watch his *uncle* give him."

Rhys stiffened. "What of it?" he finally managed in a neutral voice.

"It bore the Duke's coat of arms."

He shifted his eyes toward the lad, whose head was now even with Rhys's shoulder. Soon he would be a man to be reckoned with. "Yes."

"You gave it to him."

"Yes."

"How come he has the right to call you uncle when his father is a bastard? A bastard has no family, belongs to nobody." With a look, William challenged him to deny the charges.

"According to the law, yes. But what a man feels in his heart goes beyond the law."

He wondered when he'd come to believe that statement. In his youth, he'd often pretended he was illegitimate, that his parents had never married. He'd wanted to have something in common with Grayson. Grayson, whom the Duke adored. Grayson, who'd always had a ready smile for Rhys, always acknowledged him, always listened to him when no one else seemed to. He'd have been content to spend his life standing in Grayson's shadow—rather than Quentin's.

Crossing his arms over his chest, Rhys pressed his shoulder against the window casing. "Did you wish to address me as uncle?"

He could see William mulling over the possibilities.

William squinted up at him. "Nah, you ain't no relation, at all. It's just sometimes I wish I belonged to somebody."

"You mean a great deal to me, William."

The boy shrugged. "If you say so."

"I do say so."

As though uncomfortable with the sentiment he'd been seeking, William glanced back at the garden. "They're not very good at that game."

"It seems a lesson is in order. Shall we take a break from your studies and join them?"

Standing on the croquet lawn, Lydia was well aware that Rhys had been watching her long before he stepped through the glass doors of his study to join her. His gaze had settled on her as though it was a physical caress. She tried not to stare at him, while he strode across the lawn with William in tow, but she could not help but be pleased he would soon be close enough that she could gaze into his eyes, hear his voice, and bask in his attention.

She had a feeling he'd decided to teach her how to play croquet, but she was well versed in the rules. She'd been purposefully awkward so Sabrina could take delight in feeling more skillful.

Lydia also understood the purpose of croquet was to provide an opportunity for innocent flirtation. She could hardly wait to put her knowledge into practice.

"Hey, Lyd!"

She forced her attention away from Rhys and gave it to Colton as he raced toward her.

"They've got dogs!" he said excitedly, breathlessly, stopping beside her.

"Dogs!" Sabrina shouted, dropping her mallet before rushing up to Colton.

"They're fenced in," Colton explained. "Can we take them for a run?"

She shifted her gaze to Rhys. His mouth had curled

up slightly in amusement. She enjoyed even the barest hint of his smiles.

"Are the dogs tamed?" she asked Rhys.

"They're hounds. Used for fox hunting."

"Will they harm the children if they play around them?"

"No." He turned to William. "Why don't you oversee things? Tell Mr. Burrow I've given my permission for all of you to take the hounds out."

"Aye, Guv, I'll take care of it."

He shook his head while William, Colton, and Sabrina dashed off.

"Why did he call you Guv?" Lydia asked.

"He's having a difficult time adjusting to my new status."

"I don't understand. I thought as a second son, you would have been accorded the respect of being addressed as my lord."

He seemed to hesitate, his gaze sweeping over her, and in his eyes, she thought she detected loss and acceptance.

"For a time, I'd distanced myself from the family. I did not acknowledge them, nor did they acknowledge me. Therefore my servants merely assumed I had no connection with the peerage, but simply possessed some magical means to provide for them if they served me well."

She wondered how much more he'd reveal if she prodded gently, wondered if she had any right to. "What happened to cause the rift between you?"

"I did something they found quite unforgivable. Do you understand how to play croquet?"

With grace, she accepted his determination not to discuss the past any more than he already had.

She held up her mallet. "I can't quite figure out how to hold the blasted thing."

He grinned, his eyes twinkling, and she felt as though she'd touched the stars. Strange how a mere glimmer of happiness in him could make her almost giddy with joy.

"Allow me to demonstrate," he offered.

He moved behind her, circled his arms around her, and placed his hands over hers where they gripped the mallet.

"What is the scent you wear?" he asked.

His breath skimmed along the sensitive skin below her ear. She would have expected it to tickle, not send delightful shivers through her.

"Rose."

"It smells sweeter on you than on any bud I've ever encountered."

She angled her head slightly, giving his breath more area to travel over. Although she looked ahead, she very much sensed his head was bent close to hers. "You spend a great deal of time sniffing rosebuds, do you?"

"When a gentleman compliments you, my dear Miss Westland, you should blush becomingly and thank him."

She felt her face growing warm and responded, "Thank you."

"You are most welcome."

She waited patiently, not daring to move, her breathing shallow, while she was acutely aware of his nearness, the curving of his shoulders almost cradling her back. Then she felt his lips, soft and warm, touching the side of her neck. Her eyes fluttered closed, and she found herself leaning against him.

"The lesson here, Lydia," he whispered seductively

against her ear, "is to never let a man distract you from your purpose."

"My purpose?" she asked breathlessly.

"To learn to play croquet."

"Oh, yes. What are the rules of croquet, then?"

"I haven't a clue."

Laughing, she spun away from him. "You scoundrel!"

He was smiling broadly, actually smiling, and he was transformed into the most gorgeous man she'd ever laid eyes on. All along, she'd considered him handsome, but with a smile gracing his face, he stole her breath away.

"You asked me to teach you what you would not find in the books."

"So I did." She placed the mallet against her shoulder, holding it as though it were a parasol.

He grew serious. "A gentleman will always take advantage."

"So what is a lady to do?"

"Always remain watchful, alert, and aware of a man's intentions."

"And if she doesn't mind him taking advantage?" she dared to ask.

"Then she ceases to be a lady."

She lowered the mallet. "And yet a gentleman, while taking advantage, continues to be a gentleman?"

"There's anger in your voice."

"There's anger in my entire body!" The unfairness of his rules was preposterous.

He slowly raked his gaze over her, which only served to further agitate her. She was contemplating where best to apply the mallet: against his head or his shin.

"That, my dear Miss Westland, is the point of this

entire lesson. Anger is not to be displayed under any circumstances."

"I take it your mother never learned that lesson."

She saw his tongue gingerly working the corner of his mouth. Although no evidence of his mother's slap remained, Lydia didn't think it was easily forgotten.

"Obviously not," he murmured.

Suddenly feeling deflated, she marched up to him and glared at him. "Do you know what I think? I don't think you meant to give me a lesson at all. I think you found yourself having fun, and for some reason, you don't think *joy* should be displayed under any circumstances. I'm tempted to use your head as a croquet ball."

He looked so surprised that she might have laughed under different circumstances. Instead she put the mallet away and went in search of Colton and Sabrina.

The Marquess of Blackhurst was as infuriating as he was handsome. She was of a mind to teach him a few lessons of her own.

Chapter 10

A true lady shall favor a gentleman who
demonstrates a kind regard for both animals
and children.

*Miss Westland's Blunders in
Behavior Corrected*

The Harrington stables were vast. Lydia couldn't
imagine the joy of possessing so many beautiful
horses for the simple pleasure of riding them. Most of
the horses her family owned were used to work the
farm or cattle.

And they certainly didn't have a host of servants to
see to the welfare of the livestock. Back home, she took
care of her own horse. She didn't mind the chore. She
actually rather enjoyed it.

Today she'd decided to join Colton on his afternoon
ride. They strolled through the cavernous structure that
didn't smell much different from their barn at home.
She welcomed the scent of fresh hay and warm hide.

The rest of the family was going for another excur-
sion in the carriage to view the surrounding countryside.

"Good afternoon, Miss Westland," an older man said
as he approached her, doffing his cap. "Going to join
the lad today, are you?"

Following Colton's debacle with the Duchess, and after gaining their father's approval, Rhys had introduced the head groomsman to the family, making certain Sims understood he was to ready a horse for them any time they requested. Sims was in charge of the stables and had several younger men and some boys who worked with him. A few gawked at the visitors now, but most remained hard at work.

"Hello, Mr. Sims," Lydia said. "You've got a fine stable of horses."

"Aye, miss. His Lordship has a good eye. Any one of the beasts in here should do you well."

She smiled brightly. "Thank you. I'll take a look around and let you know which one I'd like."

"Very good, miss." He turned to Colton. "Will you be riding the same horse today as you have before?"

"Yes, sir."

Mr. Sims grinned. "Right-o, then. Let's get him ready."

While Colton hurried off with Mr. Sims, Lydia searched for a mare that she thought would be to her liking. Through a wide opening at the other end of the stable, she saw some horses canter by.

She walked to the opening and leaned against the gate that separated her from the horses within the confines of the paddock. She counted six. One neared, caught her scent, and trotted away. Her stomach roiled.

Its flanks bore the unmistakable scars inflicted by a lash or a whip. A riding crop maybe. But only if it had been held by someone with a very heavy hand. Her gaze darted to the other animals. They all bore similar scars. Tears stung her eyes at the thought of the cruelty that had been inflicted on them and all they'd suffered.

"Have you found a horse, miss?" Mr. Sims asked.

She pointed toward the enclosure. "These horses—"

"His Lordship insists no one other than himself ride these, miss. Inside, I have a fine, gentle mare I think you'd enjoy riding."

"His Lordship?" she whispered hoarsely. "The Marquess?"

"Aye, miss."

She could hardly believe it. She'd judged Rhys to be caring. How could she have been so incredibly mistaken?

"Lyd, what are you doing?" Colton asked, as he approached. His eyes widened with horror at the sight of the horses. "God Almighty! What happened to 'em?"

She could see her brother was hurting for the horses as much as she was. Growing up on a farm, they always had the utmost respect for animals and would never dare dream of abusing one. What sort of monster did? "They've been terribly mistreated," she said.

"Aye, miss, they have, but that's not your worry now, is it?" Mr. Sims asked. "Come along. Let's get a horse readied for you."

He turned away, but Lydia could hardly take her eyes away from the sight of the battered animals.

"I never noticed these before," Colton said. "Why would anyone do that to a horse?"

"Because he was cruel. That's the only reason."

"You think Uncle Rhys did it?"

"Who else? Mr. Sims said he was the only one who rode them." She wrapped her arm around Colton's shoulder and led him back into the stables. It always took her by surprise to realize he was nearly as tall as she was.

But the realization distracted her for only a heartbeat, before her thoughts returned to the horses and

Rhys. She'd never suspected he was a man capable of such brutality.

He'd insisted he wasn't kind. She'd refused to listen. Now she'd seen the proof of his claims. She was revolted by the knowledge that she'd allowed him to kiss her, had flirted with him, had even fancied herself falling for him.

Rhys heard the yelling the moment he stepped out of the silversmith's shop. Apparently he wasn't the only one, because people began streaming out of the shops and heading toward the end of the street where the commotion seemed to be originating.

His height afforded him a better view than most, and yet he could scarcely believe what he was seeing as he neared the carpentry shop. Mr. Bower, a tenant who farmed a good deal of Harrington land, stood in his wagon, with the reins in one hand and a whip in the other. He yelled down at some woman who was screaming up at him.

Rhys wended his way through the crowd of curious onlookers, not an easy task when they were all vying for a closer inspection of the turmoil. Usually this village was as quiet as a church. He could hardly fathom the excitement these quarreling people were causing.

"Pardon me. Excuse me. Make way, please," he ordered as he tried to diplomatically move people aside.

He neared the wagon. A woman climbed on board. Not a woman. A lady. A finely dressed lady. Not only a lady.

Lydia.

By God, she was furious.

"Give me that whip, you goddamned sorry son-of-a-bitch!"

She reached for it.

Bower shoved her back.

She teetered. Her arms flailed.

Rhys's breath backed up painfully in his lungs, and he quickened his pace.

Bower pushed her again. Losing her balance completely, Lydia cried out.

As she fell backward off the wagon, Rhys thrust someone aside and caught Lydia. She flung her arms around his neck as though she didn't quite trust him not to drop her.

When releasing her was the furthest thing from his mind.

They were both breathing hard, their gazes locked. Passion fueled the violet of her eyes, eyes framed by the longest lashes he'd ever seen. He wanted to look into them until he became lost, until his past transgressions melted away. Her parted lips were so incredibly close to his that he would need to lower his head only a fraction in order to taste them. The temptation was almost more than he could tolerate.

He became acutely aware of the side of one of her breasts flattened against his chest, the warmth of their bodies easing through the cloth, mingling, saturating the skin of the other.

He had carried many a woman to his bed, but none had felt as right in his arms as she did. None had felt as though she belonged. None had made him regret so profoundly that he could offer nothing more than this.

"Put me down," she hissed through bared teeth.

Apparently he'd mistaken fury for passion. He became increasingly mindful of the people surrounding him, jostling about in an attempt to determine exactly what was going on here.

He tipped his head slightly in acquiescence, and slowly lowered her feet to the ground, relishing the length of her body unfurling against his. She stepped back, and the cool air rushing between them restored his senses.

"Miss Westland, perhaps you'd care to explain what this commotion is all about. From my vantage point, it appeared you accosted Mr. Bower here."

"Aye, that she did, m'lord. A wild woman, to be sure—"

He cut a scathing glare at Bower that abruptly silenced the man. He turned his attention back to Lydia. "Miss Westland?"

"Not that you would care, but his wagon is loaded with too many supplies. It's too heavy for one horse to pull. He was using that whip on the poor animal. I was trying to stop him."

"And placing yourself in great peril during the process."

"I can defend myself. The horse can't."

"I see." Indeed he did, now that he looked beyond Lydia to the wagon. Heavy furniture had been loaded into it. He glanced up. "Mr. Bower, I don't fancy getting a crick in my neck while discussing the matter with you. Will you please step down?"

That Bower didn't want to was evident in the mulish expression that crossed his face, before he climbed off the wagon. As soon as Bower's feet were planted firmly on the ground, Rhys smashed his balled fist into the man's face. Bower hit the side of the wagon before sliding to the ground.

Lydia's mouth dropped open, as did the mouths of most of the people standing near enough to have seen what had transpired.

"I have no tolerance for a man who abuses a woman," Rhys said with remarkable calm, trying desperately not to imagine what might have happened to Lydia had he not been quick enough and close enough to catch her.

"But, m'lord, she was carrying on—"

"I witnessed her behavior, Mr. Bower. The prudent thing for you to have done would have been to go in search of a constable. Or myself. Now if you'll please stand, we'll discuss this matter like civilized gentlemen."

Bower hesitantly worked his way to his feet, eyeing Rhys the entire time as though he didn't quite trust him not to strike him again. Rhys was incredibly tempted to oblige the man by fulfilling his expectations of another blow.

Instead Rhys turned to the crowd. "The entertainment is over. I suggest you all return to your business." He glanced at Lydia. "You may, of course, stay."

"Of course."

He couldn't quite comprehend the reason she seemed cross with him. He had, after all, come to her rescue like a gallant knight.

Bower flinched when Rhys went to straighten the man's jacket and dust the dirt off his clothes. Rhys wasn't normally so quick to deliver a punch, but then where Lydia was concerned, he seemed to seldom behave as himself.

"Now, Mr. Bower, Miss Westland is quite correct. Your wagon carries far too much weight for this horse."

"But, m'lord, I've only got the one horse, and I don't fancy making two trips into the village when it takes away from me time in the field. But me new wife fancies some new furniture."

"You keep beating that horse like you were, and he's going to die, and then you'll have nothing at all, you idiot!" Lydia pointed out.

Bower's face turned a mottled red. "That horse has been pulling me wagon long enough for me to know what he can and can't handle!"

"Enough!" Rhys demanded. "You will lighten the load."

"But, m'lord—"

"I'll send some of my men with a wagon to pick up the remaining items and deliver them to your home," Rhys told him. "In the future, you need only send word to Harrington that you have supplies or furniture or whatever needs to be delivered, and I'll see it is taken care of. To spare your horse and your time."

The man nodded with obvious resentment. "Very good, m'lord. I'll get some chaps to help me unload the wagon."

"Thank you, Mr. Bower. One last thing. It would improve my opinion of you considerably if you were to offer an apology to Miss Westland."

Bower glared at Lydia. "I 'umbly apologize, miss."

The tone of his voice more aptly conveyed that he wished some misfortune to befall her. Rhys would have to pay Mr. Bower a visit later and teach him a few manners, but further public chastisement would only serve to embitter the man.

Lydia nodded curtly, seeming as happy to receive the apology as Bower was to issue it. Bower lumbered off in search of someone to help him unload the wagon.

"He'll beat that horse the next chance he gets," she said.

"To ensure that he does not, I shall speak with him again on the matter later," Rhys said.

She furrowed her brow as though he'd spoken in a language alien to her. He'd never had much luck in understanding women's minds when they were revealed to him through conversation, let alone when he could see within their eyes that the wheels were turning. Wherever she was headed with her thoughts, he decided it would be best if they simply moved on to more pressing concerns.

Tugging on his glove, Rhys glanced around. "Where is your brother?"

"By now he's probably back at the house."

Now it was his turn to wonder at her meaning. "I beg your pardon? I thought you'd planned to go riding together this afternoon."

"We started out together. Then I saw the village and wanted to take a closer look. He figured I'd want to do some shopping, and he wasn't interested. So he headed back."

"Then who accompanied you to the village?"

Shrugging, she shook her head. "No one."

"Are you telling me that you rode here without the benefit of chaperone or escort?"

"I suppose I am." She gave him a pointed glare. "I'll see you later."

"Where are you going?"

"Back to the manor."

"You can't ride back alone."

"Why not?"

"Because it's simply not done. A *lady* does not ride about the countryside alone."

She blanched at that, but jutted out her chin in defiance. "I do it all the time back home."

"Well, you shan't do it on my watch. I'll escort you home."

"I don't need an escort," she insisted.

"I'll not have your father berate me for not seeing to your welfare. Unfortunately, the silversmith has not yet finished the task which I've set to him. I was going to have a spot of tea at the inn just up the road. Perhaps you'd care to join me."

Ah, he could see those little wheels of indecision turning.

"Mrs. Forest is known for her deliciously wicked chocolate desserts," he offered in an attempt to entice her.

"No."

He sighed deeply. "Very well. I'll escort you home and then return to finish my business."

"That's not necessary."

"I fear it is, Lydia. What sort of gentleman would I be if I did not look after your welfare?"

She leaned toward him, her eyes narrowed. "I know exactly what sort of *gentleman* you are, my *lord*."

The derision in her voice took him off guard. Was she still seething over the abuse of the horse, or did she have cause to be upset with *him*? If so, what in God's name had he done?

"What sort of gentleman is that?" he asked.

"Hypocritical. Cruel. Unmerciful."

Devil take it! She could easily be describing Quentin. Rhys had been the scapegoat for far too many of his brother's actions. By God, not with her. Not with her.

He'd wrapped his hand around her upper arm before he'd realized what he was about. Her eyes widened, her nostrils flared, and those damned lips parted. His body reacted as though she'd suddenly fallen onto a bed of silk.

He wanted to crush her to him, not in anger, but in

passion. If he were a wise man, he would allow her to return home alone, or he'd find someone else to escort her.

Apparently wisdom did not run in his family.

"I believe a lesson is in order."

"I don't want you teaching me anything. Unhand me," she said in a low voice.

He did so, but only because his fingers were in danger of brushing against the side of her breast. And what would happen to his control then?

"Please, join me at the inn," he said in as level a voice as he could muster, hoping to give away none of the confusion swirling through him. Was this not the lady who had asked him to teach her? The lady who sat with him in his father's bedchamber until the wee hours of the morning?

She gave a brief nod. "Very well. Don't touch me. Don't talk to me."

He arched a brow. "May we at least sit at the same table?"

"I suppose."

"Very good."

Although in truth, he thought his words bespoke of an overly optimistic view for their time together.

Lydia couldn't believe she'd allowed Rhys to browbeat her into joining him for tea. Although *browbeat* was a bit harsh. He'd seemed as gentlemanly as her stepfather while he'd spoken to her.

It was the shiver that had cascaded through her body when he'd grabbed her arm that had caused her to lash out at him. She didn't want to find herself drawn to this man who could so abuse animals.

Abusing animals was only a step away from abusing people. What did she know about him, really?

He'd been raised alongside her stepfather. Yet he hadn't. They'd never allowed her stepfather to forget who he was or more importantly, *what* he was.

Now she was having afternoon tea with a man who jumbled up her emotions. Why did he have to be so devastatingly handsome, sitting at a table near the back of the inn, where the sunlight eased through a window and washed over him?

He was upholding the conditions she'd placed on joining him. He wasn't touching her or talking to her. He was, however, managing to communicate with her. And she wasn't altogether certain how she felt about that.

Warm, tingly, flustered, short of breath.

His intense gray gaze had not left her since they'd sat. It stayed on her while he sipped his tea and ignored the cream-filled pastry slathered in chocolate that the serving girl had placed before him. Lydia had gobbled down hers as though she were at a watermelon-eating contest back home.

"What?" she finally snapped.

A glimmer of a smile touched his eyes. "I was wondering if you might like to feast upon my pastry as well."

She shifted in her chair, her eyes darting to the thick chocolate on his plate. She didn't know why the chocolate here tasted so much better, creamier, and richer. It was impossible to resist.

"It's unladylike to eat two."

"It's unladylike to wolf it down without catching a breath between bites."

The heat of embarrassment scalded her skin, boiled her simmering temper. She tossed her napkin on the table. "I'm going home."

Lunging partway across the table, he grabbed her wrist. She froze, glaring at him.

"Please, don't go," he pleaded quietly. "That was uncalled for and rude. Boorish. Impolite. I was being an ill-mannered lout." A corner of his mouth quirked up. "You may, of course, feel free to stop my self-flagellation at any time."

"Why would I when I think you deserve it?"

"For teasing you about your enthusiastic response to the chocolate?" He shook his head slightly. "I don't think so. There is more at stake here, and I can't figure out what. Most women would have been grateful to have been rescued from a brute such as Bower. You seem to resent my intrusion."

"Not your intrusion. You."

Slowly unfurling his fingers from her wrist, he straightened. "I see."

The wounded look in his eyes almost brought tears to hers. Was that his ploy? To seem cruel, and then appear hurt? Yet so often he'd been kind.

"I saw your horses," she blurted.

Deep furrows creased his brow. "My horses? Of course you saw them. I assume you rode one into the village."

"The ones in the paddock behind the stables."

"Ah, *those* horses."

"Mr. Sims told me that you don't allow anyone else to ride them. They've been horribly abused."

"Indeed they have been, but not by my hand."

"Then whose?"

"Quentin's."

Lydia felt the force of that one word like a physical blow. The tightening of the muscles in Rhys's jaw, the hardening of his eyes, the firm set of his mouth told her that more than resenting his brother, he resented that she'd assumed the worst of Rhys.

The anger she'd been holding against him flowed out like the water of a lake through a busted dam. Relief rushed in.

"I'm sorry. Mr. Sims—"

"Is not one to speak ill of the dead. No one, by God, is willing to speak ill of the dead. Almost makes me anticipate my death."

Reaching across the table, she wrapped her hand around his clenched fist where it rested beside his teacup. "I should have realized it wasn't you who'd taken a whip to those horses."

"And why, pray tell, should you have realized that?"

A thousand answers rushed through her mind. Instinct? Attraction? No, it went beyond that. It was an indefinable something that resided in her very core so that when she looked at him or gazed into his eyes, she felt as though she'd discovered the better part of herself in him.

"I can't explain it," she finally confessed. "I just should have known."

She withdrew her hand and eased back onto the chair. "Why didn't you stop Quentin as you did Mr. Bower?"

"Two reasons. The first is that it is most difficult to alter the behavior and actions of any man when he outranks you, because he is held in higher esteem by the nature of his birth."

"And the second," she prodded, when it seemed he would not continue.

"I had not been to Harrington in years. I was unaware Quentin had begun to reveal his cruelties so flagrantly. Yet even so, some are still blind to his faults."

Her heart wrenched. "Your mother."

"Quite so."

"I'm sorry. I shouldn't have suspected the worse. I should have asked you—"

"Let it go, Lydia."

Her name rolled off his tongue, reminding her of something thick and warm to hold the chill at bay on a wintry night. Why did he have this effect on her? Why did he make her want to rise to her feet and settle onto his lap? Wrap her arms around his neck and bring her mouth to his?

He did have the most luscious mouth she'd ever seen. He pressed his thumb against his parted full lips. She watched, mesmerized, while his tongue stroked the underside of his thumb. Once. Twice. Three times. And she imagined placing her own thumb there, allowing him to dampen her skin.

His eyes glittered with mischievousness, as though he knew the trail down which her wayward thoughts were headed. Then he leaned toward her, and his thumb caressed the corner of her mouth, making her lips yearn for more, her pulse to race.

"The next time you take me to task," he said in a low, sensuous voice, "I suggest you do so without having a bit of chocolate teasing me at the corner of your mouth."

She jerked back as though he'd slapped her. Humiliation swamped her. She snatched up her napkin and wiped her mouth.

"Too late. I've already taken care of it."

She watched in amazement, while he returned his thumb briefly to his mouth, and she wondered if he tasted her as much as he tasted the chocolate.

"You should have said something." Her chastisement lost its impact when spoken with a squeaky voice.

"You are quite right. But I was too distracted wondering how the flavor of your skin would enhance the enjoyment of the chocolate."

And based on the taste he'd just received, Rhys knew that it enhanced it a great deal.

Confound it! What was he doing speaking to her in this manner? Why, when he was around her, did he seem incapable of controlling his thoughts, his tongue, or his body?

She was staring at him with wide, curious eyes as though he'd yanked her from her home and dumped her into a foreign land. Quite likely, she often did feel that way. Traipsing about the countryside on her own? Getting into a brawl with a man twice her size? What was he to do with her?

Certainly not what he wanted to do, what he craved doing. He had to put them both on an even keel. He swapped his pastry laden plate with her empty one.

"Finish off my pastry," he ordered.

"After you've insulted me twice—"

"No insult," he rushed to assure her. "Mere teasing on both counts." And unavoidable temptation.

She lifted her fork and peered at him through half lowered lashes. "Don't you like chocolate?"

"I prefer to taste where it's been."

He could not have spoken truer words, and he considered that biting off his tongue might be appropriate. He could see her running his words through her mind as though she were trying to determine how he could enjoy where chocolate had been. Unfortunately, he'd never be able to demonstrate for her exactly how he preferred to have his dessert.

"Do you want me to scrape off the chocolate so you can have the pastry back?"

He laughed. She was such an innocent delight.

He shook his head. "No, you finish it off. I rather enjoy watching the pleasure you take in eating sweets."

"I do have a weakness for chocolate," she admitted as she scooped up her first bite.

Unfortunately, he was beginning to fear he had a *weakness* for *her*. He relished every moment spent with her and wanted one more. One more conversation, one more smile, one more touch . . . one more kiss.

He wanted what he knew he did not deserve.

Chapter 11

Lydia stepped out of the inn and glanced down the main street that ran through the center of the village. Bower's wagon was gone, but she could see where he'd left a good portion of his furniture. Simply because Rhys had insisted.

Her family, her stepfather was influential in Fortune. She knew beyond any doubt he could have stopped Bower from making his horse carry such a heavy load. But he wouldn't have been able to accomplish the same results as effortlessly as Rhys had. Had her stepfather punched the man, the man would have no doubt fought back.

As much as she understood about the intricacies of the aristocracy, she was amazed to witness the power Rhys wielded simply because of his birth. His title. He'd only held his position for a few months. Yet people kowtowed to him, as though he'd worn the cloak of a marquess his entire life.

She was quite simply amazed.

She darted a glance at him. Tugging on his gloves, he gazed around the village and nodded in acknowledgment to those who caught his eye. Life here was incredibly different. Certainly in Fortune, everyone acknowledged one another, but she sensed equality there. Her family was well-off, no two ways about it. But people didn't bow to them as they practically did to Rhys.

"The silversmith should be finished with his task by now," Rhys said. "Where shall we meet?"

"I could go with you," she offered.

He seemed to hesitate, and she wondered briefly if he was embarrassed to be seen with her in public. Hidden away in the corner of an inn was one thing, but to walk brazenly through town might be considered quite another.

He angled his head slightly and held out his arm. "If you wish."

"Do you wish?"

His gray eyes warmed as he gave her the barest hint of a smile. "Indeed I do."

Smiling brightly, she placed her hand on his arm. "Lead the way, my lord."

She was acutely aware he kept his steps short, slow, leisurely. He did not have the loose-jointed walk of a cowboy, yet he had a powerful grace to his stride that mesmerized her.

"Was there something in particular you were looking for when you came to the village?" he asked.

She shook her head. "It just appeared quaint from a distance, so I wanted to have a closer look."

"Your brother didn't share your interest?"

She laughed lightly. "He lacks the maturity to appreciate what an incredible opportunity we have to experience something so unlike what we have at home."

"Do you not have villages?" he inquired.

"Not like this. We don't have thatched roofs and flower boxes at the windows. We have square buildings with false storefronts. Hot, dusty streets. Fortune has grown and flourished, but it's more like a child still struggling to understand itself. This village seems comfortable with its place in the world."

"You're quite the philosopher."

"Are you mocking me, sir?"

His eyes warmed. "No, Lydia. I am intrigued by you."

He stepped toward an entry. "Here we are."

Before he could open the door, it was opened for him. A wizened gentleman wearing spectacles, with thick lenses that made his eyes appear huge, ushered them inside. "My lord, I have the watch all ready for you."

"Very good, Mr. Crump."

Lydia couldn't help but be curious about the watch, especially since he'd given one to Colton. While Mr. Crump scurried across the store and eased behind a glass counter, Lydia followed Rhys until he was standing before the silversmith.

Mr. Crump brought out a silver watch, resting on blue velvet. On its circular cover had been carved the same image that was on Colton's watch.

She watched as Rhys slowly trailed his gloved finger over the etching. "Very nice, Mr. Crump. Please wrap it carefully, and I'll take it with me."

"Very good, my lord."

"You're replacing the watch you gave Colton," she speculated softly.

"Not exactly. I simply discovered I was in need of one similar to the first."

"Because you don't want your mother to know what you did."

He looked uncomfortable, avoided her eyes. "It's a rather long story, but has nothing to do with my mother."

She considered prying further, but as it was, he made her feel as though she was intruding where she had no business. Turning away, she browsed through the little shop, while Rhys finished dealing with Mr. Crump. Perhaps she should have waited outside.

Being around Rhys was too confusing. At times, she thought he had an interest in her. Mostly, however, she felt as though she was nothing more than a pain in his backside.

Riding alongside Rhys, Lydia fought to keep her attention focused on the scenery, but her gaze constantly betrayed her and wandered back to Rhys. Unlike Colton, who had complained about the odd English saddle, Rhys seemed completely at home in it. Powerfully elegant.

How he could be both powerful and elegant seemed contradictory, and yet he was. He was exactly what she'd told her brother Johnny she was searching for in a man. His presence had dominated the village. Something about his persona implied he'd never cower before anyone.

How difficult it must have been for him to grow up in the shadow of a brother who did not deserve to cast one.

"I don't understand how your mother could prefer Quentin over you. I've only been here a short time and already I'm well aware he was not a nice man."

"He was quite good at manipulating people, skilled at hiding his true self."

"How could he hide what he did to those horses?"

He shifted his attention to her, and she felt the full weight of his gaze. "I imagine he found some way to justify his treatment of the animals. He no doubt told anyone who would listen that they were disobedient."

She shuddered. "Thank goodness he had no children." She tried to recall what else she knew of Quentin. "Was he married?"

"For a time." He pointed across the land. "If you've no objection to a bit of rougher riding, the scenery is much more pleasant if we cut across the estate."

"I'm used to rough riding," she assured him, delighted by the thought of a challenge.

Something primal flashed in his eyes, and she had the feeling he'd read something more into her statement, something not entirely innocent.

He urged his horse off the main road and into a canter. She easily followed, quickly catching up with him. She wasn't fond of the sidesaddle. At home, she would have worn a split skirt and ridden astride. When she'd packed her trunk, she'd assumed a riding habit would be more appropriate here. She had to admit that she did feel more like a lady, although a secret part of her wouldn't have minded challenging him to a race. But she wasn't quite used to the saddle and didn't want to risk losing.

She enjoyed the subtle rolling of the land. The dark green countryside, the abundance of trees. The graceful sweep of the blue sky. The same sky she looked at while she worked in the fields. Strange, how it suddenly seemed much more beautiful when she wasn't toiling beneath it.

He brought his horse to a halt near crumbling pillars of stone nearly lost within the foliage. She wouldn't have even noticed them if he hadn't directed her toward them.

"What is this place?" Lydia asked.

"The remnants of a forgotten castle."

"It can't be forgotten if you remember it," she said.

"I suppose not."

She waited while Rhys dismounted and walked over to her. Raising his arms, he placed his strong hands around her waist. Resting her hands on his broad shoulders, she held her breath while he slowly lowered her to the ground, his gaze locked on hers.

Warmth swirled through her. She was aware of her bodice rasping lightly against his shirt, her skirt brushing his trousers, the toes of her shoes touching his. Aware that she now looked up at him where before she'd looked down, and in the looking, she was drawn into the gray of his tempestuous eyes.

Desire rolled over his face the way storm clouds billowed across the land, darkening as they sought to release all they'd gathered. He wanted her. She was certain of it. She trembled with the knowledge that she desired him as well.

Several young men had given their attention to her, yet she'd never known such awareness, as though an invisible rope had been lassoed around them and was bringing them closer together.

Abruptly he released her. She didn't know if it was because the sensations threatened to overwhelm him as they did her—or if he was upset that he experienced them at all. She squelched her disappointment and followed him as he strode away from her.

He came to an area she was certain had once been the base of a wall. He stood there gazing at what nature had mostly reclaimed.

"I thought castles had moats," she said, awed by the history she sensed in the place. Hundreds of years might have passed since this place had fallen.

A corner of his mouth quirked up. "Not all of them. Certainly not this one. At least I've been unable to find any evidence of it. Once when I was much younger, I thought I'd found a secret passage that might lead me to the dungeons. But it was nothing more than a badger hole."

"So you came here to explore," she said.

He turned, crossed his arms over his chest, and leaned against the edge of the remaining wall. "I came here to think."

"And is that the reason you're here now? To think?"

"I am not sure why I came. I felt a need to share this place with you when I have shared it with no one before."

She glanced around. "I think it's beautiful. But sad as well."

"You have a romantic bent. I fear it will make your heart easier to break."

"You flatter me by worrying about my heart at all."

He grinned. "Are you quoting from your books now?"

"I'm trying to improve my wit. I can hold my own in a conversation about cattle or crops or the weather. I'm not exactly sure what the gentlemen here want to talk about."

"Indeed there is a talent to successfully carrying on a meaningful conversation about nothing. I suppose I should provide you with a list of appropriate topics."

"I'd be very grateful if you did."

"Is it so very different in Texas?" he asked quietly.

"Yes. I can't explain all the differences. Some are subtle."

"Do you really ride over the countryside by yourself?"

She nodded. "Sometimes. Sometimes I ride with a man."

He shifted his stance as though she'd piqued his attention. "Indeed?"

She smiled warmly. "Our rules are different. We don't bother with chaperones. I've gone on picnics with young men in the area, and my parents were nowhere to be seen. Your society seems to expect everyone to misbehave while mine expects them to behave."

"Interesting commentary on our differing worlds."

She'd been looking into his eyes, unaware he'd moved as close as he had, close enough that she smelled the lemony fragrance that graced his skin, along with the masculine scent that hovered beneath. Close enough that she felt the heat of his body through his clothes.

He cupped her chin, his thumb stroking the corner of her mouth. "You don't kiss like a woman who has *behaved.*"

He lowered his mouth to hers. Her eyes slid closed, and it was as if every nerve ending in her body unfurled. How could a kiss touch her in so many different places?

He was right. She was no stranger to men's advances, and yet no kiss she'd received before his made her feel limp, as though her bones were simply melting away. His arm came around her back, pressing her closer against him. Gripping his shoulders, she angled her head to give him easier access, to announce her acquiescence to his questing tongue.

He responded with a guttural groan, totally barbaric, completely in tune with their surroundings. Ancient and primal. A beast whose tether had been loosed.

Rhys wanted her as he'd never wanted any woman. Here on the ground, beneath the trees, against the crumbling wall. She still tasted of chocolate, as his tongue plundered and his mouth ravished.

He skimmed his hand along her ribs until he felt the weight of her breast filling his palm. Heavenly perfection.

He'd brought her here simply because they'd been close to reaching their destination of Harrington, and he wanted more time with her. Alone. Without others about. Without the pall of death to steal her smiles and the joy from her eyes.

She was at once an innocent and a temptress whom he had not the strength or desire to resist. Her beauty, blossoming from deep within her, had the power to cause ships to sail and knights to crusade.

A distant part of his mind cautioned him that he could not claim her as he wanted. To possess her would be to ruin her; to ruin her would be to destroy her. He'd destroyed once before. He could not risk doing it again, even though his body ached with need and his heart cried out for deliverance.

Breathing heavily, he tore his mouth from hers and turned away. "You are a witch, to tempt me as you do."

"And you are a coward, to push me away as you do."

Startled by her comment, he jerked around and stared at her.

"I'm not as innocent as you think," she insisted, her breathing as labored as his. Her mouth still carried the dew of his kiss. Her half-lowered eyes belonged in a bedchamber.

He raked his gaze over her. "Tell me you are not a virgin, and I will take you here and now."

She looked away.

Reaching out, he cupped her chin and turned her attention back to him. "You *are* as innocent as I think. Even if you were not, Lydia, you would not want the likes of me. I betrayed my brother, betrayed my family. Be grateful I have no wish to betray either Grayson or you."

"They betrayed you," she said.

He shook his head sadly. "They turned away from me, but only because I gave them sufficient reason to do so."

"What did you do?"

He considered telling her all, but he had no desire to see her look at him with revulsion. So he ignored her question about his past and concentrated on the present, on his need to leave her as innocent as he'd found her.

"Grayson trusts me to be a complete gentleman where you are concerned." He stroked his thumb over her lower lip. "I have no intention of disappointing him. He was a far better brother to me than Quentin ever was."

"But you don't mind disappointing me?" she asked softly.

"Trust me, Lydia, you'll be far more disappointed than you are at this moment if we continue along the path we've been traveling. You told me that you wanted respectability and love. Neither is within my power to give."

Chapter 12

~~~◦◦◦~~~

Lydia was acutely aware of the uncomfortable silence stretching between her and Rhys. It had been there as they'd ridden home. Built as they'd handed their horses off to the stable boy. Deepened as they now trudged up the steps to the manor.

She wasn't sure what to make of him or what to think about what had passed between them. How could he act now as though nothing had happened when her body still shimmered with unfulfilled promises?

She had but to glance at him to remember the press of his lips against hers, the skimming of his palm along her ribs, the feel of his hand cradling her breast.

That she'd come close to drowning in the sensations he'd elicited within her should have frightened her. Yet all she seemed able to do was feel disappointment that he'd halted his exploration and gone no further than he had.

As a woman who valued her virtue, she knew she

should be grateful he'd shown such remarkable restraint. As a woman only just beginning to explore the unknown territory that existed between a man and a woman, she was curious about all she didn't know.

"Are you going to ignore me from here on out?" she asked quietly, as they neared the top of the stairway.

He glanced over at her, his eyes the gray of a sky warning of the tempest to come. "Were that it was that easy. Unfortunately, I am aware of every breath you take."

A small thrill of pleasure speared her. So he was not as unaffected by what had passed between them as he appeared to be.

"Is that so awful?" she asked.

"For reasons which I have no desire to explain . . . yes. I think it would be best if we dispensed with sharing dinners in the evening or any other moments for that matter."

As though unwilling to discuss the situation further, he walked up the remaining steps. She followed like a faithful dog, while part of her wanted to grab his arm, spin him around, and demand he explain everything. He was unfair to remain mysterious where her heart was concerned. She wanted explanations. *Deserved* them.

A servant opened a door, and Rhys stepped aside, politely inclining his head to indicate she should precede him into the manor. With a glare she knew would have sent her brothers scrambling to get as far away from her as they could, she strolled with as much dignity as possible into the manor.

"My lord, you've returned home at last," the butler said as he staidly approached them.

"I was not under the impression I had a curfew," Rhys said.

"I should say not, sir. However, His Grace instructed me to tell you and the young lady—as soon as either of you returned—that he wishes for you to join him in the drawing room."

Rhys leaned closer to the servant. "You mean in his bedchamber."

"No, my lord." The servant's eyes sparkled as though he was handing out gifts on Christmas morning. "His Grace has apparently had a remarkable recovery. If I may say so, my lord, it's somewhat of a miracle."

"Indeed, Osborne, you may say so." Rhys turned to Lydia. "Shall we go to the drawing room?"

She nodded and fell into step beside him. Once they were out of the butler's earshot, she said quietly, "Rhys?"

"Yes?"

She stopped, forcing him to do the same. "Don't get your hopes up."

"Whatever do you mean?"

She hated to be the bearer of possible bad tidings. "Sometimes," she began softly, "it seems to me people have a momentary *recovery* only to leave us shortly thereafter. As though they're being given a chance to say good-bye."

He nodded thoughtfully. "Perhaps that is the case here. Regardless, we shall be grateful for it and not keep my father waiting any longer."

He extended his arm toward her.

"Should I curtsy?" she asked, as she laid her hand on his arm.

"No." He winked, actually winked at her. "It would be appropriate, however, to address him as Your Grace."

She wrinkled her nose. "I knew that."

"I know."

She honestly didn't know what to make of this man who seemed to warn her off one minute and tease her the next. She wondered if Rhys was as confused by his actions as she was.

With her heart thundering, she walked with him down the elaborately decorated hallway. She was on the verge of truly meeting a duke this time, not simply watching one as he slept. He would be as aware of her presence as she was of his.

"I should take a moment to straighten my hair, change into a gown—"

"You look lovely as you are," he interrupted.

Glancing up at him, she nodded gratefully. "Thank you."

Something akin to satisfaction warmed his eyes, before he turned down the corridor. A footman bowed slightly and opened the door. She still couldn't get accustomed to never having to open a door.

Rhys escorted her into the room. Her mother and father sat together on a sofa. Colton and Sabrina lounged quietly on nearby chairs. But what really caught Lydia by surprise was the sight of the Duchess.

Regally she sat in a plush chair beside an even larger chair, her hand resting on the arm of an elderly gentleman. He was dressed as though he expected to attend a social function that evening, his silver hair combed back, his gray eyes twinkling.

"Ah, the prodigal son returns at last," he said, with a shaky voice that betrayed his infirmity, because hovering within its shadows were the remnants of its booming characteristics.

"I must say, Father, that you've given us all a jolly nice surprise today. It's good to see you looking so well," Rhys said, and Lydia heard the true pleasure in his words.

"I would be a poor host if I did not join my guests for at least one meal, wouldn't I?" Harrington asked.

"Considering that you have been quite under the weather, I should think all would have been forgiven."

"It's easier to obtain forgiveness from others than it is to obtain it from oneself. Introduce me to your lady."

Rhys cleared his throat. "She is not my lady, Father. She is Grayson's stepdaughter. Our paths crossed in the village, and I escorted her home. May I have the honor of presenting Miss Lydia Westland?"

Her heart was pounding so loudly that she almost didn't hear her introduction. And she didn't care what Rhys had told her in the hallway, the man sitting before her had nobility carved into every line of his face, the set of his shoulders, and the depth of his gaze.

She released her hold on Rhys, stepped nearer, and curtsied. "Your Grace, it is an honor to make your acquaintance at last."

He leaned toward her and said in a low voice, "So you're the one who whispers with my son in the middle of the night and keeps him company."

"I thought you were asleep."

"Only too tired to open my eyes, dear girl. I wonder if my son has opened his."

She felt a hand come to rest beneath her elbow as Rhys helped her to straighten. The Duke glanced around her to where her parents sat.

"Lovely girl, Grayson."

"I had little to do with that, Your Grace."

Lydia was acutely aware that within this room, her stepfather was formal with this man who had sired him, and she wondered if it was out of respect for the witch sitting beside the Duke.

"Perhaps you had naught to do with the siring, but I see your influence here. Your own children offer much to be proud of. Don't you agree, Winnie?"

Lydia jerked her gaze to the woman lovingly patting her husband's hand. *Winnie?* It seemed too soft a name, too teasing a name for the shrieking shrew she'd seen in the hallway twice now.

"Of course, dear," the Duchess said.

"I should like for us all to dine together this evening," the Duke said, and even in his weakened state, his voice was riffed with command.

"If that's what you'd like, dear, then I shall see that it is so," the Duchess said. "I'll instruct Cook to make all your favorites."

She rose gracefully to her feet. "I shall see to it immediately. If you all will excuse me."

Lydia couldn't help but stare. The lady walking out of the room was completely regal in her bearing. Lydia had just seen a side to the Duchess she'd never suspected existed. She couldn't help but be impressed that for this occasion at least, for her husband, the Duchess was putting aside her personal feelings of revulsion for Grayson Rhodes.

"If you'll excuse me, Father, I have some matters to see to as well," Rhys said.

"Of course. Although I do hope you'll consider playing the piano for us this evening."

Rhys flinched as though a whip had been taken to his back. "Perhaps I can convince you that you'll be more entertained by a reading from Miss Westland."

The Duke turned his expressive eyes on her and patted the chair beside him. "Sit here, Miss Westland. I've a desire to know you better."

She eased onto the chair, not certain if she really should, concerned with the appropriateness of taking the chair the Duchess had just vacated, but thinking it would be unacceptable to deny the Duke's request.

"I shall take my leave now, Father," Rhys said.

"Yes, yes," the Duke mumbled distractedly as he waved his hand in the air.

She was vaguely aware of Rhys leaving, more aware that she could see some semblance of her stepfather in the man sitting beside her.

"Have you heard Rhys play?" he asked.

"No, Your Grace."

"I'm most surprised by that. He plays when he is melancholy." He winked at her. "We shall have Rhys play tonight."

"I don't think we should force him if he doesn't want to," Lydia said.

"Life is nothing more than being forced to do what we'd rather not."

"I don't believe that."

"Then I suspect you would find living in our world not to your liking."

She swallowed hard, wondering what exactly he'd overhead in the shadows of his bedroom.

He turned his attention away from her. "Now, Grayson, tell me more about Texas."

Rhys caught up with his mother in the foyer. When she had a mission, she could be quite a ball of energy.

"Mother?"

She turned, dabbing the corners of her eyes with a

white linen handkerchief. She gave him a sweet smile. "I thought he looked rather well, didn't you?"

He thought his father was giving a good imitation of looking well, but couldn't bring himself to admit the truth. "Yes."

"Not fully recovered though," she whispered, as though she feared she would jinx the Duke by saying the words loudly enough for anyone else to hear them.

He shook his head sadly. "No."

Taking a deep breath, she nodded. "Then we shall make the most of this evening. Your father has three favorite desserts. I'm not sure which one he would favor."

"Why not ask Cook to make all three?"

Her eyes sparkled. "Splendid idea! I shall do just that. The seating arrangements will be a bit tricky."

"Might I suggest we dispense with formality for this evening?"

"Splendid idea. Besides, I doubt *Debrett's* provides information on seating the *sort* of guests we've been burdened with."

She wrinkled her nose as though she caught a whiff of something foul-smelling. Rhys couldn't help but think that she would forever consider certain personages as beneath her.

"I'm certain your father will want Grayson at one elbow," she mused. "I'll place you at the other. I'll sit at the foot of the table."

He'd noticed in the drawing room what he'd noticed his entire life. Whenever his father was in his mother's presence, she fluttered her hands over him. A touch on his hand, a combing back of his hair, a straightening of his clothes. Her sitting at the foot of the table would not do for this evening.

"I think you're correct in your assumption. He'll want Grayson beside him. However, you are much more attuned to Father's needs than any of us. I think you should sit close to him, because you'll sense more than anyone when he is tiring."

She nodded briskly. "You're quite right. It's been a while since we were of a like mind, you and I."

Indeed it had been.

She pursed her lips. "This girl. This Lydia. What were you doing with her?"

"As I said. Our paths crossed in town, and I escorted her home."

"Was she alone then?"

"Yes."

"That's terribly bold of her."

"Quite so. Apparently it is not uncommon in Texas for a woman to ride unescorted."

"Heathens," she muttered before turning, her heels clicking briskly over the marble floor. She wagged a finger in the air, not bothering to look back at him as she announced, "He'll want you to play this evening! It will go better for you if you simply make your peace with his request now and do it."

He watched her disappear down the corridor. Strange how he'd almost forgotten there were moments when he actually enjoyed her company. Equally astonishing was the knowledge that she would play her role of duchess well this evening. It was not in her nature to be less than regal when the situation warranted and when her audience was the man she loved.

Sitting at the far end of the table, Rhys was acutely aware that his father barely touched any of the food placed before him. His mother valiantly pretended not to notice as one course after another was brought out.

The dinner conversation had been amiable. He was grateful Grayson's family had been given the opportunity to see his mother at her best, because more often than not, he was proud of her. That she failed to feel the same about him was his fault, not hers.

"Grayson, you mustn't wait so long before coming home again," his father said, weariness laced through his voice.

"With all due respect, Your Grace, I feel as though Texas is my home."

His father offered up a slight smile. "That is the way it should be. Don't you agree, Winnie?"

Rhys watched as his mother elegantly dabbed her napkin at her mouth before replying, "Of course, dear. Would you care for a bit more dessert?"

The fact that his father had not yet dipped his spoon into the custard seemed to have escaped her notice.

His father shook his head. "I look at the bounty that surrounds me, and I know no hunger."

His mother laughed lightly and glanced around the table. "His Grace has always been a bit of a philosopher and poet. I suspect that is the reason he was so fond of attending plays in his youth."

"I attended plays because I had a soft spot for a lovely actress," he murmured.

Rhys lifted his glass of wine and drank all that remained in one swallow before signaling for more to be brought to him. He wanted to yell at his father for ruining the pleasant evening.

His father met his gaze across the length of the table. He didn't know what his eyes reflected, but his father looked away. Taking the hand of his Duchess, the Duke pressed a kiss to her fingertips.

The Duke's public display of affection was unheard of in this household, and Rhys was certain that fact was apparent to their guests since his mother wore a startled expression.

"Winnie, I can't recall ever telling you that I love you," his father said quietly.

His mother fluttered her free hand against her chest. "Your Grace, I'm certain—"

"No, Winnie, I never did tell you, and I do love you. More than I ever thought possible."

His mother released a tiny whimper and pressed a clenched hand to her mouth. "Don't do this to me now!"

He smiled slightly. "If not now, when? Come here, dear girl."

She didn't hesitate when he tugged on her hand. In front of their guests, she climbed onto her husband's lap. "I shan't forgive you for leaving me."

"I know," he cooed. "I know."

Rhys caught Grayson's attention and signaled for him and his family to leave quietly. As they did so, Rhys met and held his father's gaze over his mother's quaking shoulders. He raised his glass of wine in a silent salute, acknowledging what he understood with startling clarity: his father was not only a poet and a philosopher, but a damned fine actor.

Chapter 13

Lydia sat in the drawing room. A few lamps provided the dim light that seemed so appropriate for the occasion.

The Duke was almost swallowed by the oversized, overstuffed chair in which he sat. The Duchess was perched on the arm of his chair, her fingers stroking his face, neck, hair, and hand. Lydia was suddenly viewing the woman in a whole new light. She could not imagine the sorrow of losing a spouse.

Yet her mother had lost her first husband and married another man. Although Lydia barely remembered life with her first father, she knew beyond a doubt her mother was happier with Grayson Rhodes.

They sat side by side, holding hands, their younger children at their feet. Lydia had been certain the Duchess would have a conniption fit when the children had plopped onto the floor, but she seemed to have eyes only for her husband.

Even though her son was now entertaining them.

The music Rhys played was strangely dark, yet hauntingly beautiful, evoking images she wasn't quite certain she wanted to explore. She imagined shadowy rooms and hot bodies pressed together.

She gave herself a mental shake. Surely no one else's mind was filled with these lustful, carnal thoughts. She blamed her wayward imaginings on this afternoon, when he'd come so close to taking her down a path she'd never known how desperately she wished to travel.

She watched his fingers—long, slender, strong, skillful—dancing over the keys, and she could well imagine them plucking the buttons loose on her gown. His head was bent, heavy strands of black hair falling forward to brush his brow, his cheek. She longed to brush them back and watch them fall again. Over and over.

She wanted to go to him, press her breasts against his back, wrap her arms around his shoulders, and let the music flow into her through him. Although others were in the room, she felt as though only he and she existed, as though he played only for her, as though he was pouring himself into the music, pouring himself into her.

The music drifted into silence, and yet its existence continued to hang in the air as though to tease her ears. Rhys stood and bowed slightly, obviously not comfortable as the center of attention.

Lydia expected the Duke or Duchess to clap, or at the very least to announce their approval of his entertainment. When neither did, Lydia blurted, "I thought your playing was beautiful."

Rhys angled his head slightly. "You are too kind, Miss Westland."

Hardly kind. The thoughts running through her mind bordered on murderous. She could forgive the Duke his silence. He was ill. But the Duchess? How could she not praise her son's efforts?

"The hour is late, Father. You must be weary," Rhys said.

The Duke barely nodded. "Grayson can help me get to bed."

"As you wish," Rhys said. "Mother, shall I escort you to your chambers?"

She nodded and rose to her feet, bending slightly to kiss her husband on the cheek. "I shall see you tomorrow afternoon."

"I look forward to it."

She walked toward the door, stopping briefly before Lydia's stepfather and raising her brow. "Take care with him."

"Of course, Your Grace."

She placed her hand on her son's arm and strolled from the room. So regally. Lydia was torn between despising the woman and admiring her.

"Lydia, will you take Colton and Sabrina to their rooms?"

Lydia turned her attention to her mother, realizing she'd been so focused on Rhys and his mother that she hadn't noticed when her stepfather had moved to stand beside the Duke. She didn't imagine the elderly gentleman wanted them to see him being carried as though he was a child. He'd been in the dining room when they'd entered, had already been sitting in this room when they'd been fetched to join the family here. How humiliating it must be for a man who had been ruler of so much to suddenly find himself a beneficiary of everyone's tender mercies.

"Lydia?" her mother prompted again.

"I will," she said, "but first . . ." She stepped nearer to the Duke, searching his aged face. Rhys had spoken on behalf of his mother—urging the Duke to tell her that he loved her. Lydia's mother would speak on behalf of Grayson, making certain the Duke understood what a fine man his illegitimate son was. Who would speak for Rhys?

"I think, Your Grace, neither you nor your wife fully appreciate all Rhys offers."

The Duke chuckled low. "Fancy him, do you?"

She darted a quick glance to her stepfather, who was scrutinizing her. She wasn't certain anyone would understand her feelings for Rhys. She wasn't sure she understood them herself. She met the Duke's gaze. "I simply noticed he seems to bow to everyone's wishes except his own."

"A man who is to be duke should bow to no one."

"Yet you bowed to convention when it came to marriage."

"Lydia," her stepfather warned. It wasn't often he growled at her, and she knew she was close to being disrespectful. But she wanted the Duke to realize that his lastborn son was as fine a man as his firstborn.

"No, Grayson, leave her be. I like her spunk. But Winnie won't allow you to be the new Duchess of Harrington," the Duke said. "She'll find Rhys some boring wife to bear him boring children."

Not if I can help it hovered on the tip of Lydia's tongue. She bit back the words. "It never crossed my mind to become the new Duchess of Harrington."

"As you wish, girl."

She curtsied slightly. "If you'll excuse me, I need to

put the children to bed, and then I think I'll take a walk in the garden. I could use some fresh air."

Rhys stood at the window of his bedchamber and watched Lydia stroll through the gardens, captured in moonlight. That she had complimented his performance pleased him beyond measure.

How had she become so important to him in such a short while? He continually berated himself for seeking her out, and yet he seemed unable to resist her innocence.

Tarnished by all he'd seen and experienced, he worried he would taint her if he spent any more time with her. He should at this very moment go to his father's bedchamber and visit with him while his father was more alert than he'd been in some time.

Rhys convinced himself, however, that his father was no doubt weary and in need of rest after such an eventful day.

Rhys was equally tired, but how could any man resist the temptation that awaited him in the garden? Even as he cursed himself for his weakness, he turned on his heel, strode from his room, and walked out of the manor house.

He found her at the far end of the lawn where roses grew in abundance and their scent still lingered on the breeze. She sat within a white gazebo, its walls serving as a trellis for the climbing flowers.

That she seemed neither surprised nor startled to see him appear within the opening gave him a moment's pause, made him briefly wonder if she'd lured him out on purpose. If she'd known he'd been watching her.

But then he decided it didn't matter. She was here,

and only she was important. Still, he kept his distance, not trusting his hands to remain off her, his mouth not to give in to the temptation to kiss her.

He walked around the circle until he stood opposite her. Then he leaned his hips against the railing. Through its opening she would be able to see the rolling hills of Harrington, while he saw nothing but her.

Now that he was here, he could think of nothing to say. It was simply enough to be in her presence, to locate her scent among that of the roses. To enjoy the sight of her silhouette in the shadows. She should have been lost within them, but her pale lilac gown and her hair that looked as though it had been spun from moonbeams gave her an edge against the darkness.

"I knew you'd come," she said, her voice floating toward him as gently as the clouds passed before the moon.

"Did you?"

"I saw you standing at a window."

"Perhaps I was simply looking for a star to wish upon. Perhaps I noticed you not at all."

"You noticed me. I can always feel when you're staring at me."

"Staring makes it sound as though I'm being rude, invading where I am not wanted."

"What would you call it then?" she asked.

Longing for. A desperate yearning.

"I suppose staring is as good a word as any," he said, unwilling to admit the truth of his obsession.

He glanced off in the distance, but nothing had the power to hold his attention as she did, and he soon found himself once again looking at her. The temptation to move closer was almost more than he could bear.

"I adore the way you play the piano," she said.

He dug his fingers into the railing, relishing the bite of wood cutting into his palms. "I thought it a very dark piece," he admitted.

"I was mesmerized by it."

"What sort of images did it conjure in your mind?"

She looked away, presenting him with her profile. As though he were an artist, he committed the sight of her to his memory, the sweep of her long throat, the curve of her cheek, the slope of her shoulders. No aspect of her beauty went unnoticed by him. And he found every part of her beautiful. He could not have explained his reasoning, and he suspected a few rare men existed who would disagree with his assessment of Lydia. But he only cared about what he saw.

"The images," he prodded.

"I found them very"—she bent her head—"sensual."

"I thought of you as I played."

As she turned her head toward him, he felt her gaze come to rest on him.

"Did you?" she asked.

"You've managed to bewitch me, and that is not good for either of us."

"Why?"

"You are a woman who favors the glitter of London. I prefer the seclusion of Harrington. You want a man who is untarnished. I am so far removed from being one that all the polishing in the world will not make me shine."

"Is that the reason you push me back every time I come close?"

"It's one of many reasons."

"And what if I don't want you to push me back?"

She rose to her feet, and it suddenly occurred to him that coming out here was a very bad idea.

"You cannot be both a temptress and a lady," he warned.

"Why?"

"Because a temptress has no virtue, while a lady must always maintain and guard hers."

She crossed the gazebo, coming to stand beside him, not close enough for him to touch, but near enough that with no effort at all he could have her within his arms. She looked out on the countryside.

"I thought it was romantic that your father told your mother he loved her tonight during dinner."

"It was a lie."

She snapped her head around. "Do you have to be so cynical?"

"I'm a realist. I thought I would find satisfaction in his telling her, but instead I saw a measure of deceit in his actions."

"Where is the harm in it when his words made her so happy?"

"I believe a relationship is better served with honesty."

"You would never tell a woman you love her if you don't?"

"Never. But then never do I expect to love a woman."

"Not even me."

"Especially not you."

"So if I were to press my body against yours, you wouldn't react?" she asked.

"A man may lust without love."

"Can a man love without lust?"

"You tell me that you wish to be accepted by Society, and then you carry on conversations which are entirely inappropriate."

"You're pushing me away again," she said in a voice

that seemed to shimmer over his flesh. Low, provocative, inviting.

Then he was no longer pushing her away, but drawing her nearer.

He was not surprised that she welcomed his advance and sank against him in surrender. He settled his mouth firmly against hers, his tongue waltzing with hers, an ancient rhythm.

She tasted of the wine she'd sipped during dinner and the chocolate she'd nibbled when dessert was served. Her taste was rich, yet sweet, and laced with innocence. Her fingers clutched his jacket, and a purr vibrated within her throat.

Raging desire shot through him. If he'd thought to call her bluff, to tame her with actions rather than words, he'd grossly underestimated her power over him.

Or perhaps he'd simply chosen to ignore it. From the first kiss they'd shared, he'd learned she wasn't a demure lady. She eagerly returned his kiss now as she had before. She was an active participant in what with most women he'd found to be passive enjoyment. The ladies he knew preferred to be acted upon, to have their senses heightened, while he was left to find his own way.

Lydia gave as much as she took. Her hands alternately touched his cheek, ran through his hair, and rubbed his shoulders. She was as aware as he that passion encompassed every aspect of a person: heart and mind, body and soul.

He glided his hand along her silky skin, revealed by the low cut of her gown. He trailed his fingers over the lush curves, bringing his hand down to cradle the delicious mound of one breast. Had he thought her smaller than most?

She was perfect in every way, every manner. He slid

his mouth from hers. With a moan, she dropped her head back, giving him access to the flesh he so desperately desired. He skimmed his lips along her throat, the scent of roses increasing as he reached the hollow at its base.

Ah, so here was where she'd placed her perfume. He imagined her closing her eyes as she did so, her finger applying the tantalizing drops. Had she thought of him as the perfume dampened her skin?

Dampened her skin as he wished to dampen the silken haven between her thighs? A haven where he might find solace.

He licked her throat before journeying farther down. The scent faded away for only a brief time. He smiled, imagining her sliding her finger between her breasts to dab her perfume against a hidden spot only he would know of. A place his tongue now explored.

Shivering within his arms, she dug her fingers into his shoulders. He had but to peel back the bodice of her gown a little to reveal the treasure he sought. He closed his mouth around the satiny orb, his teeth around her hardened pearl. He tugged, suckled, and lathed her flesh with his tongue. She whimpered and jerked.

"Rhys!"

His name, a breathless whisper in the night. His name. Not an errant husband's or a scorned lover's.

Damn her! Damn her for imagining she was within his arms and not another's.

He told himself that he wanted her all the more because he could not have her, but the truth mocked him. He wanted her because she was all he was not, all he'd long ago lost. Innocence and beauty. She still believed in dreams.

Her hands closed around his upper arms like a vise,

while he felt her lethargically slipping away. He snaked one arm around her waist and held her against his hard body, his throbbing body.

In the moonlight, he could see her watching him through half-closed eyes, waiting, waiting, trusting, wanting, silently pleading for the release he could give her. The pleasure he could grant her.

With his head bent, he continued to play his lips and tongue over her bared breasts, giving attention to one and then the other, suckling and stroking, caressing and nipping, while his free hand gathered up her skirt until it was bunched between them, held in place by two bodies pressed together so tightly not even the breeze could ruffle the cloth.

Skimming his fingers up her warm, velvety thigh, he heard the sharp intake of her breath, welcomed the heating of her skin beneath his mouth, and rejoiced in the quivering of her body.

He trailed his fingers down, then back up. Down again, capturing her knee, lifting it, slowly, provocatively until he hooked it over his hip, held it with his arm, spreading her until the sweet, musky perfume of her desire wafted upward.

He skimmed his fingers back along her thigh to the heart of her womanhood. This time he moved aside the last bit of delicate lace that served as a barrier to her fulfillment. She whimpered again, her body shimmering against his palm, as he threaded his fingers through her curls. She was sinfully hot and moist. Velvet and silk woven together. Swollen. Ripe with desire.

He slowly stroked her. She released a tiny cry, a resounding plea.

He returned his mouth to hers, deepening the kiss as his fingers increased their pressure. She writhed against him, a woman seeking to escape, a woman desperate to remain. She suckled his tongue as though she wanted to draw him into her.

He captured her cry as her body arched. He slid his finger into the silken cavern where her body pulsed with the force of her journey into ecstasy.

He slid his mouth to her ear, breathing heavily, listening as her quick breaths filled the night air. She slumped against him, her arms limp across his shoulders, her face pressed to his chest.

He had pleasured many a woman in a similar manner, but never before had he felt such satisfaction, such enjoyment, such . . . pleasure. Victorious. He felt victorious.

It mattered not that he still ached with need. With her trembling in his arms, he found a fulfillment such as he'd never known.

"Goodness gracious," she said on a sigh. She lifted her gaze to his and laughed, a tinkling of pure joy like a thousand bells ringing out the jubilation. "My books certainly never explained anything like this."

The rumble started deep within his chest, like thunder preceding a storm, and when the laughter erupted from within, he nearly wept for having gone so long without hearing it. It held no cynicism, no biting edge. It was simply joyous.

"Imagine how it would have been if you hadn't instructed me to curb my enthusiasm," she said.

Laughing harder, he pressed his forehead to hers and shook his head. "Perhaps by morning I shall remember what lesson it was that I came out here to teach you."

"Something about lust and love, I believe," she murmured.

Ah, yes, lust and love. He'd thought he was the master of one and a stranger to the other. Now he was no longer sure of either.

"There's more that happens between a man and a woman, isn't there?" she asked quietly.

"Not for us."

"Why?"

"Because I find myself caring for you more than I should, and I would not see you hurt."

He eased back slightly, and her skirt floated back into place. "It would probably be best if you returned to the manor ahead of me. We would not want the servants' tongues to wag."

She cradled his cheek. "How can you give so much to me and think I wouldn't be happy with everything else you have to offer?"

Taking her hand, he turned his head and pressed a kiss to her palm. "Because everything else would fall far short of what I just gave you."

"I don't think you know your own worth."

"I know exactly what I am worth. I also know you can ill afford me."

Chapter 14

Lydia awakened, not certain why, with darkness hovering around her. She put on her night wrapper and peered into the hallway. Muffled sobbing escaped through the open door that led into the Duke's bedchamber.

She crept down the hallway, not wanting to intrude, but wanting to be available if needed. Peering inside, she saw the Duchess holding the Duke's hand, her head bowed, while a woman who seemed to be more of a companion than a servant—perhaps she was the nurse— rubbed the Duchess's quaking shoulders. The Duke looked to be completely and forever at peace.

Lydia had not expected to feel such sorrow for both the Duke and his Duchess.

Her parents stood off to the side, holding each other. Lydia crossed over to them, and her stepfather welcomed her into his arms.

"I'm so sorry," she said in a low, respectful voice.

For him, she *had* expected to feel the immense sorrow that welled up inside her now.

"He went peacefully with those who loved him nearby. A man can ask for no more than that," her stepfather said.

"Is there anything I can do?" she asked.

"No." He released Lydia and drew her mother against his side. The woman who would comfort him and lend her strength. "I'll be all right."

Lydia glanced around the room, noticing Rhys was absent, knowing he'd probably been there earlier. Had probably been the one to deliver the sad news.

With her emotions raw after their encounter in the garden, she'd decided not to join him there that evening. Now she wished she had.

She kissed her stepfather's cheek, squeezed his hand, and then walked out of the room.

In spite of the manor's grand size, it suddenly felt very small as Lydia made her way along the shadowy hallways. Everything was incredibly quiet, as though even the flames in the candles and lamps were in mourning and had retreated into silence, with no sputtering or crackling to keep her company.

She'd known where she'd find Rhys. She'd known she'd find him alone with his grief. And she'd known her heart would nearly shatter at the sight of him moving his fingers over the piano, creating melancholy chords that reached into her soul and wrenched her emotions.

Who would offer comfort to Rhys?

Not his mother. Not a wife or a lover. Not even a friend.

He lifted his head and pierced her with a gaze that reminded her of an untamed, trapped animal. His hands stilled, but it seemed as though an eternity passed before the haunting strains drifted completely into silence.

"You may address me as Your Grace now," he said in a low voice devoid of emotion.

She took a step toward him. "Rhys—"

"I was never supposed to be the Duke!" he roared, as he came to his feet, swiped at the nearby harp, and sent it crashing to the floor. He plowed his hands through his hair, his gaze darting around him as though he desperately wanted a sanctuary in which to hide.

"You'll make a wonderful duke," she promised.

His harsh laughter echoed around them. "Oh, my dreamer, you don't know the things I've done."

"I know you've rescued children and horses and even your mother in a way."

"Leave, Lydia," he commanded as he moved into the shadows that hovered in the corners. "Leave."

"I can't."

"You don't know what I'm feeling right now; you don't know what I'm capable of."

His voice seethed with fury. She didn't know with whom he was angry: himself, his father, perhaps even his mother. Maybe he was even angry with Lydia.

She wasn't afraid of the anger. He was wounded, deeply, with no one to ease the ache in his heart, no one to offer him comfort.

"I know you hurt," she said soothingly, as she crept closer.

"Hurt? You think I hurt because he's dead?"

She nodded, her chest tightening until it ached. "You loved him, Rhys. You can deny it all you want, but he was your father and you loved him."

He shook his head. "No."

"Yes," she insisted.

He shook his head more fiercely. "No. Don't you understand? I was nothing to him. Simply the spare. Hopefully never to be used, but on hand, in case the unthinkable happened. He did not love my mother. Passion did not drive him to her bed, but obligation, obligation to provide an heir and a spare."

Reaching up with trembling fingers, she laid them against his neck, felt the rapid beating of his pulse, the warmth of his skin. "You're not a spare to me," she rasped, tears for his anguish burning her throat.

"No one has ever loved *me*," he croaked. "I'm so damned alone, Lydia."

The flames burning in the nearby fireplace reflected in the tears welling in his eyes.

"No, Rhys, you're not alone. As long as I'm here, you're not alone."

He drew her to him as the shore draws the ocean, with yielding insistence. His mouth was moist and hot against hers, his tongue sweeping inside as though he felt a desperate need to journey through every part of her mouth.

She angled her head and felt a tear on his cheek slide onto hers. He growled low in his throat, as he crushed her to him. Her breasts flattened against the hard planes of his chest. She slid her arms up over his shoulders, marveling again at the strength she felt shimmering beneath her fingertips. She could run her hands over him all night and never grow tired of doing so. She scraped her fingers up into his hair.

Sensations swirled through her as desire burned deeply within her like a fire on the prairie with nothing to contain it. She was vaguely aware of his fingers drawing her wrapper aside and loosening the buttons on her nightgown.

A distant part of her mind began quoting rules of comportment—just as she had earlier in the garden—as though she still possessed her senses and would care that a lady would not sigh with pleasure as her clothing was peeled away and a man's mouth was suddenly blazing a hot trail along her throat.

She knew she was going to lose the battle to remain a lady again, yet in the losing, she would win. Because Rhys was all that mattered, and she would willingly give him anything he needed.

She shivered even as she burned. She dropped her head back, and he nipped at the tender flesh of her shoulder.

"Tell me you want me," he growled.

"I want you," she repeated, dazed by desire.

She'd wanted him in the garden. For all he'd given her before, she'd felt slighted, cheated, that he'd withheld himself, had not sought his own pleasure with her.

She'd wanted him from the first moment she'd laid eyes on him. How could anyone not see what a good man he was?

She saw it. She saw it in all the little things he did, things she'd never considered a nobleman would care about.

He moved his lips lower, his tongue licking and tasting, his mouth kissing. She gasped as he closed his mouth around her nipple. She felt a tug as he suckled, a tug that seemed to reach through her body to touch the most intimate of places. Before Rhys, she'd never realized how connected different parts of her body were.

Her knees weakened and trembled, and she might

have crashed to the floor if he hadn't been supporting her, easing her to the carpet, following her down.

When she'd asked him to instruct her, she'd had no idea the lessons he could teach. This time, however, she was determined the lesson would not fall short. This moment was not hers, but *theirs*.

She tried to work the buttons free on his shirt, but her fingers quivered.

He moved his mouth to her ribs, his breath wafting over her flesh as his lips paid homage to each bit of skin he revealed as he worked her clothing aside.

"Your shirt," she said breathlessly.

Sitting up, he jerked his shirt over his head, and she wanted to laugh, because she hadn't needed to bother with buttons after all. Stretching out his body beside hers, raising himself up on an elbow, he began unbraiding her hair.

"I want your hair loose," he said, a fevered pitch in his voice and a purpose to his fingers.

Reaching up, she shyly pressed her palm to his bared chest. Velvet against steel. Then her hair was free, and he was fanning it out around her, across her shoulders, her chest.

"Glorious," he told her just before he returned his mouth to hers.

Eagerly she welcomed the kiss, while her fingers outlined each of his ribs, then each muscle, her hand easing lower, following the light sprinkling of hair down until it reached the waistband of his trousers. She heard his breath catch as much as she felt it.

He dragged his mouth from hers, his breath coming in harsh, heavy gasps as though he were fighting to draw in each bit of air. Raising himself up on his knees, he held her gaze, while he worked her nightgown down, down, down . . . past her hips, her knees, her feet.

She'd always thought she'd feel a measure of embarrassment at this moment—the first time she was fully exposed to a man's gaze. Yet she felt nothing beyond gladness that she was sharing herself with this man.

"Dear God, but you are beautiful," he whispered, as he glided his hand along the length of her. "So beautiful."

He quickly unfastened his trousers and shed them, revealing the magnificence of his body, the power of what he had to offer her.

She would have told him that she thought he was beautiful as well, but he kissed her again, deeply, hungrily, pressing his chest against hers, his hand cradling her hip, rolling her toward him until she felt his heat pressed against her stomach.

Moaning low, he skimmed his hand up the inside of her leg. She shivered as his fingers reached the apex between her thighs. His exploration was gentle but thorough, as sensations mounted deep within her and expanded outward.

That she was moaning and writhing beneath him might have mortified her if her needs weren't so strong. He led her toward the pinnacle and then eased away.

Digging her fingers into his shoulders, she urged him to complete what he'd started. He parted her thighs further and nestled himself between them.

She bit her lip as he stretched her, filling her . . . only to retreat.

"No," she rasped.

He stilled, his breathing labored. "No?"

"Don't stop."

He released a low chuckle that sounded like relief. "Thank God."

He lifted his head and held her gaze. "I don't know how to make it not hurt."

She cradled his cheek, welcoming his bearded stubble scratching her palm. She adored every aspect of him. "I love you, Rhys."

He lowered his mouth to hers, capturing her cry as he buried himself inside her. She dug her nails into his back, holding onto him as she kept herself as still as possible.

He kissed the corner of her mouth, a sensitive spot below her ear. "The worst is over. 'Tis time to dream, my little dreamer."

He began to rock against her, and the burning lessened, while another sensation began to take hold. Something far more intense than what she'd experienced in the garden. He was offering a new promise, a stirring so deep, so profound that it frightened her to think of the promise being kept, terrified her to think of it being broken.

Her body tightened around his, and instinctually she moved in rhythm with him, meeting each thrust, greedy for the next.

Then the promise was upon her . . . "No!"

"Yes," he commanded, as he ground his body against hers and catapulted her over the edge.

She cried out as she at once arched and somehow still managed to curl around him. His guttural cry quickly followed, his body shuddering as he folded his arms around her and pressed his face against the curve of her neck.

Lethargically she realized that tiny jerks continued

to cascade through him. Several moments passed before she realized it wasn't that he was caught in the throes of passion, but that he wept.

She trailed her fingers up and down his damp back and watched the firelight and shadows play over his glistening flesh. He was mourning at last, could let go of the past, and embrace their future.

What had he done?

Rhys tasted the salt of his tears coursing toward his lips and wanted to weep all the more.

Sanity had returned at last, but at what price had he lost his hold on it? And more importantly, what would the cost be to Lydia?

"I love you," she'd said.

But she could not, because she did not know him, didn't know all the dark secrets he harbored deep within himself.

Of all the women he'd carried to his bed, not one had granted him true affection. The fault could only rest within him.

With one hand, he managed to erase the evidence of his tears. Slowly he lifted his head and met Lydia's gaze.

She looked at him with languid eyes, a woman who had been well and truly sated. Yet for all his experience, he had taken her too quickly, too roughly. He'd used none of the finesse or skills he'd acquired over the years.

He'd completely lost his head, and all semblance of control.

She bestowed upon him a lovely smile, a smile that he did not deserve. He shook his head slightly. "We should not have done this."

Her smile withered as hurt filled her eyes. "Rhys—"

"Shh." He combed his fingers through the strands of her hair that lay against her cheek. "You were a virgin. I have compromised you."

"I wanted to be here."

"Be that as it may, the fact that I showed no restraint is unforgivable." And that he continued to show none was disconcerting. Yet here he remained, raised up on his elbows, still cradled within her body, stroking the silky smoothness of her face as though his fingers intended to memorize every aspect of her.

Her smile slowly returned, her eyes growing as warm as her skin where it still touched his.

Lying beneath him, Lydia studied the manner in which his gaze roamed over her—with such tenderness that it caused her heart to ache. He had no reason to chastise himself for his actions when she'd never known such joy, such incredible fulfillment.

He was her tormented love, yet she was certain that over time she could help him smile more often, laugh heartily, and enjoy all life offered. Convince him that he was indeed loved and loved deeply.

He eased off her, and the chill of the night crept over her skin. Sitting up, she began gathering her clothes and putting them on, while he did the same with his.

His back was to her. She couldn't resist running her fingers over his shoulders, along his spine. He stilled.

"You are not to worry," he said quietly. "Following my father's funeral, I shall talk with Grayson and put matters to right."

Joy spiraled through her with the knowledge he would ask for her hand. They would marry and be happy. She would see to it.

Wrapping her arm around his waist, she pressed a kiss between his shoulders. She laid her cheek against his warm skin.

"I don't think you know how happy you make me," she whispered.

Chapter 15

A lady need have no fear of marriage when her affections fall on a gentleman of unblemished reputation.

Miss Westland's Blunders in Behavior Corrected

Lydia knew it was probably unseemly to have a spring to her step when she walked about the manor, strolled in the gardens, and visited the stables. But she could not contain her elation. The grass had never seemed as green, the trees as full of leaves, the birds' songs as sweet, and the sky as blue. Everything was vibrantly beautiful.

Rhys loved her. He hadn't spoken the words, but she didn't need them when he'd shown her how he felt. Soon he would speak with her stepfather.

As she sat in the sitting area of her bedroom, thumbing through *Harper's Bazar* and searching for an appropriate wedding gown, she could hardly fathom how quickly her life had changed.

That she'd found such a deep love in so short a time was almost unbelievable, and even though she knew the acknowledgment and celebration would have to

191

wait awhile longer, she bounced between euphoria and anxiousness.

Three days had passed since the elder Duke had been laid to rest. The Duchess had immediately packed up her belongings and moved to the dower house, apparently a smaller house on a stretch of land not too far away. Lydia suspected her hasty retreat had come about because she couldn't stand to be in the proximity of Grayson Rhodes and his *abhorrent* clan.

The Duchess had tolerated them while her husband was alive, but now she was free to do as she would.

Lydia had not been saddened to see her go. The manor seemed more at peace with her absence. Although she would always welcome the Duchess into her home, she wouldn't feel slighted if the woman never accepted an invitation.

"Lyd, when do you think we'll be going home?" Sabrina asked from her place not far from Lydia's feet. Despite all the chairs, her sister preferred lying on her stomach on the floor.

"I'm sure you'll be going home soon," Lydia replied as she studied the lines on the gown that had caught her fancy. She tried to imagine how she would look wearing it into the chapel.

"But you'll be coming, too," Sabrina said.

Lydia cursed her careless tongue. She lowered the periodical and met her sister's questioning gaze. "I might decide to stay a little while longer."

"Why?"

She couldn't very well announce to her younger sister—before Rhys had spoken to her parents—that she was going to get married. She wondered if she'd have time to send for Johnny and Micah. Would she and Rhys be married in London or here?

She had so many questions, but ever since the night she'd lost her innocence within Rhys's arms, she'd had no opportunity to speak with him. He'd been unavailable for meals. She didn't know exactly where his bedchamber was. She'd been unable to find him in his study or in the library. He never joined her in the morning room or on the croquet lawn or in the garden.

She knew he had many affairs to see to after his father's death, and she fought not to feel neglected. Soon they would be able to spend every night together wrapped in the cocoon of their love.

"I like England," she told Sabrina, hedging with the truth.

"But you won't stay long, will you?"

Forever. She would stay forever.

A quick knock saved her from having to answer. The door opened and her mother strolled in, a hesitant smile on her face. She looked as though she wanted to appear happy, but wasn't altogether certain she was filled with joy.

"Rhys just had a long talk with your father and me," she said.

Lydia's heart kicked against her ribs, and she fought to maintain her composure. "And?"

"He's suggested we go to London."

Lydia smiled brightly. "London," she repeated, pleased they would be married there.

"Yes, he thought I would like to visit with my sister, and he seemed to think you attending the balls would facilitate your finding a husband. Lydia, did you tell him that you hoped to find a husband while you were here?"

Lydia's smile withered and died. "He wants me to go to London to find a husband?"

Her mother nodded, obviously as confused as Lydia was. "Since he's in mourning, he, of course, won't be attending any social functions, but he said he could still manage to sponsor you and ensure that you found a good match. I don't understand why he is even proposing such a thing unless you've said something to make him feel that we expect you to marry an aristocrat."

Lydia's chest tightened and ached to such a degree, she could barely draw in a breath. Surely her mother had misunderstood what Rhys had told them, had misconstrued his intentions.

"Lydia, what did you tell Rhys?" her mother asked.

Lydia shook her head. She'd told him nothing. She'd made love with him. Why was he talking of parading her around London?

"We discussed the Season on occasion," she managed to force through her dry mouth.

Setting her periodical aside, she stood. "He must have misunderstood what I wanted. Do you know where he is?"

"We left him in his study."

She nodded, trying to contain the tremors rippling through her. "I'll speak with him."

"I'm all for going to London, because I would like to see Elizabeth. I'm not against you attending balls while we're there, but I simply don't understand why he feels he has an obligation to find you a husband."

"Yes, well, I don't understand his reasoning either, but I'm certain before the afternoon is over that I'll get to the bottom of this misunderstanding." She strode from the room, her thoughts as scattered as autumn leaves by the first breath of winter.

What he was proposing was preposterous! She wanted to marry *him*, not someone she met at a ball in

London. Maybe he wanted to give her a Season and then ask for her hand in marriage. Yes, surely that was it. He wanted her to experience London without being tethered to him in the beginning.

She hurried down the stairs. Yes, yes, that had to be the basis for his suggestion. It was entirely inappropriate for them to become betrothed so soon after his father's death. Taking her to London was a gift. He didn't really plan to act as her sponsor and find her a husband.

Not when she'd already shown him with her words and her body how deeply she loved him.

Arriving at the entrance hall, she turned toward his study. Her heels clicked impressively over the marble, beating out a steady tattoo that seemed to echo like drums during a battle. Only she and Rhys weren't at war. They were simply not communicating very well.

The young footman standing guard outside the study did not move to open the door as she approached. Instead he simply bowed his head slightly.

"His Grace has indicated he has no wish to be disturbed, while he works on his ledgers," he informed her.

"His Grace can go to hell."

The footman's eyes nearly popped out of his head.

Lydia reached for the door handle, and he grabbed her wrist. She glared at him, and his cheeks flamed red.

"Miss Westland, I must insist you not disturb His Grace."

She considered making a scene, but it wasn't this poor man's fault his master had suddenly lost his senses. Instead she gathered her dignity around her like a tattered cloak, spun on her heel, and marched down the hallway.

Rhys had to have known she would have questions about their trip to London. That he would instruct his man to forbid her from seeing him was unconscionable.

Stepping into the garden, she began trudging toward the other side of the house, her temper heating with each stride she took. Until this moment, it had never occurred to her that he'd actually been avoiding her. She'd given him the benefit of the doubt and assumed his duties in regard to the estate had kept him away. She was no longer so sure.

She recognized the glass doors through which he'd once emerged to join her in a game of croquet. If they were locked, she'd grab a mallet and break them.

She'd worked herself into a fine fury by the time she tried the door. That it opened with a resounding squeak of its hinges should have calmed her somewhat. Instead it only served to ignite her temper further.

She entered the room and glared at the man who sat behind the desk, continuing to scribble something across his ledger, ignoring her in the process.

"Did you really think you could keep me out?" she demanded.

His head came up abruptly as though he was only now aware of her presence. He set his pen aside, leaned back in his chair, and sighed. "No, I suppose I didn't."

As he stood, he grandly swept his hand over his desk, indicating one of the chairs opposite him. "Please, come in and sit down."

She shut the door and *did* walk in, but she had no intention of discussing this situation while sitting.

"My mother tells me that we're going to London."

"It is a favorable market for husband hunting."

"And you think I need to *hunt* for a husband?"

He looked away momentarily, while she fought to stop shaking. He could not be this dispassionate. Not after all they'd shared, all she'd given him.

"I've compromised you, and as I stated before, I intend to set the matter to rights."

His cold words caused shards of ice to form around her heart.

"I thought you'd intended to ask my stepfather for my hand in marriage."

"Then you misconstrued my meaning."

Misconstrued his meaning? He'd held her tightly, with their naked bodies entwined. He'd wept. What was there to misconstrue?

"In your mind, finding me a suitable husband will set matters to right?"

"Indeed."

"You think a man is going to be content with soiled goods?"

He blanched. "I doubt during the heat of passion he will notice you are not virginal."

"You noticed that I was."

"I shall bestow upon you a dowry the likes of which will make him not care."

She spun around with a heavy weight pressing on her heart, her chest tightening until she thought it would cave in on her, and her pulse racing. She pressed a trembling hand to the lips he'd kissed voraciously. "You're selling me."

"I am attempting to right a wrong I did you."

She turned around and stared at him, this man she thought she'd known. "Why are you doing this? Don't you feel anything for me?"

She watched the muscles of his throat work as he swallowed.

"I feel *everything* for you," he rasped.

She took a step closer. "Then why?"

"You want the glitter and lights of London. I have

done things that are best kept hidden in the dark."

"What things?"

He slowly shook his head. "Not even for you will I give voice to my sins."

"What if I said I don't care what they are? I forgive you for them without knowing any of your sins. My love for you is that strong, Rhys."

"No love is strong enough for this."

She flattened her palms on his desk and leaned toward him. "Mine is. We won't go to London. I won't enjoy the Season. It was just a dream—"

"That you shall have. It is all I can give you, for I will never give you marriage."

"What if I'm with child?"

The blood in his face quickly drained away, and he dropped his gaze to her stomach. "We shall pray you are not."

He might as well have stabbed a rusty bayonet through her chest. She shoved herself back from his desk and straightened her shoulders.

"It seems, Your Grace, I have made a grave error in judgment. I welcome your generosity in offering to sponsor me while I'm in London. I shall persevere to make you proud. As for a dowry, my father is fully capable of providing for me. I won't have you further cheapen what passed between us by offering to *pay*"— she spat the word, not bothering to disguise her disgust with his proposal—"for me."

Rhys watched her walk across the room with a regal bearing that would have done a queen proud. She flung open the door and marched through it without looking back.

With mouth agape, obviously confused as to how someone who had not come through his door was now exiting from it, his footman peered into the room. "Your Grace, I'm dreadfully sorry—"

Rhys held up a hand. "Just close the door."

When it was shut tightly, he sank into his chair. Tremors racked his body as he fought to keep himself from calling her back. Letting her walk out of this room, out of his sight, had been the hardest thing he'd ever done in his life. Unfortunately, he feared this moment was only the harbinger of his torment to come.

Chapter 16

Standing on the steps leading into the manor, Rhys watched while the coaches on the cobbled drive were readied for their journey to London. He would travel in the first one alone. Grayson's family would be in the one behind his. The servants he'd brought with him from London would follow in the third and fourth.

They'd never set foot in his family's London residence, but then it had been some time since he had as well. While in London in recent years, he'd stayed in a house Camilla had provided for him. Smaller than her residence, of course, but still part of her deceased husband's holdings. He hoped he could arrive in London quietly and avoid being forced to call on her or anyone else of rank.

He was certain curiosity would abound regarding the new Duke of Harrington, but other peers eluded the glitz and glamour of London's social scene. He would not be the first reclusive lord, nor did he expect he'd be the last.

He heard the heavy front door behind him open. He glanced over his shoulder to see Grayson's little chatterbox leading the way, incredibly animated. He could not imagine trying to keep up with her energy.

Grayson and his wife were doing their best to calm Sabrina and answer all the questions she was popping off about their trip to London. Colton seemed unimpressed with the whole affair. Rhys could certainly relate to that sentiment. He'd rather not go himself, but he wanted to ensure Lydia chose a bit more wisely in London than she had here.

Lydia's soft voice wafted through the front opening as she thanked the servants for the care and attention they'd given her while she was in attendance. He stiffened, greedily anticipating the sight of her. He'd made an excuse to avoid dining with them each night since his father's passing. If only he'd heeded his own counsel and avoided her since she'd arrived, he would not now find himself in a position of feeling as though he needed to be her benefactor.

Then she glided through the doorway and regret slammed into him with such force that it caused him to take a step back.

She wore a traveling outfit of violet that deepened the hue of her eyes. The innocent young woman who had stumbled over her introduction to him looked to be a woman with a purpose, no longer naïve. No longer a dreamer.

But a woman who had been slapped in the face by harsh reality.

She angled her chin haughtily. "Your Grace, it was so kind of you to arrange our journey to London."

"It was the least I could do, Miss Westland."

She gave him a pointed look that clearly conveyed she thought there was a great deal more he could do.

"Your Grace? Your Grace?"

He glanced down at the urchin tugging on his sleeve, taking his attention away from the beauty who would soon grace only his memories. "Yes?"

"How long will it take?" Sabrina asked.

"We will travel for most of the day. This evening we shall stay in an inn. Then tomorrow we'll again travel for most of the day. By tomorrow afternoon, we'll be in London."

Colton groaned and dropped his head back as though someone had cracked a whip across his back.

"Colton, behave," Abbie scolded.

"But two long days inside the coach listening to Lyd *ohing* and *ahing* everything she sees and Sabrina asking how much longer is enough to drive anyone crazy," the boy grumbled.

Rhys could not agree with the lad's assessment. He thought it would be quite enjoyable to witness Lydia's excitement, when she saw things for the first time.

"Colton, I'm taking my horse to London," Rhys said. "He'll be tethered to the last coach. Perhaps you could see your way clear to ride him for a bit this afternoon."

"You mean it?" the lad asked.

"His Grace isn't one to speak falsely," Lydia said, before Rhys could respond.

The cold edge to her voice made it sound as though he had indeed spoken falsehoods. Her glittering eyes said it even more clearly. He suddenly remembered Colton warning him about Lydia's bad side. It was a lonely, frigid place to be.

"I have never spoken untrue," Rhys said through clenched teeth.

"Did I not just say that?" she asked lightly.

"It is the manner in which you said it."

"I think, Your Grace, you are looking for and finding innuendo where it does not exist."

"I feel as though I've walked in on the middle of an argument," Abbie said, her gaze darting between Rhys and her daughter. Even Grayson had narrowed his eyes.

"Lydia, has something happened we need to know about?" Abbie asked.

Lydia smiled sweetly as she reached out and squeezed her mother's hand. "Of course not, Mama. I'm simply practicing my repartee. You know how much I like to put into practice the things I read in my books. Besides, I'll need it in London if I'm to be a success. I was thinking I should travel in the coach with His Grace, so I might continue to practice."

Rhys felt every muscle in his body tighten into a painful knot.

"Lydia, I'm not certain that's a good idea," Abbie said. "We've imposed so much already."

"But I have so many questions about the Season that the Duke could answer for me along the way. Besides, he offered to teach me what I didn't know."

"When was this?" Grayson asked.

"One morning when he discovered me studying my books," Lydia said, her gaze never faltering from Rhys.

"I'm not sure it's appropriate, Lydia," Abbie said.

"He's offered me his protection, Mama. According to my books that makes him a trusted chaperone. Besides, we're traveling in a caravan. Papa will be only a scream away."

"Why would you scream?" Grayson's voice contained a savage edge.

Laughing, Lydia moved over to him and hugged him. "Now everyone is being silly. He's family, for goodness' sakes, and we'll be traveling in the coach in front of yours." She lifted her face to Grayson, looking all the world like an innocent again. "Please, Papa, I do have so many questions, and I can't find the answers in my books."

Grayson studied Rhys. "It's up to you—whether or not you want Lydia to travel in your coach."

"Please, say yes," Colton piped up. "It'd give me more room to move around."

Rhys considered suggesting that Colton travel with him, so he'd have all the room he needed. But to deny Lydia's request would no doubt open a Pandora's box of speculation and suspicions, and while they were well deserved, he preferred to handle this matter as diplomatically as possible. That Grayson had blithely accepted Rhys's desire to offer Lydia a Season as mere kindness and a way to repay his mother's inhospitality was a godsend.

"I shall be most honored to have Lydia travel in my coach."

The look she flashed his way indicated that having her travel with him would not come without cost.

Sitting across from Lydia as the coach traveled toward London, Rhys was acutely aware of every aspect of her being. The slow rising and falling of her chest. The sparkle in her eyes as she gazed out the window. The gentle fragrance of flowers that surrounded her.

She'd spoken not a word since entering the coach.

He would accuse her of being coldhearted, but he knew she was anything but glacial. She was as warm as sunlight in a meadow.

Yet she seemed too proper, too perfect, sitting there with her hands folded in her lap. Silent. The injured lover seeking to heal her own wounds.

He shifted on his bench seat, as he imagined Colton did for much of the journey. "You're being most disagreeable," he finally uttered.

Keeping her profile to him, she did little more than shift her eyes in his direction. "On the contrary, Your Grace. I've agreed to go to London. I've agreed to attend the balls. I've agreed to find a husband. I pray every day that I am not with child. How much more agreeable would you have me be?"

He could not prevent his gaze from drifting down to her waist, nor could he prevent himself from wondering if she were indeed carrying his child. It pleased him to think of her having his son or daughter, while at the same time he was horrified to consider the ramifications. How his past might affect his child. If he were not accepted in polite society, neither would his offspring be.

He'd always taken such care with the ladies Camilla sent him. He'd always made use of a condom if a lady wanted to reach her fulfillment with him nestled inside her. With Lydia, he'd given no thought to protecting her, only possessing her. How could he have taken so little care with the one lady who meant so much to him?

"I would have you ride in the other coach," he finally admitted.

She shrugged. "You need only have said so."

"And have Grayson wonder exactly what the undercurrents were within our strange exchange at the manor?"

"Guilt has obviously made you delusional, so you are reading messages which do not exist into the conversation."

Reaching across the coach, he grabbed her arm and shook her. "Stop it, damn it! This is not you."

She jerked free of his hold, scooted into the corner, and glared at him. "How would you know?"

Balancing himself, he moved until he sat beside her. He cradled her cheek against his palm. "A part of me feels a need to apologize for not walking out of the room that night, before you were close enough for me to smell your sweet fragrance. But another part of me, a greater part of me, is incredibly grateful you gifted me with your love, even though you refused to believe I was so undeserving."

"Rhys—"

He touched his thumb to her lips. "The hardest thing I shall ever do is give you up to another. That I will be a better man for having done it will be little consolation in the lonely years that follow. Trust me to know there would come a time when you would hate me and when the dream you thought you'd achieved would become a nightmare."

"I don't know if I want to marry an English lord when he can't be you."

"Many good men are in London, and we shall find you the best."

"When I first thought of coming to England, I have to admit I thought it would be wonderful to marry a man with a title. But after having seen your parents, I'm no longer sure. It never occurred to me there would be marriage without love."

"You shall have love in your marriage. We will not settle for less."

He slid his arm around her and drew her head within the crook of his shoulder.

"I wish you'd tell me what you did that is so awful," she said.

"You would loathe me, and that I could not bear."

She snuggled up against him, her hand coming to rest beneath his jacket, against his chest. "Mama said we'd stay at your house in London."

"I thought it best. I am the only one in residence so there is ample room. Although I believe Ravenleigh's house is large, he does have five daughters to accommodate."

"Will you attend the balls?"

"No." His being in mourning was the perfect excuse. The less he was seen, the better. "I shall, however, interview any gentlemen who express an interest in calling upon you."

"Shouldn't that be my stepfather's job?"

"His position is not as . . ."

She tilted up her lovely face. "He's illegitimate."

"Quite so."

"His birth shouldn't make any difference."

"But in my world, it does make a great deal of difference."

Moving away from him, she straightened. "I actually do have a lot of questions."

He leaned back into the corner of the coach, crossed his arms over his chest, and smiled ruefully. "Then by all means, let the lessons begin."

"Don't know why we hafta go back to London," William grumbled.

Rhys took the jacket the lad offered him and slipped it on. "London is an excellent place for Lydia to find a husband."

"But I liked it in the country."

Rhys studied his reflection in the mirror, wondering why he cared how he looked. "Things will be much different for us in London now."

"I'll never be like you."

"We should hope not."

He gazed past his image to the bed where William sat, looking forlorn. The inn had made rooms available to him and his entourage for the night. Dinner would soon be served in a private room. Life should have been good. Instead he found it lacking. It seemed William did as well.

"You don't much like wearing the cloak of servant, do you, lad?" Rhys asked.

William shrugged. "I ain't complaining."

"Perhaps while we're in London, you might serve as Colton's companion. The Ravenleigh household is overrun with girls. I suspect the boy would welcome having another male around when they're visiting."

"You mean be his valet?"

Rhys turned and smiled. "I mean, be his friend. Your duties to me will be suspended. You'll have no lessons while we're in London, except for what you learn from Colton. But I will expect you to apply yourself more diligently to your studies when we return to Harrington."

"Why do you care so much about me studies?"

"Because I have great expectations where you're concerned. You were not meant to be some man's servant, but rather your own master. We simply have to determine how best to achieve that end."

* * *

Lydia had been staring out her window at the inn, certain the faint lights she saw in the far distance were those of London, when she spotted Rhys walking along a rolling hill. She now trudged along the same path he'd taken.

Dinner had been an incredibly informal affair. Sabrina had almost as many questions to ask Rhys as Lydia had asked him in the coach. He'd been patient with his answers during both occasions.

During the meal, Lydia had simply watched him, trying to understand him, while searching for a way to heal her heart.

She loved him. She loved his patience, his kindness. The way he rubbed his bottom lip when he listened. The way he smiled with amusement, using his eyes more than his lips.

She even loved him for wanting to protect her. However, she couldn't help but resent that he kept so much hidden from her, judged himself through his eyes, and would not allow her to judge him through hers.

He turned his head slightly as she neared.

"I should think you would have learned your lesson about joining me when I am alone at night," he said quietly.

"You're very skilled at seduction, Rhys, but make no mistake—nothing that's happened between us would have taken place had I not wished it to."

"I could prove you wrong."

"I wasn't issuing a dare. Try to seduce me, and you'll succeed because I want you. Why would I deny myself the pleasure of your touch?"

"Are you admitting to coming out here for the purpose of seduction?"

"No. I came out here because I was curious as to whether that hazy light in the distance is London. I thought maybe you would know."

"It is."

She laughed lightly. "It's a much larger town than Fortune, then."

"You will see things you've never seen. It's possible you'll hear things you would prefer not to hear."

"What kind of things?"

"Things about my family. About me."

"I've told you before that I don't care about your sins. I'm drawn to you, Rhys. I feel like I'm caught in large waves, tossed toward the shore, then pulled back out to sea. You can't tell me that you aren't attracted to me at least a little."

"My feelings are of no consequence."

"They matter to me; they matter to me a great deal."

"You've told me that you long for respectability."

"I think all women do."

"Precisely. That is the very reason I shall never marry."

"Because you're not respectable."

"Because I've done things that cannot be respected. My mother, as you may have noticed, can barely tolerate my presence. She holds me accountable for Quentin's death."

She rolled her eyes. "Your brother got drunk and fell into the family pond. How can you be responsible for his carelessness and poor judgment?"

"I told you that I'd betrayed him, betrayed my family."

Rhys had been standing here, pondering his past, wondering what he should reveal to Lydia. He had no wish to harm her further. As far as he knew, Quentin had kept Rhys's betrayal within the family. But there was always the chance he might have told someone during one of his drunken stupors. Rhys would prefer Lydia hear the truth from him.

"Are you trying to convince me you're as cruel as he was?"

"Cruelty had nothing to do with it. Therein lies the irony. For I had not meant to be cruel, and yet I was."

She moved closer to him and placed her hand on his arm. "You are anything but cruel. You made my family feel welcome. You rescued the horses that your brother treated badly."

"But I could not rescue Annie."

"Annie?"

"My brother's wife. She possessed the disposition of an angel. She came to me one night, and I did not have the strength of character to turn her away. There in my father's house, in the bedchamber beside my brother's, I took my brother's wife as though she well and truly belonged to me."

"You slept with your brother's wife?"

Her voice reflected the horror his actions deserved.

"At least your stepfather thought your mother was a widow when he visited her bed. I knew Annie was not. I knew she was to get herself with my brother's child, to provide an heir. I knew she was not free. Yet I showed no restraint. Rather I revealed my true self. The weak man I am. The weak man you do not deserve."

Lydia couldn't help but feel a measure of revulsion. But Annie had gone to Rhys. He hadn't sought her out. She'd believed the worst about him when she'd seen the scarred horses. She wouldn't believe it now.

"How old were you?" she asked.

"Nineteen."

Relief coursed through her. "You were so young. You're no longer that man."

"Am I not? Three nights later Annie took my brother's straight razor and slashed her wrists."

Lydia's legs suddenly went numb and weak. She stepped to a tree and pressed her back against it to provide her with support. "Not because she slept with you?"

"She left a letter. 'Darling Rhys,' she wrote. 'Forgive me for what transpired between us in your bed for I cannot forgive myself.' You can well imagine my family's reaction to her words, to the truth of my betrayal. That night I ran away. Only once in all the years before my brother's death did I return to that house. I was turned away. But one cannot ignore the heir. And so here I am. Where I was never meant to be."

She shoved herself away from the tree and cautiously approached him. "Rhys, her death must have been awful for you. I understand you've probably been riddled with guilt. But I know you. I know it was not your intent to harm her. My love for you does not lessen with this confession."

"Confession? Lydia, that night was only the beginning of my sins. The others are buried so deeply within the shadows of London that I can only pray they remain where they are. It is not what I did with Annie that makes me unacceptable, but what I dared to do in the years since. Your opinion of me would change; your love for me would die."

"Then tell me everything."

"Nothing will be gained, and everything lost." He walked away.

"I won't stop loving you," she vowed into the night, determined to find a way to prove it.

* * *

Rhys had never before presented his card. He did so now at the Earl of Ravenleigh's London home, waiting in the entrance hall while Grayson's family stood nearby. The butler had taken his card and was off to inform His Lordship of the Duke's arrival.

It appeared to be a very nice residence, not as ostentatious as his own, but then not everyone possessed his mother's garish tastes or her need to surround herself with clutter.

A high-pitched squeal emanated from the stairway. Rhys looked up to see a young woman rushing down the steps.

"Mama! They're here!"

Mayhem and madness followed that pronouncement.

Lydia released an echoing squeal as she hurried across the foyer. Then she and the young woman were wrapped in each other's arms while four other girls—completely devoid of decorum—were scurrying down the stairs.

A woman who greatly resembled Abbie in appearance hurried out of a distant hallway, the one down which the butler had recently traversed. She was followed by a man whom Rhys recognized as Ravenleigh.

That Abbie and her sister embraced did not surprise Rhys. That Ravenleigh was heartily shaking Grayson's hand did astonish him.

Yet all he could think was that this welcome was the sort Grayson should have received upon arriving at Harrington. Shrieks of joy rather than shrieks of anger.

He couldn't stop himself from smiling at the sight of Lydia's happiness. She was again the hopeful woman she'd been when she'd arrived at Harrington, before he'd disappointed her by not offering for her after she'd given so much of herself to him.

She and the other girl—Lauren, he remembered now—were no longer hugging, but swinging held hands as though they needed the touching to confirm each other's existence. How natural they seemed. How unaffected.

He had little doubt Lydia could hold her own in London. He simply wasn't certain if it would be better if she left without reaching for her dream, because the experience would surely change her in ways he had not.

"Your Grace, I was sorry to hear of your father's passing."

He jerked his attention to Ravenleigh, who was now standing before him. Under the circumstances he decided to overlook the slight not greeting him first had been. "It was not totally unexpected. Still, the passing of a parent does manage to take one unawares."

"Exceedingly so, I'm afraid. The ladies are going to take tea in the garden. Elizabeth has a penchant for growing roses which I'm certain she wishes to show off. We'll usher all the younger children upstairs for sweet cakes. Perhaps you'd like to join Grayson and me in the library."

"I appreciate the invitation, but I'd merely planned to see that they were welcomed and then be on my way. I shall send my carriage around for them later."

"I can't believe you're actually here!" Lauren said enthusiastically as she wrapped her arm around Lydia's and led her through the garden.

Lydia could hardly believe it herself. She and Lauren had written to each other over the years expressing how much they wanted to share the balls and London. And now here she was. Yet all she seemed capable of doing was wondering when Rhys would return.

Her mother and Aunt Elizabeth sat at a table beneath a tree, sipping their tea and talking. Lauren hadn't bothered to ask if Lydia wanted tea. She'd simply ushered her into the garden.

"I wanted to get you away from them, so we can talk privately without ears listening," Lauren whispered, when they were a good distance away.

She leaned close and touched her shoulder to Lydia's. "What is going on between you and the Duke?"

Lydia's heart jumped around in her chest. "Whatever do you mean?"

"My goodness, Lydia, the man barely took his eyes off you the entire time he was here. And the *way* he looked at you"—she fanned her face with her hand as though she were suddenly burning with a fever—"if a gentleman ever looked at me like that, I swear I'd marry him tomorrow."

Lydia would marry Rhys as well if he wasn't saying one thing and doing another. He loved her, but not enough to risk marrying her, for fear in marrying her, he'd hurt her. Yet she was certain their love was strong enough to withstand any storm. But a man who had never known love could not begin to fathom its power.

Lydia shook her head, but she couldn't prevent the tears from forming. "He has no interest in marrying me."

"Oh, my!" Lauren grabbed her arm and pulled her behind a trellis covered in vines and roses. "You love him?"

More tears surfaced as Lydia pressed her hands to her mouth and nodded.

"So much," she rasped. "I'm trying to be a lady

about it. I've read all these books on how a lady comports herself, and nothing explains how to act when your heart is breaking."

Lauren put her arms around Lydia and drew her close. "What do your parents say?"

"They don't know." She wiped her eyes, sniffed, and pulled back. "And you mustn't tell them. Rhys simply told them that since we were here, I should have a chance to visit London, attend a ball, and that he's willing to help me find a suitable husband."

"How damned English of him."

Lydia released a small laugh. "Isn't it, though?"

"So he's willing to find you a husband, but not step into the shoes himself. Well, we'll just have to see about that."

"What do you mean?"

"As fate would have it, my friend Gina is hosting a ball the night after tomorrow. You remember her, don't you? She lived in Fortune for a time."

"I remember her. She worked in the cotton fields with us."

"That's right. She and I have remained friends over the years. When she came to London last summer for a visit, I took her to a ball, and she had a marriage proposal that very night."

"You're kidding?"

"Absolutely not. She married the Earl of Huntingdon, and they're quite happily married now, as you'll see. I'll expect nothing less for you."

Chapter 17

Lydia trembled with anticipation, shook with trepidation.

She felt as though she'd waited her entire life for this moment of walking into a London ballroom. Four crystal chandeliers with gas flares provided light for the room that was a colorful sea of men and women dressed in such finery that Lydia wished she'd had time to have a more fashionable dress sewn.

Although Lauren and Aunt Elizabeth had assured her that she looked lovely, she suddenly felt dowdy and ill-prepared. Where was Rhys when she needed him? Who would whisper in her ear with gentle encouragement and anticipate her mistakes before she made them?

She understood that he was in mourning, but for tonight, she dearly wanted him here. How was it she could so desire his presence when he refused to embrace the emotions that existed between them?

"Gina and Lord Huntingdon had a rough go of it when they discovered Gina's father had left them with nothing except debt," Lauren whispered behind her fan. "But now they are so madly in love that I think Huntingdon considers himself to be far richer than he would have been with the money Gina's father had originally promised him."

"Are you telling me that he married her for her father's money?" Lydia asked.

Rhys had told her love wasn't often a consideration for marriage, but she'd hoped his assessment of marriage among the aristocracy had been tainted by his cynicism and his own parents' situation.

Lauren nodded. "Not at all unheard of. As a matter of fact, be grateful the Duke is willing to interview any gentleman who shows an interest in you. It's often difficult to tell by looking when a man has fallen on hard times."

"I'd just be grateful if one looked my way with something more than morbid curiosity," Lydia mused.

"They will. It just takes a while for them to warm up to foreigners. Come on. Let me introduce you to Lord and Lady Huntingdon."

Lydia took a deep breath. Within her tightly fitting kid gloves, her palms began to sweat, although she knew she had no reason to be nervous. She'd memorized the various forms of address. More importantly, she knew Gina.

Their host and hostess turned to them. Lydia wouldn't have recognized the woman if Lauren hadn't already told her whom she'd be meeting. Gina looked far prettier than Lydia remembered her as being. She wondered if love was responsible. Was it such a transforming emotion?

"Gina, you remember my cousin Lydia Westland, don't you?" Lauren asked.

Gina gave Lydia the warmest, most welcome smile she'd ever received. "Of course I remember her. Although it's been years since we've seen each other. How do you like London?"

"I've only been here a few days, but I think it's wonderful," Lydia admitted.

"I despise it," Gina said, still smiling. "Devon's almost finished up his business here. Then, thank goodness, we can return to the country next week."

She squeezed the arm of the gentleman standing beside her. "Lydia, this is Devon, my husband."

But in her voice, Lydia heard he was also her love.

He gave his wife an indulgent grin before bowing slightly to Lydia. "My wife is not one to stand on ceremony. It's a pleasure to meet you, Miss Westland."

"It's the ceremony I love," Lydia admitted.

"I can barely tolerate it," Gina said. "So many rules. I have better things to do with my time than memorize rules."

Lauren laughed. "Ah, Gina, bless your heart, you never change."

"Thank goodness for that," Lord Huntingdon said.

Gina fluttered her hand. "Go on and enjoy yourselves. See if you can break as many hearts as Lauren has."

Lydia followed Lauren as she made her way around the ballroom, occasionally stopping to make introductions.

"I can't believe you've had this gaiety every summer while I've been picking cotton," Lydia said quietly, more grateful than ever that she wore gloves to hide the tiny scars where plucking bolls had pricked her fingers.

"It's an entirely different life, that's for sure," Lauren said. "It's a shame Harrington couldn't be here."

"I know," Lydia said, looking around wistfully. She wanted to share this moment with him. "I feel like something's missing."

"What could possibly be missing?"

"I'm not sure. I've anticipated this moment for so long that I suppose it has no choice except to be disappointing."

"You won't be disappointed once the gentlemen start asking you to dance." Lauren wiggled her finger toward a corner. "Do you see that tall gentleman over there?"

"How could I miss him?" Lydia asked. He was at least a head taller than the tallest man standing near him. And so incredibly thin as to be gaunt.

"He always stands out in a crowd. He's the Earl of Whithaven. And over there, do you see the very petite woman with the blond hair?"

Lydia nodded.

"That's his wife."

"What an odd pair," Lydia mused.

"I would think so as well except that she is so obviously in love with him. You should see the way she looks at him when they dance. For all they say that the aristocracy does not marry for love, I sense there is a change afoot. Marrying for property or political alliance is giving way to matters of the heart. It's been ever so romantic to watch."

"My goodness, Lauren, you almost sound British."

Lauren laughed lightly. "I should hope so. Nine years in this wretched country, trying to fit in."

Lydia was taken aback by her statement. "I thought you loved it here."

"I adore certain aspects of it. But there is so much

ceremony that sometimes it becomes a bit much. You can see that Gina doesn't care. She introduces people like she was still in Texas. Upon further consideration, hers might not have been the best ball to start you off with. I love her dearly, but she has no interest in conforming. And look at us. We've been standing here for the longest while the music plays and others dance. Young men stand along the walls like fossils. Have you ever seen even the homeliest of women in Texas sit out a single dance?"

Lydia smiled with remembrance. "I suppose you have a valid point."

"Of course, I do. Everything is so proper here. There are times when I consider it all splendid, and other times when I wish for something more. Oh, listen to me. This is supposed to be your night. We really must find you a dance partner." Lauren's jubilant smile enhanced her beauty. "And here comes a possibility now."

But the Duke of Kimburton, while polite to Lydia, was obviously interested only in Lauren and promptly escorted her onto the dance floor. Lydia glanced around at all the glitz and the glamour and suddenly wished what she'd never expected to wish at this moment.

She wished she was anywhere but where she was.

The Earl of Whithaven stood in a distant corner, away from the maddening throng, and studied every man. Daring each to meet and hold his gaze, making a mental note of those who looked away too quickly, too guiltily.

His height gave him a decided advantage. He planned to make the most of it this evening, and during every other evening while he was in London. His gaze darted to his wife. His lovely, treacherous wife.

"Whithaven, what's wrong, man? You look as though you found your dinner disagreeable," Viscount Reynolds said.

He shifted his attention to Viscount Reynolds and the Marquess of Kingston. Trusted friends both. He stepped farther back into the corner, and they promptly joined him, sensing that discretion was in order.

"I believe"—he swallowed hard and forced out the detested words—"I believe my wife is having an affair."

"Daphne?" Kingston asked.

"She is the only wife I have," he responded tartly.

"But she adores you, man. It's always been quite obvious," Kingston assured him.

"No longer. I'm certain of it."

"How can you be so sure?" Reynolds asked.

To no one else, other than these two, would he confess the truth. "A few nights ago, I joined Daphne in her bedchamber. To, of course, exercise my rights as her husband."

"Of course," Reynolds murmured.

"Quite so," Kingston mumbled.

"She suggested things—" He stopped, unable to continue as the memories bombarded him.

"What sort of things?" Kingston asked.

"Things I would do with my mistress but never my wife."

Both men's eyes widened and their mouths dropped open.

"Where would she learn of such things?" Reynolds asked.

"As I said. She has obviously taken on a lover."

The gentlemen glanced around the room.

"And you think he is here?" Kingston asked.

"I would not be at all surprised. He must be a peer. I

cannot expect a lesser man to attract the attention of my Daphne. Certainly he would not be worthy of it."

"Have you considered," Reynolds began, "that she has perhaps visited the infamous Gentleman Seducer?"

Whithaven scoffed. "He is but a myth."

"Perhaps grounded in truth. There has been much whispering going about."

He shook his head. "She has no need to pay for a man's services. Good Lord, look at her. She is lovely beyond description."

"I daresay there is not a gentleman in attendance who does not wonder if the rumors about this mysterious roué are true. I, for one, have been more attentive to my wife in hopes of keeping her from visiting this fellow, should he be flesh and not myth. I've even heard it rumored he has a penchant for chocolate," Kingston told them.

"You don't say?" Reynolds murmured.

"Where did you hear this?" Whithaven asked.

"My wife," Kingston admitted.

"How would she know?"

Kingston looked uncomfortable but revealed, "She said she overheard a lady mentioning she'd paid him a visit."

"Not my Daphne."

"No, of course not," Kingston hastened to assure him. "I've no doubt it was a woman of little consequence."

Whithaven once again began a slow perusal of the guests. "By God, when I do discover who her lover is, I shall kill him."

Sitting beside the window in the front parlor, Rhys thought the constant ticking of the clock on the mantel might drive him stark raving mad. Through the open doorway, he had a clear view of the entrance hall. For the past hour he'd expected Lydia to return home at any moment.

His gaze continually jumped between the doorway and the book resting on his lap, continually jumped from the doorway to the single word on the page he seemed unable to move beyond, jumped in rhythm to the damned ticking of the clock.

It did not help matters that Grayson and Abbie were also in the room. Apparently they *were* reading, because he occasionally heard the soft rasp of pages being turned.

He should have attended the ball. He'd even contemplated going to Huntingdon's residence and creeping around to peer in windows until he spotted the room in which the dance was being held, until he caught sight of Lydia and could rest assured she was enjoying herself.

He'd often listened distractedly while Camilla had gone on and on about how important it was to be considered part of the Marlborough House Set. Lydia was attending a ball hosted by an American, being introduced by an American. She would no doubt be seen as a tourist. He did not think she would be shunned, but the possibility existed that she would not be welcomed with open arms.

He could only hope he was making much ado about nothing. She was lovely, graceful, and so full of life she was bound to draw a gentleman's fancy, and in so doing, her evening would be victorious.

Blast it! Knowing the peerage as he did, he should have taken greater measures to ensure she had the type of evening she'd always dreamed of. But he'd feared revealing himself in a public forum, of causing unwarranted harm.

His little dreamer would do well. Her poise and charm would win over the finest of gentlemen. He was certain of it. She would be the toast of London. He would be interviewing possible suitors in the days to come.

Perhaps that was where his worry initiated, from deep within his secret yearnings. He truly didn't want her with someone else. Walking on another man's arm, kissing another man's mouth, sleeping in another man's bed, opening herself up to another man's passions.

He heard a loud pop. He looked down at his lap to discover he'd somehow managed to crack the spine on his book. As a rule he valued books and treated them with utmost respect. He would have to find a binder to fix this one.

"How long do these parties go on for?" Abbie asked.

Her twang was more pronounced than Lydia's. Strange how he'd never noticed before. He could well imagine Lydia practicing until she sounded more like Grayson than her mother.

He glanced up at the clock. A little after two. "I should think she will be arriving home at any moment."

Home. It had been years since he'd thought of this house as his home. Although it was well and truly his now, the ghosts from his past continued to haunt him. And he had no desire for them to inflict themselves on Lydia.

Outside, the clatter of hooves and wheels neared and came to a stop. He discreetly slipped his fingers between the curtains, separating them enough so he could peer through the window. He saw Lydia alight from Ravenleigh's carriage.

He could hardly describe the joy that the sight of her brought to him. How lonely it would be when she was another man's wife and no longer visiting him.

"She's arrived," he said quietly.

He heard the front door open, and the butler murmur a greeting. While Grayson and Abbie immediately rose, Rhys schooled his features not to reveal how desperately he wanted to know exactly how her evening had gone. She was not his to care about as he did. To express any sort of outward interest was not to be done.

He caught a glimpse of her strolling past. He attributed the lack of a spring in her step to weariness from dancing all evening.

"Lydia!" her mother called out.

Lydia came back into view, peeking into the room. "Mama, I didn't know you were going to wait up."

"Of course, we would! We've all been anxious to hear about your evening. Come tell us about it."

She hesitated before entering the room. Her dance card and ivory fan dangled from her wrist. She looked like a wilted rose, one plucked and left without water—not one that had blossomed and then faded as it should.

"How was it?" her mother prodded.

Standing in the center of the room, looking uncertain, Lydia smiled softly. "Just as I thought it would be. I wish you'd been there. So many ladies wearing beautiful gowns. Gentlemen dressed in their finery. There was an orchestra." She finally met Rhys's gaze. "Back home, we usually only have a fiddle player or two."

"Did you dance?" Abbie asked.

She nodded slightly, slipping the hand where her dance card dangled behind her back. "Oh, yes."

Her mother smiled brightly and hugged her. "I'm so glad. I was worried you wouldn't have a good time."

"How could I not when I've wanted this night my whole life?"

Her mother patted her cheek. "It's late and I know

we're all tired. You can give us all the details tomorrow." She slid her arm around Lydia. "Let's get you tucked into bed."

"Actually I don't think I can sleep just yet," Lydia said. "I have a couple of questions I'd like to ask His Grace before I forget. Just some etiquette questions." She looked past her mother to him. "If you don't mind answering them."

"I don't mind at all," he assured her, finding himself glad he would have a few moments alone with her.

Her mother bussed a kiss across Lydia's cheek. "I suppose a few minutes will be all right. You'll get Mary to help you undress?"

"Yes."

Rhys watched as Grayson kissed his daughter's cheek and murmured good night, before he and his wife quit the room. While avoiding his gaze, Lydia moved gracefully to the sofa and sat. With her eyes downcast, she slipped her fan and dance card off her wrist and set both aside.

"Did you really dance?" he asked quietly.

She lifted her gaze to his, tears pooling in her eyes and spilling onto her cheeks. He felt as though his heart had just been flayed.

"Lord Ravenleigh and Lord Huntingdon both honored me with a dance." She released a tiny whimper and pressed her gloved hand against her mouth. "Oh, Rhys."

His book landing on the floor with a thud, he surged to his feet. He crossed over to her, sat beside her, and took her in his arms. Her tears began in earnest then, her delicate shoulders shaking with the force of her anguish.

"Shh, shh, my darling, it's all right," he murmured.

"It was awful. I didn't expect to be the belle of the ball, but I had hopes I would at least be noticed by someone."

"I'm sure you were."

She leaned back slightly, her eyes searching his for the truth. "Then why didn't anyone ask me to dance, why didn't anyone approach me or speak to me? Lauren had so much attention paid to her. I don't blame her for not spending more time with me. Honestly. I just felt like such a wallflower."

"When I have little doubt you were the most beautiful blossom there."

"Don't do that, Rhys, don't flatter me when you care so little for me."

"How can I convince you that it is because I care for you so much that I will not consider marrying you?" He rained kisses over her face, tasting the salt of her tears. "It breaks my heart to see you so unhappy, but marriage to me would only deepen your sorrow. Of that I am certain."

"I know I'm being silly," she said breathlessly, as he trailed his mouth along the ivory length of her throat. "But tonight was to be the realization of my dream."

He dipped his head lower, running his lips and his tongue along the gentle swells of her bosom. She dug her gloved fingers into his hair.

"I wanted you there so desperately. I kept thinking you'd surprise me and appear."

Lifting his head, he held her tear-filled gaze. "I promise you that the next ball shall be all you've ever dreamed of." His voice was hoarse with his need to ease her pain. He'd lessened other ladies' heartache, and he knew that his gifts rested not in the telling, but in the showing.

"How can you be so sure?" she asked softly.

"Trust me." He stroked his thumb over her lips. "You'd better go to bed now. I'll take you up."

He stood and extended his hand. He could not explain why it felt so right to close his fingers around hers and draw her to her feet. Continuing to hold her hand, he led her from the room and up the stairs.

He escorted her down the hallway to the door that led into the room in which he'd slept when he'd visited here in his youth. Now he occupied the largest bedchamber, the one designated for the Duke, one that joined the room where the Duchess had once slept.

"I'll let Mary know you need help preparing for bed."

She shook her head. "Don't disturb her. It's late, and I really don't want to see anyone."

"You can't sleep in your clothes."

"I think I'm just going to sit and stare out the window."

He glanced around the hallway. All the doors were closed. All was quiet.

"At least let me unfasten your gown," he offered.

Her eyes widened fractionally.

"So you might rest comfortably," he hastened to add.

She nodded slightly. He opened the door and followed her into the room. A lamp burned low. The coverlet had been turned down.

He closed the door. She spun around, but he saw no fear in her eyes. Only inquisitiveness.

"It would not do to be seen unfastening your gown," he explained quietly.

She nodded once more and presented him with her back.

"Sit on the bed while I remove your slippers."

"Maybe I should send for Mary."

Coming up behind her, he whispered. "I have the talent to make you forget about this night, but only if you're willing." He touched his lips to the nape of her neck. "Be willing, Lydia."

Be willing? Lydia thought. Where he was concerned, when was she not? In a shadowy corner of her mind, she thought she was desperate to even contemplate sharing another night with him. But she loved him.

She was already ruined. What was one more night of bliss?

She stepped away from him and sat on the bed, her heart beating like the wings of a hummingbird. Anticipation shortened her breath. Kneeling before her, he placed her foot on his thigh. While he removed her slipper, she combed her fingers through the curling strands of his hair.

"No one tonight was as handsome as you," she whispered.

He set her shoe aside. Holding her ankle, he rubbed her foot up and down his firm thigh, making her toes curl and uncurl. A delightful sensation ran the length of her sole.

"Although I was not in attendance, I know that no lady was as beautiful as you."

"You're so talented at flattery."

He shook his head. "Not flattery, Lydia. The absolute truth. I swear to you that I have known many of London's ladies, and none shine with your beauty."

He placed her other foot on his thigh and was soon setting that shoe beside the first. Standing, he took her hands and brought her to her feet. He placed a gentle kiss on her lips, almost a kiss of farewell before turning her so her back was to him.

She felt him working the fastenings of her gown while his lips played lightly along the side of her neck. His breath was warm, his mouth warmer.

During some distant evening, she might reflect on this moment and recognize she'd been wanton, but for now she wanted nothing more than to have what he would give her. He spoke of love. He demonstrated love. Yet he would not commit to it as though never having had it showered on him, he feared its power.

She thought he would have removed her clothes quickly, but his fingertips, lips, and tongue paid homage to each inch of her back that was revealed as he slowly cast aside her clothes, piece by piece, until she was completely uncovered like a newly displayed piece of artwork.

She continued to stand with him at her back. She felt the gentle tugging on her hair as combs and pins were removed. All this was improper, the two of them in this room, alone. But after an evening when everything had been so incredibly proper, when she'd worried over every moment, every look, every introduction, when she'd wanted so desperately to belong, she welcomed knowing that with Rhys, for now, she *did* belong.

Her hair tumbled around her. She was suddenly as she'd been before the party. Simple, unfettered.

Anticipating what was to come.

She went to turn, but he placed his hands on her shoulders.

"Not yet," he said in a voice so low that she almost didn't hear him.

He brushed the curtain of her hair over onto one shoulder. Then he began his sensual assault. Slowly, so slowly, he did nothing more than move his mouth across her shoulders, over her back, along her spine. A kiss here, a nip there, a swirl of his tongue that almost made her knees buckle.

His hands framed her hips. She glanced over her shoulder to see him lowering himself to his knees. She felt the press of his kiss high against her backside.

"Did you know you have a dimple?" he asked in a rough voice that somehow reminded her of the music he'd wooed from the piano.

He played her as skillfully as he had the ivory keys, each touch serving a purpose, each hesitation building the anticipation. She felt as though he'd poured warm brandy through her veins.

She shook her head lethargically. "I didn't know," she whispered.

He drew a circle on her skin. "I adore it."

He placed his mouth lower, against the curve of her buttocks, lower still to her thigh, to her knee, then up and over to the other side. Then back again.

Her hands furled and unfurled. She wanted to touch him, to kiss him as he did her. To have what he'd promised her: a night to remember.

"Rhys?"

"Lie on the bed. Face down."

She did as he commanded. The sheets were cool against her skin. She turned her head to the side and watched as he removed his clothes, piece by piece, no hurry, no rush, as though he understood what each of his movements did to her. How simply observing him caused her heartbeat to quicken, her flesh to heat, and desire to stir the embers of passion to life.

She hadn't forgotten how beautiful he was in his naked splendor, but she appreciated the sight of him all the more for having gone so long without seeing him like this. He was more than ready for her. And she for him.

As he neared the bed, she started to roll over for him. Reaching out, he touched her shoulder. "Not yet."

Straddling her hips, he held himself above her, leaning low and whispering near her ear, "If you feel a need to scream, bury your face in the pillow to muffle the cry."

She wanted to scream now with the burning need to have him inside her, rocking against her, heightening her pleasure while fulfilling his.

He skimmed his hands along her sides, over her hips. He returned his mouth to her back with feathery kisses and light touches. It was as though he were discovering all her secret, sensitive spots. Places she'd never dreamed existed.

He shifted, no longer straddling her, and his lips were trailing once again over her legs, kissing the backs of her knees while his hand kneaded one foot and then the other. Feet she'd expected to use for dancing all night—not standing and wishing.

Her body began writhing and undulating as she sought surcease. She was hot, so hot. No matter where he touched her, she felt a tug low in her belly. No matter where he kissed her, she felt a tingle between her legs.

"Rhys?" she whispered desperately.

He moved up, lying his body over hers, but not in hers, once again straddling her hips. He breathed as harshly as she did. He slid his hands beneath her, one cupping her breast. He squeezed and kneaded the pliant mound while his other hand glided along her stomach and then arced downward to nestle within her curls.

She released a tiny whimper as he continued to work his magic with his fingers.

"The pillow," he reminded her hoarsely.

She buried her face in the pillow, stifling her scream,

as he carried her to new heights, her body bucking, but held firm beneath his weight.

Her heart pounded as her limbs, if at all possible, sprawled over the bed. He slid his finger inside her, too late, she thought, for much purpose, until he whispered low, "I love the way that feels."

She noticed it then, her body's gentle pulsing and throbbing. She smiled lethargically.

He slid his hands away, levered himself away from her, and rolled her over. She went willingly, her melted bones happy to follow.

"Now for the other side," he said in a seductive voice that promised more pleasure.

He stretched out beside her, shoulder to hip, and blanketed his mouth over hers, their tongues waltzing to what was becoming a familiar rhythm. But the familiarity did not lessen the excitement. Rather it enhanced it.

Lydia thought that must be an aspect of love. To never grow weary of a lover's touch, to anticipate each kiss as though it were the first. To discover new wonder and delight in a caress, a stroke.

The pressure of his hands was deliciously sweet. On her shoulder, her breast, her hip. One hand traveling the length of her, while the other massaged her neck. His foot rubbed hers; then slid up to rub her calf. Back down to her foot.

Subtle movements, careful pressure as though they were in no hurry but had all night to simply enjoy the presence of the other.

This was love, she thought. A quiet joining. Two souls, two hearts, two bodies.

Why could he not understand that she was willing to

accept his past, look beyond it to their future? If giving everything to him could not convince him of her commitment to him, what would?

She slid her fingers along his neck, up into his scalp; then down again to his shoulders. She felt his muscles bunching with his movements.

He brought his knee up and nudged her thighs apart. He nestled his body between her legs. She wanted him there every night, until she was old and frail. She wanted to sleep with her body curled around his. She wanted to awaken with his face beside hers on the pillow.

His mouth began a slow, leisurely sojourn over her breasts. His tongue circled her nipple. She arched her back, raising her body to meet his.

He murmured sweet nothings, gentle words telling her how beautiful she was. She never felt as beautiful as she did when he was with her.

He moved his mouth lower, along each rib, lower still to her navel. With his tongue, he outlined her as though in reverence before sliding lower.

He pressed his mouth to the heart of her womanhood. His tongue stroked, velvet against silk, igniting the flames. She ran her feet up his thighs, buried her fingers in his hair.

"Rhys." His name on her lips was a sweet benediction, whispered over and over.

His mouth worked its magic, his tongue swirling, stroking, thrusting. He skimmed his hands up her body until his fingers were taunting her nipples and her spine curved upward.

The tension mounted, the sensations grew. She turned her head to the side and stuffed the corner of the pillow in her mouth to muffle her screams, as he propelled her into a realm where nothing existed beyond the pleasure.

She came to herself vaguely aware of the tears on her face, and his cheek pressed against her stomach. She looked down at his dark head.

"As beautiful as that was, Rhys, I feel empty without you filling me."

He lifted his gaze to hers. "I won't risk getting you with child."

She saw no point in reminding him that she might already be. He eased off the bed.

"Don't leave me yet," she ordered.

He hesitated before lying beside her and drawing her into his arms.

"Why are you so willing to give, but not to take?" she asked.

His answer was only silence and the tightening of his arms around her.

Chapter 18

Rhys stood in Lady Sachse's cluttered drawing room awaiting her arrival. That she was willing to receive him was a promising sign. That she'd left him waiting for nearly an hour didn't bode well for the meeting.

Swallowing his pride had left a bitter taste in his mouth, but for Lydia's happiness he would endure all sorts of unpleasantness. That he'd been unable to resist pleasuring her again was unconscionable. He still did not remotely believe marriage was an option for them. Even if he could initially offer her the glitter of London, with him at her side it would soon lose its sheen. Of that he was utterly convinced.

"Well, well, well, I certainly never expected to welcome you into my home after our last parting," Camilla said, as she swept into the room.

She approached him with her hand held out, fully

expecting what he would unwillingly give. He took her offering and kissed the back of her hand.

She spun away from him. "The news is that the Duke passed away. Not that I'm sorry to hear it, since you no doubt benefit immensely from his passing." She glanced over her shoulder at him. "You wear the rank well."

"It is not yet a comfortable fit," he contradicted her.

She faced him. "Rumor also has it that you're serving as benefactor for the old Duke's bastard's daughter."

"She is Grayson's *step*daughter."

She arched a thin brow. "Then it is true." She sat regally in a chair and glanced up at him. "Why would you make such a generous offer?"

"Why would I not?"

She ran her hand over her skirt. "I was at Huntingdon's ball. It did not go well for the girl."

"Her lack of success is the very reason I am here."

She smiled, as though he'd simply confirmed what she'd suspected. "You need me again, Rhys. How that must gall you."

Indeed it did, but he kept his facial features as blank as possible.

"Ravenleigh has influence. His wife not as much— being American," he said.

Her smile broadened. "There is something to be said for true British blood running in one's veins."

"You have influence, Camilla."

"Indeed I do."

"I wish for her to meet with more success when she attends her next ball—"

"She must first be invited."

"Which you can arrange."

"Without a doubt. But what of me, Rhys?" She rose

and began to pace. "They've finally managed to determine who is to be heir to Sachse. It seems I was not the only one incapable of breeding, and those in the family who did succeed have for the most part produced only girls. After much effort they tracked down some distant male cousin, and according to the solicitor, the heir was hesitant to leave his studies. He is a lad in short pants who will have a guardian, who no doubt will not favor me."

Her agitation increased with each sentence uttered. "I will be moved into the small dower house. God knows what they'll determine is an adequate allowance. My husband, may he rest in hell, did not leave a will with any stipulations regarding me. I am at the mercy of the new Earl who is due to arrive at any moment."

She spun around and faced him. "What of me, Rhys? How do I benefit if I see that this girl is accepted?"

"You will become my duchess."

That she had hoped for such an announcement, he had little doubt. That it still took her by surprise was evident by her open mouth and her slowly sinking into the chair.

"Do you mean it?" she asked hesitantly.

"Have you ever known me to speak falsely?"

She shook her head slightly, and he could fairly see the possibilities spinning in her mind. "It is not enough that you have given her your endorsement. You must attend the next ball as well. The title carries weight to be sure, but not as much as the man who wears it."

"I'm in mourning."

"If you were a woman, it would be unacceptable. As a man, you will garner a few frowns, but everyone is exceedingly curious to meet the new Duke of Harrington. I believe you'll be forgiven for your breach of etiquette.

We can announce our engagement at that time."

He wasn't certain which he dreaded more: attending the damnable ball or having his engagement to Camilla cut in stone.

"If that's what you wish."

She laughed lightly. "Oh, that's definitely what I wish, Rhys. As for our wedding—"

"The specifics on that will wait until Lydia has been satisfactorily situated. I'll not be distracted from my purpose where she is concerned."

"Which is?"

"To find her a suitable husband among the aristocracy."

"You care for her."

It was issued as a statement, not a question, one he found rather irritating.

"She is delightful," he admitted. "That aside, I simply wish to see her happy."

"Then why not marry her yourself?"

He bestowed upon her a pointed glare that indicated he thought she was an idiot for even asking.

"You fear your sins will be uncovered. My ladies wish to keep their secrets as much as you do."

"We shall hope that is the case. Regardless, I am not willing to risk hurting her."

"Whereas I cannot be hurt."

"You know going in *what* you are marrying." He wasn't referring to the title, and well she knew it. "You'll overlook it to gain a title. I think she wants so much more." *She deserves so much more.*

"Then we shall see that she gets it."

He shifted his attention to the doorway where the butler had just entered. Camilla leaned to the side of the chair and glanced back over her shoulder. "Yes, Matthews?"

"His Lordship has arrived."

Rhys had never seen Camilla grow as pale as she did now. For all the cold armor she wore, he sometimes suspected she wasn't as strong as she seemed.

"You mean the Earl of Sachse?" she croaked.

"Yes, my lady."

She rose unsteadily to her feet. "Then by all means, show him in."

Rhys wasn't certain what compelled him to move forward and squeeze her hand. She gave him what looked to be a terribly forced smile.

"Perhaps they'll appoint me his guardian, and then I can have everything," she said.

"My lady, the Earl of Sachse."

Rhys looked toward the doorway and decided that the Earl didn't need a guardian, and if the way Camilla's fingers were closing tightly around his were any indication, she'd reached the same conclusion.

"My lord?"

The tall, well-tailored man bowed slightly. His brown hair, unfashionably long, fell across his brow. "Lady Sachse."

"Please, do come farther into the room so we needn't shout."

He walked into the room, glancing around as though feeling quite lost. When he was near enough, Camilla said, "Your Grace, my I have the honor of presenting . . ."

Obviously she'd paid little attention to the heir's name when she'd received notification that he'd been located. How typical of her.

Sachse blushed. "Archie Warner, Your Grace."

"His Grace is the Duke of Harrington," Camilla explained. "My betrothed."

Rhys shuddered as though she'd just applied the chisel to the stone in order to begin carving what could not be changed. Sachse looked completely delighted.

"Well, congratulations are in order to be sure! I had no earthly idea!"

"At this point in time, no one does," Rhys hastened to assure him. "We have yet to make a formal announcement, and until we do, I would prefer that we keep the news to ourselves."

"Of course, Your Grace," Sachse said. "That goes without saying. I have never been one for idle gossip."

"Then we are of a like mind, Sachse." Rhys found himself taking an instant liking to the man.

"I would have waited to discuss Rhys's suit with you, my lord," Camilla said, "but I was under the impression you were still a boy in school when I was told you did not wish to leave your studies."

He laughed. "My studies? I'm a teacher up north."

"A scholar then."

"Indeed."

She swept her hand to the side. "Shall we all sit?"

"I would be honored to join you," Rhys said, "but I'm certain you and the Earl have pressing matters to discuss, and I do not wish to intrude—"

"It would be no intrusion, Your Grace," Camilla said.

"Then let me simply confess that I cannot stay for I have guests who require my attention."

She smiled falsely. "Of course. Allow me to walk you out. If you'll excuse me, my lord?"

"Oh, indeed. Do not mind me." He strolled over to a table where a book rested—as decoration only, Rhys was certain—and turned back the cover.

Rhys walked from the room with Camilla following

close enough behind him to have stepped on his heels a number of times.

"Coward!" she spat once they were in the hallway.

He grinned. "You'll have him wrapped around your little finger before the day is done. You don't need my assistance."

"He is not at all what I expected."

"Not a callow lad, that's for certain. I should imagine he won't have any trouble at all finding a suitable lady in London. Perhaps you should have waited to become *betrothed*."

She angled her head haughtily. "Don't be ludicrous. Settle for an earl when I can have a duke? Not if my life depended on it." She patted his arm. "Be sure to look overjoyed when you announce our betrothal."

She left him then to make his own way to the door. His life was a maze of regrets, but if he could see that Lydia was happy, he thought he could forgive himself almost anything.

"You should have seen it, Lyd. There was blood everywhere and people were hollerin'. You could tell from looking at 'em." Colton scrunched up his face, wrapped his hands around his throat, stuck out his tongue, and made choking noises.

Sitting in the front parlor of Rhys's home, Lydia tried to look appropriately horrified. Snuggled on her lap, Sabrina squealed and buried her face against Lydia's chest.

"Colton, behave," her stepfather chastised. "The whole point behind having those particular wax figures in a separate room is to spare the ladies' sensibilities."

"Thank goodness for that," her mother said with a

shudder. "I've heard enough from Colton to squelch any desire I might have had to see what was inside that room."

Colton puffed out his chest with pride. "Only me, and Pa, and William got to go into the Chamber of Horrors. You would have liked seeing what Madame Tussaud did, Lyd."

While her curiosity was piqued, she decided if she did visit the exhibit, she'd pass by that particular room without peering inside.

"You took William with you?" she asked.

"Sure did. Uncle Rhys said it was okay if he went with us."

Her stepfather cleared his throat. "Colton, I've explained about how you are to address—"

"Uncle Rhys don't care if I call him uncle." He gave Rhys a pointed stare. "Do you?"

Rhys sat in a chair that made him appear to be an outsider looking in.

"Not at all," he remarked.

Pleased with the answer he'd been given, Colton beamed his smile around the room. "Honestly, you shoulda been there, Lyd," he reiterated.

"I can visit with you anytime, but not with my cousin. I had an enjoyable time shopping with Lauren this afternoon, thank you very much. No blood, no gore."

"Shopping. Boring." Colton flung himself back in the chair.

"I liked the animals in the zoological gardens," Sabrina said, sitting straighter, as it became evident that Colton's time as the center of attraction had drawn to a close.

Lydia tugged on Sabrina's braid and smiled. "Did you?"

She nodded enthusiastically. "I saw an elephant and a lion and a—"

Lydia touched her finger to Sabrina's mouth knowing her sister had an impressive memory and would no doubt list every animal she'd seen and then some. "Why don't you draw me pictures of all the different animals you saw?"

She wrinkled her nose. "I wish you'd go places with us. We've seen all kinds of things, and you missed every one of them."

"I've seen lots of things, too. I've just seen different things."

"Why can't you go with us?"

"It's difficult to explain," she told her sister.

"Are you still studying for that test you were telling me about?"

Trust Sabrina to remember things said that were better forgotten. "I simply enjoy shopping for clothes more than I like looking at animals."

"I think we've seen just about everything there is to see in London," her mother said. "I'm so glad you've had your dream of attending a ball in London. I'm more than ready to return home."

Lydia shot her gaze at Rhys. Her dream wasn't to attend a ball. It was to have a successful Season. To live a life beyond that into which she'd been born.

Obviously aware of her trepidation, Rhys eased up in his chair. "I thought we'd agreed Lydia would enjoy the remainder of the Season."

Her mother darted a glance at her stepfather before settling her attention on Rhys. "You'd mentioned finding Lydia a husband. She assured me that she wasn't interested." She looked at Lydia. "I thought you were going to explain—"

"I want a Season, Mama. Not necessarily a husband. Although if I find one, I won't be disappointed."

"Lyd, are you gonna get married?" Sabrina asked. "Is that the test?"

"Colton, take Sabrina to the kitchen for some cookies," her mother ordered.

Sabrina slid off Lydia's lap, patted her hand, leaned close, and whispered, "You'll pass the test, Lyd. I know you will." Then she followed Colton out of the room.

Her mother rose to her feet and began to pace, more agitated than Lydia had ever seen her. Her stepfather simply sat as still as stone and studied Lydia.

"How long is a Season?" her mother asked.

"It'll last through July," Lydia supplied.

"That's almost two more months. You can't possibly expect us to stay when we've already been gone for over a month. I know Johnny and Micah are capable of handling the businesses, but it was never our intent when we left to stay away for such a long time."

"You can go home, Mama. Simply leave me here."

Looking frightened, her mother sank onto the sofa and took Lydia's hand. "I don't believe I can do that. Go home and leave you here? You're my little girl, Lydia."

"Mama, I want to experience everything London has to offer. Concerts, operas, plays, and walks in the park. Dinners and balls and courtship. I don't mean to sound ungrateful for the life you've given me in Fortune. I just yearn for more. Besides I'm no longer a little girl. I've become a woman."

Out of the corner of her eye, she saw Rhys stiffen. He knew as well as she did that it was within his arms that she'd truly become a woman. She could reveal everything that had passed between them, and her stepfather would insist on a shotgun wedding in this very room before the sun set.

Only she didn't want Rhys under those conditions. She wanted time to prove to him that they were meant for each other. Meanwhile, she could enjoy the glitter of London.

"I could stay with Aunt Elizabeth," she suggested. "Lauren has asked me countless times in her letters to come visit. I know they won't mind."

"While we were at Harrington, I offered my protection to Lydia," Rhys said quietly. "That offer stands. I am practically her uncle."

He looked uncomfortable as he said it. She was certain her parents would think it was because of his relationship to her stepfather—the bastard. But she understood that his discomfort came about because they were not related at all. And they'd shared experiences forbidden between a true uncle and his niece.

He shifted his gaze to her stepfather. "I assure you that I am well aware you have very high standards regarding the type of man you'd wish for Lydia. I would personally interview any gentleman who expressed an interest in her—as I promised to do before we left Harrington. She could spend each afternoon here, with a chaperone, of course, to receive callers."

"We don't want to inconvenience you," her mother said.

Lydia ground her teeth together.

"It's no trouble, I assure you," Rhys answered.

She thought her mother looked as though she'd suddenly aged ten years. But Lydia knew that sooner or later she had to exert her independence. Now, while she was where she wanted to be, was the perfect time.

"Mama, you and Papa have always taught me that if

I wanted something I should reach for it, work for it, remain determined to get it," Lydia reminded her. "I will do whatever I have to in order to stay in London until the end of the Season. I'm here. Why can't I stay for a while longer with your blessing?

"It won't cost you a single penny. I have my own funds, money I've set aside over the years. I'll use it for everything I need."

"Lydia never has been frivolous," her stepfather said. "I should imagine she has more than enough to get her through the Season."

Her mother looked at him as though she had no idea who he was. "You're in favor of her staying?"

"I know what it is to want something and to be told you can never possess it." He got to his feet, crossed the room, and joined her mother on the sofa. "Lydia is a grown woman. We can't hold on to her forever. I see no harm in her spending some time here without us. Besides, if you take her home now, she'll only come back next year. You'll simply be postponing the inevitable. Lydia has spoken of London for years. It's a harmless dream. Let her have it."

"That's easy enough for you to say. You're a man—"

"I was a scandalous rogue, my sweet. I know the dangers in London. I know not all men are to be trusted. If Rhys gives me his word as a gentleman that he will protect Lydia, then I believe him. And if he breaks his word, I'll kill him."

"You'd have to stand in line behind me," her mother said.

Lydia knew her mother was not issuing an idle threat. Another reason she thought it wise not to mention how involved her relationship with Rhys had become.

Rhys cleared his throat. "I shall endeavor to ensure

neither of you has reason to wish me ill. I'll look after your daughter as though she were the rarest of jewels."

Not exactly what Lydia wanted from him. She'd rather he look after her as though she were his wife.

He looked off to the side. "Yes, Rawlings. What is it?"

Rawlings walked farther into the room, silver tray in hand. "An invitation has arrived, Your Grace. For Miss Westland."

"Oh!" Lydia popped up and removed the invitation from the tray. With trembling fingers she opened it. She pressed a hand to her mouth, smiling broadly.

"It's from Lord and Lady Whithaven. I've been invited to the ball they're hosting next week."

She knelt in front of her mother. "Look at it, Mama. Isn't it the most beautiful invitation you've ever seen? I arrived too late to get a written invitation from Gina. She simply accepted my presence because she and Lauren are such close friends." She flattened the card against her chest. "This is an official invitation."

She looked at her mother imploringly. "Oh, Mama, please say I can go."

"Who is this Lady Whithaven?" she asked.

Lydia shook her head. "Lauren pointed her out to me, but I wasn't actually introduced to her. Someone I met must have spoken to her on my behalf."

She gazed over at Rhys, who seemed neither pleased nor surprised by the invitation. "Do you know Lady Whithaven?"

"We have a passing acquaintance."

"So you can reassure Mama that Lady Whithaven won't corrupt me?"

"Lydia!" her mother exclaimed. "I don't expect anyone here to corrupt you. I simply don't know these people. In Fortune I know everyone. It's so large in London, so crowded, with too many people. I could never be comfortable here. I don't understand why you think you would be. But I can see you're determined to at least experience it fully." Gently she cradled Lydia's chin. "So stay. Have your Season. Then come home."

"Promise you'll write every day."

"I will." Lydia hugged her mother tightly. "I will."

Her entire family was gathered in front of the Ravenleigh house. The Harrington coach was waiting to whisk them off, so they could board their ship and sail back to Texas. Lydia hadn't expected this moment to be so difficult.

Tears stung her eyes, as she leaned away from her mother. Tears of joy, because she was going to stay. Tears of sadness, because she'd never in her life said good-bye to her mother. She hardly knew where to begin. Her books didn't advise her regarding this situation.

She could see her mother valiantly fighting back her own tears as she turned to her sister. "Elizabeth, you take care of my little girl."

"I will. Don't worry. I've had nine years now in this country. It's much tamer than Texas, believe me."

Lydia glanced over at Lauren. She was practically bubbling with joy because Lydia had been granted permission to stay. She expected them both to take London by storm now.

"Will you write to me, too, Lyd?" Sabrina asked.

She looked down at her sister and tugged on her braid. "Every day. And you'll have to send me pictures every day."

"I will." Her voice warbled.

Lydia knelt and drew her sister close.

"I'm going to miss you, Lyd."

"I'll miss you, too."

"You won't stay forever, will you?"

She was very much aware of Rhys watching her. His presence provided her with the strength to let go.

"Not forever," she hedged. Even if she did marry and live here, she would visit home often. She wondered at what point children stopped thinking of the place where they grew up as home.

She released Sabrina and quickly found Rhys holding her elbow, helping her to rise. Awareness shot through her, and she realized it was indeed wise that she would no longer be staying at his house. She had no will to resist him.

She turned to Colton and held out her arms.

He scrunched up his face and hunched his shoulders. "Ah, Lyd," he muttered.

"You won't see me for months and months. Give me a proper good-bye."

He shuffled over like a man approaching a hanging tree. And then his arms came around her with such strength and tightness she almost lost her balance. How like a male to put on an unemotional display in front of others when he privately felt as sorry to see her staying behind as the others.

Was there ever a way for a woman to understand the complexities of a man?

Colton suddenly broke free as though he realized he might have revealed too much of what he felt. She ruffled his hair. "Give Johnny a hug for me."

"Not on your life!" he yelled with disgust. "I ain't hugging him. Bad enough I had to hug you."

She smiling gaily, trying to maintain control for

what would be the most difficult of good-byes. Her stepfather stepped in front of her and took her hands.

"When I first saw you, you were a skinny little thing with large eyes. You listened to my stories with wonder and awe. How was I to have known then that watching you grow up would be one of the greatest joys of my life? I did not give you to your mother, but she has shared you with me. I could not love you more than your own father would have had he lived.

"Love is a journey, Lydia. Sometimes you have to travel far to find it. Sometimes you discover it has been beside you all along. I lived a good deal of my life without it, and I would not wish that on you.

"But in your search, remember this: choose well and wisely. But should you not, know our affections for you will not falter and that your home will always be where we are."

"I love you so much, Papa." She flung her arms around his neck. Tears rolled onto her cheeks. He was the one who'd taught her to dream of things that stretched far beyond Fortune.

He held her tightly, rocking her gently. "All I want is for you to be happy."

She nodded, her cheek rubbing against his. She moved back and began swiping the tears from her eyes.

"Here, use my handkerchief," Rhys said.

She took the linen with the single initial, an R, embroidered in crimson decorating the corner. She dabbed at her tears, part of her questioning if staying was the right thing to do. Part of her knowing she had no choice. Otherwise, she would always wonder what might have been.

Her stepfather held out his hand to Rhys. Rhys hesitated, before grasping her stepfather's hand.

"I shall do all in my power to ensure her happiness," Rhys said.

"I've no doubt you will," her stepfather said. "I hope in the process you'll find your own happiness."

Rhys nodded brusquely before releasing her stepfather's hand and stepping back. She wondered if he were capable of being happy.

"You'd best be off," Rhys said. "I would not want you to miss your ship."

"Quite so. We've already cabled Johnny to let him know when to expect us. Wouldn't want him to send a posse out to track us down," her stepfather said lightly.

"Posse?" Rhys murmured. "Yours is quite a different world, Grayson."

Lydia didn't think she'd ever heard Rhys call her stepfather by name. She was more surprised by the affection he seemed to have woven into the word.

"If I had it to do over, Rhys, I would have taken you with me," her stepfather said quietly.

"But life does not give us second chances. We must make the best of what we have and be content."

Like the fluttering of a butterfly's wings, her stepfather's gaze came to rest on her briefly.

"Do not be so certain second chances do not exist," her stepfather said. "The secret is to recognize them when they are offered, seize them with both hands, and make the most of them." He turned away. "All right, now! We need to be off."

Another flurry of tight hugs and hastily given kisses on the cheeks followed. Lydia stayed as close to her parents as she could, while everyone clambered into the coach.

"Remember to write!"

"Have a good journey!"

"We love you!"

"Take care now!"

"Don't worry! We'll look after Lydia!"

"Have fun, Lyd!"

"I will."

A last squeezing of hands, a final farewell.

Then the coach was rolling away, clattering over the street. Lydia pressed a balled fist to her breast to prevent the unexpected ache in her heart from growing.

Rhys came to stand behind her. She felt the warmth in his nearness; the strength and sturdiness in his presence.

"You'll be too busy to miss them," he said somberly.

She shook her head. "No, love doesn't work that way." She angled her head thoughtfully and gazed back at him. "But you don't know enough about love to realize that, do you?"

Lauren grabbed Lydia's hand. "Come on. We need to begin planning our strategy for the Whithaven ball."

With one last look at Rhys, Lydia followed Lauren into the house. What she intended was to plan her strategy for convincing Rhys they belonged together.

Chapter 19

"The seamstress did an excellent job in so short a time," Lauren said.

Glancing at her reflection, Lydia had to agree. The gown of white satin revealed her shoulders and the barest hint of her breasts. The sleeves were puffed and made of lace. Draped gauze and ruffles flowed across the skirt and along the train. Everything was trimmed in the palest of pink. A pink that matched the rose buds nestled in her hair, hair piled on her head in the loveliest of curls.

Lydia, Lauren, and Aunt Elizabeth had made the rounds of all the best shops in London. Lydia felt as though she was truly ready to make her debut. Her new debut. Tonight she would be a success.

And Rhys would be beside her.

She looked at Lauren, sitting up in bed, beneath a mound of blankets.

"I wish you were going with me," Lydia said.

Lauren sneezed and wiped her nose. "I feel rotten. A cold in summer is the worst. But it should only last another day or so, and then we can go to the balls together. Besides, it won't hurt for Harrington to have you all to himself."

"He tells me that he loves me, but he won't marry me."

Lauren laughed. "He may change his mind after seeing you tonight. Make him jealous. Flirt and dance with every man save him. Drive him mad from wanting you."

"You make it sound so easy."

A brisk knock and the door opened. Aunt Elizabeth peered inside. "The Duke is here."

Lydia took a deep breath. "Wish me luck."

"You won't need it. You look smashing."

Clutching her fan, she followed Aunt Elizabeth down the stairs. "I don't know why I'm more nervous tonight than I was before."

Her aunt squeezed her arm. "You look lovely. Harrington is determined that things will go well for you tonight, so I'm sure they will. Besides, Lady Sachse is offering her endorsement, and that should go a long way."

"Lady Sachse?"

Her aunt looked surprised. "I thought you knew. She's with Harrington. She'll serve as your chaperone, and she's well connected among the aristocracy. More so than I am. I simply never could force myself to care about all these things."

They entered the foyer, and Lydia nearly forgot to breathe at the sight of Rhys dressed in his evening finery. His black, swallow-tailed coat fit him perfectly.

"My goodness, Rhys, you failed to tell me that she was beautiful."

Only then did Lydia become acutely aware of the woman standing beside him. She was much younger than Lydia had expected of a chaperone. Her brown hair was swept high on her head. Her brown eyes took in every aspect of Lydia's appearance.

"I was under the impression you'd seen her before," Rhys said quietly.

"Well, yes, but since we weren't properly introduced I paid little attention."

He bowed slightly. "Lady Sachse, may I present Miss Lydia Westland."

"You may indeed," Lady Sachse said. "My dear Miss Westland, Rhys has spoken so highly of you. I am quite honored to make your acquaintance at last."

Lydia curtsied. "I'm honored as well."

"Although most of my friends consider Americans to have atrocious accents, I must admit I find yours quite charming," Lady Sachse said.

Lydia wasn't certain why she felt as if she'd been insulted. She smiled. "Thank you."

"You will be thanking me for a great deal more before the evening is over." She patted Rhys's arm. "Come. We must be off to pick up Lord Sachse."

"Your husband?" Lydia asked hopefully.

Lady Sachse laughed. "Oh, no. My dear husband, may he rot in hell, has long since passed away. Archie is a distant cousin whom we will also introduce to London tonight. He graciously took up residence in a smaller Sachse property while allowing me to remain in the larger house. And Harrington graciously offered us his carriage for the evening. So shall we be off?"

* * *

They picked up Lord Sachse and introductions were made. Lydia liked him immediately. He had a ready smile and seemed as fascinated with London as she was. While they traveled to their destination, she and Lady Sachse sat side by side while the gentlemen sat opposite them.

Now they were walking up the steps into Whithaven's residence, following the flow of people. When Lydia entered the entrance hallway, she realized that although Gina's party had been pleasant, it was apparent Lady Whithaven enjoyed giving parties much more.

The festivity was obvious. Fresh flowers adorned almost every inch of the floor and tables. A small group of musicians played in the entrance hall while people walked through. A distant doorway led into what Lydia could see beyond was the ballroom.

"I must confess this is my first ball, and I am terrified of putting my foot wrong," Lord Sachse whispered near her ear.

She smiled at him. "You'll do fine."

"I wish I could look as calm as you."

"I'm nervous as well," she assured him.

"Do you know Whithaven?" he asked.

"No. I've seen the couple, but I haven't been introduced to them."

He grinned. "Then I shall follow your lead as introductions are made."

As they neared the doorway, with Rhys and Lady Sachse entering the ballroom, Lydia could see the couple Lauren had pointed out as being Lord and Lady Whithaven.

Lady Whithaven was truly lovely. She had the greenest eyes Lydia had ever seen. Eyes that suddenly widened when they fell on Rhys. All blood drained from her face as though she'd seen a ghost. Lydia thought the poor woman might swoon as Lady Sachse made introductions.

"I must say," Lord Whithaven said in a booming voice, apparently not noticing his wife's reaction, "that we've all been rather curious about you, Your Grace. It seems no one could remember meeting Quentin's younger brother."

"Quentin and I were not close in years. Neither did we run in the same circles."

Lady Whithaven lowered her gaze and said softly, "Your Grace, we are most honored to have you in our home."

"I am most honored to be here, Lady Whithaven, and to make your acquaintance at last," Rhys said in a low voice.

She lifted her gaze to him, but it seemed to Lydia that the woman wanted to be looking at anyone other than Rhys.

"And may I present Lord Sachse," Lady Sachse said too loudly, as though she, too, had noticed Lady Whithaven's discomfiture and was hoping to distract everyone from it.

"Lord Sachse," Whithaven said. "This seems to be the Season of unknown lords."

"Unknown lords, unknown ladies, to me as well. I daresay I shall have a time of it, trying to remember who everyone is," Lord Sachse said.

"I wouldn't worry overmuch," Whithaven said. "Lady Sachse knows everyone. She'll no doubt help you put names to faces."

"Indeed I shall," Lady Sachse said. "On behalf of the Duke, allow me to present Miss Lydia Westland. The

Duke and I have high expectations regarding the success of her Season."

It was as though her pronouncement was edged in gold.

Lord Whithaven smiled fully at Lydia, giving her his undivided attention. "We are honored to have you."

She bowed. "Thank you, my lord."

"Ah, an American. Not to worry. We shan't hold that against you, will we, my dear?"

Lady Whithaven still seemed rattled as she looked from Rhys to Lydia. "Of course we won't hold it against you." She held out her hand. "Come, I shall introduce you around."

And with that, Lydia was led into the throng.

While Camilla escorted Sachse around the room, introducing him to those who mattered, Rhys stood off to the side near a pot of large fronds. He could sense whenever a lady's startled gaze came to rest on him. He would offer her the barest of nods in acknowledgment, and the lady would quickly look away.

A few gentlemen tried to engage him in discourse. But he had no interest in a lengthy conversation. He merely used the opportunity to make them aware of his relationship with Lydia, and his desire to see her well settled.

Beautiful Lydia, who tonight was the brightest star in the room. No matter where she wandered, he saw her. Smiling with such warmth and joy. Dancing with the finest of gentlemen. Her confidence illuminated her face. He could imagine many a gentleman falling under her spell as he had.

His chest tightened with that thought. He would not deny her happiness, and yet he didn't like to think of her experiencing it with another.

The music ended, and the gentleman with whom she'd been dancing escorted her off the floor and returned her to Rhys.

He waited until the man was out of earshot, before saying, "You liked him."

"I like them all. Tonight is *exactly* what I thought London life would entail." She peered up at him. "You haven't danced."

"I'm in mourning."

She tapped her fan on his arm and batted her eyes. "I'm not certain I like Lady Sachse."

"You should like her very much. She is well connected. Many of these ladies owe a great deal to her, and *these* ladies influence the gentlemen. Do not be fooled. A gentleman may carry the title, but by God, it is his wife who wields its power."

The orchestra again began to play.

"My dance card has an empty spot on it for this dance," Lydia said quietly.

"That will not do." He held out his hand.

She gave him a deliciously wicked smile. "I thought you were in mourning."

"For you, I will make an exception."

She slipped her hand into his, and he led her onto the dance floor. He placed a hand on her waist, while she placed her hand on his shoulder.

"You were made for this," he said quietly, as he guided her through the waltz. "The glitter of London. I've never seen anyone wear it so well."

"I didn't think you'd attended many social events."

"I haven't, but that doesn't mean I haven't an opinion on the matter."

"So many ladies seem surprised to see you here."

"Because I am in mourning."

"That excuse will only take you so far, Your Grace. There's an undercurrent that I can't quite explain."

"Let it go, Lydia. Secrets shared in the dark are best kept there."

"If it's a secret, why do I feel as though everyone knows what it is?"

"Only a very few know, and they will hold their tongues. You should not concern yourself with the ladies, but rather the gentlemen. You are husband hunting, after all."

She glanced around. "I don't think I could ever grow tired of this. It's everything I've always dreamed of and more."

And he intended to ensure she held on to it.

Whithaven was grateful he'd finished welcoming his guests. Although their parading by him gave him an opportunity to scrutinize every man, he had yet to determine who was fornicating with his wife.

The desire to know burned within him. It had taken every ounce of breeding he possessed to stand beside her and not let it show how much he'd come to despise her.

"Still searching for a phantom?" Reynolds asked quietly.

Whithaven glared at Reynolds and Kingston. "No phantom. I went to get a piece of jewelry out of the drawer for her, and I found this stuffed in a back corner."

He unfurled his fingers.

"I take it that is not your handkerchief," Kingston murmured.

"With an R embroidered on it? In crimson? I should say not. Perhaps it's yours, *R*eynolds."

"Good God, don't be ludicrous. Does it stand for his first name or his last? Or his title?" Reynolds asked.

"Perhaps it stands for roué," Kingston speculated. "Not the man's initial at all, but rather a symbol of how he has decided to dedicate his life."

Whithaven crushed the cloth in his fingers and returned it to his pocket. "I would suggest you gentlemen search through your wives' things."

"Invade her drawers?" Reynolds asked, clearly appalled by the notion.

"This man exists. Whether he is one of us or not, he exists. And by God, I shall rout him out."

"Come, Rhys. It's time for you to make your announcement," Camilla said.

Rhys stared at her, uncomprehending. "What announcement?"

"That we are to be married. I told you that I would want an announcement made at the first ball we attended."

He remembered now that she *had* told him. He'd simply been so focused on what he wanted for Lydia that he'd forgotten what he owed Camilla. He glanced around the room, his gaze quickly finding and settling on Lydia. She was laughing, enjoying herself, a gentleman escorting her back to him.

"Our solicitors have yet to meet in order to work out the details," he reminded her.

"A mere formality. Patience has never been my strong suit. I wish people to know that you intend to make a duchess of me."

"Perhaps we should wait for a more opportune moment," he said.

"Whithaven will be calling for you at any second. What can be more opportune than that?"

As though her voice had reached Whithaven's ears, the Earl was suddenly standing on the platform where the orchestra was seated and calling out in his large, booming voice, "May I have your attention, please?"

The murmuring fell into immediate silence. Lydia and her escort stopped and turned to look at Whithaven. Rhys remembered the debacle of Grayson's arrival, because he'd put off what he knew would be unpleasant.

This moment promised to be ten times worse. Not for the world would he hurt Lydia, but a part of him could not help but wonder if this way was for the best. Any hope she had of a life with him would die as surely as the flame on a candle was snuffed with little more than the pressure of two fingers.

"I know we all felt sorrow at the passing of the Duke of Harrington. Tonight we are honored to have his successor in our midst, and we welcome him. I have been informed he has a rather special announcement to make."

"Make it count, Rhys," Camilla whispered. "Or your lady shall find this is the last ball she attends."

"For you, Camilla, I shall follow in my father's footsteps." He made his way toward Whithaven, realizing that indeed he had far more in common with his father than he'd ever realized. He would marry one woman while forever loving another. How had his father managed to find the strength to do it?

Years of marriage to the old Sachse had proven Camilla barren. Rhys did not have to concern himself with how his children would feel to know their father did not love their mother. For that he was grateful. He would find an heir elsewhere in the family.

As he stepped onto the false flooring, he gave Whithaven a brusque nod before turning his attention to the crowd.

"I am new to the title and certain to make many missteps along the way," he said, "but I am certain of this. I shall love only once and that it shall be forever. It is with honor that I announce my intention to ask Lady Sachse for her hand in marriage."

Escape! Escape! It was all Lydia could think. She had to escape. Turning her shoulders this way and that, she wended her way through the crowd until she reached the doors that led into the garden.

She had no strength in her hand as she struggled to turn the knob. No strength in her legs as she stumbled outside. She was trembling and nauseated, while chills cascaded through her. She staggered to the railing and gripped it with icy fingers.

He'd sworn to her that he would never marry. And now he intended to marry Lady Sachse!

Lydia had been such a fool. She'd asked him to teach her what her books didn't. And he'd taught her how painful a shattered heart could be.

She'd wanted to stay in London to have more time with him. She'd thought if he saw her in lovely ball gowns, if he saw that she was poised and graceful, if he saw that she truly belonged in this world, then he'd cast his doubts aside.

Instead he'd cast her aside.

"Miss Westland? Are you well?"

Lord Sachse. She recognized his voice, heard his concern for her. Tears stung her eyes. She took a deep, shuddering breath. She had to get control of herself.

She swallowed hard, trying to eliminate the tingling in her jaw. She would not be sick here.

"Yes, my lord, I'm fine, thank you."

"Are you certain? I saw you leave, and you seemed quite pale."

"The crowds," she stammered. "I'm not accustomed to the crowds. In Texas, you can walk forever and not run into anyone. In there, suddenly I felt like the walls, the people, the paintings, everything was closing in on me."

"I thought perhaps it was the shock of the Duke's announcement," he said kindly.

She shook her head quickly. "No, of course not. Why would I care who he intends to marry?"

"I noticed the way you looked at him while you danced." He cleared his throat. "I must apologize. I am an absolute buffoon, hardly well versed in protocol. Perhaps my bumbling efforts would best be served by bringing you a bit of punch. Then perhaps you would do me the honor of dancing with me."

She nodded, wondering how in God's name she would make it through the remainder of the evening. "Yes, yes, to both." She turned her head slightly, trying to be polite without revealing her tears. "Thank you. And you're not a buffoon."

He bowed slightly. "You are most gracious. I won't be but a moment."

He dashed off, and she gave her attention back to the garden smothered in darkness. She really didn't care if he never returned. She was torn between weeping uncontrollably and maintaining a measure of decorum. Weeping was winning the battle.

"Lydia?"

Oh, God. Rhys. She wouldn't weep in front of him, wouldn't let him see how badly he'd hurt her. She would rise to the occasion and show him what a true lady she was.

"Your Grace. Congratulations are in order." She cursed her voice for quivering.

"A dozen times I'd considered telling you, but I was always at a loss for words," he said quietly.

"You seemed to have had no trouble finding the words only moments ago when you announced your intention to marry."

"I know you must think I took advantage—"

She spun around, her fists clenched, her chest aching. "Why her? Why her and not me?"

"It's complicated."

"I'm not simpleminded, Rhys. Explain it to me."

"I can't."

She laughed, a hideous sound that erupted from within her and reached hysterical heights before she managed to control it. "You can't or you won't?"

"I won't."

She looked past him to where Lord Sachse stood, crystal cup in hand, obviously not certain if he should intrude. She smiled brightly and held out her hand. "My lord, thank you."

He approached cautiously and gave her the cup. She drank the contents in one long swallow, then ran her tongue around her mouth in a way that she was certain would make Rhys's gut knot up. She extended the cup to him.

Startled, he took it.

"If you'll excuse me, Your Grace, I'm going to go have some fun."

She placed her hand on Sachse's arm and allowed him to lead her back into the ballroom.

"Well done," he whispered with a smile just before he took her into his arms for their dance.

She might have believed him if it weren't for the fact that she felt such a fool for loving so desperately a man incapable of loving her. Because if he did love her as he claimed, why would he not risk everything for their happiness?

"Dear God, you love her."

Standing in a corner with his intended beside him so that they could receive well wishes from the guests, he could not help but notice Lydia—no matter where she was or with whom. She had danced every dance since she reentered the ballroom. A different gentleman each time.

Her smile grew, her eyes sparkled, and she laughed lightly. If her heart was breaking, she was doing a splendid job of putting it back together. For which he was grateful. Better to have harmed her a little, than to have broken her completely.

"I said—"

"I heard you," he replied.

"You're not going to spend the remainder of your life comparing me to her, are you?"

He actually smiled, although he doubted his expression carried any mirth. "There is no comparison to be made."

Lydia far outshone the woman standing beside him: in beauty, elegance, grace, humor, kindness, compassion. The list was without end. She possessed the finest aspects of a lady. Something she had not learned from her books. The intricate weaving of her soul that had created a woman he would love until he died.

"She is a success tonight, Rhys. You should take comfort in that."

"I fear I nearly broke her."

"Don't flatter yourself. She'll get over you quickly enough."

"I can only hope."

As for himself, he would never get over her. She would be his last thought when he took his final breath. Beautiful Lydia who called out his name during the throes of passion.

Sweet Lydia. A dreamer who had fallen in love with a realist.

"He did what?" Lauren asked, sitting up in bed.

"He declared his intention to marry Lady Sachse," Lydia said, repeating what she'd announced when she'd burst into Lauren's room only a moment earlier.

Clutching her handkerchief, Lauren sniffed. "I don't understand."

"And you think I do? Driving home in the carriage with him and that horrid woman was almost intolerable. I thought I'd suffocate."

"Lady Sachse is highly thought of."

"Well, I don't think much of her." Lydia dropped into a chair, not softly as a lady ought to, but as someone facing defeat.

Lauren blew her nose and settled back beneath the covers. "My head is so stuffed that I can hardly think."

"I'm sorry. I know I shouldn't bother you now—"

"No, no." Lauren fluttered her hand. "I didn't mean that. I'm simply confused. I was absolutely certain that you held his heart."

Lydia had felt the same. She'd thought all he really

needed was time. Time to see that she wore the glitter of London well and that she belonged. Time to realize she belonged with *him*.

"He says because he cares for me so much he won't marry me. He claims that he's done something he's ashamed of, something that would destroy me."

"That makes no sense," Lauren said. "If that were the case, why risk harming Lady Sachse?"

"Exactly."

"So, he must have lied to you about the possibility of scandal. Obviously, Lydia, he's toyed with you."

Could that be? Could she be that naïve? He'd frequently mentioned her innocence, but she didn't feel that he'd taken advantage. For some reason, he would risk hurting Lady Sachse, but not Lydia. Why?

"He toyed with you," Lauren continued, "and wanted to dash any hope you had of marrying him. Thus, his announcement that he intends to wed Lady Sachse. So you will move on to someone else."

Yes, that made sense. He wanted her to move on.

"Oh, Lauren, until he made his announcement, tonight was everything I'd ever thought London would be and more. I danced every dance. The gentlemen were charming. The formality. The beautiful gowns. The orchestra. I adored all of it so much more tonight because I was accepted, drawn into the center of it all. I don't want to leave it."

"Then don't. My goodness, Lydia, there are gentlemen aplenty. We shall simply have to find you one more deserving than Harrington. My stepfather can interview them for you."

"No, Rhys offered to provide that service. I like the idea of forcing him to see that other men find me worthy."

"That's a girl!"

Lydia sighed, unable to embrace Lauren's enthusiasm for the idea. She was trying to be strong, trying to be brave, when all she really wanted to do was crawl into a ball and weep. Strange, how at this moment she recalled the Duchess sitting beside her Duke. The woman had given no indication that she'd abhorred the presence of their guests. She'd maintained her dignity.

Lydia had never thought that she would hold the Duchess up as an example of proper behavior. Upon reflection, it seemed she'd learned almost as much from the woman as she had from her son.

It was easy to hold up her head when the world was to her liking. Lydia was determined to prove to Rhys that she was not easily defeated when things didn't go as she'd hoped.

And if at all possible, torment him in the process.

Chapter 20

A lady must recognize that levity in a gentleman is not to be tolerated, and therefore,
must not be encouraged.

Miss Westland's Blunders in
Behavior Corrected

True courtship was not at all as Lydia had envisioned it would be.

She and her aunt had arrived at Rhys's house shortly
after lunch. They were taking a stroll through the garden when the Earl of Langston had arrived. Lydia had
been summoned. Her aunt had decided to continue to
enjoy the garden. After all, Rhys was Lydia's stepfather's brother. She trusted him. As Lydia knew, chaperones meant much more to the English than to the
Americans.

The Earl of Langston had been shown to the parlor,
where she'd quickly joined him. Now they both sat quietly and properly in plush chairs with a small table between them. He had a delicate teacup set on a saucer
balanced on one thigh, his bowler hat on the other.

She couldn't imagine any man she knew in Texas
drinking from a teacup without breaking it, much less
balancing it on his thigh. She hadn't dared to pick up

hers for fear it would rattle and betray her nervousness.

Although it wasn't the Earl who had her on edge, it was the Duke standing stiffly before the window, his back to them as though he wanted to give them privacy. Privacy for what, she couldn't imagine. English courting seemed to comprise little more than darting glances at each other and blushing.

She judged the Earl to be not much older than she was, and he was extremely pleasing to look at. His blond hair formed a curly halo around his head. His long sideburns were more peach fuzz than true whiskers. His posture was beyond reproach, his clothes well tailored. If she believed in judging a book by its cover, she'd have to admit the Earl might make a fine husband.

But she found herself wondering how his kisses might compare with those Rhys had bestowed on her. Would the Earl be capable of heating her body with nothing more than a light touch? Did he possess the ability to make her laugh? Or even to smile? Would he over the years fill her with joy?

Or as Rhys had also done, would he anger her beyond reason, betray her heart and call it compassion.

"I say, Miss Westland," the Earl began in a deep baritone that nearly had her jumping out of her skin, "I've often wondered why it was that North America went to war against South America. Perhaps you would be so kind as to enlighten me."

She stared at the man with the raised eyebrow who seemed to be looking down his narrow patrician nose at her. She felt the color rise in her cheeks, because she didn't have a clue regarding the war to which he was referring.

"I'm sorry, my lord, but I don't recall that particular war."

"You don't say? I rather thought it was all the talk some years back. I remember my father discussing it and mentioning the war's bitterness was responsible for the assassination of your President Lincoln."

She angled her head thoughtfully. "Are you referring to the War Between the North and South?"

Smiling brightly, he nodded enthusiastically. "Yes, by Jove, I believe that was it. Why did North America take such an interest in a neighbor so far away?"

It occurred to her that he might be teasing her. Maybe he had a wry sense of humor, but the seriousness in his eyes indicated he was indeed searching for an answer to his question.

"Not North America. The northern states of America. They fought the southern states."

His smile dwindled. "I'm not quite certain I follow what you're saying."

She sighed, unable to determine exactly how involved he wanted the history lesson to be. "Well, the United States is divided into states, as I'm sure you know."

He neither nodded nor confirmed in any way that he did indeed know that little fact.

"It was a very complicated war. Slavery divided the states, forced those in the South to decide they no longer wanted to be part of the Union, part of the United States. They wanted to establish their own government so they could govern themselves, establish their own laws."

He began blinking rapidly and shaking his head. "But I distinctly remember it was the North against the South."

"Yes, the northern states against the southern states."

"North America against South America."

She shook her head. "No, not really."

"Then I don't understand."

"Good God, man!" Rhys bellowed from his corner, startling Lydia and causing her to issue a tiny screech.

Apparently he'd scared the Earl of Langston as well, because his cup and saucer landed at his feet with a small kerplunk and a faint ringing as china tapped against china. Thank goodness, the thick carpet prevented the pieces from breaking, although Lydia thought the cup might have chipped. The Earl now stared openmouthed at the Duke.

"Have you never taken a history lesson?" Rhys demanded to know. "Have you never gazed upon a map?"

"Certainly, Your Grace, I've managed to accomplish both."

"Then how is it you are unable to comprehend what Miss Westland has adequately explained?"

"I . . . I don't know."

She watched in stunned fascination as Rhys withdrew his watch from his pocket, clicked open the lid, glanced at it, and snapped it closed. "Your time is up, sir."

The Earl bobbed his head like an apple in a bucket of water. "Yes, Your Grace." He lunged to his feet, looked down at his teacup and up at Lydia, his face reddening. "I'm frightfully sorry."

She rose as well and smiled. "Don't worry about it."

"It was my immense pleasure to visit with you, Miss Westland. Will you do me the honor of allowing me to call upon you again?"

She was on the verge of saying yes when Rhys barked, "No, sir, we will not so honor you."

"Very good," the young man said, repeatedly bowing as he scurried out of the room.

When the door closed behind him, Lydia turned to her benefactor. "You were rude!"

"He's densely slow. I was appalled by his lack of knowledge."

"Because he doesn't know the particulars of a war that took place in another country and began nearly two decades ago?"

"You are an extremely intelligent woman, Lydia. I will not have you marry a man who will bore you to tears five minutes after he's placed his signature upon the marriage documents."

She took a step toward him, angling her chin. "And you're going to be the one to determine who will bore me to tears and who will not?"

He took a step nearer to her. "Indeed I shall."

She took another step closer. "What qualifications will you use to determine that he won't bore me?"

Another step. "He'll keep abreast of current affairs."

She took another step, placing herself close enough that she could almost feel the heat of his body. "And you think that will be enough to keep me entertained?"

"Hardly. He shall also have a thorough knowledge of history, both British and American."

"Do you intend to give him some sort of examination?"

"Perhaps I will."

He dropped his gaze to her mouth. She parted her lips slightly and ran her tongue around the inner edge, watching as his eyes darkened and his own lips parted.

"What else must he know?" she asked, surprised by the husky nature of her voice.

"He must know the art . . ." His voice trailed off.

"Paintings, music, theater," she mused.

"Of seduction." He lowered his mouth—

The door opened and he jumped back before his lips could press against hers. Having grown dizzy with anticipation, Lydia was surprised she remained standing as the room spun around her.

"Yes, Rawlings," Rhys demanded.

Hearing the dignified click of the butler's steps, she strolled to the window, looked out on the garden, and wished for a fan to cool her heated skin. Why was she so unable to resist him—even when she was furious with him?

"Two more gentlemen have come to call on Miss Westland," Rawlings said.

She glanced over her shoulder in time to see Rhys lift the men's cards from the silver tray held by Rawlings.

"Viscount Sandoval," he read aloud before shaking his head and returning one card to the tray. "We are not at home for anyone less than an earl. You may tell the Earl of Carlyle, however, that we are available, and you may show him in."

"Very good, Your Grace."

"Please send a maid to clean up the spill the previous suitor made. Miss Westland and Carlyle will enjoy their tea by the window."

"Very good, Your Grace." He made a very stately exit.

"You're going to tell the Viscount we're not at home when we are at home?" she asked incredulously.

"Did your books not explain that it gives no insult when you tell someone you are not at home?"

"I think you're being rude again."

"Be that as it may, I am quite serious that we will not consider anyone of a lesser rank than earl."

"Even if he's intelligent?"

"I have a set of standards, Lydia. We shall endeavor

to find a man who meets all the requirements, not merely a handful of them."

"Perhaps you should further enlighten me as to what these qualifications are since I'm the one who'll be marrying the man."

A tap on the door, and her discussion with Rhys came to an abrupt halt. The door opened, and Rawlings walked in followed by a young man. He had straight brown hair and bushy side whiskers. His puppy-dog brown eyes spoke of intelligence.

"Carlyle," Rhys said succinctly. "You are welcome to join Miss Westland by the window."

"Thank you, Your Grace." He hurried over and smiled brightly at her, obviously assuming he'd passed her benefactor's first test.

Lydia sat, and he quickly followed suit.

"Carlyle, Miss Westland and I were just discussing America's civil war. Are you familiar with it?"

"Indeed I am, Your Grace."

"Perhaps you would be kind enough to share with us what you know."

"Certainly."

While Rhys positioned himself before the fireplace, Lydia smiled at her latest suitor, as though she truly cared about the different reasons that had caused a fracture in her country. His eagerness was charming. His knowledge immense. And when he was sitting, it was almost—almost, not quite—impossible to tell that when he stood, he barely reached Lydia's shoulder.

As her latest suitor turned to leave the room, Lydia closed her eyes. She'd bounced back and forth between the chairs by the window and those in the center of the room. Now she was again in the middle of the room where her afternoon had started.

"We are no longer home, Rawlings," Lydia heard Rhys say from the doorway.

Thank God for small favors was all she could think as, with a sigh, she leaned back and rubbed her temples. She'd had four more visitors after Carlyle. One obviously had an affinity for eating foods heavily spiced with garlic. One had been more interested in stuffing the little cakes into his mouth than carrying on a conversation. One had been aged—"like fine wine," he'd joked upon introduction—and had held a horn to his ear to improve his hearing. One had spoken passionately about the girl he wanted to marry if only his obligations to his family didn't require him to marry someone who could help replenish the family coffers.

"Is your head hurting?" Rhys asked quietly.

She moaned in the affirmative. "I never knew courtship could be such a pain."

Although he moved silently through the room, she felt his presence behind her before he placed his hands over hers at her temple.

"Lower your hands," he ordered.

"And why should I do that?"

"Because I can help make your headache go away."

She placed her hands on her lap, and he moved his fingers in a slow circular motion against her temples.

"Where does it hurt?" he asked.

"Everywhere."

He skimmed his hands along the sides of her face, stopping momentarily at the sensitive spots below her ears, before stopping at the base of her neck. He began slowly, gently kneading the tight muscles that sloped down to her shoulders. The change in the pressure and the angle of his hands told her that he'd knelt behind her.

"I would meet with more success at eliminating your pain if you would not object to me taking your hair down. Mary can put it up before you join your aunt."

She didn't particularly want his hands to stop working their magic as he removed her pins, but she imagined he could do a great deal more for her if her hair wasn't fashionably tidy. She decided his statement must have been rhetorical, because before she could give him permission, he'd already begun to pluck her pins free with one hand while the other continued to squeeze and rub.

She recalled a challenge her stepfather had once issued to the children to rub their tummies and pat their heads. They'd all fallen over laughing at their efforts. She had a feeling Rhys would excel at that task.

Her hair began to fall, and the simplicity of not having it piled elaborately on her head eased her headache somewhat. Rhys burying his fingers into her hair and stroking her scalp caused the pain to abate even further.

And when he moved her hair aside and placed his lips against the silky curve of her neck, all the pain vanished.

"You're very good," she said lethargically, as her entire body seemed to melt into the chair.

His hands continued to knead her head, rub her temples, and stroke her ears, while his hot mouth and tongue traveled up and down her neck.

"Is this helping?"

"Definitely. You should consider hiring yourself out."

His hands stilled, and his mouth hovered over her skin. "Pardon?"

"You're much better than a headache draught."

The door suddenly opened, and his fingers flinched against her scalp. Lydia turned her head to see Lady and Lord Sachse standing in the doorway.

"Well, my, my," Lady Sachse said, "I suppose I was wrong when I told Rawlings we had no need to have our arrival properly announced."

Rhys glowered at Camilla. He'd thought her continual habit of showing up uninvited had ended when he'd walked out of her house. He extricated his hands from within the wonderful abundant thickness of Lydia's curls and pushed himself to his feet. "Lydia had a headache after an afternoon of dealing with suitors."

"Well, then, I look forward to head pains after we're wed," Camilla said as she stepped more fully into the room. She angled her head. "Stop shooting darts at me with your eyes, Rhys. It doesn't become you. And you, my dear, needn't bother to pin up your hair. It's really quite beautiful."

Lydia stopped frantically trying to gather up her hair. She cast a quick look at Rhys as he came around to stand in front of her. He gave her a curt nod, and she dropped her hands to her lap.

Camilla made herself at home by sitting in a nearby chair. Lord Sachse moved in to stand beside her, but Rhys was acutely aware the man's gaze never strayed from Lydia.

"Archie has never been to London before," Camilla began. "I can't quite fathom that myself, but be that as it may, I decided to show him a bit of the city, so we've been out riding about in the carriage."

"It's a nice day for it," Rhys murmured, striving not to show how much he resented the intrusion, while at the same time immensely grateful for it. Touching Lydia always seemed to be an unfortunate way to go, because he seemed to have no restraint whatsoever where she was concerned.

"Indeed it is," Camilla said. "And while we were out, I was struck with the most splendid idea. I thought the four of us—you and I, and Miss Westland and Lord Sachse—might attend the concert at Royal Albert Hall this evening."

Rhys shook his head. "As I've indicated, I wish to find a suitable match for Miss Westland. Sitting in a theater hardly suits that purpose."

"Don't be obtuse, Rhys. The Royal Albert Hall is a splendid place to be seen. You don't want the London gentlemen to believe Miss Westland cares about nothing more than dancing. Being American, she is at a decided disadvantage. She needs to be seen as having a bit of culture, not being totally barbaric."

"I assume you're aware that I *am* in the room," Lydia stated defiantly.

Rhys snapped his attention to her. Camilla did the same. Sachse's attention had never wavered from Lydia.

Lydia gave Rhys a pointed look. "I'd like to attend the concert." She looked at Camilla. "As for my having a bit of culture, I'll have you know that a traveling Shakespearean theater group put on a wonderful performance of *Hamlet* in Uncle Harry's saloon. I enjoyed it immensely."

Sachse coughed, no doubt trying to hide his laughter, while Camilla seemed uncertain what she should say. Rhys as always was charmed with his little dreamer.

Camilla finally managed, "I'm not sure how the

Royal Albert Hall will compare with Uncle Harry's *saloon*. You will no doubt find it lacking, but shall we give it a go?"

"Retract your claws, Camilla," Rhys said, his voice vibrating with warning.

"I believe Miss Westland is fully capable of defending herself, Your Grace," Sachse said. He smiled warmly at Lydia. "I must admit to being entirely without culture. Although Shakespeare is one of my passions, I've never had the luxury of attending a play. Neither have I attended a concert such as I hear this one is. I would be honored if you would accompany me this evening."

"I would be honored to do so, my lord," Lydia said, returning his smile.

"Then it's all settled," Camilla announced as she stood. "You will send your carriage around for us, won't you, Rhys?"

"Of course."

She smiled brightly. "Then we'll see you this evening."

She began strolling from the room. Sachse gave a polite bow. "Your Grace. Miss Westland. I look forward to this evening."

He followed Camilla out and shut the door. Lydia came to her feet, and her hair tumbled around her, down her back, stopping short once it had curled over her backside. Rhys grasped his hands behind his back to stop himself from reaching for her.

"You won't be happy if you marry her," Lydia said.

His happiness never had been a consideration. His only concern remained *her* happiness. "She and I are cut of the same cloth."

"She acts as though she owns you."

In many ways, perhaps she did. Certainly she knew more about him than most.

"How is your head now?" he asked, having no interest in a discourse on his selection of a bride.

She rubbed her neck. "It's fine. I think I'll see if Aunt Elizabeth is ready to leave, so I'll have time to take a nap before we go out tonight."

He took a hesitant step toward her. "How are you feeling otherwise?"

Sadness touched her eyes. "I should have had my menses by now."

"Perhaps your body simply has not adjusted to being in England."

She gave him what he thought she intended to be a smile, but instead looked like a weary, disappointed imitation. "We'll hope that's what it is."

She strolled from the room without another word. He strode to the cabinet to fix himself a stiff drink.

Damnation! Part of him desperately wished he'd be forced to marry her, while a part of him feared dragging her into his hell.

"Truthfully, my dear, how does this compare with Uncle Harry's *saloon*?" Camilla asked.

Sitting with Lord Sachse on her left, Rhys on her right, Lydia stared in wonder at the majestic domed ceiling, the balconies circling above her. She might have thanked Rhys for separating her from the she-cat, but Lydia was determined that nothing would spoil her evening.

She could hardly take it all in. "It's magnificent."

"Does it hold a few more people than Uncle Harry's *saloon*?"

"Camilla," Rhys said softly, a warning purring in his voice.

Lydia looked past him to where Camilla sat. "You can be as mean-spirited as you like, you won't ruin my enjoyment of the evening."

Camilla angled her head haughtily. "My dear, I had no plans to even attempt to ruin this night for you."

Liar, Lydia thought. Unable to contain her excitement over the building, she squeezed Rhys's arm. "I wish Mama could have seen this place. Much more impressive than the Chamber of Horrors."

"Perhaps she'll have reason to return to London, and we'll be sure to bring her."

We'll? She'd thought once she married someone else that Rhys would be out of her life completely, forever. Spending any time at all with him now was bittersweet.

She greedily devoured any moment he gave her, knowing each success carried him further away. She still couldn't understand why he'd subject himself to life with such a coldhearted woman as the one who sat beside him now.

What was it that gave Camilla such a strong hold on him?

With Rhys looking into her eyes, Lydia was in danger of forgetting another person completed their party. She turned to Lord Sachse, who seemed inordinately pleased she'd done so.

"What do you think of the place?" she asked.

He smiled warmly. "I feel quite overwhelmed."

"I think I could use every complimentary word in the dictionary and fall short of giving this building its due."

He leaned a little nearer, as though to impart a secret. "I have heard it said that the organ should be considered the eighth wonder of the world."

"Do you think they'll play it tonight?"

"I should hope so."

She sat back and sighed deeply. "I think it's magnificent." She laughed lightly. "I said that already, didn't I?"

"Indeed you did, but I, for one, never tire of hearing your enthusiasm."

"Sometimes my enthusiasm can be very unladylike," she assured him.

"I should never find honest enthusiasm such. What of you, Your Grace? Do you not find the lady's enthusiasm most enjoyable?"

Rhys was watching her intently, and she wondered if he was remembering the times he'd curbed her enthusiasm—and the times he hadn't.

"Her enthusiasm adds immensely to the enjoyment of my evening," he said.

"And you, Lady Sachse?" Lord Sachse asked.

She pressed a hand to her chest. "For a moment there, I thought everyone had forgotten I was here."

"You must forgive us, dear lady," Sachse said. "I suspect you find it rather tedious to have to listen to those of us who are not accustomed to the majesty this building offers."

"On the contrary, I am pleased my suggestion to attend tonight has met with such approval."

"You were very kind to include me in your plans," Lydia said, trying to set aside her dislike for the woman, striving to be as gracious as she believed a lady should be.

"Not at all, my dear. The more you are seen, the more likely you are to catch someone's fancy. The sooner you are wed, the sooner shall I be."

Lydia snapped her gaze to Rhys. She saw a muscle in

his cheek tighten as he stared straight ahead. His situation with Lady Sachse was beginning to make sense. He'd told her many among the aristocracy married for reasons other than love. His reason for marrying Lady Sachse was suddenly obviously, painfully clear.

Lydia had been mistaken. Lady Sachse did have the power to ruin her enjoyment of the evening.

Rhys had despised watching Lydia's enthusiasm for the evening wane. She blamed exhaustion from her earlier excitement, claiming it had worn her out.

But as the carriage traveled through London, Rhys suspected Camilla's unfortunate comment was more to blame. Damn the woman for not knowing when to hold her tongue.

Lydia was no fool. She would piece the puzzle together, and in all likelihood, she would not fancy the picture she saw.

Sachse sat beside him now while the ladies sat opposite. Camilla, at least, was keeping her sharp tongue behind her teeth. He was of a good mind not to carry through on his offer to marry her, but he understood Camilla's claws were far reaching. He'd bargained with Satan's bride, and now he would reign in hell.

The carriage slowed and stopped. Before Sachse could react, Rhys said, "I'll see Miss Westland to the door."

The footman helped her out of the carriage. Rhys followed, walking beside her. He'd expected to have to rush after her, but there was no hurry to her step. He was not certain what he wanted to say or why it had bothered him so much to notice that Sachse had not taken his eyes off Lydia during the entire concert.

That the man was quite taken with her was obvious.

But he knew as little of London as she did. He was not nearly worldly enough. Rhys could only hope another gentleman would offer for her. And soon.

Gracefully she ascended the steps, stopping well short of the door.

"You bargained with her," she said softly, not meeting his gaze.

"She is well connected with the Marlborough House Set. She has influence where I do not."

"She's the one who is making sure that I have invitations to more balls than I could possibly attend."

"Yes."

She glanced up at him then. "In exchange for what?"

He shrugged as though it was of no consequence. "She will become my duchess."

"She'll make you miserable."

"I'll see you happy, Lydia, at any and all cost."

"You don't love her."

"No, but neither does she love me. It is a fair trade."

He saw tears welling in her eyes, before she looked away. "The price is too high to you."

"Not if I say it isn't."

"If I don't get married—"

"Nothing will change for me. I will still marry Camilla. Our agreement was that she would see you accepted into polite society. She has succeeded. That she has graciously agreed to wait for our wedding until you are settled is a credit to her."

She shook her head.

"Whether you marry or return to Texas, I shall wed her. You might as well finish the Season and continue your search for a suitable husband."

"You're selling yourself."

"It is not the first time."

Her head snapped around, her eyes searching his face.

"You have not lived in the world I have seen, Lydia. Not all of London is glitter and gold. Marriage to Camilla will be silver at best."

"And at worst?"

"Tolerable." He cupped her chin, holding her gaze. "Find your happiness, so I might rejoice in it. For the price has already been paid."

Chapter 21

⌒⌒⌒

Rhys was not one to panic easily, but as he alighted from his carriage in front of Ravenleigh's house, he couldn't help but be alarmed. Lydia's note had been delivered to him only a short while ago. It had simply stated she was not up to receiving gentlemen today.

What the deuce did that mean?

He had a strong suspicion that after her discovery the night before—the bargain he'd struck with Camilla in order to reap benefits on Lydia—she'd decided she no longer wanted to be the belle of London. She was too independent by half, too certain her love could withstand all things.

How tempted he was to put her to the test.

He strode through Ravenleigh's door—a man on a mission. It did not improve his disposition to see Lauren gliding down the stairs.

"Your Grace, I saw your carriage arrive. Is something amiss?"

"I've come to talk with Miss Westland. If you will please fetch her for me."

"I can't do that."

In the process of removing his gloves, he stilled. "Pardon?"

"She's not quite well."

"What do you mean she's not well?"

Lauren blushed. "She simply wants to stay in bed."

"Is she fevered?" he asked as he rushed past her and up the stairs.

"No, Your Grace."

"Is food not agreeing with her?"

"I don't believe she's tried to eat."

"Breathing, then. Is she having difficulty breathing?"

"No, Your Grace."

All sorts of images ran through his mind. Devastating illnesses. The air in London was not as fresh as the air in the country. He would return her to the country where she could breathe the purest of air.

He reached the hallway. "Which room is hers?"

"Your Grace, this is entirely inappropriate—"

He spun around and pinned her with his most intimidating glare. "Which room?"

She pointed to a nearby door.

He gave her a brusque nod. "Thank you."

He crossed over to it and flung it open without begging entrance. She was curled on her side on the bed. The only light was that which spilled in from the hallway, and yet he could still see that she was incredibly pale.

His throat tightened as he knelt beside the bed and took her limp hand in his. "Lydia?"

Her eyes fluttered open, and she gave him a weak smile. "I sent you a note. Didn't you get it?"

"It told me nothing." He brushed strands of hair from her brow. "You're ill?"

"No, not really. But neither am I with child."

He heard the disappointment in her soft voice, felt a stab of regret in his own heart. He slid his gaze to where he knew her hips were resting beneath the covers. "It's for the best," he said distractedly, unconvincingly.

He shifted his attention back to her. "Is it this bad for you every month?"

He could see a little color returning to her cheeks.

"Not usually. I guess it's just all the traveling and excitement. I'm just worn out."

Nodding, he glanced toward the doorway where Lauren hovered. "Keep the door open. Fetch Lydia a cup of hot tea. Three teaspoons of sugar, half a teaspoon of cream, and two drops of lemon."

Lauren promptly left.

"You know exactly how I like my tea," Lydia said with wonder in her voice.

Lifting her hand, he pressed a kiss to her fingers. "I know a good many things about you."

"Did you know I go swimming in the nude?"

His eyes widened as the image scalded his senses.

"In the creek back home," she added. "Everyone does."

"All I had at Harrington were a pond and some rivers."

"I wanted to be a lady so badly, Rhys."

"You are the finest lady I have ever known."

"A lady wouldn't have been distracted worrying about whether or not she was with child."

"I believe you are quite mistaken. I think a good

many ladies worry about that very thing. Gentlemen can be persuasive when they set their minds to it, and most are adept at escaping chaperones now and then."

"I always thought my mother must have been mortified, because everyone in Fortune knew what had gone on between her and Grayson when they weren't married. My father, John Westland, made no secret that it wasn't his baby she carried."

"You say that as though you no longer hold the same misgivings."

"Understanding now how badly it hurts to know I'll never have your child . . . I would have gladly borne the shame of his birth and loved him all the more because he was yours."

Her declaration almost robbed him of speech. "You shall have children. Lots of children."

"But they won't be yours. You can't comprehend how much I love you, can you?"

"I understand you can't possibly know how much you would come to loathe me."

"With all my heart, I believe you're wrong."

"Fortunately, I have not the courage or strength of conviction to test you."

"I'd win."

And in the winning, she'd eventually lose.

"I'm totally confused," Lauren said.

She sat on the edge of Lydia's bed while Lydia sipped her tea. Rhys had only recently left, after ensuring she would be well cared for.

"By what?" Lydia asked.

"The Duke. My God, Lydia, you should have seen him. *Nothing* was going to keep him away from you. Absolutely nothing. I know it was inappropriate to allow him into your room, but he was like a man possessed." She leaned nearer. "Or a man madly in love."

"I know he cares for me, Lauren. I simply don't know how to convince him that I'm willing to risk everything for him. When I opened my eyes and saw him here, I felt such gladness. I can't explain it. He touches something so deep inside of me. The gentlemen I've met make me smile, make me feel happy, but Rhys manages to make me feel as though I could soar." She sighed. "Listen to me, prattling on like Sabrina."

"What are you going to do?"

"I don't know." She took another sip of tea. "I suppose I'll simply have to fall in love with someone else."

"Do you think that's possible?"

"I don't know, Lauren. But I don't want to think that I'll spend the remainder of my life this miserable, this disappointed."

Lydia much preferred being courted outdoors. She strolled through Hyde Park with her latest suitor. The lovely park seemed to be *the* place where everyone who was anyone happened to walk by.

Although she wasn't exactly certain she was being courted. Lord Sachse walked alongside her, very stately looking in his top hat.

Lady Sachse had arrived mid-afternoon and announced that a stroll through the park was in order. Rhys had consented, and so here they were, with him and his intended ambling along behind Lydia and her escort.

The park wasn't nearly as stuffy as the cluttered parlor where she constantly feared knocking something over and breaking it. She enjoyed the fresh air and the twittering of the birds in the trees. Life surrounded her here, and she could almost overlook her disappointment that she wasn't carrying Rhys's child, that he wouldn't set his intended aside for her.

"If I may speak boldly, Miss Westland, your heart does not seem to be in the husband hunt," Sachse said quietly.

She darted a quick glance over at him. "I had a vision of London with its balls and glitter. Sometimes I wish I'd held on to the dream instead of touching the reality."

"I am a scholar, Miss Westland, more comfortable with my books. I certainly never expected to have such fortune land in my lap, as it were. I must confess that securing myself a wife so I may leave the glitter behind appeals to me greatly."

She angled her head thoughtfully. "So how is your wife hunt going?"

"Not at all well, I'm afraid."

Smiling, she patted his arm sympathetically. "I can't imagine why. You're handsome, intelligent, enjoyable—"

"But I am not the Duke of Harrington."

She stumbled over her feet, and he quickly grabbed her elbow, helping her to balance herself.

"I'm not sure I understand what you mean," she said, although she was afraid she knew exactly what he'd meant.

He grinned. "I have an older sister, Nancy. She is a dear girl, Miss Westland. Beautiful, really. Like you. Although her outer appearance is appealing, it is her inner beauty radiating outward which truly makes her lovely to behold. You remind me of her."

She blushed. "Thank you for the compliment, my lord."

"You are most welcome. Although I must confess it is not your beauty which so much reminds me of her."

"My wit?"

He shook his head, his grin growing. "Her husband is the homeliest fellow you'll ever see."

Wide-eyed, Lydia stared at him, hardly knowing how to respond to so caustic a statement.

He tilted his head toward her. "It's true, I'm afraid. No one in the family could believe it when this chap caught her attention, but my sister looks at him the way you look at the Duke, and her husband looks at her the way Harrington looks upon you."

She glanced away. "And how is that?"

"As though no greater love existed."

She dared to meet his gaze. "I'm certain you're mistaken."

"I'm certain I'm not."

"You're impertinent."

He had the audacity to grin broadly. "It is my lack of breeding. I should probably apologize."

"Yes, I think you should."

"I would if I thought you were truly insulted. Now tell me if I have judged correctly."

"Harrington has announced his intention to take Lady Sachse as his wife," she reminded him succinctly.

"Indeed, he has."

They continued on. Lydia thought when she returned to Texas she would discuss with her family the possibility of setting aside some land for a park. They had an abundance of farmland where she could walk whenever she wanted, but she liked the idea of landscaping an area simply for the enjoyment of people to amble through.

Although here some people traveled by in carriages

and others rode on horses. All were dressed in their finery as though on display. She supposed that was part of the reason Lady Sachse had suggested the stroll through the park.

"You know, Miss Westland," Lord Sachse began, and she looked over at him, "I have been pondering your situation, and it has occurred to me that the fastest way to bring a dog to heel is to yank on his leash."

Startled by his comment, she said, "I beg your pardon?"

"I would very much like to offer myself to you in marriage."

As though he'd anticipated that she'd stumble again, he'd already placed his hand beneath her elbow and was offering her support.

"What?"

"I think we are well suited. Certainly you are beautiful and intelligent. I enjoy your company, and I think you enjoy mine."

She didn't know what to say. She'd always romanticized that her love would go down on one knee and whisper poetry before asking her to spend the remainder of her life with him.

"This is quite unexpected, my lord."

"You need not look so frightened. I don't think our marriage will come about."

She nodded. "You're probably right. Rhys has managed to find fault with every gentleman who has called on me."

"He shan't find fault with me. Lady Sachse will see to that. Although I suspect when faced with the reality of losing you, Harrington will step in and offer his own suit."

"What if Rhys doesn't 'come to heel' as you suggested?"

He shrugged. "Then I marry a very lovely lady with whom I think I would be quite happy."

She shook her head. "He won't marry me."

Reaching out, he tucked a strand of hair behind her ear. "You did not see the way he watched you when we were at the concert. My dear Miss Westland, I believe he would die for you."

"Do stop scowling, Rhys. It doesn't become you," Camilla said, her hand resting on his arm.

Rhys concentrated on relaxing his facial muscles—not an easy task when Lydia's laughter continued to float back toward him. What the deuce was Sachse saying to her that caused her such delight?

"Is there anything about me that you feel does become me?" he asked drolly.

"Your title," she answered without hesitation.

He sighed heavily. "I have the impression that ours will be a cold marriage."

"Colder than you think. I shan't be sharing your bed."

He snapped his head around. "Pardon?"

She angled her chin slightly without meeting his gaze. "I have no objection to your finding your diversions elsewhere."

"I should hope not, if you're not willing. You can't be serious. Never? You have no plans whatsoever to ever share my bed?"

She darted a quick glance up at him, coloring rising in her cheeks. "I have my reasons."

"Suppose you enlighten me."

"I have no desire to be compared against every other woman who has graced your bed."

"You placed them there," he reminded her. "Afraid your performance might fall short? Is that the reason you never visited my bed?"

"My reasons are personal and have nothing whatsoever to do with you. We shall simply continue where we left off when Quentin, may he rest in hell, took his fall into the pond."

"I was not aware you knew Quentin well."

"There is much about me that you don't know. It's best if we keep it that way."

"Is there anything about you, anything that I don't know, that will come back to haunt Lydia?"

"Of course not. But they are my secrets, and I prefer to keep them to myself."

He wasn't certain why a sense of foreboding came over him. He needed to see Lydia well situated, and then whatever his marriage to Camilla became, he would accept. After all, she had twice helped him when no one else would.

Chapter 22

There were moments when Rhys wondered how he could possibly go through with his marriage to Camilla. He was fairly certain they would be happiest if they led completely separate lives. She'd already indicated that she would not object.

For him, time spent with Lydia was blissful torture. He hoarded every smile, laugh, and word like a miser. A portion of her that he could store away and take out in later years to reflect upon. How could every moment spent with her be both joyous and sorrowful?

He sat in his drawing room, a book of Shakespeare's sonnets on his lap. He'd reread *Hamlet* earlier, before moving on to other reading. He'd imagined Lydia's enjoyment as she'd watched the play performed in Harrison Bainbridge's saloon. He suspected she'd been as overwhelmed there as she'd been at the Royal Albert Hall. She took such joy in life. She held none of the cynicism so central to him.

He would hear of her from time to time, he was certain. Perhaps on rare occasion their paths would cross. And he would forever be left to reflect on what might have been had he not made such ghastly mistakes in his youth, had he possessed a stronger character.

He turned his attention back to Shakespeare. The man had been wise in all things. If only Rhys were half as knowledgeable, perhaps now he would not find himself facing years of loneliness. Even marriage to Camilla would not ease the ache in his heart. Rather he suspected it would only cause it to increase.

He glanced over as he heard the hushed entry of his butler. "Yes, Rawlings?"

"A young lady has asked to see you, Your Grace."

His first thought was that Lydia was here, and his heart beat with the anticipation of seeing her. But Rawlings extending the silver tray with the card resting on it assured him it was more likely to be Camilla, although she was not prone to presenting him with her cards.

He lifted the card, read the name, and felt trepidation slice through him. Nodding, he rose to his feet. "Tell Lady Whithaven I will see her."

He straightened his clothes, retrieved his jacket from the chair where he'd laid it earlier, and slipped it on. He combed his fingers through his hair and rubbed his chin. He was in dire need of a shave. He was certain the lady only wanted reassurances that he would hold her secret close. He thought it would behoove him to look reputable when he gave such a promise.

She strolled into the room and stopped, as petite and lovely as ever. A footman closed the door behind her. Only then did she approach Rhys, her red-rimmed eyes roving over him. She'd obviously been weeping, and it pained him to have caused her any worry or concern.

He bowed. "My dear Countess."

She shook her head slightly as though caught in a dream. "I didn't know it was you."

"I never intended for you to know, but a situation arose which required I reveal myself."

She pressed her fingers to her lips while unshed tears welled in her eyes. "She said you were the kindest and gentlest of men."

"I am honored Lady Sachse spoke so highly of me, but I assure you—"

She shook her head vehemently, while more tears gathered and spilled onto her cheek. "Not Lady Sachse," she rasped. "My dear friend Annie."

Rhys thought his legs might buckle beneath him. "Annie?"

"I didn't know you were Quentin's brother. Until you attended our ball, I had no name to associate with you. I knew you only as Lady Sachse's lover. I had no idea who you truly were. Now that I know, I am obligated to confess all. May I sit?"

"By all means." A splendid idea, because he thought at any moment he would no longer be able to support himself. "May I offer you something to drink?"

"Yes, please," she said as she sank into a chair near the one he'd been sitting in earlier. "I would welcome strong spirits if you have them."

He had an intense craving for them as well.

"I have just the thing." He poured the last of his brother's whiskey into two glasses and handed her one. He cautioned, "Sip it. It burns and warms and brings a sense of peace."

"I fear nothing shall bring me peace."

But she did sip the whiskey, while he took a generous swallow. He'd come to favor the strong drink and had contemplated asking Grayson to send him more.

She set the glass on the table between them and eased up in the chair. "I am certain we must have met at Annie's wedding, but I was newly taken with Geoffrey and hardly noticed anyone else."

"I must confess to remembering little of their wedding. I was sixteen and only in attendance because duty dictated. I made my escape as soon as it was allowed."

"Annie was most unhappy with Quentin. He had rather . . . morbid tastes." Her cheeks reddened. With a visibly shaking hand, she reached for her glass and took another sip of whiskey before setting it aside.

She gave him a tremulous smile. "I can see why so many ladies sought your counsel. You give a lady a chance to form her thoughts."

What he was trying to do was form his own. He moved until he was kneeling before her. Taking her hand, he squeezed it. His chest tightened into a painful knot. "I am so sorry. I didn't know Annie was your friend. I can never forgive myself for causing her to take her life—"

"I hold Quentin completely responsible."

"Then you do not know the whole tale."

"I know much more than you think. I know he abused her in bed. I know he sent her to you and told her if she did not seduce you, then he would make her life more miserable than it was."

His hand went limp around hers. "Sent her to me?"

She nodded, her eyes reflecting her own horror at what Quentin had done.

"Why would he do that?"

"He was a voyeur. Your rooms shared connecting walls. Annie said he could see into yours without being seen himself. He'd sent servants to you before, and he was bored with that distraction. He wanted to tempt you with an unforgivable sin."

Rhys lunged to his feet, his heart thundering, his stomach roiling. He'd been nineteen, only just beginning to experience the pleasures a woman's body could offer.

"He watched," he rasped, unable to believe it, unable to get beyond the sense of violation he felt.

He spun around and pierced her with his gaze. "You are mistaken. He would not have sent her to me when it was his place to get her with an heir. He would not have risked my seed taking hold."

More tears spilled onto her cheeks. "She was already with child."

He staggered back, dropped into a chair, and bowed his head. It could not be.

"She had told him only that day. He wished to celebrate. Dear God, but he was the vilest of creatures. I dared not tell anyone because I did not wish to tarnish my dear friend's memory. Following her death, I heard the rumors that it was the second son who had betrayed the first, but I alone knew it was the first who had betrayed the second. Although I suppose Lady Sachse knew as well."

Rhys's head came up. "Lady Sachse. How did she know of it?"

"I'm not exactly sure. I know only that Annie mentioned that Lady Sachse had sought to comfort her. But Annie maintained that all the comfort in the world could not lessen her disgrace, her abhorrence over what she'd done. She was quite beside herself when she came to see me. That night she took her life. I lay the blame at your brother's feet."

Rhys scraped his fingers through his hair. "I knew he

was demented, but this revelation sickens me. You've mentioned it to no one?"

"No. I would not have had the courage to come to you tonight except that you looked so unhappy at my ball. Unhappy and yet announcing your intention to marry Lady Sachse—which is a marvelous pairing. You were both incredibly kind to me. I suppose once you are wed that she will cease to be as generous and will no longer share you with her lady friends. I am amazed she did so at all. If you were mine, I think I would keep you to myself."

Yes, there were many things he was beginning to think Lady Sachse had kept to herself.

"Rhys Rhodes. By God, we should have guessed," Reynolds said.

From within the shadowy confines of his carriage, Whithaven watched as his wife climbed into hers. He clutched the linen handkerchief while his anger boiled.

"At least now the monogram makes sense," Reynolds mused.

That Reynolds had found an identical handkerchief bearing the same crimson initial among his wife's things brought Whithaven no comfort.

"Some years back I remember there were whispers that he'd betrayed his brother," Kingston told them. "I suppose we should not be surprised he would betray you as well."

"Don't sound so superior," Reynolds said. "Simply because you didn't find evidence of a handkerchief doesn't mean he hasn't bedded your wife."

"I keep my wife well pleasured. Make no mistake about it. I daresay she has no cause to look elsewhere for her satisfaction."

"Are you saying I have not your skills in bed?"

"I am saying if the shoe fits, wear it."

"I'll have you know, of late my wife can scarcely keep her hands off me, so *this* fellow cannot be as talented as rumored."

"But at some point, obviously, it was not you she wished to put her hands on."

"Gentlemen," Whithaven growled. "Fighting among ourselves will hardly make this problem go away."

"What do you propose?" Reynolds asked.

Whithaven narrowed his eyes as another carriage came around the corner. It bore the ducal crest.

"I say we find out where he's going."

It took Rhys less than ten minutes to find the first peephole in what had been Quentin's bedchamber. It was hidden behind a painting of a fox hunt and looked in on the room where Rhys had slept when he was younger and in residence.

A room where he'd lost his virginity to a seductive upstairs maid who'd visited him in the middle of the night when he was sixteen. He thought he might be ill.

By the time he arrived at Camilla's, he'd remembered every sexual encounter he'd experienced in that bed. Not a single one of them initiated by him.

He was shaking with such fury and a sense of violation when he walked through her door that it was all he could do to follow her butler into the solarium without smashing objects along the way.

Stretched out on a fainting couch, she smiled at him. "My dear Rhys, what brings you here so late at night?"

"You never told me that you knew Annie."

"Annie?"

"Quentin's wife."

"Ah, yes. Annie." She gracefully glided a hand toward a nearby table. "Have some wine, Rhys."

"I believe I'll pass."

She shook her head with a *tsk*. "Suit yourself."

She poured herself some and gulped it down.

"How did you know Annie?" he demanded.

"Does it matter?"

"I believe it does. The night you and I met, I'd just left my brother. He was in residence here in London. I was walking away from the house when you happened by in your carriage. You knew who I was. I did not think to wonder at the time how you knew, when I'd never before set eyes on you. How did you know who I was?"

"I am certain our paths must have crossed at some time."

He banged his fist on the table, and she jerked.

"I want answers. We made a bargain back then. You took me to your smaller town house. You offered me shelter, food, anything I wanted if I would make myself available to you. I was desperate and accepted your offer. Only you never came to me. Never. You sent other women to me."

"You were young, virile. I was generous to share you."

"How did you know I was virile?" he growled.

"Rhys—"

"I found peepholes in my brother's room. So I ask you again. How did you know I was virile?"

"Because I watched you!"

He felt as though someone had just bludgeoned his heart.

She drank greedily, her hand shaking so badly that the wine spilled onto her gown.

"Why?" he rasped.

"The old Sachse, my dear departed husband—may he rest in hell—was a cruel man. He and Quentin were friends, two sides of the same bad penny, as it were. They had an appetite for voyeurism, and a young man still in his prime could provide them with quite a bit of entertainment."

A shudder rippled through Rhys that he thought would fracture him in half. He walked to the table, poured himself a full glass of wine, and swallowed it down in one long gulp before daring to look at Camilla. "Have you nothing stronger to drink?"

"In the cabinet."

Caring only that its contents were as dark as his thoughts, he grabbed a decanter, splashed the liquid liberally into the glass, and quickly downed it. "How many times did you watch with them?"

"Only once. I could tell you that they forced me to watch you"—he could see her blinking back tears, striving to maintain her composure—"but I wanted to reassure myself that the . . . act . . . was as disagreeable for every other woman as it was for me."

She sat up on the chaise. "My God, Rhys, the care with which you touched Annie." She shook her head, her tears brimming. "It was the first time I ever wept."

"And in your smaller town house, where you allowed me to live . . . how many times did you watch me there?"

She lowered her gaze.

"Damnation!" He swiped his hand across the table, sending the contents spilling and crashing to the floor.

"You are well and truly sick of mind and revolting of heart!"

"I know," she whispered plaintively.

He wanted to double over from the pain of it. "Did your ladies know we were being watched?"

She jerked her head up, a horrified expression on her face. "No, of course not."

"Why, for God's sake why?"

"Because I discovered old Sachse wasn't the only man who had no finesse when it came to bedding his wife. I believed that at least once, a woman should be with a man who didn't plow into her as though she were a field to be furrowed." She came to her feet. "And because my husband was a sadist. I was sixteen when we married, and by the time I was knowledgeable enough to realize that what he'd convinced me was the way of things was only *his* way . . . it was too late for me. Even your skilled touch would not carry me to the heights I've seen you carry others. And so I found my satisfaction in giving you to other ladies."

He turned his back on her.

"I don't expect you to forgive me—"

"That's damned good of you, because I won't."

"I do hope that you might understand—"

He spun around with such force that she staggered back and fell across the chaise.

"Understand?" he demanded. "I was a damned whore! I knew that, I accepted that. But to also know that I was on exhibition for your amusement. My God, if you were a man I'd beat you to within an inch of your life."

She straightened, wiped away her tears, and met his gaze. "At least now you know why we will have a chaste marriage."

"We won't have a marriage at all."

She sniffed and angled her head. "You can't cry off. I shall sue you for breach of contract, breach of faith. And I shall not play nicely."

"Are you threatening to expose my past?"

"I'm not threatening, I'm promising. You have much more to lose than I, and if I learned one thing from your abhorrent brother, it was how to spin a yarn so that I come away the victim. I shall have everyone's sympathy while you shall have nothing but their disdain."

"I don't give a damn what anyone thinks."

"Perhaps not. But I do believe you care what Lydia thinks. She has stayed in your house. Who would think she has not been part of our games?"

"Don't even contemplate harming her with innuendo."

"Then don't consider crying off. I wish to be a duchess. It's all that's left to me."

"Do you not fathom that I prefer not to ever set eyes on you again?"

The familiar scheming look came into her eyes. "All I want is the title. After we're wed, you may go to the far corners of the earth and I won't care." She gave him a sad smile. "Protect your little dreamer, Rhys. You know I have sharp claws and no heart."

He turned and strode from the room. Let her make of his departure what she would.

He didn't much care for threats or bullies, but Camilla had read him right. He did care about Lydia and was willing to do whatever was necessary to see her happy.

He hurried down the outer steps only because he wished to be away from Camilla as quickly as possible, but once he reached the pavement, he had no desire to go anywhere. His footman opened the carriage door, and Rhys merely shook his head, surprised by the effort that simple action took.

"Take the carriage home. I wish to walk."

He stood there a moment, listening to the clatter of the horses' hooves, the whir of the wheels. Fog had settled in, and he quickly found himself alone in the muggy air.

How in God's name had he brought himself to this moment? He'd been so eager with the first woman, so grateful for her attentions, but she hadn't returned to his bed the next night. He'd thought the fault had rested with him. So he'd begun searching for answers in obscure books that he could find only on the darker side of London, books that revealed various positions for lovemaking, writings that described ways to increase pleasure.

Until the night Quentin's wife had come to him. Sweet Annie, who had simply asked him to love her, and even though he'd known it was wrong, he'd heard her crying in the room next to his too many nights not to invite her into his bed. They'd made love so tenderly, slowly, gently that when they were finished, they'd clung to each other and wept for what might have been. For what shouldn't have been.

Quentin had sent her to him. Three nights later she'd taken her own life and left him a note of apology—a note Quentin had discovered. A note that had ignited Quentin's temper and drawn both his parents into the room. A note that revealed that Rhys had bedded his brother's wife, was responsible for her death. That shamed him into running.

What sort of sick and twisted mind had his brother possessed?

Rhys was brought back to the present by the sound of footsteps. He hadn't realized how far he'd walked.

He glanced over his shoulder. Three shadows emerged from the fog. Before he could react, pain arced through his jaw. And he realized that his darkest nightmare was about to descend on him.

Chapter 23

Lydia awoke to a tapping. She opened her eyes to the darkness, disoriented and confused. What had made that sound?

Click. Clink.

She eased out from beneath the covers, shivered, and scurried to the window. Parting the drapes slightly, she peered out.

William stood outside, tossing little pebbles against the house. She opened the window. "William?"

"I didn't know where else to go," he called up in a hushed whisper.

"Wait there."

She grabbed her night wrapper from the foot of the bed and slipped it on as she hurried down the stairs. She opened the front door to find him waiting for her. He looked as though someone had died.

"What's wrong?" she asked.

"It's His Grace. Said he'd flay me back if I sent for a

doctor, but he needs one bad. He likes you. Thought maybe you could convince him to come to his senses."

"Is he sick?"

"Worse than that." He grabbed her arm. "Come on, please."

Horrible visions rushed through her head. Perhaps his appendix had burst. Or he'd come down with some disease: cholera, the plague. Did they still get the plague in England? Hadn't it wiped out most of the population of Europe at some time?

Rhys would no doubt scold her for not knowing the specifics.

"How did you get here?" she asked.

"I ran. That day you came to live here, I came to say good-bye to Colton. He showed me which room was yours. Didn't think I'd ever have need of knowing."

"Let me get dressed, and I'll have a servant bring a carriage around."

He nodded, and she retreated back inside. All she could think was that she'd be lost if Rhys died. How could she even contemplate marrying Sachse when her heart so totally and completely belonged to Rhys?

At Rhys's home, William led her inside and dashed into the library. Lydia went in after him and immediately spotted Rhys slumped in a chair beside the fireplace.

"Oh, my dear God," she rasped, as she rushed across the room and knelt before him.

His beautiful face was cut, bruised, and scraped. One eye was nearly swollen shut. "My God, what happened?"

Through his one good eye, he glared at William. "I told you to go to bed."

"Figured you didn't really know your own mind. Thought she'd do you some good, Guv."

Lydia gently touched her fingers to his bleeding cheek. His torn clothes were further ruined where flecks of blood had splattered on them. "What happened?"

"I stumbled when stepping out of my carriage," he muttered through clenched teeth.

"I'm not stupid, Rhys. I have three brothers. I know what the results of a fight look like when I see it."

"To say it was a fight would imply I'd taken part, had a chance to defend myself. It was more of a thrashing."

"Why?"

Shaking his head, he looked away.

Stubborn man. She prodded his chest, and he issued a low moan before slapping her hand away.

She gave him a pointed look. "Your ribs are probably broken. Let me send for a physician."

"No. I can tend to myself."

"I don't know why men think sending for a doctor is a sign of weakness. My brothers have a tendency to avoid doctors as well. If you won't let me get you a physician, then you'll have to let me tend to you."

He snorted. "Go back to Ravenleigh's, Lydia."

"A doctor isn't always available in Fortune. I know quite a bit about tending injuries."

"Bring me a bottle and leave me be."

She turned to William. "Get him a bottle from the liquor cabinet and a glass."

"No glass. Tonight I have no wish to be refined."

"Fine, but I think you'll find it easier to drink with a glass." While William fetched the alcohol, Lydia tried to assess Rhys's injuries. She lifted his hair off his brow and grimaced. "How many men?"

"Three."

"I hope you gave as good as you got."

"Under the circumstances, I decided to take what I had coming like a man."

"So you didn't resist?"

He barely shook his head.

"Here you go, Guv."

Rhys lifted the bottle to his mouth, grimacing and moaning as he tipped it up. Lydia put her hand beneath it to hold it steady while he gulped the brew, no doubt hoping for quick oblivion.

"Surely you're gonna do more than that for him," William said.

"Yes. Go to the kitchen and see if you can find me a cut of beef, the larger the better. Also we'll need warm water, towels, scraps of linen."

"I'll find 'em all." He scampered off.

Lydia let go of the bottle and sat back on her heels.

"Don't look so worried, Lydia."

"I can't play these games, Rhys. I can't pretend not to feel something that I feel."

"Then you are dooming yourself to a life of misery if you stay in England and continue to pursue an aristocratic husband. Happiness in marriage is seldom to be found."

"I don't believe that. I can't believe the unhappy marriages I've seen here are the rule and not the exception."

"No?" He leaned menacingly toward her. "The gentlemen who beat me did so because they objected to the fact I'd entertained their wives."

She blinked in confusion. "They beat you because you played the piano for them?"

He released a harsh, ugly laugh. "No, my little dreamer, I seduced, pleasured, and bedded them."

His callous words caused pain to pierce her heart. She'd never expected him to speak so crassly about his relationships with other women.

"It disappoints you to know Annie wasn't the only married woman with whom I've slept."

"Of course it does. I believe in the sanctity of marriage. I thought Annie was an exception."

"No, Lydia. *You* were the exception."

She didn't like the way he said that, as though there was more at stake here.

"So you had affairs—"

"An affair indicates a lengthy time together. For me, it is usually only a few nights."

A few nights? Was he easily bored with women? Had he grown bored with her? Was that the reason he now seemed to favor Lady Sachse?

"Is what happened tonight behind your reason for not marrying me?"

Silence.

"I love you," she said.

"Love me? Love a man who not only slept with married women, but was well compensated to do so?"

Her entire body tightened with his implication. Surely he didn't mean . . . "You mean like a woman in a . . . a brothel?"

"Precisely."

Revulsion caused her stomach to roil. "Why?"

"Why not? My family had turned me out. I know where ladies are most sensitive." He trailed his finger from her temple to her chin. "Behind her ear, along the length of her spine, behind her knee."

She scooted back, beyond the reach of his touch. "No."

"Ah, yes, Lydia. You were more sensitive than most. Easily seduced."

She shook her head. "No, you didn't take advantage."

"Didn't I? I am a master of pleasure. I have dedicated my life to it. Ask any of the women whose husbands attacked me tonight, and you'll find that I gave them what their husbands never did.

"I have studied poetry until I can whisper the most beautiful false flattery into a lady's ear. I have unraveled the ancient arts and discovered secrets that can carry a woman to heights she's never before achieved. I can make her forget how *sad* an evening was."

He'd said something similar before. Tears stung her eyes. "The night of my first ball—"

"I replaced your unhappy memories with glorious sensations, did I not? Just as I'd promised? Each touch was well planned. Each caress served a purpose. Each stroke of my tongue was designed to help you forget."

She shook her head. "No, no, you were never false with me."

"I am a man who has bedded countless women, and loved none of them, who suffered through their touch because of what they could gain me. How can you ever be sure, my little dreamer? Will you always wonder if my words were practiced, whispered to someone else before I whispered them to you? I have given countless women memories to replace those they wished to forget. Why should you be any different?"

"Because you love me."

"I've told you before that I do not have love to give. Lust I know well. Love I know not at all. You have confused one with the other. Perhaps you need another lesson."

He slowly came to his feet. She couldn't stand the doubts plaguing her, the thought of him touching her as he'd touched so many others—not with love, but only with lust.

She scrambled to her feet and raced toward the door.

She heard his harsh voice calling after her. "That's right. Run, Lydia, run!"

She dashed outside and into the carriage. As the driver guided it through the streets of London, Lydia curled into a ball and wept. She didn't know the man she'd just left. Perhaps she'd never known him.

"Where'd Miss Westland go?" William asked as he walked in carrying a box laden with the things Lydia had requested.

"She left." Rhys located a glass and poured himself a stiff drink. He downed it even though it stung the cuts on his lips and his jaw ached when he opened his mouth.

"Why?"

"Because she's a true lady."

She'd been repulsed by his confession, reacting just as he'd always known she would if he revealed the truth regarding what he had been.

As much as her leaving had hurt, as hard as it had been for him not to pull her into his arms and hold her close, he knew all had happened for the best.

She would be safe now, spared the humiliation that was sure to follow.

He had little doubt gossip would run rampant and most of the truths would be trampled until all that remained was the ugliness of the entire affair. He didn't want to contemplate what would happen if the gossip reached the ear of the Queen. If she decided he was unworthy of his titles, he could well lose them. With many of the husbands in the House of Lords, he thought it possible his family could lose everything. At the very least his family's good name would be ruined.

"I thought you fancied her," William said.

"You thought wrong."

He didn't fancy her; he loved her—more than life it-self. He'd do anything to see her happy—even if he had to destroy himself in the process.

Chapter 24

H er heart was shattering. Lydia actually thought she could feel the fissures widening as the pain intensified until it was almost unbearable.

His words, his touch, his kiss—all the skills of a master seducer. He excelled at pleasuring women, pleasuring them for compensation. What sort of compensation did they offer him? She supposed she should consider herself fortunate that he'd shared his talents with her—and not taken payment for the privilege.

She opened her trunk, trudged to the wardrobe, and yanked down a gown. She tried to wad it up, to mash it into a tiny ball, her fists bunching it, and striking it—

"Lydia?"

She dropped it into the trunk, fell to her knees, and began folding it, stuffing it, flattening it—

"Lydia!"

She wanted it so tiny that she'd never see it again.

Hands grabbed her shoulders and twisted her around.

"Lydia, what's wrong?"

"He doesn't love me." She searched Lauren's concerned face. "Oh, Lauren, I wasn't special. Everything was a lie. Everything."

A heart-wrenching sob broke free as the tears welled in her eyes and rolled onto her cheeks.

Lauren wrapped her arms around Lydia and pressed her close. "Whatever are you talking about? The servants brought me an urgent message from the Duke stating that I was to see to you immediately. And here you are, dressed and packing. Whatever is going on?"

He'd sent a missive? How thoughtful. He probably feared she'd take her life as Annie had, and he'd have that on his conscience. But she'd kill Rhys before she'd kill herself.

Yet even her fury with him could not lessen the agony of his betrayal. Unable to control the flow of hot tears, she nodded with her cheek pressed against Lauren's delicate shoulder. "I went to see Rhys. They beat him, and I wanted to help—"

"Who beat him?"

She shook her head. "I just want to go home now."

Lauren began to rock her. "Oh, Lydia, what has happened?"

Her shoulders trembled as she released the force of her grief, her despair. She thought her ribs might cave in on her, might squash her lungs. If she ceased to breathe, she would not care. If her heart stopped beating, she would welcome the end of her agony.

She wanted to take a bath. She felt dirty. Ashamed. She'd given herself to him in love, and yet for him every touch had been a practiced execution. He'd used his mouth, tongue, and hands to help her forget her first ball.

Who would help her forget this night of despicable revelations?

"Here now, come sit in the chair and tell me what happened."

Lydia felt as though the very air was crushing her. Her feet dragged across the floor as Lauren guided her to the chair. She dropped into it with all the decorum of a cow. She no longer wanted to be a lady.

She wrapped her arms around herself and began to rock. Through her tears, the room was little more than a blur of colors. She heard a drawer open and close. Then she felt the soft linen patted against her cheek.

"Let's dry your tears and you can tell me everything," Lauren said.

Closing her fingers around the cloth, Lydia took the handkerchief from her cousin. "I just want to go home."

"Did Harrington do something untoward? Lydia, did he hurt you?"

"More than I thought humanly possible. I've never in my life known such pain."

"Shall I wake Papa? Does he need to take the Duke to task?"

Shaking her head, she reached out and clutched Lauren's hand. "We mustn't tell anyone. Ever," she rasped.

Trying to gain control of her heartache, she wiped the tears from her eyes and swallowed hard. "He told me that he'd done things best left in the dark. He said I'd hate him if I knew . . ." She let her voice trail off. She didn't want to give life to the words, to say them aloud.

"Do you hate him?" Lauren asked.

She shook her head. "I don't know. I just know that I hurt so badly. I thought I knew him." She wiped away the fresh tears. "He sold himself."

"You mean his skills?"

Lydia nodded.

"Like at the docks, unloading ships and such?"

Lydia felt the pain of betrayal and more tears surface because she was going to have to say it aloud. She shook her head. "He sold himself to women."

Confusion washed over Lauren's face. "What did they pay him to do? Rearrange their furniture?"

Lydia groaned. She didn't think Lauren was being deliberately obtuse, she just thought it was impossible to comprehend exactly what Rhys had done. "They paid him so that he would pleasure them."

Her eyes widening, Lauren dropped onto the edge of the bed. "You're not serious?"

Pressing a hand to her mouth to contain the wail she wanted so desperately to release, Lydia nodded again.

"Is he the Gentleman Seducer?"

"The what?"

"Rumors have been adrift for some time that there was a gentleman in London who entertained married ladies. I know one young lady who married a man she couldn't stand simply so she'd have an excuse to be accepted by the Gentleman Seducer. He's supposed to be extremely skilled. Do you think he could be Rhys?"

Dear God! She'd once overheard Johnny talking with some friends about the colorful names prostitutes had. Was Rhys no exception? "I think I'm going to be ill."

"Shall I have some tea brought up? The English believe it's a cure-all for everything."

Nothing would cure this, but still Lydia nodded, every movement more difficult to make than the one that came before it.

"Wait here."

Wait here? As though she had the will to do anything else.

Lauren hurried out of the room, closing the door behind her. With a shuddering sigh, Lydia dropped her head back. She didn't want to think about Rhys with all those other women. She didn't want to think of them paying him. Paying him, for God's sake. She honestly didn't know who was more revolting: the women or Rhys.

She pulled the handkerchief through her fingers, over and over. She felt as though she didn't know Rhys at all. How could she have been so naïve, so stupid as to believe he cared for her?

She lifted the handkerchief to wipe away more tears, and her gaze fell on the solitary initial. R. His.

He'd given her this handkerchief the day her family had left. She'd held on to it, hadn't washed it, but had simply tucked it away. She brought it to her nose now and smelled his lingering scent.

The lemony fragrance awakened so many memories. All the times he'd given in to temptation. All the times he'd warned her away. He'd warned her away far more often than he'd given in.

Lauren returned to the room. "Here you are. Your tea. Just the way you like it."

She set it down on the spindly-legged table beside Lydia.

Lydia shifted her gaze from the handkerchief, to the steam rising above the cup, back to the linen. "Did you know how I prepared my tea before Rhys told you?" she asked.

"I knew you liked lemon and sugar and cream. But

not the exact amounts. No one notices that sort of thing."

"Rhys did." She rose from the chair, walked to the window, and gazed out.

"Lydia, you mustn't despair. You can publicly denounce him. Your Season can be saved."

"I'm not sure I'll ever go out in public again."

Having handed his card to the butler, Rhys waited within Whithaven's foyer. He turned at the sound of approaching footsteps, halfway expecting to see Whithaven himself. Instead the butler was merely returning.

"His Lordship is not at home," he announced.

Rhys looked past the man to the hallway from which the servant had emerged. "Is that so?"

"Indeed, Your Grace. Perhaps you'll find him in residence another day."

"I doubt it." Rhys started walking toward the hallway, ignoring the stammering of the servant insisting that the Earl was not at home. While he doubted he had any influence, he did still possess rank.

Rhys flung open a door, and the Earl popped up from behind his desk, as tall and lanky as ever.

"You know, Whithaven, you're easy enough to spot in a crowd, but to think a mere hooded mask would hide your unusual height and thin bearing to the point I would not recognize you was foolhardy, man."

"My lord, I tried to stop him—" the butler began.

Whithaven held up his hand. "It's quite all right. Please, close the door."

Rhys ambled farther into the room.

"You've got your nerve, showing up here," Whithaven said.

Rhys gave him a withering look. "And you have your nerve beating me without explaining what I'd done to deserve such treatment."

"You know damned well what you've done. My wife has been beside herself since you showed up at our ball."

"I was invited."

"Apparently, sir, you had a life in the shadows before you inherited your titles." He angled his pointed chin and looked down his nose haughtily. Not many men could literally look down their noses at Rhys. Whithaven could. "The Gentleman Seducer, indeed."

It was all Rhys could do not to flinch. He'd loathed the way Camilla had referred to him, cheapened him . . .

"How exactly, may I ask, did you determine who I was?"

"You may ask. I will not answer."

Rhys impaled the man with his eyes.

Whithaven averted his gaze. "I suspected something was amiss with my wife. Unknown to her, I've been following her around London."

"Did your wife tell you of our time together?"

Whithaven looked as though he might be ill. "Get out of my house."

"Until I am brought before the House of Lords on some sort of charges, I still outrank you, sir, and I will know what you know."

Whithaven straightened. "Very well. Rumors are beginning to surface that Lady Sachse ran the house in which your *liaisons* were carried out. Terribly unseemly of her."

"Ah, rumors are beastly things. Yes, she initially provided for me as I'm sure you do *your mistress*"—

Whithaven's eyes bulged at that—"but she's frightfully frugal and was somewhat tight with my allowance. What is a gentleman to do?"

"Not offer his services for hire like a commoner. Where was your pride, man?"

"You cannot lose what you never possessed, but I am not here to discuss my transgressions, but rather your idiocy. Your wife loves you."

"She has a strange way of showing it."

"I ask you again, did she tell you what transpired when she visited with me?"

"Good God, no, and I don't want to know."

"Nothing happened."

"Ha! *That* I do not believe. She would not be walking around here with reddened eyes were that the case."

"I'll admit she scrambled onto my bed, but only so she could lie in comfort while she wept. You were with your mistress. She came to me wanting nothing more than someone to hold her. Once she began to cry, that is all I offered."

He sneered. "You're saying you didn't fornicate?"

"I'm saying she was not unfaithful, merely unhappy. You would be wise to get rid of your mistress. Focus your energies and time on pleasing your wife. As for the gentlemen who joined you in accosting me last night, I can rather guess who they might have been. You may reassure them that their secrets, particularly about their *shortcomings*, are safe with me. But if they wish to discuss the matter more fully, I'll be available this afternoon."

Whithaven was moving his mouth as though he wished to say something but couldn't quite wrap his mind around what he wanted to say. Rhys turned on his heel and began to walk from the room.

"Did you actually bed any of our wives as it's rumored?"

Rhys halted and looked over his shoulder. The one thing he'd never done was compromise the truth. It was tempting to do so now, but if he did, what would he have left? Nothing. "Unfortunately, there is always a seed of truth in any rumor, but I swear to you, sir, your wife was not one of them."

Walking out of the room, he wished he'd be able to say the same thing to every gentleman who might be curious enough to pay him a visit today. He was almost to the front door when he heard the patter of slippers across the marble floor. He glanced toward the stairs, and there she was—the lovely Countess.

Her eyes widened in horror as she cautiously approached. "Your Grace, what in the world happened to you?"

Although his jaw protested, he gave her a wry grin. "A man does not do this to another if he does not love his wife. He wouldn't have cared that you'd come to see me."

"Geoffrey did this to you?"

"I have since explained to him that you did nothing except cry in my arms."

She reached up to touch his bruised cheek, then dropped her hand to her side. "He found your handkerchief in a drawer. I shouldn't have kept it. I'm frightfully sorry."

"No need to apologize, Countess. I would ask, however, that you do what you can to protect Miss Westland. She is innocent in all this."

Rhys heard the soft clearing of a throat. Lady Whithaven snapped her gaze toward the hallway from which Rhys had just emerged. He had no reason to look. If he never set eyes on Whithaven again, it would be too soon.

She looked back at Rhys, tears in her eyes. "Rest easy. I shall see to Miss Westland. In Annie's memory."

"Thank you." He continued on, out the door, and toward his carriage.

When he arrived home, he alerted Rawlings to the fact that he would no doubt have a few visitors that afternoon. He would be home to all of them, one at a time. Then he called William into his office and penned a missive for the lad to deliver.

"Do you remember where we lived just before we moved to Harrington?" he asked as he folded and sealed the letter.

"The one that kept us warm, where all the ladies came?"

"That's the one."

"Aye, my lord, I remember."

He didn't see any point in correcting William on his proper form of address; after all, he probably wouldn't be a duke for much longer—not if those who had seats in the House of Lords had their way. "Think you can find it again?"

William looked offended that Rhys had asked.

"Absolutely."

"Good." He held out the missive. "I want you to deliver this to Lord Sachse. If he is not at home, I want you to find out where he is and deliver it to him there. It's imperative I see him today."

Lydia sat in the chair, staring out at the rose garden. Her heart continued to beat but without meaning. The world had never seemed so dull, empty, devoid of joy.

Lauren was insisting Lydia attend the Kimburton

ball that evening. All Lydia wanted to do was get on a boat and go home. The glitter had certainly become tarnished.

The door opened, but she didn't look to see who it was. Life went on around her, but she had little desire to participate.

"Lydia, you have a gentleman caller," Lauren said.

She twisted around in the chair, unexpected hope filling her. "Rhys?"

"No, Lord Sachse."

She furrowed her brow. "What does he want?"

"Well, silly goose," Lauren said. "I don't know. He's talking with Papa right now. Let's get you presentable so we can find out."

What Lord Sachse wanted was to make good on his offer to marry her. She could hardly believe it as he sat beside her on the sofa in the parlor, awaiting her answer. She'd thought of this moment a hundred times while she'd been in Texas: gaining some lord's attention, falling in love with him, having him fall in love with her.

Between her and Sachse, if she searched hard enough, she could find affection. She wondered if she'd ever care for him to such an extent that he could break her heart as Rhys had. Would she ever again dare love any man to such a degree that she would risk her heart?

Or had Rhys ruined any chance of future love for her? Would she hold herself apart, afraid, uncertain, not knowing if her shattered heart could ever be healed?

A quiet knock on the door saved her from having to give Sachse her answer.

"My lord? There's a lad out here to see you. Says he has an important message for you that can't wait," the butler said.

Sachse gave her a smile. "I'd better see what it is."

She followed him into the hallway, where she was surprised to see William waiting. He wore a very serious expression as he handed Sachse a note. She desperately wanted to ask after Rhys, and yet his previous life was as he'd promised her it would be—abhorrent to her.

Sachse read the note before turning to Lydia. "It seems Harrington wishes to see me. A matter of some importance."

"Is he all right?" she asked, unable to keep the concern out of her voice, unsure why she continued to care.

"I'm sure he is, but I'd better see what it's about. Lad, did you want to ride back in my carriage?"

William pulled a watch out of his pocket, the watch Lydia had seen Rhys pick up in the village. He snapped it open and studied it carefully. "I've got a bit of time. Think I'll walk, but thanks for the offer."

Lydia touched his shoulder. "Join me for some sweet cakes before you go."

After she said good-bye to Sachse, she took William to the garden, where she had a servant bring them some sweets. She doubted many lords gave their valets the kind of gifts Rhys gave his: expensive watches and readings at night.

William was stuffing a little cake in his mouth when Lydia asked, "Where did you get the watch?"

His eyes bulged as he worked hard to swallow. "I didn't steal it if that's what you're thinking. Guv give it to me."

"Why?"

He shrugged. "He said a bloke ought to have a watch."

"That's a very nice one."

He squirmed in the chair as though uncomfortable under her scrutiny. He finally admitted, "Could be on account I mentioned how lucky Colton was to have a watch with all that fine carving on it."

That she could believe. "Why do you call him Guv?"

"On account I was calling him that for so long I keep forgetting he's His Lordship now . . . or His Grace. Just keeps changing, ya know?"

"So when you started working for him—"

"Well, I didn't work for him, not at first anyways. We was partners, him and me."

That was interesting. Lydia leaned forward, and although she knew it was very unladylike, she set her elbow on the table and her chin in her cupped palm. "What sort of business did you have?"

"Weren't really a business. Like I said, we was partners. If one of us found a job, we'd cut the other in on it. Helping each other out: loading things, lifting, carting stuff. Good, honest work it was."

"How did you meet?"

His gaze darted to the cakes. "You got a lot of questions. Maybe you ought to ask him."

She shoved the plate closer to him. "You can eat the cakes while you tell me how you met."

He accepted the bribe and after finishing a cake, continued. "I was working as a pickpocket at the time. The man me mum sold me to had standards, you see."

Her stomach roiled at the idea that his mother had sold him. She wanted to comment but didn't want him to lose the flow of the story.

He took another bite of cake. "He expected us to bring in a certain amount of money, and if we didn't, he didn't feed us. Sometimes he beat us. I was sort of desperate one day, on account of the pickin's being slim, and I saw this bloke who sorta looked like a gent, but not really. Like maybe he'd been a gent at one time. So I figured he might have something valuable on him. Only I was a bit slow, what with me arm bein' broken the day before, and he caught me at it."

He'd slipped into a harsher accent, the way she suspected he'd talked before Rhys had taken him in. "The gentleman?"

"Right. He had me by the scruff of me shirt, holding me up against the wall. 'Guv,' says I, 'have mercy. Let me go.' Only he wanted to know who beat me. Never seen a bloke look so angry. Only he wasn't mad at me. Turns out he was mad at the bloke what hit me. Told him me tale, trying to get him to have mercy on me and let me go. Only he said if I'd come with him, I'd never get beaten again, never go hungry.

" 'No, thanks, Guv,' I says. 'I've heard about blokes like you.'

"Told me he wasn't one of them blokes and if he ever did anything I didn't like, I had his permission to slit his throat. Then he handed me this." William reached down and pulled a knife from his boot. "I says, 'You don't know me, Guv, but I bloody well know how to use a blade.' "

"And he said, 'You don't know me. I'm a man who knows how to keep his word.' So off with him I went."

"And found your odd jobs around London," Lydia added.

"That's right."

"But you didn't stay working at odd jobs?"

"Ah, no, that was a stroke of bloody good luck, that was."

He finished off another cake.

"Tell me about your good luck," she prodded.

"I come close to dying, I did."

"And how was that lucky?"

"Well, I was bad sick. Burning up with the fever. Don't remember a lot of it. Remember Guv carrying me around, trying to get me into a hospital, but they didn't want the likes of us dirtying their halls. Then he took me to the house we're living in now. I remember Rawlings. He didn't know if he should let us in. There was a lot of yelling. Then another bloke come to the door. The yelling got louder. We finally left."

Rhys had told her that one night his family had turned him out. What must it have cost him, knowing he was responsible for Annie's death, to have returned? But he'd suffered the indignity for William's sake.

"And that's when Her Ladyship pulled up in her fine carriage," he finished.

"Her ladyship?"

"Right. Lady Sachse. She took us in."

Lydia's heart began to pound. "Lady Sachse took you in?"

He nodded enthusiastically. "She give us this nice, warm house. Had a doctor come fix me up. Then her friends started coming to see Guv. I became his valet. Sometimes we'd go for strolls in the parts of London good folks don't like. That's where he'd find his servants. Like Mary."

Lydia sat back, hardly knowing what to say. Rhys had bombarded her with all the ugliness in his life, all the actions he'd known she'd find reprehensible. And only now did she realize how unbalanced his confessions had been.

She'd listened to *what* he'd done. She'd never insisted he explain *why* he'd done them. She needed to know why. William's story had explained a good deal, but it contained some gaping holes. She knew someone who could probably fill in the holes. Lydia was determined to get answers.

Standing in his library, Rhys mused that he'd been completely unprepared for the parade of visitors that afternoon. One gentleman had been blistering mad that Rhys had *not* slept with his wife.

"What the hell is wrong with you not to recognize what a beauty she is?" he'd demanded to know.

Rhys had merely mumbled that in hindsight he could now see he had indeed been quite blind. He'd decided against agitating the man further by asking if the suggestion he'd given the man's wife on ways to help him not release his seed quite so soon had been of any help. Perhaps it was the woman's beauty that got the man so worked up to begin with that he couldn't quite contain himself long enough to get her with an heir.

Most of the gentlemen who visited were quite pleased to learn their wives had never passed over his threshold. In truth, during the time he'd been *kept*, as it were, by Camilla, he hadn't truly pleasured that many women. Several, like Lady Whithaven, simply wanted a man's comfort or his advice. For those who did want more, he'd happily obliged.

After all, he'd owed Camilla a considerable debt. She'd managed to have a physician tend to William, had saved the lad's life while Quentin had merely sneered at him and demanded he leave. Going to Quentin had been difficult, swallowing his pride to do so, but he couldn't tolerate the thought of another death on his hands.

Now he turned to the Earl of Sachse, who had responded to his summons. "May I offer you something to drink? Port? Cognac?"

"No, thank you. I doubt this is truly a social call."

"No, it's not." He indicated a nearby chair. "Will you at least sit?"

"I don't believe."

Rhys leaned his hips against his desk and wrapped his hands around its edge, needing the sturdiness it offered for what he was about to do. "I noticed you seemed to have an interest in Lydia."

"More than an interest. I wish to marry her. I'd just broached the subject with her when your missive arrived."

Rhys dug his fingers into desk. Bless William for his talent at tracking—not much different from Colton's claim. Rhys would have to ponder that notion later.

"How is Lydia?" he asked.

"Heartbroken, but not defeated."

Relief washed through Rhys. He'd been terrified that he might have been too brutal in his attempt to force her to hate him. He'd immediately sent a missive to Lauren last night because he hadn't wanted Lydia to be alone.

Now it seemed she'd have not only Lauren at her side, but Sachse. He was unprepared to feel as though a red hot poker had been stabbed through his heart. He'd planned to convince Sachse that Lydia was an innocent, would make him a fine wife. But it seemed he had no need to convince the man of anything.

"I'm pleased to hear she is continuing on, even more pleased to hear you wish to marry her."

"I couldn't give a damn if you're pleased. You came close to ruining the girl."

"I'm well aware of that fact. I want to assure you that nothing untoward passed between us." What had passed between him and Lydia had been based on love, not gain. Although she would never believe that now. His harsh words had seen to that.

"I don't need your reassurances. It is quite clear to me—and everyone else—that Miss Westland is a lady of the highest caliber, above reproach."

Rhys was grateful to know Sachse's sentiments were echoed by others. "Do you know if she'll be at Kimburton's this evening?"

"Yes. I assume you won't be in attendance."

"You assume wrong."

It seemed Rhys had finally managed to say something to surprise Sachse.

"I am not skilled at the games the aristocracy plays, but I was under the impression, based upon all the whispers going about London, you would not be welcomed at Kimburton's or anyone else's social gathering," Sachse said.

"Your impression is correct, and all the more reason I must go, and why you must ensure Lydia is there. It is imperative she give me a public snubbing; otherwise, she risks censure herself. Having you beside her will make it go easier for her, I should think."

"I can't imagine Miss Westland issuing a cut direct to anyone, much less to you."

He nodded. "It will be against her nature, but it must be done. As an Englishman, you understand that. You must ensure she comprehends its importance. She must in no way give any indication that she is anything but reviled by my presence."

"And after tonight?"

"She won't see me again. I'm quite good at disappearing."

"You love her."

"What I feel for her is unimportant. All that matters is that I do what I must to lessen the harm that could come her way."

Sachse took a deep breath and seemed to relax. "I shall do my part, Your Grace."

"Then I would ask one more favor of you."

"And that would be?"

"To love her well."

Arriving at Lady Sachse's, Lydia tried to at least appear to be a lady, but she was trembling with such fury that it was difficult. She'd known from the beginning she hadn't trusted or liked the woman. She found little comfort in knowing her suspicions were justified.

Nor did she find comfort in Lady Sachse's apparent sorrow. She sat in the darkened room with the drapes drawn closed, a half-filled decanter on the table beside her chair, a glass in her hand.

"My life should have been ruined," she whispered.

"Do you ever think of anyone besides yourself?" Lydia asked as she strode across the room and jerked the drapes open.

The woman screamed and covered her eyes. "Close those immediately."

"No, I want to see you clearly when you explain to me how you could do to Rhys what you did."

"And what did I do? I gave him a roof over his head, coal for his fires, fine clothing, food, servants. He wanted for nothing."

"Except love and acceptance."

"Oh, he was loved and accepted. My God, girl, my ladies adored him."

"The ladies who went to see him. How is it they didn't know who he was?"

"He was young when he ran off, nineteen I believe. He had yet to make any dent at all in the social scene. As the spare, he held little interest to anyone. Besides, Quentin commanded attention.

"By the time I saw Rhys again, he'd aged considerably—if not by years, at least by appearance, by experience. The hard life he'd endured during those years was clearly carved into his face. I created a fantastical story about his origins. A commoner with a talent for seduction. A roué. A man who'd dedicated his life to sensual pleasure."

Lydia's revulsion for this woman continued to grow by leaps and bounds.

"How did they find out who he was?" Lydia asked.

Lady Sachse gave her a pointed look, and Lydia's heart sank. "Because he attended a ball," she whispered.

"He wished to see you meet with success. I thought my ladies would hold their tongues. Apparently someone didn't."

For her Rhys had risked exposing his past. Because of her dream, he was more of an outcast than he'd ever been.

"Who all knows?" she asked.

"Unfortunately, the rumors are rife over London. Before the day is done not a single peer will not have asked his wife if she visited Rhys." Unsteadily she placed her glass beside the decanter and looked at Lydia imploringly. "He has told people I was not privy to his actions. Why would he do that? Why would he spare me the shame I so rightly deserve?"

"It's not in his nature to hurt people. I have seen him turn his cheek far too many times. Tell me what I need to do to help him."

With tears in her eyes, the Countess shook her head. "It is too late. Everyone knows what he did, and they will soon know everyone he did it with. There is no hope for him. He is well and truly ruined. He will be ostracized, reviled, shunned. Accept it, girl, and get on with your life."

"And if I can't?"

"You must. It is the kindest thing you can do for him. His greatest fear was that he would drag you into the sewer with him. Do not let his efforts to protect you be for naught. You must show you are better than he. You must. Or you will destroy what is left of him. That I can promise you."

Chapter 25

A true lady will not reveal either through actions or words that her heart is breaking.

Miss Westland's Blunders in
Behavior Corrected

The Duke of Kimburton's ball was without a doubt the most elegant affair Lydia had ever attended. With Lord Sachse and Lauren at her side, she was also aware the guests were more interested in the latest gossip than they were in dancing.

Not only were they whispering about the wicked Duke of Harrington, but they were also speculating on the recent rumors that the new Earl of Sachse was to wed an American heiress. Lydia had yet to give him her answer. Strange how it seemed as if her dream had suddenly shifted around her until she wasn't quite certain what it was anymore.

Tonight it was easy to get caught up in the glitter of London when it sparkled so magnificently.

"This is one of the grandest events of the Season," Lauren whispered.

"I'm surprised we were allowed through the door," Lydia said.

"Don't be silly. No one blames you for the Duke's indiscretions. Besides, it doesn't hurt to have the attentions of Sachse. Especially when Lady Sachse is a victim in all this scandal as well."

A victim? The woman had instigated and been responsible for most of it, as far as Lydia was concerned.

"How is Lady Sachse holding up?" Lauren asked.

"Quite well," Lord Sachse responded. "I visited with her only briefly this afternoon, but she seems to be rising above all this."

"I'm not surprised. In all matters, she places herself first," Lydia said quietly.

"Lydia!" Lauren whispered harshly. "Your acceptance into polite society has been facilitated by Lady Sachse's influence."

But at what cost to Rhys?

"Miss Westland?"

Lydia turned to see Lord and Lady Whithaven. Glad for the distraction, she smiled warmly. "Lady Whithaven."

The Countess took her hands and squeezed gently. "My dear, you look lovely this evening."

Lydia blushed. "Thank you."

"My dear husband was hoping you would honor him with a dance later."

Lydia looked past her to the Earl. "Yes, I'd be honored."

"The eighth dance would serve me well," Lord Whithaven said. "And you must comprehend the honor I am bestowing upon you, since I fully intend to dance every other dance with my wife this evening."

Beaming with joy, Lady Whithaven patted her husband's arm. "Isn't he simply delightful?"

"Yes, he is," Lydia assured her. Much more so than when she'd last seen them.

Lady Whithaven turned to her husband. "You were going to introduce Miss Westland to your cousin, were you not?"

"Oh, yes," Whithaven said, as he glanced around. "A marquess, but I must find him first. So many people at this gathering. As soon as I spot him, I'll bring him right over. He'll want a dance. A most agreeable fellow. Above reproach."

Lady Whithaven again took Lydia's hand and squeezed. "If you need anything, my dear, know we are here for you."

She and her husband walked away.

"That was interesting," Lauren said. "It's always been obvious Lady Whithaven loved her husband. Tonight he seems equally besotted."

Before Lydia could respond, she heard a voice that grated on her nerves.

"My dear Miss Westland."

She forced herself to smile. "Lady Sachse."

"If I may say, you look quite stunning this evening."

Lydia was taken aback. She heard no cattiness in the woman's voice. "Thank you."

"My pleasure, dear. Miss Fairfield, you are equally stunning."

"Thank you, Lady Sachse," Lauren said.

"And Lord Sachse," the Countess purred, "you are as handsome as ever."

"And you, dear lady, are as charming as ever."

"Hardly. It's simply that everyone has been so kind to me this evening that I wanted to share my happiness."

To Lydia's great surprise, Lady Sachse took her arm

and led her a few steps away. Then she said in a compelling low voice, "Listen carefully to what I am about to say. Archie, bless him, and your American cousin have not the sophistication to comprehend the delicate situation in which you and I find ourselves. For us, ruin has been avoided. But under no circumstances, in any public forum, are you to ever acknowledge Rhys. It is imperative that you heed my words."

Lydia heard the unspoken words. Rhys would carry the weight of the scandal on his broad shoulders.

"Do you understand the gravity of what I am saying?" Lady Sachse asked.

"Perfectly."

"Splendid." Lady Sachse stepped back and glanced around.

Lydia did the same and spotted the Duke of Kimburton striding toward them. He was indeed handsome and in many ways reminded her of Rhys. Confident, he wore his title well. He smiled at Lauren and greeted her before turning his attention to Lord Sachse.

"My mother would like to meet you, Lord Sachse. As well as your lady."

Sachse smiled. "We are honored, Your Grace."

Lydia slid her gaze to Lauren, who was beaming as though Lydia had somehow managed to accomplish something wonderful.

"Miss Fairfield, perhaps you'd come with us as well," Kimburton said.

"Certainly, Your Grace."

"Will you excuse us, Lady Sachse?" Kimburton asked.

"Of course." She leaned toward Lydia. "Remember, my dear, among the aristocracy we must always travel the hardest path and never reveal how difficult the journey. Rhys understands that well. Do not disappoint him."

Lydia wanted to ask her exactly what she was talking about, but the Duke was waiting—as was his mother. As soon as introductions were made, she'd seek out Lady Sachse and demand to know what she knew that Lydia didn't.

Lydia felt eyes coming to bear on her as she followed the Duke. She wondered briefly if this was how the animals at the zoological gardens had felt when Sabrina had gone to see them. Every aspect scrutinized and measured.

She'd studied her books, had wanted to make a grand impression. Suddenly she wondered why she'd thought it was all so important. No one watched her as closely in Texas.

The Duchess sat in a large overstuffed chair as though it were a throne. The woman exuded regal bearing and grace—just as Lydia had expected of the aristocracy.

The woman smiled warmly. "Lord Sachse, I understand you are a scholar."

"Yes, Your Grace."

"Explain to me what is to happen to all of us with these American girls invading our shores."

"I suspect, Your Grace, we shall be the richer for it."

She laughed, a throaty sound of pure enjoyment. "You are either very wise or very foolish."

"Foolishly in love perhaps," he admitted.

Lydia felt her cheeks grow warm. He was kind, well-mannered, and charming. Any lady would be thrilled to have his attentions. While she was only mildly flattered.

The Duchess turned her attention to Lydia. "I must say, my dear, that you are very lovely."

"Thank you, Your Grace."

"There is scandal afoot, and yet you remain poised. I should think the Prince of Wales would like to make your acquaintance. Don't you agree, Kim?"

The Duke nodded. "Yes, Mother."

"And you, Miss Fairfield. I have been watching you, or more precisely watching my son watch you."

"He is one of the most eligible bachelors in London, Your Grace. I imagine he watches a lot of girls," Lauren said.

"Yes, I suppose he does."

As the Duchess continued to speak with Lauren, Lydia couldn't help but feel as though she'd somehow, in spite of everything, managed to pass her test. She might actually rub elbows with the royal family. What sort of elegant affairs would she attend then?

How would her stepfather's status rise? A man whose birth had denied him so much?

Lydia became aware of the din of surrounding conversation falling into silence like the ocean receding from the shore. Music ceased to fill the huge room.

"Well, this should prove interesting," the Duchess murmured. "I had not expected him to show."

Lydia glanced over her shoulder to where the Duchess was looking.

And there stood Rhys.

In the doorway, tall, proud, handsome—even with his bruised face. He'd come. She hadn't really thought he would. Thought he would have spared himself this humiliation of feeling all eyes trained on him, of knowing the low opinion held of him.

She turned completely to look at him and felt a hand close around each of hers—Lauren on one side, Sachse on the other.

"Don't do anything rash," Lauren warned.

"You must not acknowledge him," Sachse said.

Not acknowledge him? Not acknowledge the man who caused her heart to beat, her lungs to breathe? Ignore the man who had taught her what was not written in her books?

He stood there as he had been his whole life—alone.

She was on the verge of achieving everything she desired. All she had to do when he caught her attention was look away.

She had professed that his sins wouldn't change her feelings for him. She understood now that she'd been mistaken, because she realized with startling clarity that knowing everything had caused her love to deepen. She could forgive him anything.

She turned to Lord Sachse. "My lord, you are an exceedingly kind man. But I've discovered I don't wear the glitter and gold of London well."

"My dear, I believe love has the power to spin straw into gold."

Rising up on her toes, she kissed his cheek and whispered, "We shall see."

She gave Lauren a tremulous smile and squeezed her hand.

"Don't do it, Lydia," Lauren whispered.

"I have no choice."

She began wending her way through the crowd. She could see those who had already turned their backs on Rhys were suddenly looking to see why there was any movement at all.

She heard the first stirring of murmuring. She could sense curiosity piqued.

"My dear."

Someone grabbed her arm, stilling her progress. She looked to the side, and Lady Whithaven smiled at her.

"My dear, you have tears in your eyes," Lady Whithaven said. "I'm certain you're searching for a handkerchief. Here, you may use mine."

Lydia started to shake her head, to tell her that she wasn't searching for anything—she'd found what she wanted in Rhys—but her gaze fell on the handkerchief, on its solitary monogram—an R embroidered in red.

She suddenly remembered how surprised Lady Whithaven had been upon being introduced to the Duke of Harrington. And it all made sense. This woman had been with Rhys.

Lydia lifted her gaze to Lady Whithaven's face. Tears sparkled in her green eyes.

"You mustn't go any farther," Lady Whithaven whispered. "Stay here with me, and all will be well."

This woman had known Rhys's touch, known his kindness. And yet she'd already turned her back on him.

Lydia looked at Lord Whithaven. His cheeks burning red, he studied a distant corner of the room. She remembered how little attention he'd paid to his wife before. Tonight he adored her, and Lydia couldn't help but wonder what role Lady Whithaven's liaison with Rhys had played in the Earl's change of heart.

She clutched the familiar handkerchief in her gloved hand. "Thank you, Lady Whithaven. I know now, without a doubt, that all will be well."

She barely heard Lady Whithaven's gasp as she continued on.

And she knew the moment Rhys's gaze fell on her, felt it like a welcome caress—even though she was certain he had not meant it that way. She quickened her step until suddenly nothing was between them but open floor, secrets revealed, and hearts wounded.

But wounds could be healed, and in the process hearts strengthened. She stopped before him.

"Did no one explain to you that you are to turn away from me?" he asked through clenched teeth, his lips barely moving.

"They explained. So did my books."

"Then do it."

Slowly she shook her head.

"Damnation!" he hissed. "Do you not remember the first ball you attended? The sadness and disappointment you felt because you were not welcomed as you'd hoped to be?"

Oh, she remembered it. Remembered it well.

"What will follow will be ten times worse," he continued. "No balls, no dinners, no gentlemen calling. You will be ignored and gossiped about. To hold your dream of making a place for yourself among the aristocracy is within reach. Turn away from me."

"No."

"Lydia, you are worthy of a king, but not deserving of me. You need to return to Sachse."

"I need to follow my heart." She curtsied, gracefully, elegantly. Then she lifted her gaze to his. "My heart always leads me back to you."

"You don't know what you're doing."

She rose and smiled warmly. "Oh, but I do. I've always dreamed of traveling to England and falling in love—and I did. I love you, Rhys. And nothing will change that."

She watched as tears formed in his eyes, and he swallowed hard. "I would do anything to see you happy."

She held out her hand. "Then take me away from here."

He wrapped his hand around hers, drew her against his side, and escorted her out of the ballroom. Away from the glitter and gold of London.

And toward her dream.

Inside his carriage, Rhys took Lydia into his arms and kissed her deeply, desperately. As long as he drew breath, he would never forget how she'd looked as she walked toward him—a lioness, a woman who would not be tamed by society's rules.

"You are a fool," he rasped as he rained kisses over her face.

"I love you, Rhys."

He leaned back, cradling her face between his hands. He'd never thought to be this close to her again. "Grayson will kill me. As will your mother."

She smiled. "No, they won't."

"You must understand. When Annie died, I tried to hide in London's underbelly. Five years I wandered. A man can easily get lost in London. A young man eaten up with guilt could risk never finding his way out."

"But you did find your way out."

He nodded. "Eventually. I never did anything during those five *lost* years for which I was ashamed. I worked menial jobs for food and shelter. Hefting, carting around, building, cleaning. I wasn't particular. Then William got sick."

"He told me. I spoke with Lady Sachse as well."

"When Camilla made her offer, it seemed no hardship. What young man doesn't dream of women wanting him? You must understand, the things I said the other night—I wanted you to run. I did not want my past to hurt you."

"The only time it hurt me was when it kept me away from you. I love you so much."

"There is a good chance we'll have nothing. The Queen could take it all away."

"Then we'll have nothing together."

He removed his gloves, then slowly peeled hers off. He took her hands and pressed them to his lips, inhaling the sweet scent she'd placed on her wrists.

"I have searched my whole life, not truly knowing what I sought. Until I looked into your eyes, until I saw your acceptance of me. I would see you happy at all costs. I love you more than life. Will you do me the honor of becoming my wife?"

She released a joyous laugh. "Oh, yes!"

She wound her arms around his neck and kissed him passionately. With her, there would seldom be decorum. And yet when it was most needed—as she'd proven tonight—she had the regal bearing of a queen.

"Make love to me, Rhys."

How he was tempted to do just that. Instead he drew back. "No, the next time I make love to you, darling Lydia, it will be after we've signed the marriage agreement. I'll not have my son arrive only months after we are wed and have his mother whispered about. There will be whispers enough where we are concerned."

She kissed his chin. "I don't want to wait."

"We'll send for your parents tomorrow."

She pressed her head into the nook of his shoulder. "We're going to be so happy."

He only wished he could be as optimistic.

*   *   *

"You're quite ruined," Lauren announced.

Lydia closed her book. She'd been reading in the parlor for most of the afternoon, while Lauren had been sleeping. She'd gotten home rather late last night.

"But I'm so happy," Lydia said.

Lauren sat down. "You were going to be introduced to the Prince of Wales."

"And instead I'll be married."

"Everyone was quite shocked when you left with him."

She leaned over and squeezed Lauren's hand. "I love him, Lauren. I don't care that he pleasured countless of London's ladies. I care only that he pleasures me."

Lauren's eyes popped. "Did he? Last night? Everyone speculated that he did."

She shook her head. "No, we just drove through the streets of London, kissing, talking, and planning our wedding."

Lauren looked toward the doorway. "Yes?"

The butler entered with tray in hand. "Some ladies are here to see Miss Westland."

Lauren took the cards. "Ladies Reynolds, Kedelbrooke, and Wrotham." She looked at Lydia. "Are you at home?"

Lydia nodded. "Certainly."

The ladies entered with bright red cheeks and gazes that danced around the room as though they weren't certain they wanted to look directly at Lydia. Lauren invited them to sit and offered tea. They all sat quietly sipping.

Finally, Lady Reynolds said, "Miss Westland, I hope you won't consider me impertinent, but we are dying to know—do you intend to marry the Duke?"

She smiled, wanting to express her absolute joy that she could answer as she was. "Yes."

Lady Reynolds looked incredibly delighted. "Splendid. My dear girl, you are so lucky. He has such wonderful hands. Honestly, once you are wed, you must have him rub your feet."

Lydia suddenly wished Lauren hadn't invited these ladies in. It had never occurred to her that she would speak to women and know that they'd known her love's touch. It was one thing to accept he'd bedded some ladies. Quite another to sip tea with them.

"He rubbed your feet?" she dared to ask.

Lady Reynolds nodded. "I'd gone to see him because my dear husband was a bit *hasty* at times." Her blush deepened. "His Grace—of course, he wasn't His Grace then—shared with me several strategies for curtailing my husband's eagerness, and the entire time he explained the matter, he rubbed my feet. It was quite delicious."

"He rubbed my back," Lady Wrotham admitted. "I sat on his lap like a child and bawled my heart out. Hence the reason I had his handkerchief, which my husband discovered. In my marriage, I found no semblance of the passion that I read in Jane Austen's books."

"Yes, he'd given me his handkerchief as well," Lady Reynolds said. "I wept abominably in the beginning, as I recounted my sad tale."

"He fed me chocolates until I thought I would pop," Lady Kedelbrooke offered. "It was a most pleasant evening."

"Pleasant?" Lydia asked. Pleasant didn't begin to express what it was like to have Rhys make love to a woman.

"Oh, yes. He has a passion for books. As do I. We contrasted Dickens and Twain."

Chocolates and books. Foot rubs and advice.

"Have you told your husband exactly what transpired between you and Rhys?" Lydia asked.

"Oh, no," Lady Kedelbrooke said. "I much prefer my husband think I was naughty. He has been most attentive, striving to make sure I do not stray again."

When she'd never really strayed to begin with.

Lydia had no doubt some women had received much more from Rhys than what these ladies had. But she felt no jealousy or envy. She would have what all these ladies had never had.

A husband who adored her, who would be attentive, and who would never cause her to stray.

Lydia's family had arrived in force three days before. Her wedding gown had arrived yesterday. In the weeks since the *infamous ball*, as it had come to be known around London, whispers were growing quieter.

A few more ladies had come to call. Lydia was quite the envy of many.

The day after tomorrow she and Rhys would get married. She had one more thing she wanted to do.

She stood in the entrance hall of the house the Duke had set aside for his Duchess. A house she supposed in some way belonged to Rhys. Yet neither of them had been invited there. She'd given her card to the butler, a card that would soon be different, would soon carry her married name.

She heard the butler approaching and steeled her resolve.

"I'm sorry," he said coldly. "The Duchess is not at home."

Lydia smiled. "Then I'll wait here until she is."

He blinked. "Her Grace is *not* at home."

She nodded. "I heard you. I'll wait right over here by the potted plant until she returns."

He spun on his heel and walked back down the hall from which he'd come. A moment later, the Duchess was trudging toward her.

"Do you not understand when you are told I am not at home, that it simply means I am not at home to *you*?" she asked.

"I understand perfectly, Your Grace."

The Duchess came to a stop as though she'd hit a brick wall. "Then why did you tell my butler you would wait until I returned?"

"Because I want to speak to you, and I'll wait all day if I have to."

"I don't wish to speak to you, and you can wait all month. I am not at home."

Lydia smiled. "Then I'll wait all month."

"Impertinent chit!" With a flourish, she headed back down the hallway.

"Would you like a chair in which to wait?" the butler asked.

Lydia shook her head. "No, I'll stand."

And she did. While the butler occasionally checked with the Duchess, only to return with the message that she was not yet at home.

If the Duchess wanted a test of wills, she was going to discover Lydia was not one to be trifled with, not where Rhys was concerned.

"The Duchess is at home," the butler said quietly.

Lydia glanced at the hallway clock. Four hours. She hadn't had to wait as long as she'd expected she would.

She followed the butler into the parlor.

"There," the Duchess said, from her chair by the window. "You have been received. You may now leave."

"I don't think so." She walked farther into the room and studied a portrait that was hanging on the hall. The man was indeed handsome, but he also caused a shiver to skitter down her spine. "Is this Quentin?"

"Yes."

"You had two sons, Your Grace." She faced the woman. "The day after tomorrow, I'm going to marry Rhys."

"You are not telling me anything I do not know. I saw the announcement in the *Morning Post*."

"It would mean a great deal to us if you would be there."

"I am not giving my blessing on this union. Quentin is dead because of Rhys. Rhys betrayed him." She lowered her gaze. "Quentin began to drink quite heavily after Annie died. It was that drink that caused him to stumble into the family pond. Caused him to drown."

"I did not know Quentin, Your Grace. But I know Rhys is a good man."

"Ha! He sent for the Duke's bastard against my wishes."

"Do you see no good in him at all?"

"I cannot see what does not exist."

Lydia sighed deeply. She so desperately wanted to make this woman understand how precious Rhys was. But the only way to do that was to destroy Quentin. Or to reveal that Rhys had asked the Duke to tell her that he loved her. To snatch away what she held dear.

She could do neither.

"I love your son, Your Grace, with all of my heart. I have been unable to find any time in his life when he placed himself before anyone else. He is a good man, an honorable man. The day after tomorrow, all of my family will be with me in the church. Rhys will have no family. You loved your Duke. I will love mine. I would ask that you love him as well. Join us when we begin our life together. We can't change the hurts of the past. But we can see that there are fewer in the future."

"You are most ill-bred," the Duchess said. She looked out the window. "Name off all the reasons you love my son."

Without hesitation, Lydia did.

Chapter 26

A true lady shall leave no doubt within any-one's mind that she loves the man of her choosing with all of her heart.

Miss Westland's Blunders in
Behavior Corrected

Rhys stood within a small room not far from where he would enter the church. Lord Sachse waited with him. He'd wanted Grayson to stand by him, but his half-brother had a more pressing position. He was to give the bride into Rhys's keeping.

Rhys had thought the chapel would suffice since he was certain that only Lydia's family would be in atten-dance. But Lydia had wanted the church. As always, he found himself unable to deny her anything.

A brusque knock on the door, and then Camilla strode into the room. Rhys had never thought he would ever again associate with her, and yet somehow, he found himself doing just that. He'd forgiven her for her lies and deceptions, perhaps because when all was said and done, he'd recognized that she'd suffered far worse than he. She'd had an unkind husband as well as Quentin to deal with. And in her own strange way, she'd believed that she was giving the ladies of London

359

something they might never acquire otherwise.

"The guests are arriving," she announced. She crossed over to Rhys and patted his lapels. "You may thank me properly later."

"If guests are here, I suspect it is more Lydia's doing than yours," Rhys said.

"Don't be so abominably *correct*, Rhys. It doesn't become you." She patted his lapels again before stepping back. "Although I must admit, you look terribly handsome today." She turned to Lord Sachse. "And you as well."

"Thank you for the compliment, Lady Sachse."

"Honestly, Archie, you need not be so formal. We're practically related."

"We're not related at all, madam."

Rhys was startled by the man's comment and the predatory warning he heard shimmering within the quietly spoken words. Had Rhys not said the same to Lydia, in the same manner, at one time?

Camilla blushed, actually looking flustered. "Perhaps next Season you will have a bit more luck at finding a wife."

Archie shrugged. "I prefer to choose wisely rather than hastily. Now that the Season is coming to a close, however, I need to look over all the Sachse properties. I was hoping you might accompany me. I know nothing at all about managing so large an estate. You have done such a splendid job of acquainting me with London, I thought you might make a fine tutor as I learn what I must to keep Sachse from ruin."

"I am quite ready to leave London," Camilla said. "I shall be more than delighted to accompany you."

Rhys watched the exchange with interest. Camilla was a flirtatious wench, her every word and action designed to control a man. But Archie? What was his interest in Camilla?

Camilla walked over to Rhys, placed her hands on his shoulders, rose up on her toes, and placed a kiss on his cheek. "I do wish you well, Rhys."

When she stepped back, he was shocked to see tears welling in her eyes. He withdrew his handkerchief from his pocket. "Here."

Upon seeing his offering, she laughed lightly and took it. "Honestly, Rhys, you must see to having a different monogram placed on your handkerchiefs. These are known all over London."

"You are quite right. I shall see to it after my wedding."

"She is a lucky girl, Rhys. I'll leave you gentlemen now." Walking toward the door, she fluttered her fingers in the air. "Archie, I expect you to call this evening."

"It shall be my pleasure to do so . . . Camilla."

She stilled and glanced over her shoulder. Rhys had never seen her look so soft, so vulnerable. "So we might discuss our plans for touring the estates."

"Of course," Lord Sachse said quietly.

With a bob of her head. Camilla left the room.

"Take care with her heart, Archie," Rhys said in a low voice, not certain why he felt the sudden need to protect Camilla.

Archie faced him and gave him a brusque nod. "I intend to do just that. I suspect no one ever has, although you've probably come the closest."

"I must confess to never understanding why I liked her as much as I despised her."

"Perhaps because you recognized that she is not as callous as she appears. The previous Earl of Sachse—may he rot in hell—kept a journal which I discovered when I spent the night at the manor home before coming on to London. While she and I are touring the estates, I intend to convince her that I am nothing like my predecessor."

"She will not be able to give you an heir."

Archie shrugged. "We shall see. I am more inclined to believe the fault lay with her husband."

Before Rhys could say more, another knock sounded. His heart jumped, and he took a deep breath. It was time.

The door opened and his mother strode in, regal in all her bearing. He could not have been more surprised had it been the Queen herself. He'd called on his mother shortly after the debacle of the ball to announce his intention to marry Lydia. She'd refused to see him.

"Mother, what are you doing here?"

She sent a haughty glare Archie's way. "Will you please excuse us?"

"Certainly, Your Grace."

Archie left the room, closing the door quietly behind him.

"Your lady came to see me," his mother announced. "She is rather . . . ill-bred, insolent . . . stubborn. Do you know she stood in my entrance hall four hours waiting for me to receive her? Impertinent woman."

"I will not have her day ruined," Rhys warned. "If I have to cart you through the church like a sack of potatoes, by God, I will do it."

"Honestly, Rhys, must you continually compare me to a sack of potatoes? I find it most unflattering."

He stared at her, unsure how to respond. Was she teasing him? Surely not.

She approached him, and just as Camilla had before

her, she began to straighten and brush lapels that needed no attention.

"Every day you must tell her that you love her. Do not wait until you are on your deathbed. A woman needs to hear those words often."

"As does a son," he said quietly.

She stopped fiddling with his lapels and lifted her gaze to his. Tears welled in her eyes. "I loved you best. I always did. I felt guilty for that, and so I spoiled Quentin. But you were always so sweet. Until the affair with Annie. It broke my heart that you would betray your brother in that manner. And I felt that I'd failed you both. I am so sorry."

The tears rolled over onto her cheeks. He drew her into his embrace. "You never failed me."

She shuddered with silent sobs. "I felt as though I had," she rasped.

He tucked his knuckles beneath her chin and tilted her face until he could look into her eyes. "I love you, Mother."

More tears surfaced, and he had no handkerchief to give her, Camilla having taken his last one with her when she left. So he collected her tears with his glove. "Now, now, no more of this. I want to see a smile."

She gave him one, and he returned it in kind.

"Lydia will make a wonderful duchess," she said.

"Indeed she shall."

"Then you'd best get on with the wedding. I'm anxious to have grandchildren."

Rhys stood at the front of the church, quite unable to believe his change of fortune. His little dreamer had come to him seeking lessons in how to be accepted among the aristocracy, and in the end, it was she who'd gained him acceptance.

Rumors regarding his past had begun quieting. If the Queen was displeased with him, she'd yet to make her annoyance known which gave him further hope that all might be well. That and the fact that the church was packed to the rafters.

Archie stood beside him. Rhys turned slightly, and his gaze fell on his mother, sitting at the front. She smiled at him, a smile that brimmed with love. She placed her hand over her heart before pressing her fingers to her lips and blowing him a kiss.

He returned the gesture and could have sworn he heard some sighs.

The organ suddenly filled the church with the glorious chords to announce the arrival of his bride. He looked down the aisle and knew he'd never seen a more beautiful woman.

Tiers of lace cascaded over white satin. Billowy whiteness flowed along the long train behind her. A gossamer veil fell over her face to her knees. Yet through it, he could see her brilliant smile, her sparkling eyes.

She carried a bouquet of white orchids. She walked slowly, elegantly with her arm wound around the arm of the man who'd been her father since she was a young girl, the man who'd unintentionally brought her to Rhys. He could not help but believe that Fate was a mischievous lady, weaving the most elaborate of tapestries with people's lives.

But he knew the remainder of his life, at least, would be woven with threads of gold.

Lydia stopped at the front of the church, beside the pew where the Duchess sat. She pulled a flower from her bouquet and offered it to his mother. The Duchess rose and gently hugged Lydia before taking the orchid and returning to her seat.

Then Lydia was at his side, her hand on his arm, her gaze holding his, her smile radiating her love for him.

And all that mattered was that she would be his for the remainder of his life, that she had taught him—a realist—how to dream.

"What have you done with my mother?" Rhys asked from the doorway that separated his bedchamber from Lydia's. "The woman who is claiming to be the Dowager Duchess of Harrington is not a woman I know."

Smiling at her husband's reflection, Lydia slowly moved the brush through her hair. "I simply reminded her that she had another son, and a very worthy one at that."

"Where you are concerned, nothing is ever that simple."

He walked toward her. Her body trembled with need and want. He wore a silk dressing gown. It wouldn't take her any time at all to get that off him. He was holding a tiny silver pitcher, the size of a teacup.

"What's that?" she asked.

"You'll see."

He set the pitcher on the vanity and took her brush. She watched his slow, unhurried movements, the way his hand held her hair before he glided the brush through it.

"What did my father say?" she asked.

He stilled his brushing and knelt beside her. He turned her so she faced him. "He'll take William back to Texas with him."

And in his voice, she heard the cost. She combed her

fingers through his hair, trailed them over his face, and cradled his jaw. "You'll miss him."

He nodded. "We traveled together through the darkness. He has yet to find his light. While you, my darling Lydia, are all the light I shall ever need."

His kiss was the sweetest of desperations, claiming her mouth with bold strokes of his tongue. As he carried her over into the realm of pleasure she'd only ever shared with him, only wanted to share with him, she was vaguely aware he'd worked the sash on her wrapper free and was now hard at work on the buttons of her nightgown. Fifteen buttons, and his mouth never strayed from hers while his hands worked.

A talented man. She threaded her fingers through his hair, holding him in place so her tongue could dance with his. She took such delight in his eagerness, discovered that it served to ignite hers, to make her impatient.

She wanted to be on the bed, opening for him, welcoming him. He was her husband now, and this joining would sanctify their marriage, would not leave guilt hovering at the edges of her conscience. Although she'd enjoyed every encounter she'd shared with him, this one held no sorrow. She had no need to offer him comfort. He had no need to offer her any.

They were free of all constraints, free to celebrate their love. To celebrate each other.

He ended the kiss but not his attentions to her. He traced his fingers around her face, his gaze following the trail, along her throat. Lower. His hands slid into the opening of her gown, his palms resting against her warm skin, capturing the beating of her heart.

Provocatively, with the ease of a master seducer, he moved his hands, and the gown skimmed off her shoulders and down her back to pool at her waist.

"Lift your hips," he ordered.

She obliged him. He slid her nightgown over her hips, past her thighs, knees, and feet.

"I'll never grow tired of looking at you," he rasped.

"Nor I you," she promised as she leaned forward and tugged on his sash.

He latched his mouth onto her nipple while she fought to untie the knot that kept his flesh from hers. When she achieved success, she pulled his dressing gown back until it fell to the floor.

She wondered if her breath would always catch at the sight of him, if her heart would always beat more rapidly, if her joy would always expand to fill her chest to near aching.

Cradling her breast, he asked, "Do you remember when I told you that I preferred where chocolate had been?"

His kneading fingers were distracting, causing the warmth between her thighs to increase. "Yes."

He lifted the tiny silver pitcher. "Chocolate. Warm. Melted."

Her eyes widened as he trickled a line of chocolate over the breast he still held with one hand. He gave her a wickedly delightful grin, and the gray in his eyes darkened to pewter.

Then he was licking up that which he'd poured.

"Goodness gracious," she purred as she dug her fingers into his shoulders, dropped her head back, and wound her legs around his waist.

When the chocolate was gone, he continued to swirl his tongue over her breast.

"Now I understand." She sighed. "Where the chocolate has been."

"I know all sorts of little tricks," he assured her.

She raised her head, slipped her hand beneath his chin, stopping his tender ministrations and lifting his gaze to hers. "You don't need tricks with me, Rhys."

Within his eyes, he laid bare his love for her. She almost wept for the depth of it. No cynical rebuff, no protective denial. He'd lowered his walls, revealed his true self.

"Lydia, I want you to know I never made love to any of those women. I'll admit to pleasuring a few of them, but I never enjoyed a single one as much as I enjoy you. My purpose was to spoil them, to give them everything, to take nothing for myself. Not one ever gave to me as you do."

His eyes glistened with unshed tears. "Not one ever called out *my* name," he rasped.

"Rhys," she said softly.

"My God, but I do love you."

Rhys claimed her mouth with desperate urgency. She was his, now and forever. This woman who uttered his name like a benediction, this woman who claimed to need no tricks, to need nothing beyond him.

With every woman before her, he'd been extremely conscious of each touch, each stroke, each caress— determined that each should increase the woman's pleasure.

With Lydia, he was beyond thinking. He simply wanted to possess, to share, to own her as she owned him. Her hands were in his hair, then rubbing his neck, caressing his face, as though she could not get enough of him. He'd never known such joy.

He bracketed his hands on either side of her hips and drew her forward. She wrapped her legs around his waist, her thighs soft and warm against his sides. He cut off the kiss only long enough to order, "Hold on tight."

Then he pushed himself to his feet, rising with her wound around him. He had one arm beneath her bottom, one around her back, while their mouths devoured, their bodies heated.

A litany raced through his mind: she was his, totally and completely. Absolutely. She belonged to no one else, had never belonged to another man.

And he'd never belonged to another woman. She alone had dared to breach his defenses and conquer his heart.

His steps quickened, his heart pounded. He carried her across the room, laid her on the bed, and followed her down, their mouths never separating, their bodies pressed close.

She said she needed no tricks. With her, he'd never used any. He touched her for his enjoyment as much as hers. Her skin was the softness of silk, the warmth of a newly lit fire.

Her sighs spurred him on, her moans drove him mad. She caressed him as though she would never get enough of him. She rubbed his back, his sides, his back again, his buttocks. Urging him on. With her soles, she stroked his calves, his feet. He'd never been with a woman who sought to pleasure him as much as he did her. He'd never known that in the taking, he also gave.

He'd planned a slow seduction, but his resolve withered beneath the eagerness he sensed in her. They would have time, much later. For now, the fires of passion ran rampant. And he wanted Lydia with a desperation he'd never known. Wanted her selfishly, for himself.

He trailed his mouth along her throat.

"Rhys." She bucked against him, arched her hips against him. "I want you. I want you now."

Groaning low, he slid his hand between their bodies. She whimpered as he tested and stroked. She was hot and moist and ready.

He rose above her, held her beautiful violet gaze, and watched the wonder cross her face as he slowly slid inside her, inch by inch, filling her completely, claiming without remorse or guilt what he'd only recently acquired.

A woman who loved him.

Lydia welcomed his fullness, clutching her body around him. She cupped the back of his head and brought his mouth back down to hers. As he began to move slowly against her, their tongues parried and thrust in rhythm to the beat of their hips.

She tore her mouth from his. "You're mine," she growled.

"Always."

Then she surrendered with wild abandon to the passion he stirred to life within her. He quickened his strokes, deepened his thrusts. She held his gaze, watched as the tempest brewing within him darkened his eyes, silvery-gray, pewter. There was such beauty in his restraint, such power in his resolve. He would not finish without her.

She cried out his name, he called out hers as together they reached the pinnacle of pleasure and toppled off. Slick bodies trembling, tired limbs quaking. She felt his heart pounding and wondered if he could feel hers.

Closing his arms around her, he rolled them both to their sides, their bodies still joined. Lethargically she trailed her fingers along his side.

"Rhys?"

"Mmm?"

"I want you teach me everything you know about pleasure."

"You don't need lessons, Lydia," he murmured. "You possess a natural talent when it comes to lovemaking."

She pressed a kiss to his throat. "I think I do need lessons. I've been thinking about the chocolate."

"What about it?"

"I believe I'd like tasting where it's been"—she leaned back and held his gaze—"if it's on you."

He rose up above her, smiled down on her. "Then by all means, let's have the lessons begin."

Epilogue

A true gentleman shall love his lady with all
his heart and do all in his power to make her
happy.

The Duke of Harrington's
Blunders in Life Corrected

It was whispered about London that tonight's ball
was *the* social event of the Season, not to be missed
by those fortunate enough to receive an invitation. Lydia had been anticipating this evening for weeks now.

"What do you think, Mary?" she asked, gazing at her
reflection in the mirror, pleased with the lines of her
new gown.

"You look beautiful. His Grace will be most pleased,
I'm thinkin'."

"You've done wonders with my hair as always.
Thank you."

As Mary opened the door, Lydia heard laughter—a
deep rumble woven through much lighter chords—
float into the room.

Mary glanced over at her. "Sounds like the Duke and
Lady Katherine at it again."

"Indeed it does."

Knowing that she and her husband would be late

once again, Lydia headed into the room across from theirs, the room designated as the nursery. Her heart expanded, and she wondered if she would ever not feel this immense contentment at the sight of Rhys holding his six-month old daughter. He rarely gave up any opportunity to take her in his arms. He was as attentive a father as he was a husband. Lydia knew that two females more fortunate than she and Katherine did not exist in all of Britain.

She watched as Rhys moved their daughter toward the mirror until her peals of laughter echoed around him and his chuckle joined hers. Of late, Katherine had become enthralled with her image in the mirror, and her father used her fascination to full advantage. Lydia didn't think laughter had ever rung through this house as often or as loudly.

"Rhys, you do realize that it is exceedingly bad form for us to arrive late to a ball which we are hosting?" Lydia asked.

He quieted, but his smile didn't diminish. "How can I be late when I live in the house?"

"You will be late by not being downstairs to greet our guests on their arrival."

Holding Lydia's gaze in the mirror, he said, "I understand that the Harrington ball is being touted as *the* social event of the year."

Lydia couldn't contain her grin. "That's what I hear."

"How about that, Katherine?" he said. "Tonight you shall attend *the* social event of the Season."

"Rhys, you're not thinking of taking her downstairs."

"Why shouldn't I? She's as much of a joy as her mother. Everyone will adore her as much as I do." He moved Katherine toward the mirror and again her laughter bubbled forth.

"Listen to her, Lydia," he said reverently. "She sounds so incredibly happy."

"Perhaps because she is," she said as she crossed the room and laid her head against his arm until the mirror reflected the family as a perfect portrait. The dark-haired, violet-eyed babe held by her adoring father. The mother and wife who loved them both so very much. "You sound happy as well, Rhys."

"I am. More than I ever thought it possible to be. And you?"

She smiled warmly. "Do you not know without asking?"

"I know, but still I enjoy hearing the words."

Rising up on her toes, she kissed him before whispering, "My dear Rhys, with you beside me, I'm living my dream."

COMING IN JULY-
SUMMER'S HOTTEST HEROES!

STEALING THE BRIDE by Elizabeth Boyle
An Avon Romantic Treasure

The Marquis of Templeton has faced every sort of danger in his work for the King, but chasing after a wayward spinster who's run off with the wrong man hardly seems worthy of his considerable talents. But the tempestuous Lady Diana Fordham is about to turn Temple's life upside down . . .

WITH HER LAST BREATH by Cait London
An Avon Contemporary Romance

Nick Alessandro didn't think he would ever recover from a shattering tragedy, until he meets Maggie Chantel. But just when they are starting to find love together, someone waiting in the shadows is determined that Maggie love *no one* ever again. Now Nick has to find the killer—before the killer gets to Maggie.

SOARING EAGLE'S EMBRACE by Karen Kay
An Avon Romance

The Blackfeet brave trusts no white man—or woman—but the spirits have spoken, wedding him in a powerful night vision to a golden-red haired enchantress. Kali Wallace is spellbound by the proud warrior but will their fiery love be a dream come true . . . or doomed for heartbreak?

THE PRINCESS AND HER PIRATE
by Lois Greiman
An Avon Romance

Not since his adventurous days on the high seas has Cairn MacTavish, the Pirate Lord, felt the sort of excitement gorgeous hellion Megs inspires. Though she claims not to be the notorious thief, he knows she is hiding something—and each claim of innocence that comes from her lush, inviting lips only inflames his desires.

REL 0603

Avon Romantic Treasures

Unforgettable, enthralling love stories,
sparkling with passion and adventure
from Romance's bestselling authors

Avon Trade Paperbacks . . .
Because every great bag deserves a great book!

A Promising Man (and About Time, Too)
by Elizabeth Young
0-06-050784-5 • $13.95 US

A Pair Like No Otha'
by Hunter Hayes
0-380-81485-4 • $13.95 US • $20.95 Can

A Little Help From Above
by Saralee Rosenberg
0-06-009620-9 • $13.95 US • $21.95 Can

The Chocolate Ship
by Marissa Monteilh
0-06-001148-3 • $13.95 US • $21.95 Can

The Accidental Virgin
by Valerie Frankel
0-06-093841-2 • $13.95 US • $21.95 Can

Bare Necessity
by Carole Matthews
0-06-053214-9 • $13.95 US

The Second Coming of Lucy Hatch
by Marsha Moyer
0-06-008166-X • $13.95 US • $21.95 Can

Coming Soon
Does She or Doesn't She?
by Alisa Kwitney
0-06-051237-7• $13.95 US • $21.95 Can